Act Normal

To my delightful daughter-in-law,

Melissa Manchee.

We are blessed to have you as part of the family.

Act Normal

The Tarizon Saga

Book 5

by

William Manchee

Top Publications, Ltd.
Dallas, Texas

Act Normal
The Tarizon Saga

Cover Design by William Manchee

Top Publications, Ltd.
Dallas, Texas

ISBN #978-1-935722-76-2
Library of Congress #2007922321

This work is a novel and any similarity to actual persons or events is purely coincidental.

Prelude

Unknown to the inhabitants of Earth, in another galaxy millions of miles away, there existed a sister planet known as Tarizon. Both planets were settled by humans who had occupied the mother planet, Pharidon. Pharidon's civilization was so advanced that its people lived nearly a thousand years. Consequently, Pharidon became overcrowded and the planet's natural resources could not support the growing population. When the situation became critical explorers began searching for other inhabitable planets where their citizens could relocate. One of these groups of explorers came to Tarizon and another to Earth.

It is believed that these settlers brought many animals, plants, insects, and other life-forms from Pharidon to Earth and Tarizon. They were raised and nurtured by the first settlers and then released to live and evolve on their own. Although Earth and Tarizon were settled about the same time and brought with them Pharidon's advanced technology, their civilizations developed quite differently. At the time of Tarizon's Unification it was the early twentieth century on Earth. While Earth was about to experience its first World War, Tarizon had already endured its seventh.

Prior to the war Tarizon had been divided into thirty-one separate nations. These nations had been fighting amongst themselves for thousands of years. In the twenty years before global peace finally came millions of soldiers and civilians had lost their lives and much of the infrastructure of the planet had been destroyed. From out of the rubble a peace movement was born led by a charismatic holy man named Sandee Branh. Sandee had been elected Chief Minister of Lyon, the largest nation of Tarizon. Sandee claimed as a child that God had chosen him to save Tarizon from self destruction.

From the day He first appeared to him, Sandee devoted his life to spreading God's message of peace and unity. Sandee told his followers that the petty national governments should be scrapped in favor one worldwide authority. Since so many were weary of war and feared the destruction of civilization on the planet if something wasn't done, Sandee's movement gathered momentum until there was enough support to call a World Assembly.

At the World Assembly, representatives from all of the thirty-one nations hammered out the Supreme Mandate and then called for a worldwide referendum to ratify it. If the Supreme Mandate was ratified by a majority of its citizens, each nation agreed to subject itself to it and the new World Assembly. On the day of the referendum nearly seventy percent of the population voted and the Supreme Mandate was ratified by sixty-one percent of the popular vote.

The new government on Tarizon was called Central Authority and it ruled in accordance with the Supreme Mandate which guaranteed the right to assemble, to speak freely, to vote, and a fair trial for those accused of crimes against the public. It abolished slavery and provided many other civil liberties as well.

Unfortunately, Central Authority was only able to maintain order in the major cities of Tarizon. Huge domes had been constructed over these cities so water and air could be filtered and purified. A controlled environment allowed the urban population to go about their daily lives without protective clothing and risk of radiation poisoning. Some areas outside of the domes were governed by local town councils or regional governments who were pledged to uphold the Supreme Mandate but only loosely controlled by Central Authority. Much of the rural area had no government and a state of anarchy persisted.

The dominant populations of these rural areas were mutants who hadn't enjoyed the protection from radiation and pollution that the domes provided and suffered the consequences. Two political parties emerged during this time, the Purists and the Loyalists. The Purists represented the unspoiled humans who believed they were superior to the mutants and all other life-forms on Tarizon and should rule over them. Their opponents, the Loyalists, considered themselves loyal to the intentions of those who had written the Supreme Mandate. They believed all life-forms were protected by the Supreme Mandate and should be treated equally.

The Loyalist managed to maintain control of the World

Counsel for nearly forty years during which time the citizens of Tarizon enjoyed a rare peace and the planet's ecology slowly recovered. There was much hope and optimism about Tarizon's future until a series of cataclysmic super volcanic eruptions plunged the planet once again into chaos. The tremors, tidal waves, floods and toxic ash that ravished the planet for over a year left Tarizon nearly uninhabitable.

In a desperate move to save the human race and Tarizon's other life-forms, emissaries from Tarizon were sent to Earth to arrange for the reception of millions of evacuees from Tarizon. However, the best treaty that could be arranged with the U.S. Government was to allow citizens of Tarizon to come to Earth for a five to seven year visit for the purpose of mating and conceiving children in a healthy environment and then returning with them to Tarizon. In exchange for a new generation of healthy Tarizonian citizens, the United States was given advanced technology that would guarantee it was the dominant military power on Earth for generations to come.

Because the government feared the American people couldn't handle the knowledge that alien life existed elsewhere in the universe and would not approve of hundreds of thousands of children conceived on Earth, and technically U.S. Citizens, being sent off to another planet, it elected to keep the program secret. The CIA was given oversight of the program, however, it was administered primarily by military commanders from Tarizon. On rare occasions, private citizens like attorney Stan Turner, were recruited as trouble shouters to help prevent information about the government's secret treaty from leaking out to the media. These private citizens were watched closely by the CIA and the aliens.

Chapter 1

First Assignment

August 1992

The long anticipated first assignment came in August, 1992. I was sitting in my law office thinking back to the day I was recruited by the CIA. "Just act normal," Mo, my CIA contact, had told me. The only problem was there was nothing normal in my life anymore, not since my son Peter had been abducted by aliens from a planet called Tarizon. The abductors were human beings who traveled in huge spaceships the size of a football field. They traveled with their slaves, an amphibious life form that, I was told, could swim as fast as a dolphin and run as fast as a gazelle. These human aliens and their slaves had been living amongst us for decades–right under our noses and we hadn't realized it.

None of this was common knowledge, obviously. Only a handful of people knew about the Tarizonian Repopulation Project. Had the press got wind of it the American people would have been outraged. It was strictly off the radar and a great effort was made to keep it that way. When my son Peter supposedly died everyone believed he had drowned in a flash flood near Possum Kingdom Lake in central Texas, but the truth was he'd been taken hostage to make sure I did what the CIA and the aliens wanted.

It had been over a year since Peter's disappearance. They hadn't found the body, of course, since there wasn't one. I thought of going public with the whole sinister affair, but I couldn't prove anything, not really. The aliens had destroyed all the evidence and taken most of the witnesses back to Tarizon. The few witnesses who remained were not credible. Nobody had believed them in the past, nor would they believe me now, if I tried to expose them.

Even my partner, Paula Waters, didn't know that the aliens had taken Peter. She'd seen enough during Cheryl Windsor's murder trial to understand that there were aliens amongst us, but she'd chosen not to know any more. When Peter disappeared she didn't seem to make the connection. She apparently bought the flash flood story that Mo, my CIA contact, had conjured up to explain Peter's disappearance.

I thought about Jodie, our legal assistant. We hadn't talked about the aliens since the trial. She also knew the aliens existed as she had possessed one of their weapons for a brief period—a memory gun that could steal time from those within its range. I hadn't brought it up to her because I knew the aliens were monitoring my every word. If they found out that Jodie knew anything about their existence or their mission here on Earth, they'd abduct her as well and then there would be three that were gone because of me—Peter, Dr. Gerhardt, and Jodie—because I couldn't leave it alone. I just had to know the truth.

Since the day Mo revealed to me that Peter had been taken, depression came over me like a swarm of angry bees. It wasn't just the sadness and hopelessness you'd expect over the loss of a child, but fear and dread of the future. If I strayed the least bit from the narrow course set by the CIA and our so-called guests from Tarizon, what would be the consequence? Would another of my children suddenly disappear? Would they take my wife or would I wake up one day in a mental hospital unable to remember my name?

It was difficult to get up each morning and face such a bleak existence, but I still had Rebekah and our three other children to protect. Of course, I owed something to Paula too, as her law partner. She'd been supportive and patient these last few months, but I needed to start pulling my weight again in the partnership. Somehow I had to get myself together and get back to work.

I looked down at the living trust I was working on for a software engineer and his wife. He'd been one of the founders of a successful computer manufacturing company and wanted to be sure his growing estate was properly protected. I was having trouble concentrating on the task and was relieved when the telephone rang. It was a long time client and friend, Ben Stover.

"Stan. I'm so glad I caught you."

"Hey. Ben. How's it going?"

"Not so good, I'm afraid. I need you to come down here right away."

Ben lived in Waco, about a ninety minute drive from Dallas. He operated a small manufacturing business and had been quite successful. I didn't usually go to my clients' offices, particularly if they were out of town. It was much more economical for them to come to me.

"We can't talk about it by telephone?" I asked.

"No. It's too complicated and we've got some tough decisions that must be made immediately."

"Why don't you and Alice come up here? It'll be expensive for me to come down to your place."

"We can't be away from the business that long. Don't worry about the money. We'll pay for every minute of your time."

"I'm not worried about getting paid. I was just trying to save you some money."

"Just come down, Stan. We've got a bad situation here."

I sighed. "Okay, but I need to know at least a little bit about your problem, so I can be thinking about it while I'm driving down."

"Oh God. I don't know where to start," Ben said dejectedly.

"Are you and Alice okay? It's not a medical problem, is it?"

"Not yet, but you know I have a bad heart. This isn't helping matters."

"Okay, just tell me a little about it."

"It's Ralph Herman, our bookkeeper. . . . I just can't believe he'd do something like this. He's been part of the family since he came to work for us nine years ago."

"Ralph Herman," I repeated. "I don't think I've met him."

"He married Peggy, Alice's daughter by her first marriage. They're divorced now, but Ralph has always been a good employee."

"So, what did he do?"

"He's been embezzling money for a long time and concealing it pretty well."

"Oh, jeez," I moaned.

This was a common problem for small business owners. The owner usually knew how to sell his product well enough but not necessarily how to run a business. He'd have to delegate bookkeeping, collections, and office management to others and trust them to be honest. Many times they weren't and this led to problems, usually serious ones.

"Yes, damn it! I can't believe it."

"How much?"

"God, I don't know; a lot. It'll take weeks to try to figure it out. We may never know the full extent of it."

I sighed. "How did he do it?"

"I don't know. I haven't been paying that much attention to the books. I can't do everything. I trusted him! Damn it!"

"Have you gone to the police yet? I asked.

"No. That's why I'm calling you. I'm not sure if I should."

"Okay, I'll clear my schedule tomorrow afternoon and drive on down. I can be there by one-thirty, okay?"

"Yeah. I'll be here—up to my elbows in shit."

I laughed. "Okay, just hang in there. We'll figure this out."

As I'd been talking to Ben, a wave of relief came over me. I wasn't sure why, but having a serious case to work on filled me with energy. Maybe it was an adrenalin rush, I didn't know, but my mind seemed clear and focused for the first time in weeks. There was a client in trouble and I was eager to dig into the shit, as Ben put it, and do whatever was needed to make things right.

Maria, my secretary, walked in and I smiled at her. Her face lit up when she saw me. "Well, you're in a better mood, I see."

I shrugged. "Yeah, Ben Stover just called. He needs my help. You'll need to clear my calendar tomorrow afternoon. I've got to go see him."

"Sure, I'll take care of it."

She made no effort to leave but gazed out the window over North Dallas. Then I remembered she'd come in about something. "So," I said, "did you need something?"

She blinked and then smiled. "Oh, sorry. Ah. . . yes; Mo is on the phone."

My skin suddenly turned cold. The energy I'd felt drained out of me and was replaced with a feeling of great dread. Maria gave me a sympathetic look and then left. She didn't know much about Mo. He had come into my life long before she became my secretary, but she seemed to sense my fear of him. It hadn't always been that way. At first it was exciting—exciting to be involved with the CIA even if only on the fringe of their activities. But as time went on, one thing led to another and soon I was deep into their operations. It had almost cost me my life at one point, but all that was nothing in comparison to what faced me now.

"Mo. What's going on?" I said, trying to act normal as he had instructed me to do.

"How you holding up?" he asked sounding genuinely concerned.

Mo, himself, was a decent person. At least, I had thought so over the years. He had helped me many times with difficult cases and had asked little in return. He even saved my life on one occasion when an assassin was on my trail. I never suspected his generosity was calculated for a specific end. I guess I had been incredibly naive. But, I knew it was the CIA and the bureaucrats who were calling the shots, not Mo. He had tried to protect me as best he could, but I had let myself get recruited. It could have been avoided if I'd just said no thanks in the beginning.

"Better," I said.

"How about your wife?" he asked.

Rebekah. That was another story. She'd never be better. She had been more or less a zombie since the funeral. Luckily her mother lived nearby and had been able to stay with her and the children. I dreaded going home at night. There were no smiles, no small talk, just silence. Rebekah hadn't said it, but I knew she blamed me for Peter's death; and well she should. It was my fault. There was no doubt about that.

"The same," I said.

"Hmm. Sorry."

"So, what do you want?" I said bitterly.

Mo sighed. "We have a situation and we need your help."

"I'm listening, " I said, pressing the phone hard against my ear. I had been waiting for this call—wondering why the aliens would need someone like me on their payroll.

"We can't talk about it over the phone. I'm around back at the service entrance to your building in a blue BMW. Come on down."

"But—" I started to protest, then realized there was no point.

"Okay, I'm coming down."

I looked at my briefcase wondering if I'd need it, then decided I better take it. There may be some paperwork involved in the assignment or I might need to take notes. After stepping out of the elevator I turned right, took the back corridor through the mail room and passed the service elevator. As I exited out onto the loading dock, I saw the blue BMW, walked toward it, and got in.

Mo took off with a jerk and turned left toward LBJ freeway.

"Where are we going?" I asked.

"To meet Kulchz," he replied evenly.

My skin turned cold again thinking of the alien commander who was in charge of the abduction of thousands of American children. What kind of a man was he? Was he really human? The aliens looked like us. Mo had said they were human, but how could that be?

"Can I ask questions, or do I have to just do as I'm told?" I asked.

Mo smiled. "Sure, what do you want to know?"

"You said the aliens were human. How can that be?"

"I don't know. I've been told that Earth and Tarizon are sister colonies having been settled about the same time. Apparently we have common ancestors."

"Common ancestors?"

"Yes, apparently millions of years ago there was a planet out there somewhere inhabited by humans. As technology advanced and life expectancy increased, the planet got overcrowded and couldn't sustain the population. Because of this, settlers started journeying out into space searching for alternative places to live. One of those groups of settlers found Tarizon and another, Earth."

I sat back and closed my eyes trying to fathom all of this. It was just too bizarre and impossible to believe. Yet I'd seen their spaceship, the memory gun, the frogmen, and they'd taken my son. How much proof did I need? "What about the frogmen? I asked."Tell me about them."

"They call them Seafolken," Mo said. "They're slaves who man the ships and do all the hard labor."

"I thought this society was advanced. How come they still have slavery?"

"I don't know. All I know is the Seafolken are strong, fast, and have psychic powers you wouldn't believe. You don't want to mess with them."

"If they are so fearsome, how do the humans keep them in line?"

Mo shrugged. "Hell, I don't know. You can ask Kulchz. Maybe he'll enlighten you."

We were on I30 now heading east. When we got to the Lake Tawakoni exit, Mo got onto the state highway and headed south.

"Why are we going to Lake Tawakoni?" I asked.

"That's where the aliens moved their headquarters after you screwed up their base of operations at Possum Kingdom Lake. They have to land near a lake so the Seafolken can feed."

I nodded. A few miles down the road, Mo took a right onto a county road that took us deep into a wooded area. He made several more turns and each time the road got narrower and was less maintained. Soon we were on a dirt road deep in the middle of nowhere. Finally, he stopped at a gate. He got out and unlocked it.

In the distance I could see the lake. Mo got in and drove us through the gate and then stopped to lock it behind us. Nobody would find the aliens out here, I thought. I doubted I could even find my way back to Dallas, if something happened to Mo. We drove another ten minutes and finally stopped by an old, dilapidated oil storage tank. As I got out of the car, I noticed a door had been cut into the side of the tank. Mo led us through it.

The dank interior was only illuminated by a single blue light above the door. I stopped to let my eyes adjust and asked, "Where are we going?"

"Kulchz has an office underground," Mo replied, pushing me forward. "Just up ahead you'll see a hatch that will lead us down to it."

I walked forward with caution, and as my eyes adjusted to the low light, I saw a metal railing protruding up from a hatch. Mo nudged me toward the railing, so I grabbed it and started down. At the bottom I found myself in a long corridor that went in both directions. It was stark white and well lit. I waited for Mo.

"Which way?" I asked.

"Follow me," he said. As best I could tell, he went south toward the lake. A few minutes later he stopped in front of a door, looked into an eye hole, and the locking mechanism clicked. He pushed the door open and walked in. I followed him with much trepidation.

Kulchz was a tall human with broad muscular shoulders and a rugged face. He looked at me intently as I entered the spacious office that appeared to be made of glass or crystal. There were thousands of lights, control panels, and monitors of every sort. He motioned for us to sit down. The room was furnished with several chairs and a sofa cushioned by a soft, white substance. When I sat down, the seat conformed itself to the shape of my body. As I sank into it, I felt like I was floating on air.

Kulchz sat in front of a large, glowing desk. With the faint blue glow came a steady humming noise that changed pitch from time to time. I looked at it curiously.

Kulchz nodded slightly. "Mr. Turner, at last we meet."

"Yes," I said. "I figured one day we would. This is quite a place you have here."

"Yes, it will do for our limited purposes."

My hands were shaking so I slipped them under my thighs to quiet them.

Kulchz smiled. "There's no reason to be nervous, Mr. Turner. We mean you no harm and your son is doing quite well on Tarizon."

Anger swelled in me as I thought of Peter being a captive of these intruders. As if he'd read my mind Kulchz said, "He's not a captive. He's been assigned temporary quarters and has been provided a guide to teach him the ways of Tarizon."

"Really? So, he got there okay? He's not sick or anything?"

"No, he's perfectly healthy and actually enjoying himself, I believe."

A monitor clicked on and there was an image of Peter being led down a crystal hallway by a woman dressed in a white gown. As she stopped in front of a room she looked toward the camera. She was young and quite pretty. She said something and Peter laughed. He seemed quite taken with her and looked as happy as I'd ever seen him. Tears of joy welled in my eyes and I could scarcely keep from crying. Peter was alive! He was okay!

The monitor went blank and Kulchz smiled. "So, worry not about Peter. He'll be fine as long as you do your job."

"My job?" I said. "What is my job?"

Kulchz sighed. "There's been, what would you call it, a . . . ah . . . botched, I believe is the term . . . a botched extraction."

"Really? What went wrong?"

"Nothing with the extraction itself. Everything seemed to go as planned. It was staged as a parental abduction as it often is, but there is a police detective who won't accept this explanation. He thinks the wife is involved in the disappearance somehow and is out to prove it."

"Who's the detective?"

"Kramer. Will Kramer," Mo replied.

“Hmm. I don’t know him. Does he have any evidence?”

"We don't know. All we know is that this detective must be stopped, and you've got to do it."

"So, you want me to represent this woman?"

"Yes, defend her and prove she's innocent. You must stop the detective too. If he keeps digging, he might discover the truth and then we . . . well you know what we'd have to do."

I knew only too well what they'd do. The two options that had been explained to me were having my memory erased or being exiled to Tarizon. The problem with memory erasing was that it was imprecise and unpredictable. It was quite possible that months or years might be erased unnecessarily. There was even the possibility of brain damage. Living on a strange planet away from family and friends didn’t offer much appeal either.

"Yes, I guess I do. . . . So, why don't you just abduct the woman and save us all a lot of trouble? Take her to Tarizon to be with her family?"

"We can't do that. Our treaty with the U.S. government doesn't allow it nor do we want the Earth mothers on Tarizon where they might try to interfere with the home family."

"What about Peter and Dr. Gerhardt?" I asked. Did the treaty allow you to take them?"

"If the program’s invisibility is in jeopardy, then it can be done as a matter of national security, but that is not the case with this woman. We have to try very hard to resolve these kinds of problems without resort to violence or abduction."

It occurred to me that many of the alien husbands would probably have fallen in love with their Earth wives and would have insisted that they be protected post extraction. I wondered if an alien husband had ever refused to be extracted. Surely it must be difficult to live with a woman four or five years, have children with her, and then up and leave without even a word of explanation.

I nodded. "All right. What is this lady's name? Where can I find her?"

"Her name is Charlotte Wenzel. She's being questioned at the Plano Police Station right now. Sooner or later they'll indict her. You should contact her immediately."

My heart sank. What were the odds I'd have a conflict on the first case they wanted to assign me?

"I can't handle that case," I said.

"Why not?" Mo asked.

"Bart Williams, my partner's husband, works for the Collin County District Attorney's office. I overheard him say he was prosecuting that case. It would be a conflict of interest."

"You have to do it," Kulchz said. "You're the only one we have to represent her."

"I'm sorry."

"They have other prosecutors," Mo pointed out. "If you take the case, they'll just assign another prosecutor."

"True. But I couldn't do that to Paula. This is a big case for Bart. He's been waiting a long ti—"

"Do I have to remind you we've got Peter?" Kulchz said angrily.

A cold chill swept over me. I glared at Kulchz. What a bastard he was. "Okay. Okay. So, if they do indict her, where do I get the money to post the bond?" I asked.

"How much do you think you'll need?"

"Well, if she's charged with murder, it could easily be two-hundred and fifty thousand dollars."

Kulchz nodded. "We'll provide you whatever it takes to get

Mrs. Wenzel off. Just let Mo know what you need."

Mo stood up. "I'll take you back to your office so you can get started."

I got up and said, "What about Peter? Can I talk to him?"

Kulchz stood up abruptly. "No, just do as you're told and he'll be fine. When Ms. Wenzel is cleared and the investigation is over, you can come back here and see some more video of him."

"That's it?" I said angrily.

Mo took my arm and guided me to the door. I looked back, but Kulchz had already turned his attention to other matters. On the way back to Dallas I thought of Peter. He did look well. Was that really him or just some computer image? I wanted to believe it was him. I had to believe it. The alternative was unbearable. When Mo dropped me off a block away from my office building, he gave me a briefcase and said the contents should tide me over for a while.

When I got back to my office, I closed the door and opened the briefcase. It was stuffed with money—hundred dollar bills in nice neat packages. It didn't take long to count three-hundred and fifty thousand dollars. The expected bond money plus a hundred grand as a retainer, I figured. Paula would be proud and shocked that I'd gotten a decent retainer from a client—not bad, had the circumstances been different. I was eager to tell her the news but when I checked her office, she wasn't there.

Chapter 2

The Investigation

I was beginning to wonder if the firm of Turner & Waters was going to survive. Stan had been devastated by Peter's death and it was nearly six weeks before he even bothered showing up for work. Even then he was listless and had little enthusiasm for the daily routine. Luckily, after the Cheryl Windsor trial, I didn't have much going on, so I was able to cover Stan's civil cases. He did just about everything from wills to adoptions. No one could ever accuse him of specializing. He said it was because he was so hungry when he first started practice that he had to take everything that came in the door just to survive. He'd bragged that he'd never refused a case and that if he didn't know how to do something, he'd learn.

I'd certainly learned a lot in the last few weeks. I'd reviewed oil and gas leases, drafted no competition agreements, appeared at a couple of bankruptcy hearings, and even attended a homeowner's association meeting, which I hope I never have to do again. They spent three hours arguing about dog poop, barking dogs, and woodpeckers attacking their carports. What a waste of time! Fortunately Jodie, our legal assistant, had become proficient in most of these matters and did most of the paperwork, but it was still a relief to have Stan back so I could concentrate on what I loved the most: criminal defense.

The press hounded us for months about the disappearance of our client Cheryl Windsor during her murder case. The case had been declared a mistrial and without a defendant it was not likely to be retried. Eventually the crowd of reporters dwindled outside our offices until one day it was gone. The only reporter that wouldn't leave us alone was Alex Garcia of the Globe Inquirer. During Cheryl

Windsor's trial he had infiltrated our team as a bodyguard and seduced me into a fraudulent affair that nearly cost me my marriage. The scandal following the disclosure of our relationship didn't deter him from continuing to cover the story. In fact, when the trial was over it became his obsession to find out what happened the day Cheryl Windsor vanished from the witness stand in mid-sentence.

The lull at the office gave me more time to spend with my husband, Bart. He was an assistant district attorney at the Collin County District Attorney's Office up in McKinney, Texas. This was just in the nick of time as our marriage had been through some rough spots and might have fallen apart had I not had time to work on repairing it. Bart had just been assigned the Gabriel Wenzel murder case and was very excited about it. It was his first high profile case and he was under a lot of pressure to do well. Usually I was the one who got all the media attention, but I was glad Bart was finally getting some well deserved publicity.

Bart had called and asked me to join him for lunch. Not having a lot to do, I eagerly accepted the invitation. We met at Chili's in Plano which was midway between our two offices. He was pacing in front of the restaurant when I walked up. I saw that he wasn't smiling, which disturbed me because he rarely got upset over anything. After we'd been seated, I asked him what was wrong.

"You don't know?" he snickered.

"Know what?"

"Stan is defending Charlotte Wenzel."

"Huh?" I said incredulously.

"Yeah. I couldn't believe it either."

"That can't be."

"Don't you know what goes on in your own law firm? You're a partner for godsakes!"

"Honey. I'm as shocked as you about this. Stan didn't mention it to me. I can't imagine him taking on a case without consulting me. I'm so sorry."

"Now, Ralston's taken me off the case and given it to Gary Shepard."

"Oh, God! I can't belief this. Let me go talk to Stan. Maybe he didn't realize—"

"Yes he did. We've discussed the case with him."

"I know. You're right," I replied angrily. "What was he thinking? I need to talk to him. There has to be some rational explanation. This isn't like Stan. Tell me exactly what happened. I don't want to misstate the facts when I give him a piece of my mind. "

Bart took a deep breath. "You knew Ralston hired a new chief prosecutor?" He said. "I think I mentioned it to you."

"This Gary Shepard guy?" I asked.

"Yes. He's out of Houston. He's been the number one felony prosecutor for the Houston DA's office for the last six years. Ralston's been courting him for awhile. I guess he made him an offer he couldn't refuse–a big pay raise and a fat expense allowance."

I shook my head in disgust. "He should have given you some of that money. You haven't had a pay increase since you've been there."

"Yeah, tell me about it. . . . Anyway, I asked Ralston why he needed to go outside the office to get a chief prosecutor. He said he had to have someone he knew would be effective. He was worried about getting reelected. He'd promised the voters in the last election that he'd improve the conviction rate if he was elected. Unfortunately, that hasn't happened."

"Well, you and I know the voters have a short memory. As long as he's a Republican he'll get reelected. This is Collin County for godsakes."

"He's worried about the primaries. Joe Sharp has been talking about running against him."

"Joe Sharp? He's a criminal defense attorney. The republicans won't elect him."

"Ralston's not so sure about that. Anyway he's acting very paranoid these days."

"He'd better be careful. If Gary Shepard's so good, he might take a run at his job once he gets the lay of the land up here."

"Yeah, wouldn't that be ironic," Bart replied.

"Anyway, I've been working with Detective Will Kramer on the Wenzel case. He was looking at the wife as the prime suspect. When Gabriel Wenzel and his children disappeared an anonymous informant came forward and claimed that Charlotte Wenzel had contacted him about killing her husband. He claimed to have refused her, but wanted us to know she might have found someone else. Based on that informant he had obtained a search warrant for the Wenzel home and he invited me to come along. They live in Canyon Creek."

"That's a ritzy address," Paula noted.

"Yes. They obviously aren't hurting for money. Kramer was already there when I arrived. He gave me the nickel tour and said they hadn't found any evidence of foul play but had found a nice two million dollar life insurance policy."

"Oh, wonderful. Was the ink still wet?"

"Probably. She took it out just a few weeks ago. She gets two hundred thousand dollars for each kiddo too."

"Who's the beneficiary?" I asked.

"Mrs. Wenzel, of course."

"Quite a motive."

"Yes, but she'd have to be really stupid to take out a policy and then kill the insured less than two weeks later. It almost makes it look like a coincidence."

"Yeah, maybe, but not all murderers are smart," I noted. "She may not have thought it through. What do you have on the victims?"

"Kramer said they were reported missing by Mrs. Wenzel Friday evening, August 2nd, I think. According to Wenzel, her husband phoned around noon and told her he'd pick the kids up from school and spend the afternoon with them. She said fine and went shopping. They never made it home. A formal missing person's report wasn't filed until the next afternoon since the father supposedly had the children."

"What else do they have?" I asked.

"A neighbor and friend of Charlotte, Janet Kaufman, claims the Wenzels were having marital problems. She says Mr. Wenzel was unfaithful and may have mentally abused her."

"What made her think that?" I asked.

"She claims Charlotte often seemed disoriented and complained of having blackouts. She thinks Gabriel or Gabe, as they called him, liked to knock her around."

"Did she see any physical evidence of that?"

"No. She couldn't remember seeing any bruises, but Mrs. Wenzel apparently wore a lot of makeup."

"Yeah, but you couldn't hide serious bruising with makeup," I said.

"How else would you explain the blackouts?" Bart asked.

"Could be drugs?"

"Yeah. Maybe. But they didn't find anything stronger than aspirin in her house."

"Anything else?"

"According to Mrs. Kaufman Gabe had a lot of issues. She said he was a control freak for starters. They had an elaborate security system cameras and monitors everywhere designed not only to keep intruders out but to keep an eye on his family. It was almost like his wife and children were prisoners in their own home."

"So, you think Charlotte just got sick and tired of it and decided to put an end to it?" I asked.

"That's what Kramer thinks."

"But, why the kids? Mothers don't usually kill their children . . . unless they're insane," I noted.

"The blackouts could be a sign of mental illness," Bart replied.

"Maybe."

"Anyway, later that day I met up with Kramer at the McKinney police station. He'd picked up Charlotte Wenzel for questioning. When I got there, Kramer had been in the interview room for some time questioning her. I watched through the one way mirror. She's a young, pretty Asian woman. She looked exhausted and was having difficulty keeping her eyes opened. Kramer was pacing in front of the small table where she was seated. He was relentless but Mrs. Wenzel was sticking to her story. I wasn't sure Kramer was going to be able to break her. That's when I heard footsteps quickly coming down the hall. I turned and saw Stan approaching."

"Oh, God," I moaned shaking my head.

"He wanted to know why we were still questioning his client."

"His client?"

"That's what he claimed," Bart replied. "He said he'd called over to the station and told them she was not to be questioned without her attorney present."

Paula shook her head. "I'm sorry, Bart. I had no idea. I'm going to go have a chat with Stan right now. I can't believe he'd do this to you."

Bart acted like he believed me but he was still angry with Stan as was I. When I got back to my office, Maria told me Stan and Mrs. Wenzel had just gone into a conference room where I joined them. Mrs. Wenzel was a brunette. She wore a mid-length black skirt, tan top, and sandals. Stan stood up. "This is my partner, Paula Waters." We shook hands and then sat.

I wanted to say something to Stan before he got started but I couldn't do it in front of Mrs. Wenzel. He must have known Bart would get pulled off the case if he took Charlotte's case. I couldn't believe he'd stabbed me in the back.

"So, Mrs. Wenzel," Stan said. "I hope they didn't treat you too badly at the police station."

She rolled her eyes. "They take me to room and let me sit long time with no food, no water."

"I know," Stan replied. "They can be very inconsiderate."

"But, thanks to you they let me go after only eight hour."

"Eight hours. I'm sorry. As soon as I heard you were being questioned, I called them, told them I was representing you, and that the interview was over."

"So, I your client?" Charlotte asked skeptically. "I not complaining; just confused."

I frowned and gave Stan a look. What was going on? He obviously hadn't met Charlotte before and she hadn't hired him, yet he told the police he was her attorney. I folded my arms and waited with great anticipation for an explanation.

"Yes, you looked a bit surprised when you saw me."

She shook her head. "Shocked better description. I don't have money and family in Japan."

"Well, there is someone who cares about you," Stan said. "I can't disclose who it is, but they hired me to defend you." Charlotte's puzzled look deepened. "Of course," Stan continued, "I can't defend you unless you want me to. If they arrest you, they'll provide you with a court-appointed attorney—usually someone just out of law school."

Her eyes narrowed. "Court-appointed attorney?"

"Right. That's why I asked you here today—to get your consent and hopefully get started on your defense. A murder case is complex and it's important we get to work right away."

Charlotte looked at Stan for a moment seeming uncertain as to how to respond. Then she raised her dark eyebrows and said, "So, my choices are to have top lawyer in Dallas defend me, or kid outa law school 'bout a week. Is that right?"

Stan shrugged.

"Gee whiz! That such a tough decision," she smirked.

I laughed.

Stan smiled."So, shall we get started?"

She put her hand to her chin and looked up like she was thinking. "Ah. . . . Let's see. . . . Yes, I make decision. I think I go with the ace lawyer. I curious to know, though, who thinks I worth your big fee?"

Charlotte was a hoot. Here she was about to be charged with murder and she was acting like a standup comic. I wondered if she was always this funny. She'd be great fun at a cocktail party.

"I'm afraid I can't tell you that. It was a condition of my employment, but I assure you I'll do whatever I can to get you off and it won't cost you a dime."

Charlotte shrugged. "Well, okay. Why not? Go for it."

"Good," Stan said. "We've got a lot to do so let's get started. . . . Let's see. . . . First, you'll have to give us a little history. Paula and I know virtually nothing about you or your family's disappearance."

The word abduction hit me like a brick. Suddenly I knew why Stan had taken this case. This had to have something to do with the aliens. Had Stan somehow figured out that this was an alien abduction case? If so, I could see him wanting to defend Charlotte, but who was fronting the money? I couldn't imagine.

"Okay. Ah. Let's see," Charlotte started. "Gabe, that short for Gabriel, and we met about five years ago at church group. I not like him much at first. He awkward and very clueless, as they say."

"Clueless? What do you mean?" I asked.

"Dense, stupid, slow, low IQ," Charlotte said like a Gatling gun spitting out rounds. "But as I get to know him better I see him actually pretty much genius."

"Really?" I replied. "A genius?"

"Yes, he work on some super-duper secret military project. He not like to talk 'bout work much, but they don't pay idiots big money."

"Go on," Stan said. "Tell us about your marriage."

"Well, after while I see Gabe not so bad. He just a super smart geek with lots of brains, no common sense. His mother and father long gone died and he have no brothers and sisters. He need me. I knew I'd be as much mother as wife, but he have plenty of dough and want lots of kids like me."

Tears began to well in Charlotte's eyes and she swallowed hard. "We had three kids you know. Gabe was a good father. I wouldn't kill him," she said, I don't care what he do to me . . . I not that kinda woman."

"What do you mean, no matter what he did?" I asked.

Charlotte sighed. "Well it no big secret he have other girls."

"Really," I said. "How long had that been going on?"

"Pretty much all the time. He not try to keep it secret either. In his mind it no big deal—at least for man. First time I griped him out, he just shrug and ask what was for dinner."

"Jesus," I said. "You've got to be kidding."

"No. If not for kids and money, I'd kicked him out long time ago."

"What was his nationality?" Stan asked.

"He not from here. He from Turkey. I think Turkey like Japan. Men do what want, women do what told."

"So I've heard. Where did you live?" Stan asked.

"We have big house in Richardson—two stories, five thousand square feet, pool, 3 car garage, A/C, close to schools," she replied like she was reading from the real estate section of the Dallas Morning News.

"Do you work?"

"No. Gabe not allow it. He say being a mother full time job. I used to be a nurses' aid but Gabe make me quit. I not complain, though. Nursing hard work."

"Yeah, I can imagine," I said. "So, tell me about the past few months leading up the abduction of your children and the disappearance of your husband?" Stan asked.

Charlotte's slanted eyes closed for a moment and then opened. She licked her pale lips with one quick sweep of her tongue. For a moment I thought she was going to lose it. Then she took a deep breath and replied. "First thing I notice is Gabe seem to having something heavy on mind. He very quiet, work long hours, always nervous 'bout something, didn't see him much. When I ask him what wrong, he say, nothing. I wonder if he want divorce."

"Did he mention divorce?" I asked.

"No. But he not happy with me. I know that."

"Was he having another affair, maybe?"

"No. That not bother him. Something else wrong."

"Tell me about the abduction?" Stan asked.

"He tell me he going to pick up kids from school on Friday afternoon. That big surprise but I not complain 'cause I like go shopping. Hard to do with three kids.

"When I get home at four he and kids not there. At quarter to five I call school to see if any problems, but they tell me Gabe already picked up kids right on time.

"I not scared since I figure Gabe just took them to dinner or for snack. When he not home by seven-thirty, I call police."

"What did they say?" I asked.

"They say since kids with father they not do nothing yet. They say call back after twenty-four hours. By eight when they not back, I know something wrong."

"So, what makes the police think you had anything to do with their disappearance?" Stan asked.

"Gabe took out a big policy just before he go away—two million dollars on him and two hundred thousand dollars on each of the kids."

"Jeez! I hope that was his idea," Stan said.

"Yes, not my idea. He say he want to know I okay if he die."

"How did he buy the insurance?" Stan asked.

"I called agent and he come to house. You know, you're in good hands with Allstate."

I stifled a chuckle. "You set up the appointment? That kinda looks bad."

"Yes it does," Stan muttered. "So, I assume they haven't found any bodies."

"No, no bodies. Just found Gabe's car on side of road near lake."

"What lake?"

"Tawaki."

"Tawakoni?"

Charlotte nodded. "Right. Right. Lake Tawakoni."

"How did it get there?"

"They say I dump bodies somewhere and leave car on side of road. They—" Charlotte's voice broke up and she started to sob. "They . . . they think bodies picked clean by vultures and bones scattered all over hills by coyotes."

"Oh, my God," I said. "That's horrible. Why do they think that?"

"I not know. They say it clever plan." She closed her eyes and began sobbing again.

"Charlotte," I asked. "You say none of this is true, right?"

Her eyes narrowed. "It not true! Do you think I kill my own children?"

"No, of course not, but they must have some evidence," I said. "Are you sure you've told us everything?"

"Yes, I tell all."

"You didn't hire someone to kill your husband? A contract killer, maybe?"

"No. There no contract killer!" Charlotte protested. "What you talking about?"

"I heard from a reliable source that you approached someone about killing your husband," I said tentatively.

Charlotte shook her head vigorously. "No! I not hire nobody to kill my husband. That wrong."

Stan glared at me. I shrugged. "Bart said they had a witness who claimed she contacted him about killing her husband. Ah, maybe he was mistaken; I don't know."

Stan thought for a moment and then looked at Charlotte."Is it possible that you might have complained to somebody about your husband and they—"

"No. Not possible. I talk to no one."

"Okay. It could just be a jail house snitch trying to get some time off his sentence. Don't worry about it. We'll find out who it is and figure out why he's lying."

"Why someone lie about me? It not right."

We talked for some time after Charlotte had left. Before we were through I confronted Stan about taking the Wenzel case.

"You knew Bart was prosecuting the case?" I asked.

Stan took a deep breath. "I'm sorry, but a friend of hers contacted me and asked me to represent her. I told him no, but he insisted. He paid me . . . I mean us, a big retainer."

"How much?" I asked.

"A hundred grand and if that runs out there will be more. We needed the money and I needed a case to work on to get back on track. I felt badly about Bart, but I knew he'd get another case. It wouldn't affect his salary. He'd just be reassigned. I hope you'll forgive me."

I signed. "It's just that this was Bart's first big case. He was really starting to sink his teeth into it."

Stan shook his head. "I know. But the client was insistent and how often do you get three hundred and fifty thousand dollars in cash dropped in your lap."

"Three hundred and fifty thousand! I thought you said a hundred grand."

"He put up the bond money too. I hope when they arrest her, it's enough."

I thought about it. "She's a housewife, owns a home, no priors. I couldn't imagine any judge asking for more."

"Well, if they do, we can get it. I just don't want her spending anytime in jail. . . . What's this about a contract killer? I can't believe Charlotte would do that. How would she know where to find somebody like that?"

"I don't know. It's just what Kramer told Bart. I'll call Shepard right now and see if he'll tell me who the snitch is."

When I got back to my office I put a call into Gary Shepard. He answered on the first ring and I told him who it was. He seemed to be in a very good mood and said he was glad I'd called.

"I guess you heard Stan and I have been retained to defend Charlotte Wenzel."

"Yes," Shepard said. "I was surprised you'd taken the case. It seemed to have caught Bart by surprise too. Don't you two ever talk?"

"Sure, it was a mixup. Stan took the case not realizing Bart was the prosecutor."

"Really? So, are you doing it pro bono? She doesn't have a dime as I understand it."

"Well, our fee arrangement shouldn't concern you. What matters is we're on the case and we intend to protect her rights. She told us about the eight-hour interrogation."

"She did, huh. So what? We had a right to question her."

"Maybe, but not to coerce and harass her. . . . And what's this about her hiring a contract killer? I heard you had a witness."

"Bart told you about that?"

"Yes, and I want his identity so we can talk to him."

"Sorry. Can't give it to you," Shepard said smugly.

"Why not? We have a right to it."

"Because there is no snitch."

"Huh?" I said weakly. "But why would Bart have told me there was a snitch then?"

"Because he's a spy for your law firm, obviously. I suspected it the first time I met him. Then, when I started investigating your past history with this office, well, I knew he'd tell you."

My stomach turned. Oh, my God! We'd been set up. "You fed Bart bogus information?" I said angrily.

"Yes," Shepard snickered.

I let my hand drop and just stared at the telephone in disbelief. Who was this bastard? Why did he hate us so much? I took a deep breath and tried to calm myself. Finally, I lifted the receiver to my ear and said curtly, "So what? You'd have to tell us eventually anyway."

"Not if we didn't intend to call him." Shepard spat."We're on to your tricks, Paula. If you want information from this office you'd better go through proper discovery. They'll be no more favors to you. And, if you approach an employee of this office again looking for inside information, I'll file a grievance with the State Bar and ask the judge to impose sanctions."

I didn't say anything. My stomach was in a knot and I could scarcely breathe.

"Is that clear, Ms. Waters?" Shepard pressed.

I still couldn't talk and finally hung up the phone without saying goodbye. What was going on? In all the years I'd practiced I'd never run across such blatant hostility from an opponent. After I'd caught my breath, I called Bart. "Honey, you won't believe what just happened to me."

"Really, well it couldn't have been as bad as what just happened to me," he said in a low tone.

"What?" I asked.

"I just got fired! And the DA is considering filing charges against me for obstruction of justice in leaking information to you."

"Oh, my God, honey. Shepard is a demon. I can't believe he deliberately set us up."

"Yeah, well he did and now I don't have a job because of your partner. Damn him! I really liked working for the DA's office. Now what am I going to do? I'll never be able to get a decent job again without a good reference from them! I'm going to kill your partner."

The phone went dead. Oh, God! What had I done? I hung up the phone and raced back to Stan's office. He was on the phone so I sat down and anxiously waited for him. Seeing my obvious distress, he cut short his conversation and hung up the telephone.

"Paula, what's wrong?"

"Stan, oh God, what have I done?"

I explained what had happened and how Bart had fallen into Shepard's trap.

"I've never met Gary Shepard," he said, "but I'd heard from some acquaintances in Houston that he was a piece of work. He's really shown his hand by going for the juggler in the first round. He obviously isn't a gentleman, that's for sure. We'll have to be very careful and vigilant in the future."

I buried my head in my hands struggling not to cry.

"It's not your fault," Stan said. "This mess is on me. It was totally avoidable. I shouldn't have sent you off to call Bart without giving the situation more thought. We panicked a little and it cost us.

I just didn't see Ralston permitting such underhanded tactics. It's not like him. This new guy Shepard obviously is some kind of Rambo prosecutor."

"Maybe, but he's pissed off the wrong broad," Paula said, her voice cracking. "He'll pay for this, I promise you."

"I'm sure he will, but in the meantime I want you to stay clear of him. Let me deal with him."

I didn't respond. My mind was far away and I couldn't concentrate. I excused myself to call Bart. He'd never hung up on me before and I was worried that I might not be able to repair the damage that had been done to our marriage. He wasn't at home and he didn't answer his cell phone, so I left a message. Where could he be? Where would he go to contemplate the day's catastrophic events? I had no idea, but I had to find him.

Chapter 3

Embezzlement

The next day I worked a couple hours in the office and was about to leave to go to Waco when Maria advised me there was a call from Agent Lot of the FBI. A sick feeling came over me. What was I going to do? During our previous murder case we'd been in possession of one of the aliens' memory guns. I'd put it in my safety deposit box thinking it would be safe there. Unfortunately, the aliens must have tracked the gun to the bank because the gun was stolen. After it happened I got a call from Agent Lot of the FBI asking me who would break into a national bank, not touch the millions of dollars in the vault, and take only the contents of my safety deposit box.

In the spur of the moment the best explanation I could come up with was that I represented an inventor and that he had given me a prototype of his new invention for safe keeping. That left a lot of unanswered questions, but got Agent Lot off my back for the duration of the trial. Now he was back, no doubt wanting more specific information about my client and his invention so they could figure out who had robbed the bank, but more importantly, who had been able to disable the bank's state-of-the-art security system in less than a minute. I picked up the telephone.

"Stan Turner."

"Stan. This is Agent Lot. How are you?"

"Oh. Agent Lot. Fine. Any news on Dr. Gerhardt or Cheryl Windsor?"

"No. I'm afraid not."

"Hmm. That's too bad. I was hoping you'd come up with something."

"We're working on it, but what I was calling about was your inventor client. Has he contacted you yet?"

"Ah. . . . Well, he's not back yet. I did get a message from him, though. He's due back in the country in a month or so. I'm sure he'll call me then."

"He still doesn't know the prototype has been stolen?"

"No, he knows. I talked to one of his associates and told him. He knows what happened. Just as soon as he gets back in town, I'll bring him in so you can interview him."

"All right; but I'm under a lot of pressure to come up with an explanation for what happened. If your client doesn't come in soon, we'll have to come looking for him. This matter is of the utmost importance and our patience is wearing thin."

"I totally understand," I said. "I'll get word to my client of the urgency of the situation. I'm sure there will be no more delays in his return to the United States."

After hanging up the phone I let out a sigh of relief. I'd bought another thirty days, but this was likely my final reprieve. The next time Agent Lot called I'd have to produce a client and his invention. The only problem was I didn't have a client who was an inventor nor was there was a prototype of an instant air purifier. Unless I came up with a brilliant idea soon, we'd be screwed.

I looked at my watch and saw it was time to head for Waco to see Ben and Alice Stover. They were two of the nicest people you'd ever meet and I was worried about what I'd find once I got down there. They'd asked me to meet them at a local restaurant, the Elite Café, because they were afraid if an attorney showed up at the office the employees would get spooked. They were seated at a booth when I walked in Waco's most renowned diner. I walked over to them. Ben got up and shook my hand heartily. Alice was smiling broadly. I bent over and gave her a hug.

"It's been awhile," I said as I took a seat. "Hey, I'm glad you picked this place. I've heard a lot about it."

"Yes, they say Elvis used to dine here when he was stationed at Ft. Hood." Ben remarked.

"Is that right? Wow! . . . So, you guys look good."

Ben snickered. "Yeah, well. We feel like shit."

I nodded. "So, tell me what's going on."

Ben was in his late fifties, tall, salt and pepper hair, grey eyes, and always had a smile on his face. Alice was six inches shorter, brown hair, green eyes, and usually very perky. Today, however, she looked tired and worn out.

"You want a cup of coffee or some lunch?" Ben asked.

I nodded. "Sure, I'll take a cup."

Ben motioned to the waitress and she came over. "Can we get another cup of coffee?"

"Sure," the waitress said and went off toward the kitchen. A minute later she put a cup down in front of me and poured the coffee from a glass pot. I added two sugars and a little cream and then looked up at Ben expectantly.

He sighed. "About six weeks ago we got a call from one of our long time suppliers about our account. He said we were ninety days past due and our last check had bounced."

"Oh, wonderful," I said shaking my head.

"Yes. I was shocked because business hadn't been great but it had been pretty steady. There was no way we should have been late on our bills and we damn sure shouldn't have been bouncing checks."

"Right."

"So, I confronted Ralph, our bookkeeper, about it and he said the bank had made a mistake and he'd take care of it."

"Well, I was a little too shaken to just take his word for it, so I pulled the old bank statements and accounts payable records and started looking through them. I was appalled at what I found. Each month our payables were getting a little farther and farther behind and about twenty percent of our revenue was being siphoned off into a bank account I knew nothing about."

"Oh, my God," I said. "You've got to be kidding."

"I wish. Anyway, when I confronted Ralph about the bank account he claimed I'd told him to set it up," Ben said angrily. "What a son of a bitch."

"So, what did you do?"

"I called my banker and asked him how it was that an employee could set up an account in our name without our permission."

"Yeah, really," I said. "What did he say?"

"He claimed he came in, set up the account, and then took

the signature card with him for us to sign. He brought it back the next day with our signatures on it."

"You obviously didn't sign it, right?" I asked.

"No, but the signatures actually look a lot like ours, don't they, honey?"

Alice nodded. "He's a damn good forger. They almost look legitimate, but we didn't sign it."

"So, you haven't called the police?"

"No, not yet. We wanted to talk to you first."

"And you haven't taken any other action?

"No, other than fire his ass," Ben replied.

"How did he take being fired?"

"He got all bent out of shape and said if we went to the police he'd report us to the IRS and tell them about our unreported income and bogus deductions."

"What? That's bullshit," I said.

"I know that, but the IRS doesn't. He also said he'd call our creditors and tell them we were skimming money from the business and planned to file bankruptcy."

"Oh, my God. This guy's a lunatic."

Alice nodded. "I'd like to go to the district attorney and file criminal charges, but I'm afraid of what he will do."

"We can't let him get away with this," Ben said. "What should we do, Stan?"

"The guy's a thief. He needs to be put away. If you let him get away with it, he'll just go do it again to someone else."

"But what if he follows through with his threats?" Alice asked.

"Hopefully, the IRS and your creditors will realize he's a lunatic."

"I don't know," Alice said. "If someone had called me and told us one of our customers was a crook, I'd have a hard time ignoring that."

Alice was right. Someone as smooth as Ralph would have the IRS drooling over the case. He'd make it sound like Ben and Alice were more despicable than Bonnie and Clyde. "Well, we could go to court and get an injunction based on his threats."

"Yeah, but would a guy like that pay any attention to an

injunction?" Ben asked.

I raised my eyebrows and shrugged. "If he didn't, we could ask the court to find him in contempt. If we were successful, he'd go to jail."

Ben looked at me and then at Alice. "Okay, maybe we should call the DA, but a more immediate problem is how do we make payroll, pay the rent, and make our payments to the bank this month?"

"How short are you?" I asked.

"We need about twenty-five thousand dollars by Friday just to get through the weekend and that doesn't include covering our three thousand dollar overdraft. Normally we keep a checking account balance of at least twenty-five thousand dollars as a cushion, but Ralph has taken everything."

"Well, we could file a Chapter 11," I said, "but that won't help solve your cash crunch right now. You need to borrow some money or find something to sell, I guess."

"I've already cashed in our life insurance policies. That netted almost eleven thousand. We don't really have anything else of value except some real estate, but that would take too long to unload."

"Maybe you could borrow on the real estate. Have you talked to your banker?"

"He might do it," Ben said, "but even that would take a few days plus we'd have another debt to service."

"Right, but maybe in a few months you'll get some restitution to pay off the loan."

It was one of those situations that didn't have a solution, just options to minimize the damage done and hopefully allow the business to survive. I felt helpless and frustrated. I wanted to tell them we'd figure it all out and everything would be okay, but I couldn't promise that.

"There is one other option," Ben said.

"What's that," I asked.

"There's been someone who wanted to buy the business. This might be the time to unload it."

"Really? Could they act quickly?"

"I don't know. We've never seriously considered selling it, so

I've never talked to them in earnest about it."

"Perhaps you should contact them. I know you don't want to sell, but it would be a good idea to have a backup plan in case our other options didn't work out. It would be a disaster if you had to shut down."

"Tell me about it," Ben said. "We personally guaranteed the 1.2 million dollar line of credit. Plus, our lease has three more years at five grand a month. That's a million and a half exposure."

"My brother might loan us another hundred grand," Alice suggested.

Ben frowned. "He's already given us a hundred and fifty grand, honey. I don't want to gamble any more of his money. It's too risky."

"He'd do it, though."

"No! That's not an option."

Alice turned away and folded her arms. It hurt to see Ben and Alice bickering. This was each other's second marriage and they'd had eighteen good years together. I didn't want all of this stress destroying their marriage or their health. Ben had suffered a heart attack several years earlier and his health was fragile. Alice was in better shape but she'd suffered from anxiety attacks and depression in the past and couldn't handle too much stress either. This was a delicate situation for both of them.

I probably should have referred them to a local attorney, but they were like family to me and I cared about them. Attorneys were supposed to be detached and objective, but I wasn't. It would be difficult dealing with their problems at a distance too. They should really have a local attorney who was close at hand and knew the local judges. The rural courts sometimes didn't like counsel from the big city and would take it out on their clients. I explained all of this to Ben and Alice.

"We've used some of the local attorneys down here for small stuff that we didn't want to bother you with, but we haven't been very impressed with their knowledge or abilities. That's why we called you. This is the worst thing that's ever happened to us and we want someone we respect and trust to get us through it."

How could I say no? They were like family. If I walked away, they'd probably give up rather than go to another attorney. I'd seen that before. At some point circumstances got so bad that the client lost heart and the will to fight. When that happened, it was all over. As good as our judicial system was, justice didn't always prevail. Both parties needed to have equal representation and the resolve to fight for their rights. This was essential for the system to work properly. If either lacked one of these elements, the other would likely prevail regardless of the merits of the case.

After we'd worn out our welcome at the café, Alice and I went to the house for more discussions. Ben detoured by way of the office to make sure everything was all right and to collect some documents I wanted to look at. All afternoon I combed through accounting records, leases, contracts, and promissory notes to assess the condition of the business and help plan a strategy for survival. The situation was bleak but there were several scenarios that would be tolerable–selling the business being the most promising.

"If you like, I'll call the DA's office here tomorrow and tell them the situation. Their response will depend on their case load and how important white collar crime is to the local DA here. If they're interested, I'll have them contact you. Your best shot at getting some quick money is if criminal charges are brought and Ralph pleads out. Restitution will be one of the conditions of any deal that is struck. Of course, if he's spent all the money then he won't have anything to give back. It's a longshot at best."

"If he can't pay us back will he go to jail?" Ben asked.

"Probably. They're not likely to give him probation if he can't repay some of the money he's embezzled."

"Good. I hope the bastard rots in prison," Alice spat. "He's ruined our life."

It was nearly eight o'clock when I left to go back to Dallas. Ben and Alice walked me to my car. It was a nice evening and the stars seemed brighter here in Waco. I gave Alice a hug and shook Ben's hand.

"Thanks for coming up," Ben said. "I feel a whole lot better now that we've gone through everything with you."

I nodded. "Good. You guys take care."

"We will," Alice said as I shut the door and started the engine.

I waved as I drove off, then let out a breath. They might have felt better but I felt like shit. Their situation was desperate when I got there and no less desperate when I left. Short of a miracle, I didn't know how they'd survive the week.

Chapter 4

Depression

It was nearly midnight when Bart finally made it home after being fired by Robert Ralston. He was drunk, so I undressed him and put him to bed. He fell asleep immediately but I was wide awake, so I just sat there for a long time and watched him. He had put up with so much since we'd been together–my infatuation with Stan, my infidelity with my bodyguard, and all the accompanying publicity. It was a miracle he hadn't already divorced me. Depression hit me like a typhoon. What had I done to deserve all of this?

What really bothered me was Stan's attitude. He took the Charlotte Wenzel case with full knowledge that Bart was the prosecutor on the case. How could he do that? He said it was for the money, but I knew that was a lie. Since when did Stan Turner give a flip about money? There had to be another reason why he felt so compelled to take on Charlotte's case, but what could it be? Nothing made sense.

Eventually I nodded off but it was a troubled slumber. I dreamt of Bart showing up at court drunk. He was loud and belligerent and ended up in a shouting match with the judge. I woke up with a start. It was light outside. Bart was still asleep, so I got up and made some coffee. When I was on my second cup and halfway through the Dallas Morning News, Bart staggered in. I poured him a cup.

"How do you feel?" I asked.

"Like shit," he replied.

"Where were you last night?"

"Getting reacquainted with all the bars and strip clubs on Greenville Ave. It's been awhile since I've made the rounds."

"Listen. I'm really sorry about your job. I didn't know anything about Stan being hired to defend Charlotte Wenzel. I was as shocked as you were."

"He knew I'd get bumped off the case if he was defending her. Why did he do it?"

I told him what Stan had told me even though it didn't make a lot of sense. "He said to tell you he was really sorry, but he had no choice."

"Bullshit! He had a choice. He could have said no, but I suppose turning down a fat fee was just too much for him. How much did he get, twenty-five grand?"

I sighed. "A hundred, actually."

"Jesus! He's just another greedy defense counsel."

"No. I don't think so. There's something else, but I haven't figured it out yet."

Bart shook his head. "There's nothing else. It's just pure and simple arrogance. I thought Stan was different, but I guess he's not; just another self-centered, greedy lawyer."

"I don't think so and he certainly couldn't have anticipated you losing your job. I still don't see how that happened."

Bart shrugged. "Shepard set me up. He claimed I leaked confidential information to you and Stan."

"Right. That much I figured out."

"When Ralston called me into his office Shepard was already there with a gleeful look on his face. Ralston said I'd been there long enough to know the rules."

I frowned. "The rules?"

"Yes, that everything said in this office is confidential unless the prosecutor in charge authorizes its dissemination. I knew then what the meeting was all about. I'd briefed you on the case and they'd found out about it. I thought everything I'd said was between you and me. I didn't know Stan was handling Charlotte's defense. I didn't even try to deny it. I just came clean and explained my shock that Stan was on the case."

"So, that's no reason to fire you."

"You wouldn't think so, but they also advised me they were considering bringing the matter before the grand jury and recommending an indictment for obstruction of justice."

"Oh my God! What did you say?"

"I told Shepard to go to hell and then stormed out and slammed the door."

"Good. What an asshole."

"True but technically what I did was against policy and if Ralston wants to call me on it he can. I doubt he'd take it to the grand jury, though. All the assistant DAs talk to their wives. Shepard's obviously the one behind this. Ralston would have never done this on his own."

"So, what are you going to do?"

"Well, I guess I'm going to be looking for a new job. Is Turner and Waters hiring?"

I laughed. "Sure, but we've only got one case going right now and I don't think you could work both sides of the same case. Although I'd like to see Shepard's face if you announced you were defending Charlotte Wenzel."

"Yeah, wouldn't that cause a storm."

"I'm really sorry, honey," I said. "I never dreamed anything like this would happen."

Bart pulled me into his arms. He sighed. "I know it's not your fault. It's just that I was just really getting into this case and felt good about it."

I kissed him and judging by the passion that followed, he'd forgiven me.

Chapter 5

Tragedy

When I got home from Waco Rebekah was sitting on the sofa with a bag of potato chips. She looked up momentarily when I walked in and then returned her attention to Sixty Minutes without a word. Since Peter's funeral she'd lost all her enthusiasm for life. She went through the motions of getting the kids off to school, making super, and doing the laundry but she never smiled, and rarely said much of anything to anybody. I suggested we both might want to get some grief counseling but her stock response was that a shrink couldn't bring back her boy.

It was killing me to see her in such a hopeless depression when I knew Peter was alive. I wanted so much to tell her that Peter was on Tarizon and that I'd actually seen some footage of him with a young woman in a hotel. Such news would bring her back to life in an instant. If only I could figure out a way to talk to her without Kulchz or the CIA knowing about it. Unfortunately, I didn't know how their surveillance system worked, so there was no way I could take a chance at circumventing it.

After I changed into jeans and a T-shirt, I sat next to her on the sofa. "Hi, babe," I said. "Alice said to say hi."

"You went all the way to Waco to see them?"

"Yeah, they've got a serious problem. Their bookkeeper's been embezzling from them."

"Really?" she said picking up the remote and shutting off the TV. "I'm going to bed."

Without another word Rebekah was gone and I was left staring at a blank TV screen. I wondered if it was always going to be this way. I prayed that one day Rebekah would suddenly snap out of her depression and our life would return to some semblance of normalcy. I knew it would never be the same, but I'd settle for anything close. After awhile I looked up and Marcia was standing in the doorway rubbing her eyes. I motioned for her to come to me.

She rushed over and sat down. "Hi, honey. Did I wake you up?"

"No, I've been studying. I was hoping you'd come home before I went to bed. I haven't seen you all day and I didn't want to go to bed without saying goodnight."

I looked at my watch and it was a little after ten. I leaned over and kissed her on the forehead. "Yeah, I had to drive to Waco. Some clients are in trouble."

"Are you going to be able to help them?"

I shrugged. "I don't know. I sure hope so. They're really nice people."

"I think I might be a lawyer."

That caught me by surprise. I didn't believe in pushing children into a profession, so I hadn't ever suggested that they might want to be attorneys.

"Really? How come?"

"Because if I'm a lawyer and can go to work with you and see you everyday."

My heart sank. Jesus, the poor kid was desperate for attention. I put my arm around her and held her tightly.

"Honey, I'm sorry everything's been so screwed up lately. I know it's been hard on you and your brothers; but just hang in there and things will get better. I promise."

"Why won't mom talk to me? Is she mad at me?"

"No. She's not mad at you. She's mad at me and the world."

"What did you do?"

"I didn't protect Peter. That's a father's job and I failed miserably."

"But what could you have done?"

I shrugged. "I don't know. Maybe worry more about my family and less about myself and my clients."

She frowned. "Well, I don't think it was your fault."

I squeezed her and said, "Thank you, honey. You better go to bed."

She nodded, gave me a hug and a kiss, and went upstairs to her room. As I was heading for bed, the telephone rang. I rushed over quickly to pick it up as I didn't want it to wake everyone up. I wondered who would be calling so late.

"Hello."

"Mr. Turner?"

"Yes."

"Sorry to call you at home, but something's happened."

"Who is this?"

"Walter Stanley. I'm a member of the Collin Commons Homeowner's Association."

"Oh, right. I've seen your name on the roster. What's going on?"

"There's been a fire."

"A fire? Where?"

"One of our townhomes was destroyed. The fire department is still here."

"Is everyone okay?"

"I'm afraid not."

A cold tingling sensation washed over me.

"Chester Brown and his family all died."

"Oh, my God! All of them?"

"Yes, the fire spread quickly, I guess. I heard one of the firemen say they thought it was arson. They smelled gas or kerosene or something."

"What? Why would someone do that?"

"I don't know, but the Allen police want to take me in for questioning."

"Take you in? Why?"

"On account of the dispute between me and Mr. Brown over the fence. Your partner can tell you about it. She was at our last meeting."

"A fence?"

"Right."

"Okay. . . . All right. Don't say anything to the police. Just tell them you have an attorney and he's on his way. Either Paula or I will be right over."

"You can't come?"

"Well, I will if Paula can't, but I'd like her to handle this, if possible. She's got more time. I just took on another murder case yesterday and I doubt I could handle two at the same time. Don't worry, though. Paula's very good. Probably better than I am, if you want the truth."

"Okay, I've heard about her too and she seemed nice when I met her at the homeowner's meeting."

"Good then. I'll call her right now and one of us will be right over. In the meantime, keep your mouth shut. Not a word to the police."

"Right. Thanks."

After hanging up I called Paula. This was great timing because now Paula would have something to do to keep her mind off of Bart's problems and keep her away from the Charlotte Wenzel case. I needed to handle that one by myself because of the CIA connection. The phone rang several times before she answered.

"Hello."

"Paula. This is Stan."

"Stan?. . . What's wrong? It's nearly midnight."

"I know. I'm sorry. But you've got a murder case."

"I do?"

"Yes. Remember Walter Stanley at the Collin Commons Homeowner's Association?"

"Stanley," she mumbled. "Yeah, vaguely."

"Well, there's been a fire in one of the units and the entire family, all five of them, have died. Walter's being taken to the Allen Police Station for questioning right now. The father's name was Chester Brown. Apparently they've been feuding for some time."

"They think he set the fire?"

"Apparently."

"Oh, wow! I'm on my way. I'm going to bring Bart too. With five murders, I'll need him."

"Sounds good to me. I've had a long day, so I don't think I'll join you at the station. You guys can handle it, can't you?"

"Yes. We've got it covered. Go to bed."

"Thanks. I'll see you tomorrow."

Chapter 6

The Feud

One of the interesting things about law practice is how quickly things change. I'd been bored to tears since my last big trial ended several months earlier. Now, all of a sudden we have two major murder trials in progress. It didn't take Bart and I long to get out of the condo and on the road to the Collin County Sheriff's office. We were like a couple of firemen answering a call and it felt good. Bart was particularly happy because he'd be back in his old stomping ground and was sure to run into some of his old colleagues, maybe even Gary Shepard.

"Who do you think will be prosecuting the case?" I asked.

"Richard Francis would be my guess. He was chief prosecutor before Gary Shepard was hired. He's a decent guy. Of course, with five victims he'll be under a lot of pressure to make an arrest."

"Stan said Walter Stanley seemed very calm considering he was about to be taken into custody and was probably the primary suspect in the case."

"Some guys are like that," Bart said. "It may be because he's innocent and believes the system will protect him or he's guilty but thinks he's smarter than everyone else and can beat the system."

The police station was deserted when we walked in. A lone dispatcher was seated behind a counter working. As we approached, she looked up.

"Hello. Can I help you?" she asked.

"We're looking for Walter Stanley. We understand he's here being questioned."

She nodded. "He's here all right, but nobody's questioning him. Are you his lawyers?"

"Yes. Can we see him?"

"I don't know. I'll tell Mr. Francis you're here."

Bart looked at me and smiled. He was right; it was Francis. We took a seat and waited. After a few minutes a tall man with red wavy hair walked up. Bart stood up and they shook hands.

"It didn't take you long to get a new job, Bart," Francis said smiling.

"No. I got lucky. Turner and Waters is suddenly up to its elbows in murder cases. . . . You know Paula don't you?"

Francis nodded, "Yes, I think we crossed paths a time or two. How are you doing, Paula?"

"I don't know yet," I said. "I haven't talked to my client."

"Well, you must have put the fear of God in him. He hasn't given us anything but his name, rank, and social security number. I think he believes he's a prisoner of war."

I laughed. "That must have been Stan's doing. I haven't talked to Mr. Stanley yet."

"Well, he's in Room Two. You can have a minute with him and then Detective Rhodes would like to ask him a few questions."

"Sure," I said. "We just need a minute."

He nodded and Bart and I went into Room Two where we found Stanley sitting quietly behind a small interview table. I introduced Bart and we sat across from him.

"Detective Rhodes wants to talk with you here in a minute. You don't have to talk with him if you don't want to, but if you don't they will think you have something to hide."

"I didn't set the fire, Ms. Waters. I swear to God."

"Okay, watch what you say in here; they may be listening. You've seen interrogations on TV, right Two way mirrors and all." He nodded. "What do you know about the fire?"

"Not much. I was making some microwave popcorn; getting ready to watch Johnny Carson, you know, when I heard sirens. I rushed outside because they seemed so close. As soon as I got out the door, I saw the red glow in the sky and smelled a strong odor of smoke."

"So, that would have been about ten-thirty?"

"Yeah, thereabouts."

"Do you know anything about how the fire got started or who might have set it? Apparently they think it was arson."

"Yes," Stanley replied, "they told me that, but I don't know anything about it."

"At your last homeowner's association meeting you and Chester Brown were yelling at each other about something. What was that all about?"

"Mr. Brown had told one of the neighbors that he was going to put up a chain link fence to keep his kids and pets in the yard. You know how tacky a chain link fence can look. It would really hurt our property values."

"So, why was it so important to him to have a chain link fence? I know they are cheaper, but from what I understand Mr. Brown wasn't hurting for money."

"I don't think he cared either, he just wanted to piss me off and he knew that would do it. So, when the architectural control committee sent him a letter advising him that he couldn't put up the fence, he came to the meeting to protest."

"What was his argument?" I asked.

"He said it was his house and he was sick and tired of people telling him what he could or couldn't do with it."

"So, what did the committee do?"

"They told him their decision could only be overturned by the full board of directors and they wouldn't be meeting for several weeks. Obviously that wasn't acceptable, so Brown said he was going put the fence up anyway."

"Did he?"

"Yes," Stanley replied. "A construction crew came out yesterday and put up the fence. It looks horrible. Everyone is very upset. Last night there was an emergency meeting of the board of directors. They voted to hire a law firm to file suit. They wanted the court to order the removal of the fence."

"Is there anyone who can verify that you weren't anywhere near the house when it caught fire?" Bart asked.

"No, not really. I'm divorced. I was home alone."

"Did you call anybody or answer the phone between the time you got home and when the fire broke out? We need someone to give you an alibi."

"No. Sorry. It had been a tough week so I was just taking it easy. There weren't any phone calls and nobody came to my door."

"Wonderful," I muttered. "Okay, Detective Rhodes is going to come in and ask some questions. Just a few tips. Don't volunteer information. Just answer the questions he asks. If you don't know an answer just say so; don't speculate. If you're not a hundred percent sure about something it's better to just say you don't know. If a question assumes a fact that is untrue don't answer the question. Just be quiet and let me object, all right?"

Stanley nodded. "Okay."

Bart went outside and a minute later Detective Riley Rhodes stepped in. He was a small dark haired man who appeared to be in his forties. He had a small mustache below an elongated nose. He introduced himself and we all pulled up chairs around the table.

Rhodes started by asking the same obvious questions that we had asked and Stanley answered them quickly and confidently. Then he went off in another direction.

"Had you had problems with the Brown family before this matter of the chainlink fence came up?"

Stanley's mouth fell open slightly and he looked at me. I frowned wondering whether to terminate the questioning, but I figured any disputes there might have been would be well known in the neighborhood anyway, so I might as well find out what they were. I couldn't imagine there being anything serious. "Well, yes," Stanley replied. "There was the problem of the barking dog."

Rhodes smiled. "Tell us about that, Mr. Stanley."

Stanley took in a long breath. "Well, about a year ago there was a problem with his German Shepard. He was just a puppy and tended to bark a lot. It didn't bother me that much because during the day I was at work and at night when the Brown kids were at home the dog got lots of attention and was fairly quiet. During the day the dog was left outside on a long chain and barked relentlessly. It was driving my wife crazy and she called animal control several times. The Browns got fined once or twice on account of it. It was no big deal."

"That was before the divorce?"

"Yes. The divorce was final about six months ago."

"And you blamed the divorce on Mr. Brown?"

"No. No. There were other factors."

I looked at Bart and he rolled his eyes. It seemed we were getting into dangerous territory and since we hadn't explored that area with our client it was best we terminate the interview.

"Have you and Mr. Brown had any words or altercations as a result of Pretty Boy?" Rhodes asked.

Stanley swallowed hard. "A couple times," he muttered.

"Isn't it true that on one occasion you threatened Mr. Brown?"

I jumped up. "We're done here, Detective," I said. "We haven't had time to confer with our client about anything prior to tonight so it's best we postpone this interview."

Rhodes lifted his hands in surrender. "Well, I'm just gathering information. It might save us both some time and trouble if we just get it over with now."

"Yeah, well. You're probably right, but I think it would be best if we heard our client's view of the facts first before we share it with you."

Rhodes stood up. "Okay, counselors. It's been a pleasure. Tell your client to stay close to home. From what I've learned tonight it appears the feud between your client and Chester Brown got out of control tonight. My gut tells me your client is responsible for those five bodies in the morgue. I've almost got enough evidence to make a case already but the DA thinks I need a little more, so I'll keep digging. I don't think it will take long, though. It was sure nice seeing you again, Paula."

Rhodes shoved his chair aside and left the room. Bart looked at Stanley and shook his head. "Come on. Let's get out of here. It looks like we've got our work cut out for us."

I nodded, took Stanley's arm and escorted him out of the interview room. Several reporters were outside the police station and we were blinded by flashing cameras when we exited the building.

"Ms. Waters, has Mr. Stanley been charged in the murder of the Brown family?"

"No. This was just routine questioning," I replied without slowing down.

"Does your client have an alibi?" a second reporter asked.

Bart spun around and raised his hands blocking the reporters from pursuing us. "I'm sorry," he said. "We have no further comment. Thank you."

We rushed to our car and took off leaving a half dozen reporters in our wake. I was anxious to hear all the details of the Stanley-Brown feud, but it was too late and we were all too tired to go through it at that late hour. Stanley agreed to come in the next morning to get started on his defense and tell us the complete story. My gut instinct told me it wasn't going to be pretty.

Chapter 7

The Evidence

The evidence against Charlotte Wenzel didn't seem all that overwhelming. Sure, she had a financial motive with the life insurance policies, but there was no evidence she needed money or didn't love her children. Still, that was the most damning element of the prosecution's case so far, so I decided I needed to try to deal with that early on. I looked through the telephone book and found the number of the Allstate agent who had sold the Wenzels the big policy and gave him a call. He agreed to talk to me so I went over to his office.

John Shipley told me he'd been an Allstate agent for eleven years. He sold mainly auto insurance but he wouldn't turn somebody down if they asked for life insurance. Apparently that's what had happened with the Wenzels.

"Mrs. Wenzels called me and asked if I sold life insurance. She said she needed a policy on her husband and kids."

I frowned. "She didn't say her husband wanted her to get a policy?"

He shook his head. "No. She didn't mention her husband, although he was at the house when I went over there to write up the policy."

"Okay, tell me how that went down."

"Well, I arrived about six-thirty in the evening. Mrs. Wenzel showed me into the kitchen and we took a seat at the kitchen table. I explained to her the different types of policies we carried like whole life, term, variable annuities, you know; we've got quite a portfolio."

"Sure. Where was Mr. Wenzel?"

"He wasn't there at first. After Mrs. Wenzel selected the policy she wanted, I told her we'd need Mr. Wenzel to sign the application."

"So, Mr. Wenzel didn't participate in selecting the insurance at all?"

"No. After I'd completed the application, she went and got him. Of course, I explained everything to him before he signed it."

"Right. Did he have any comments about the policy? Why he wanted to buy it or anything like that?"

Shipley shook his head. "No, as a matter of fact I wasn't sure he even understood the concept of life insurance."

"What? Everybody knows what life insurance is, don't they?"

"You'd think so. But when I was explaining about his premium payments, the grace period, and our reinstatement policy, his eyes just glossed over. I don't think he understood a word I was saying. Finally, he excused himself and said his wife would take care of everything."

"I see," I said, as I was beginning to get the picture. Life insurance may not be something they have on Tarizon. It could be Mr. Wenzel didn't understand the concept, but that would mean Charlotte was lying to me. I made a note to talk to her some more about the purchase of the insurance. Her story didn't quite hold water.

"What about the insurance on the kids? How did that come up?"

"Oh, that's a standard rider we can add onto the policy. Now that you mention it, Mrs. Wenzel had said she didn't want that coverage but when I asked Mr. Wenzel to initial the box declining that coverage, he refused. He said they'd take that coverage as well."

"Was there any discussion between Mr. Wenzel and Charlotte about coverage on the children?"

"No. Not that I recall. I think when Mr. Wenzel said he wanted that coverage she just shrugged and that was the end of it."

After thanking Mr. Shipley, I headed over to the Collin Creek Mall where Charlotte claimed to have gone when she got the unexpected news that she wouldn't have to pick up her children from school. I figured it was a long shot, but if anybody could remember seeing her, that would really bolster our defense. Charlotte had given me a photograph of herself which I showed to everyone I talked to. Most of the people just shook their heads when I showed them the photo, but a few said Charlotte looked familiar. The problem was none of them could pinpoint when and where they'd seen her.

After striking out at the mall, I called Janet Kaufman and asked if I could meet with her. She had apparently given the DA some very damaging information about Charlotte and her relationship with her husband, and that I needed to thoroughly examine the source of that information. She seemed reluctant to talk to me, but finally agreed I could come by her flower shop the following day.

When I got back to the office I saw Ben and Alice Stover's file on my desk. Where was I on that? After giving it some thought, I remembered I was supposed to call the DA in Waco and see if they prosecuted embezzlement cases. I didn't know anybody down there, so I decided to talk to Bart about it. He probably knew somebody in that office and it would give me a chance to apologize to him for getting him fired. He had moved into our small conference room until we had time to get with the landlord to give us some more office space. There was a pile of books next to him and he was writing some notes onto a legal pad.

"Bart, I see you're hard at work already," I said.

He looked up. "Right. I've been brushing up on some of the issues that might become important in our new case."

"Good. Listen, I just wanted to apologize about taking on the Charlotte Wenzel case. I hope you're not mad at Paula. She knew nothing about it."

"So, she said. I just don't understand why you did it knowing I was already on the case."

Lying bothered me, so I wasn't very good at it. I just wished I could tell him the truth, but that wasn't an option, so I came as close to the truth as I could. "My client is very eccentric. He came to me and said he might be willing to fund Charlotte Wenzel's murder case, but only if I personally handled her defense. I asked him why he picked me and why he was interested in her case, but he wouldn't tell me. He simply said, "I'll fund her defense, if you agree to defend her."

"That's pretty weird if you ask me," Bart said. "Frankly it sounds like bullshit."

I shrugged. "I guess it probably does, but it's what the man told me. I'm sure he has a good reason for wanting me to defend Charlotte. Maybe they were involved or something and he cares about her but doesn't want anyone to know that he's helping her out. I've wracked my brains trying to make sense of it, but there's no obvious explanation. All I know is the money he gave me is real and Charlotte Wenzel is innocent."

"How do you know that?"

"Talk to your wife. Ten minutes with Mrs. Wenzel and it's obvious she's innocent."

"Okay, I suppose I should give you the benefit of the doubt," Bart said tentatively.

"Good. Listen, I need a favor. Do you know anyone down at the Waco DA's office?"

"Sure. Gary Wakefield. I worked with him on a drug smuggling case last year."

"Good. I've got a client down in Waco who has discovered that their bookkeeper has been embezzling. I know that white collar crime is tough to prosecute and some district attorneys shy away from it. I just wanted to talk to one of the assistant DA's down there, give them the facts, and find out if they'd seriously look at it."

"I don't know what their policy is, but Gary will be straight with you. Just tell him I referred you."

"Thanks. I'll do that."

After leaving Bart I placed the call to Gary Wakefield and told him the situation with the Stovers. He seemed interested in the case and assured me that they'd take a good look at it.

"If this guy did what you say he did," Wakefield said, "we'll definitely prosecute him. Have Mr. Stover call me. I'll send over a detective to get all the facts and take a look at the evidence. It shouldn't take us long to decide if we have a case or not."

"Great. I really appreciate that. I'll have Ben call you."

"Good. Say hello to Bart."

"I will. Thanks."

I caught Alice at the office and told her the good news. She promised to call Wakefield later that afternoon. She said they'd been able to scrape up enough cash to last them the rest of the week, but on Monday things would get dicey. I told her to keep me posted and let me know if they needed to file Chapter 11 to keep the doors open.

After I'd hung up the phone, Maria advised me that Alex

Garcia from the Globe Inquirer was on the line. I looked at her in disbelief. Garcia had punched me during an argument over Paula several months earlier and I'd ended up in the emergency room. Why was he calling me? I didn't want to talk to him. Just hearing his name made my blood boil. The press had made a big deal over the story since Alex and Paula had been romantically involved. Consequently, there was no way I was going to give that scumbag the time of day. I told Maria to tell him I wasn't in.

My blood started to boil just thinking about it. He'd lied his way onto our staff, seduced Paula, and assaulted me. He was lucky I hadn't sued him or filed charges. Now he was harassing Paula and me over Cheryl Windsor's disappearance even though the police and the FBI were still actively working that case. For some reason he was convinced we knew Cheryl's whereabouts and he wouldn't leave us alone until he got us to admit it. But that wasn't going to happen.

The next day I dropped by The Blooms Flower Shop in Addison to talk to Janet Kaufman. She was working on an arrangement when I walked in. She told another girl working there that she was going to take a break. Janet was a short, plump, redhead with a perky personality. She seemed anxious to talk to me.

"I feel really bad," she said.

"Why?" I asked.

"I think I told that detective some things I shouldn't have. I didn't realize he seriously thought Charlotte had anything to do with her husband's disappearance. I know she wouldn't harm anyone, particularly her husband and children."

"I'm glad to hear that. However, some of the things you told the detective are a bit troublesome."

"I know. I tend to run off at the mouth. I feel so bad."

"Did you tell the DA she was mentally unstable?"

"Not exactly. I said the way Gabe treated her it was a miracle she could maintain her sanity."

"How did he treat her?"

"Well, he was the ultimate control freak. He planned out what she'd do everyday–where she'd go, who'd she see, and even what she'd do at home during the day."

"Jeez. That is a bit controlling. Did she complain about that?"

"Yes, constantly. I told her she had to stand up to him, but she was deathly afraid of what he'd do to her if she defied him."

"I think you told the detective he beat her. Is that right?"

"Yes, I'm sure he did although I never saw him do it. "

"Did she tell you he beat her?"

"No, but several times she came over after they'd had an argument. Each time she was a mental wreck–crying, shaking, scared to death. I felt so sorry for her. She refused to talk about it, but I'm certain he must have done something to her. There wasn't any other plausible explanation."

"So most of what you told the police was speculation?"

"I guess," Janet said. "I found out about it after the fact, but I really think I'm right. He was abusing her mentally, maybe physically."

"What about the blackouts? You told the police she had memory lapses," I said.

"Yes, she was constantly complaining about that. She'd wake up and have no memory of several hours or even days sometimes."

"Does she drink?"

"Sure, but not any more than the next girl."

"Have you ever seen her drunk? That might explain the blackouts."

"She's not an alcoholic. I'd know if that were the case. But she did like her gin and tonics and an occasional bloody Mary."

"Tell me about the day Mr. Wenzel and the children went missing. Did you see or talk to Charlotte that day?"

"Yes. She called me just after lunch to see if I wanted to go shopping with her. I told her I couldn't because I had a meeting scheduled with my son's teacher."

"Do your children attend the same school as the Wenzel children?" I asked.

"No, they go to a private school. Gabe wouldn't allow them go to public school."

"Did she say anything else to you in that conversation?"

"No. Just that she was going to Collin Creek Mall to look for a dress."

"Did she say anything about Gabe picking up the kids?"

"Yes, she was very surprised he volunteered to do it without her asking. It wasn't like him to spontaneously do things with the kids."

"Didn't that make her suspicious?"

"It should have, I guess, but it didn't. She was just glad to have a couple of free hours. She's not the suspicious type."

"What about Gabe's affairs? Do you have any knowledge of him being unfaithful?"

"Sure, there was the nurse. I saw them together at a bar once. Then there was the airline stewardess who had the audacity to call Gabe at home. I was on the phone with Charlotte when Brenda beeped in. I'm sure there were others."

"How did Charlotte react to his infidelity?"

"She didn't like it obviously, but she tolerated it more than I would have."

"Would she have been angry enough to kill Gabe?"

"No. She loved her children and their life together. She wouldn't have done anything to jeopardize that. I'm certain of that."

I thanked Janet and left. I didn't think she would be much of a witness for the prosecution. If that's all the DA had there wasn't much danger that Charlotte would be indicted. I called Mo on my cell phone and gave him an update. He thanked me and said he'd tell Kulchz, although I suspected Kulchz didn't need updating.

When I got back to the office there was a message from Alice Stover. When I called her back she told me they'd spent the morning with a Detective Winston from the Waco Police Department. She said Winston had done a background check on Ralph Herman and discovered that he'd done this before in San Antonio. He was arrested for it but since it was his first offense he got deferred adjudication and didn't have to go to jail. Apparently Detective Winston was enthusiastic about the case and had a meeting scheduled with the DA later that afternoon to discuss going to the grand jury with it.

"That's great news," I said. "Maybe they'll find out where your money went. I just hope it won't take too long."

"Tell me about it," Alice replied. "I don't know what we're going to do on Monday when our cash runs out."

"Well, Ben's working on something isn't he?"

"Yes. He's over with Vince Gully right now trying to sell off one of our plants. If he's successful, we'll unload a lot of debt and pick up a hundred grand in cash. That should buy us another couple weeks, if we're lucky."

"Good. I hope that works out. Let me know if there's anything I can do."

After I hung up the telephone I started cleaning off my desk to go home. I liked a clean and orderly office. It made me feel more in control if I went through every file on my desk each day to be sure I didn't overlook something. As I was finishing up, Maria advised me Gary Shepard was on the line. That surprised me because it was rare that a prosecutor would call a defense attorney before there was even an indictment.

"Stan, just wanted to let you know we found a body of a child near Lake Tawakoni. It was in pretty poor condition having been exposed to the elements and badly mutilated by the wildlife, but it matches the description of one of the Wenzel children."

Shepard's news stunned me. I knew it couldn't be one of the Wenzel children. But if the body was a close match and couldn't otherwise be identified, it would add a whole new dimension to the prosecution's case. It could even be enough to support an indictment. Still reeling from the news, I stuttered "Ah . . . Really? . . . Who found it?"

"Some hunters stumbled across the body this morning. We got a call from the Hunt County Sheriff's office."

"Have you checked for missing persons in the area?"

"Yes. That's standard procedure. There's been no missing children reported."

"Hmm. . . . Well, I'd like to see the body and I'll need a copy of the autopsy report when it becomes available," I said.

"I'll have someone call you when it's finished."

"Thanks," I said and hung up the telephone.

I couldn't believe that Gary Shepard was actually acting professionally for a change. I wondered why he'd suddenly become Mr. Nice Guy. Was he feeling guilty about getting Bart fired, or was he just trying to gloat that he finally had a body?

Chapter 8

Bitter Neighbors

An ad in the Dallas Morning News real estate section touted the Collin Commons Townhomes as being the ideal solution for those who wanted to own their own homes but couldn't afford the high cost of single family dwellings or didn't want to worry about yard work and onerous home maintenance. These zero-lot-line townhomes were priced well below single family dwellings of similar quality yet they included access to a clubhouse, swimming pool, and playgrounds. The ad went on to say that the Collin Commons Homeowner's Association took care of all management responsibilities for the common areas and handled maintenance of all townhouse units.

As I was studying the ad, Maria walked in and advised me that Mr. Walter Stanley had arrived. I told her to let Bart know and then show him in. Stanley looked pale and seemed nervous as he took a seat in a side chair in front of my desk. Bart slipped into the other chair moments later. We all exchanged greetings.

"Did you get any sleep last night?" I asked.

Stanley shrugged. "Not a lot. It was pretty unsettling being dragged down to the police station. It really hit me when I got home. Five people were dead and I was the prime suspect."

"Yes, it is a very serious situation," I said. "That's why we have to get right on this and figure out who else had a motive to set that fire. But, before we do that, finish your story about Pretty Boy and the other altercations that you had with Chester Brown."

Stanley shook his head. "They were nothing really," he sighed. "One Saturday my wife was on edge because Pretty Boy had been barking all morning. When she saw Mr. Brown drive into his driveway she told me to go talk to him. I didn't want to confront him because

I'm a chicken at heart, but she said if I didn't go, she would. . . . I didn't want that, of course. God knows that would have been ugly. So, I went over and told him the dog was really upsetting my wife and I'd appreciate it if he'd make him shut up."

"What did he say?" I asked.

"He said he'd been telling the dog to shut up all morning, but he wouldn't listen to him. So, I suggested he get rid of him. He didn't like that idea much. He said his kids loved the dog and he wouldn't deprive them of him."

"So, how did you leave it?"

Stanley shrugged. "I was going to blow it off, but then, I saw Brenda coming, so . . . well . . . I told him that I'd have to get a gun and shoot the damn dog."

"Wonderful. Did that impress Brenda?"

"No. She said threats weren't good enough. She wanted me to actually do something."

"Like what?"

"I don't know. She said shooting Pretty Boy would be too dangerous. People might hear the gunshot and look out their windows. She said a better solution would be to poison him."

"Really? Jesus, she said that?"

Stanley nodded. The thought occurred to me that he was better off without Brenda, but then again, I'd never met her so she might have had other redeeming qualities. I decided to change the subject.

"You weren't the only one who was upset about the chainlink fence, were you?"

"No, there were others, but none were so upset. I mean, I can't imagine someone setting Chester's house on fire over this."

"Well, tell me who they are anyway. We should check them out."

Stanley gave us a run down of the two neighbors on either side of Chester Brown and the chairman of the architectural control committee, Curtis Richmond, whose responsibility was to enforce the covenants, bylaws, and the will of the Board of Directors. Richmond seemed like a good suspect since Brown had defied him and his committee by installing the chainlink fence despite the committee's rejection of his request for a variance to allow the project. I asked him what he knew about Richmond.

"He's retired now. I think he worked for a defense contractor while he was active. He moved over to that job when he retired from the army. He was a colonel, I believe; served in World War II and Korea."

"How about his family? Is he married?"

"His wife died about a year ago. He took it pretty hard. They'd been married forty-nine years and their kids had planned a big fiftieth wedding anniversary shindig, but Mae died a week before it was scheduled."

"Wow! That must have devastated him."

He nodded. "Yeah. That's when he took over the chairman's post. He needed something to keep him busy."

"So, what was his reaction to the chainlink fence going up?"

"He was pretty pissed off about it. He called the special meeting and asked the board to authorize him to hire an attorney and file suit."

"Did he confront Mr. Brown about the fence going up without the architectural control committee's approval?"

"I didn't see it, but I understand he and Mr. Brown had a screaming match when the construction crew started working."

"How did you hear about that confrontation?"

"Barbara Heinz, one of his neighbors, was there and told me about it. She said they nearly came to blows over it."

Bart shook his head. "I can't believe anybody would get that upset over a fence."

Stanley sat up in his chair and looked at Bart incredulously. "Do you have any chainlink fences in your neighborhood?" he asked.

Bart shrugged. "Well, ah . . . I guess not."

"Exactly. They look despicable. A few of those in your neighborhood and your property values plummet."

"I guess," Bart said tentatively.

"But, you wouldn't physically attack someone over a fence?" I asked. "Or, set their house on fire?"

Stanley sat back in his chair and took a deep breath. "No, of course not; but I wouldn't have had any qualms about suing the bastard. I was looking forward to that, actually. The only problem was the damn attorneys wanted such a big retainer it would have required a special assessment to fund the lawsuit. Nobody in the Commons will vote for a special assessment unless it's a dire emergency. Now, . . . well, now . . . shoot, I don't know what's going to happen. We not only have a chainlink fence, but a burnt-out house as well. It's a good thing I don't need to sell my unit anytime soon."

After talking to Stanley I wasn't so sure he was innocent. He obviously had a motive and showed no grief over the death of the Brown family. This bothered me somewhat. But as his attorney it didn't matter whether he was innocent or guilty; he was entitled to the best defense Bart and I could provide him. Unlike Stan, who often said he'd only defend someone he was sure was innocent, I had no such policy nor did I think an attorney should pick and choose his clients. The only prerequisite to becoming my client was whether they could pay the fee. After all, practicing law was a business just like any other business. If you wanted our services, you had to be willing and able to pay. That thought led me to ask Stanley about our fee.

"A hundred thousand dollars?" Stanley gasped.

"Yes, at least that. Five people died. This will be a long, involved case. It will go on six months or better. They could ask for the death penalty."

Stanley turned a little green. "Shit. I only have about twenty thousand in savings."

"What about family. Will anyone loan you the rest of it?"

"No. I couldn't impose on my family. I've got a profit sharing plan. It has forty-two thousand in it right now. I could borrow off it, I suppose, but I'll have no money for my retirement."

"The retirement money won't do you any good if you're in Huntsville or six feet under," Bart noted.

Stanley closed his eyes and shook his head slowly. "Damn it. . . . Maybe they won't indict me."

"I hope for your sake they don't, but since you're a suspect you'll need us to protect your rights. We can start with a five thousand dollar retainer. That should allow us to begin a preliminary investigation. Maybe we can identify other potential suspects and get the police looking at them rather than you."

Walter swallowed hard. He went on and on about how unfair all this was, but eventually he wrote us a check. We talked a little while about the parameters of the investigation and then he left. Bart and I brain-stormed a bit longer and came to the conclusion that we should talk to the arson investigator, the architectural control committee chairman, and Brown's neighbor. We'd also have to dig into the Brown family in case the fire had nothing to do with the chainlink fence and the Collin Commons Homeowner's Association, although I thought that unlikely.

Chapter 9

Lies

Gary Shepard called the next day and advised me the little girl's body was in the morgue in Greenville, if I wanted to bring Charlotte to see it. The estimated age of the child was five or six. So if it was one of the Wenzel children it would be the eldest whose name was Jill. I knew it couldn't be her since she was on her way to Tarizon, but I had to go through the motions of taking Charlotte there for show. I called Charlotte and advised her of the situation. She became hysterical.

"Is it my Jill?" she sobbed.

"They don't know for sure. It's probably not her, but they need you to take a look at the body just to rule her out."

"Oh, my God! What if it her? How Gabe let this happen? He be dead too, I bet. He never let someone hurt little angels. That what he call them."

I bit my tongue. If Charlotte only knew the truth about her beloved Gabe. If she only knew he was using her and had planned this abduction from the day he first met her. What would she think about that? This whole Tarizon project made me sick. Trading human beings for technology was obscene and I feared I'd surely go to Hell for being a part of it. Depression swept over me quickly as it often did these days.

The dread of continuing the charade and dealing with Charlotte's understandable fear held me rigid in my chair as if the force of gravity was twice its normal strength. Finally, I struggled to my feet and went to my car. By the time I'd picked up Charlotte and driven all the way to the Greenville morgue it was late afternoon and near closing time. Storms were lurking about when we pulled up to the curb in front of the building. A gust of wind seemed determined to rip the door off when Charlotte opened it. I ran over and held it for her as she got out. Just as we got inside it began to rain hard.

"That was good timing," I said. "I hope it's a quick shower. I didn't bring an umbrella."

Charlotte didn't respond. She just stared straight ahead as I guided her to the reception desk. A sign behind the receptionist's read: Arthur C. Black, M.D., Medical Examiner. I told the person on duty why we were there. She said someone would be out to escort us to the viewing room. We took a seat and waited. Charlotte buried her head in her hands and sobbed. I took her hand and held it, wishing again that I could tell her the truth. A moment later a thin man in a white coat came through a swinging door.

"Mr. Turner?" he said and extended his hand. "I'm Dr. Ross, one of Dr. Black's assistants."

We shook hands. "This is Charlotte Wenzel," I said.

He nodded. "Right this way."

We followed Dr. Ross down a stark white corridor turning right, then left, through one corridor after another like rats in a maze. Finally he stopped at another set of swinging doors, turned and smiled. "Brace yourself, Mrs. Wenzel. The body is right inside."

Charlotte staggered a little so I put my hand on her shoulder to steady her. Dr. Ross pushed open the door and we followed him in. The body was on a table covered by a sheet. We walked over to it. Charlotte began to shake. I put my arm around her. Dr. Ross pulled the sheet down exposing the child's peaceful face.

"Jill! My poor baby! What has he done to you!" She screamed. She started to go to her but I held her back. What was going on? How could this be Jill? Had Mo and Kulchz lied to me? Dr. Ross covered the body again and I escorted Charlotte out of the room. She was crying hard now, so I just held her until she started to calm down. This couldn't be Jill I kept telling myself. How could it be Jill?

"I'm sorry," I said. "I didn't think it would be Jill. So often it's a false alarm."

"Who killed my baby? Was it Gabe? How could he have done this? Are all my angels dead?"

I held her tight again. "I don't know, but I'm going to get to the bottom of this. I promise you."

Somehow I found my way back through the maze of corridors to the door to the reception area. As we passed through it, I was shocked to see Detective Kramer and Gary Shepard.

"Oh, shit! You've got to be kidding me?" I spat. "Not now. Can't you see my client's been through hell."

"Sorry, Stan. If she's in hell it's of her own making."

Kramer grabbed Charlotte's shoulder and swung her around to cuff her. "Mrs. Wenzel, you're under the arrest for the murder of Gabriel Wenzel and your children."

He read Charlotte her rights and escorted her outside.

"Don't talk to them! Not a word, Charlotte," I shouted. "Not a goddamn word!"

Shepard stepped in front of me and said, "Don't worry, counselor. We don't need a confession. We've got all the evidence we need to send your client to death row."

"Don't count on it, Gary. She's innocent and I'm going to prove it."

Shepard smiled, shook his head, and started to leave.

"And I'll make you pay for what you did to Bart and now Charlotte."

Shepard spun around and glared at me. "And just how are you going to do that?"

"I'm going to make sure you never become district attorney in this county. You might just as well pack your bags and leave town, because if you think you're going anywhere in Collin County, forget it."

Shepard rolled his eyes, let out a snort, and stormed out of the morgue. I just stood there a moment trying to fathom what had just happened. Suddenly I realized Dr. Ross and a half dozen of his staff were staring at me. I forced a smile, nodded, and forged out into the torrential downpour. By the time I got to my car I was drenched. I drove around for awhile confused and disoriented. I wondered what I should do. I saw a bar coming up on my right. I didn't usually frequent bars, but a lot of attorneys did and seemed to enjoy what they found there. Maybe I could wash away my troubles with a bottle of booze. What the hell did I have to lose?

I went inside and ordered a bourbon straight up. I didn't usually drink straight liquor, but today it seemed like the thing to do. It tasted horrible, but I endured the sting in anticipation of the buzz I was expecting to make me feel better. Before I knew it I'd had four or five drinks and was feeling light headed.

Fortunately, I had a knot in my stomach that wouldn't go away. It was a painful reminder that Charlotte was being processed into the county jail and I had to arrange bond. I needed to go see Roger Rand and quickly. I left the bar and headed for my car. The sun had come out by then and the combination of the bright light and alcohol in my system made me stagger a little. I looked around for cops. I didn't want to get arrested for public intoxication. I wondered if I could drive.

After giving myself a little sobriety test, I decided I could manage it, and got in my car. Luckily Roger Rand's office wasn't too far away. I could have just put up the cash that Mo had given me, but then I might have to explain where it came from. With a bond only Roger and I would know the cash existed. I felt sure he wouldn't mind since he'd get to pocket twenty-five thousand dollars for an afternoon's work and there'd be no risk at all since the cash was up for collateral. The only problem was getting his cooperation without making him suspicious. A few minutes later I was sitting in his office.

"Sure, but what's the catch?" Roger asked.

"Nothing. This is just payback for all the favors you've done for me over the years."

"I haven't done you enough favors to deserve twenty-five grand for doing nothing."

"Listen," I said. "The truth is this money is coming from someone who wants to remain anonymous."

"A boyfriend?"

"Yeah, right. A well-known boyfriend who can't afford the questions if the relationship is exposed."

"Hey, I can't afford to get nailed for obstruction of justice or nothing like that."

"You won't. We'll dot all the i's and cross all the t's. This is strictly a legitimate deal and if there are any questions, I'll take the heat."

"All right. What do you want me to do?"

"After the arraignment, go up to the Collin County Sheriff's office and post Mrs. Wenzel's bond. Bring her back to my office when she gets out."

"All right."

I handed Roger the key to the safety deposit box where I had stashed the money along with a stack of 250 one-hundred dollar bills. Roger took it and smiled broadly.

"You won't be able to get into the safety deposit box," I said. "because it's in my name; but I won't be able to get into it either because you have the key."

"How do I know the money is there?"

"I put it in the bank across the street. We can go over there now and you can count it."

"Couldn't you go to the bank and claim you'd lost the key?"

"I could but that would be a lot of hassle and require me to swear falsely. That would be a federal offense and you could blow the whistle on me. I think you know I couldn't afford that to happen."

"I trust you, Stan. I just have to be careful. This business is my only livelihood."

"No problem. I totally understand. I want you to be comfortable with the arrangement."

We went to the bank and Roger counted the money. When he was satisfied it was all there, he set off to post Charlotte Wenzel's bond. That gave me just enough time to brief Paula on the new developments and tell her to be expecting Charlotte at the office. In the meantime I needed to find Mo. He had a lot of explaining to do.

Chapter 10

Working Together

Stan's unexpected call about Charlotte's arrest appalled me. I couldn't believe even Gary Shepard could be so cruel to arrest her just after seeing her daughter lying on a table in the morgue. Stan asked me to handle the arraignment and take Charlotte home after she got out on bond. He said to tell her he'd be in touch soon. I was surprised Stan asked me to do this. He hadn't let me get near Charlotte's case since the day Bart had been fired. I guess he felt so badly about what had happened, he didn't want me to be reminded of it.

It was nearly seven o'clock when Roger Rand finally got Charlotte to the office. She was an emotional wreck. Luckily Roger had kept her out of the general population at the jail so she hadn't been assaulted or harassed by inmates; but she was emotionally distraught over seeing her daughter's body and knowing it was likely her other children were dead too. I took her home and called her friend Janet Kaufman who agreed to come over to her house and stay with her.

Since it was late, I called home to tell Bart I was on my way. He said he had an appointment to see Colonel Richmond and that I should meet him there. He gave me the address. I wondered how fruitful talking to Richmond would be. If he had any sense, he wouldn't talk to us. When I got there he and Bart were sitting on the front porch talking like they were best buddies. I walked up to them. Bart stood up.

"Colonel, this is my wife Paula Waters. We're working on this case together."

Colonel Richmond nodded but didn't get up. Bart motioned for me to take a seat next to him. "The colonel was just telling me about the fire," Bart advised.

I nodded. "Go on. I'd like to hear about that."

Colonel Richmond continued. "It was right about bedtime when I smelled smoke. We usually go to bed at eleven. I asked my wife if she had left something on the stove, but she assured me she hadn't, so I went out in the back yard. The smell was stronger outside and I quickly saw that the smoke was coming from the Brown's house."

"So, what did you do?" Bart asked.

"I didn't fiddle," Richmond said, "if that's what you think."

"Fiddle?" Bart asked.

"You know. I didn't fiddle while Rome burned. I called the fire department for godsakes. What do you think I did? If his house was burning, my house could have easily gone up in smoke too. These are zero lot lines homes. If one burns they all burn."

"But that didn't happened," I noted.

Richmond looked at me like I was a lunatic. "No. It didn't because I got my hose out and sprayed my roof and the side of the house. I'd be damned if I'd let my house burn on account of that asshole."

"Are you referring to Mr. Brown?"

"Yes, Mr. Brown. That son of a bitch brought this on himself by being selfish and obstinate. He knew what the rules were when he bought the condo but he didn't care about any of us. He just had to put that god awful fence up. He's as guilty of murdering his family as the person who set the fire."

Colonel Richmond's attitude about the Browns was difficult to understand. He seemed to be blaming the family's death on Chester Brown, one of the victims, rather than the arsonist who set the fire. I wondered if that was intentional. Was he trying to bolster up his own alibi by reporting the fire himself and then stating the obvious that his home had been at great risk too?

"Do you think he could have anticipated that someone would burn down his house over a fence?"

He shrugged. "I don't know. People expect the rules to be followed."

"Did you see anyone loitering around the Brown property or in the neighborhood before the fire broke out?"

"No. I reckon not. Course I can't say that I was paying that much attention. I usually work in the garage during the afternoon. I've got a couple carpentry projects that keep me pretty busy."

"I understand you were considering filing a lawsuit against the Browns over the fence," Bart said.

"You're damn right I was. That's my job as chairman of the architectural control committee. If people don't follow the rules, then I take them to court."

"But that would have cost money and taken you away from your carpentry," Bart noted. "A fire is much cheaper and more effective."

Colonel Richmond stood up and glared at Bart. "I suspect you ought to leave now. I've told you all I know."

I looked at Bart trying hard not to smile. He'd taken a bite at the Colonel and drawn blood. I just hoped the Colonel didn't have a revolver laying around; or a match. The door slammed hard behind us and I burst out laughing. Bart looked back and then at me.

"What's so funny?"

"You handled that like a prosecutor."

"Well, that's what I am; or used to be."

"I know. But defense work is different. You don't want to go around making enemies. Now the Colonel won't give us the time of day and he'll be expecting us to try and blame the fire on him."

"Damn. I guess you're right. It's going to take me awhile to get used to being a defense counsel."

I took Bart's hand. "It's okay. I don't think Colonel Richmond did it. It's just too convenient. If he was going to set fire to the Brown's home, he'd have arranged to be out of town or at least miles away when it happened."

"I'm not so sure," Bart replied. "Sometimes we don't see what's right in front of our face."

"So, what now? We have two suspects without alibis," I said.

"We keep digging," Bart said. "I'll start looking into Mr. Brown and his family. Maybe you should get the roster of the homeowner's association and start talking to the other members.

Somebody might know something."

I nodded. "Sounds like a plan; but right now I'm kind of hungry. You feel like a steak?"

"Yeah," Bart replied. "Outback is on the way home."

"That's right. I'll meet you there."

We both got in our cars and took off. It was fun working a case with Bart. It made life so much easier. In the past we were always being torn away from each other by our work, but now the opposite was true. Every day we seemed to get closer and closer. In retrospect, I could almost thank Stan for getting Bart fired.

Chapter 11

Malfunction

After I hung up the phone with Paula, I called Mo. While I was waiting for him to return the call, I went into another bar. This one was called "The Hole." The name turned out to be quite appropriate but I wasn't looking for ambiance, so I found an empty stool and took a seat. I needed another drink and I was sure the booze here would taste about the same as it did anywhere else. While I was drinking a woman sat down next to me and asked if I was looking for company. I said no, but she hung around anyway. She made several attempts to start a conversation, but I was in no mood to talk, so I ignored her. All I wanted to do was talk to Mo. Why hadn't the bastard returned my call!

I studied my cell phone and wondered if I could have missed the call. Had my battery gone dead? The indicator said my batter was low, but still had a little juice. Finally I realized Mo and Kulchz already knew that I was on to them. I couldn't believe they'd deceive me the way they had. I guessed they'd thought the body wouldn't be discovered and I'd never be the wiser. I wondered what went wrong–why Jill was dead. What did this mean? Was everything they told me a lie? I reached in my pocket and pulled out the telepathic modulator. The TM, as Mo called it, looked like an oversized cigarette lighter. He had given it to me when I was recruited by the CIA for this project. He said if I ever needed help to squeeze it and my thoughts and needs would be communicated instantaneously to a support team that was always standing ready nearby for any eventuality.

I turned the object round and round in my hand and wondered what would happen if I squeezed it. Was there a penalty for sending out a false alarm? I was about to try it out when I remembered Peter. If I screwed up my assignment, they might take my failure out on him, or if not him, on the other members of my family.

"Can I have a light," the woman said extending a cigarette hanging loosely from her lips. She may have been a looker in her prime, but those days had long passed. I looked at her and then down at the telepathic modulator. I started to laugh. The woman stiffened up and glared at me. I got up to leave but felt a strong arm on my shoulder. I turned around and saw a three hundred pound brute hovering over me.

"The lady asked for a light," the brute said.

"Yes, I know. But I don't have a lighter."

The brute looked down at the telepathic modulator. I don't know if it was the booze or a death wish, but I started to laugh again. The brute began to crush my shoulder. A river of pain shot through me. I struggled to get free but his grip was too tight. Instinctively I squeezed the TM.

When I awoke my shoulder was killing me. I rolled over and discovered I was engulfed by a soft white substance. It was a sofa, a very comfortable sofa. The room looked familiar–ultra Tarizonian. In the corner I saw blinking lights from a giant control panel. It was Kulchz's office or home or whatever he called it. I sat up.

"Stan. How are you feeling?" a voice from behind me said. I turned quickly and saw Mo mixing himself a drink at Kulchz's crystal bar.

"I don't know. My shoulder feels like someone branded me. What happened?"

"Your security team had to rescue you from a bar room brawl. That's not like you, Stan. I didn't even know you were a drinker."

"I wasn't, but times have changed. My son is being held hostage and my wife won't talk to me. I have to lie to my partner a dozen times a day and now I find out you and Kulchz have been deceiving me. I thought Jill was on Tarizon?"

Mo shook his head. "I told Kulchz we should tell you the truth, but he was sure the body wouldn't be found."

That piece of information gave me comfort. It told me that Kulchz and his people were not invincible. They made mistakes; they were only human after all. I got to my feet feeling a little less pessimistic but still mad as hell.

"So, what happened? Why is Jill dead?"

"There was a malfunction," a distant voice said.

I looked over to where I thought the voice had been coming. Kulchz, dressed in a white gown, strolled toward us.

"What sort of malfunction?" I asked.

"It's hard to explain in your language," Kulchz said, "but if the ship can't land, people are brought aboard through a transporter tube. It's a device that creates an electronic stream that acts almost like one of your conveyor belts. It allows a person to float very quickly up to the ship. Unfortunately, there was a malfunction when Jill was being brought aboard. She fell to her death."

"Why didn't you retrieve the body and take her back to Tarizon?"

"It was dark and the ship was behind schedule. The pilot decided he couldn't afford to hang around and look for the body. He reported the incident and we sent in a search team the next day, but for some reason we were never able to find the body. We think an animal must have gotten to her and dragged her away."

I shook my head. "I can't believe this. That poor little girl is dead. She had her whole life ahead of her."

"It was an accident. Unfortunately, accidents happen," Mo said.

"Do you know how hard it's going to be to clear Charlotte now? They have a body and the rest of the family is missing. I don't know if I can get her off now."

"You must try," Kulchz said. "It's our obligation under the treaty."

"I know. I want to get her off. If I don't she'll probably be executed. It's just that there's so much evidence against her. I'm going to have to come up with some kind of credible alternative to what Shepard thinks happened. The problem is I can't imagine what that would be."

"You'll think of something," Mo said. "But you've got to stay out of bars."

I laughed. "Yeah, well when you don't have anyone to talk to, telling your sad tale to a bottle is about the only alternative."

Mo looked at Kulchz. Kulchz took a deep breath and sighed.

"Yes, not having someone to talk to is difficult. Mo and I have been discussing that problem."

"You have?" I said looking up at them.

"Yes, it isn't good to keep all of your anxiety within you," Mo said. "It will eat at you and ultimately destroy you. That is why Kulchz is going to assign you a guide."

"A guide?"

"Yes. We use them on Tarizon to help guests adapt to our planet," Kulchz said. "The concept works well there and I think it will work well here."

"I don't understand. What's a guide?"

"It's a companion of the opposite sex. In your case it will be a woman from Tarizon. She will stay with you and you can talk to her freely. She'll be the outlet you need to cope with your stressful life."

I just stared at Kulchz in amazement. "Wait a minute. I can't be hanging around with another woman. I have a wife."

"You can't talk freely to Rebekah even if she would talk to you. Your guide will be intelligent and fully knowledgeable about your assignment. You can discuss everything with her without concern for confidentiality. She'll cook for you, listen to your problems, entertain you, and take care of your every need."

"But I have a wife," I protested. "I'm not going to betray her even for the CIA."

"You don't have to sleep with your guide, if you don't want to," Mo said, "but I think you need someone to talk to. She'll be much better than a bottle."

I started to argue some more, but the idea of having someone to talk to felt good. It had been very lonely since Peter had disappeared. I felt isolated and depressed. Having someone who understood what was happening would be great. I took a deep breath.

"Okay, I guess she could be my intern," I reasoned. "I could tell everyone she's planning to go to law school and working for me to get experience. That way if we are together a lot no one will be suspicious."

"Yes," Kulchz said. "That's good. Fortunately, there is a ship due tomorrow and there's a guide aboard that we can reassign to you."

"That soon?" I said anxiously. I wondered what she would be

like. As I was picturing her in my mind I heard Kulchz' voice.

"In the meantime this might make you feel better."

A monitor above my head flickered and came on. The scene was a restaurant where many people were eating. The camera moved in on a table with an elderly man and two younger people. Tears began to well in my eyes as I recognized Peter. He was eating what looked like pizza with a pretty young woman. The elderly man was talking to them and they all seemed very happy. The monitor flickered and went off. I looked at Kulchz.

"You see, Peter is fine," Kulchz said."He's having a good time on Tarizon, so you don't have to worry about him. The man you saw is a counselor. That's like a judge here on Earth. Peter is to be his aide. He'll be doing important work."

I started to ask the question that had been bothering me since I'd seen the first video. How could Kulchz get a video file from another solar system so quickly? Even if the signal traveled at light speed it would take months or even years to get to Earth. But Peter looked so real and I wanted to believe he was alive, so I kept my mouth shut. I had to assume they'd somehow developed almost instantaneous communications with their planet. This whole affair was mind boggling to me anyway. Kulchz turned and walked away. Mo grabbed my arm and motioned that we should leave. On the long drive home all I could think about was Peter. He did look okay and he seemed to be happy. If only I could tell Rebekah. It wasn't fair. None of this was fair. She had a right to know her son was alive. I had to tell her.

Chapter 12

Other Suspects

My canvass of the Collin Commons neighborhood didn't produce any witnesses to the fire, but I did get a lead on another suspect. It seems there were rumors that Mr. Brown had been involved with a young divorcée, Ruth Willis. They had met at a company picnic and sparks flew between them almost immediately. For the sake of convenience, Ruth moved into a condominium just down the street from where the Browns lived. That made it easy for Chester to slip away and be with Ruth a few hours almost every day. Apparently Gladys Brown suspected something and hired a private investigator to follow her husband. Infidelity opened up a number of possibilities which Bart and I were discussing one morning at breakfast.

"One of the neighbors told me all about Ms. Willis' divorce," I said. "Before she met Chester Brown she was happily married. But her husband cheated on her, so she kicked him out of the house. He still loved Ruth and didn't want the marriage to end, so he pleaded with her to forgive him, but she wouldn't. It got pretty silly with Mr. Willis coming to the house banging on the door demanding to be let in and flower trucks coming almost daily with deliveries that Ruth refused to accept. When she went out, he'd follow her and eventually confront her. Finally she got a restraining order to keep him out of the neighborhood and away from her job. When that didn't work she finally had to move."

"So, you think he found out about Chester Brown's affair with his ex-wife and decided to do something about it?"

"It's a possibility," I said.

Bart considered that and then said, "I've got another possibility too."

"What's that?"

"It turns out Mr. Brown is a software engineer for Technology Institute or TI as it's called. His company is doing work on a top secret project for the defense department. Apparently Mr. Brown's services were in high demand and security at TI was very tight."

"Really?"

"Yes. Unfortunately since his work is classified, nobody would talk much about what he was doing exactly. I suspect if other companies wanted his services and couldn't get them, the next best thing would be to knock him off. That would, at least, even the playing field."

"Hmm. That's hard to believe. I mean, this is America. We don't have to worry about being killed by our business competitors, do we?"

Bart chuckled. "Listen, my naive little wife, corporate espionage is rampant all over the world and people die every day so that one company can get a leg up on another one."

"That's horrible. It shouldn't be like that," I said. "Life is sacred. You shouldn't have to be worried about someone killing you to make a buck."

Bart took my hand and smiled softly. "I know. That's why we became prosecutors, remember." He laughed. "And now look at us, we're defending criminals."

"Alleged criminals," I corrected. "Maybe Stan is right. We should only defend those who we believe are innocent."

"They all say they're innocent and as long as you believe them it's okay to defend them. Sure, you may be wrong a time or two, but at least you believed you were seeking justice. That's what's important."

We decided I would continue to pursue the Brown-Willis affair and Bart would dig into Chester Brown's employment some more and try to identify TI's competitors. This case was turning out to be more complicated than it first appeared, so I decided to call our client to see if he wanted us to continue work even though he hadn't been indicted yet.

"I don't know," Stanley said. "I've already given you

$5,000.00. I hate to spend a lot of money unnecessarily."

"I know. That's why I'm calling you. We've developed a number of leads that are worthy of further development." I filled him in on what we'd come up with so far.

"That's good work. What would you do, if it were you?"

"It's important in a murder case to get right on it quickly before the trail gets cold. I suspect the reason the DA hasn't indicted you yet is that they are finding the same thing we are. There are a lot of potential suspects out there. If it were me, I'd want my own team working hard to find the real killer, so I'd never get indicted. Do you realize how your life will be turned upside down if you're arrested for murder?"

"Oh, yes. It would ruin me. Go ahead. Keep digging and find out who killed Chester Brown. I'll spend my entire profit sharing plan if I have to keep from going to jail."

"Good. We'll keep you posted."

I felt bad about taking Stanley's money, but he was right. It was worth all of his pension plan, and then some, not to be arrested for murder. He'd immediately become a public spectacle and branded a demon for killing five innocent people. Even if he was acquitted his life would never be the same. A lot of people would think he'd gotten away with murder.

After hanging up, I looked at my notebook. My next entry on my list of things to do was talk to the arson investigator, Charles Stewart. I needed to know all the particulars of the fire. Fires usually had a signature and I wondered if there had been any other fires with a similar one in the recent past. It was possible that the fire was a random act and that the Browns' weren't murdered at all. When I finally caught up with him, Stewart dismissed that possibility.

"Yes, we've compared this fire to every other fire in the Dallas Metroplex in the last five years. There is nothing about this fire that would tie it to any of the others. In fact, it has a pretty unique signature."

"How's that?"

"It appears the arsonist used a delayed triggering device–a quite sophisticated one that would set off the fire hours after it had been installed. I think we are dealing with a professional here."

"A professional?" I asked.

"Yes. The arsonist either had military or commercial training in handling explosives or he hired someone with that kind of training to set the fire."

"Really?"

"Yes, the fire was expertly designed to spread quickly and trap the victims inside."

"How did they do that?"

"The victim had a number of propane canisters. Apparently he liked to barbeque. He had quite a setup on the patio. It utilized two canisters and it appears he kept three backups. The perpetrator put the five canisters at strategic places around the house. Each probably hidden so they wouldn't be seen. On each there was a blasting cap triggered by a telephone receiver. All the arsonist had to do was make a phone call and the whole place went up. Kerosene was placed in glass jars near the canisters so when they were set off there'd be plenty of fuel to help intensify the fire. There is no doubt that this was cold-blooded murder, Ms. Waters. There is no doubt about it at all."

"Well, you know Mr. Brown was working on a top secret military project."

"So I heard."

"Yes, and I understand there was a lot of competition between defense contractors for whatever they were working on. I'm told that Chester Brown was key to the project, so I would think you'd be looking at these competitors, particularly given the professional manner in which the Brown family was murdered."

"We're looking into all possible scenarios including the possibility that your client started the fire."

"But I thought you said it was a professional job?"

"That's what it looked like, but it may have been staged to look like a professional job to throw us off. We don't know if the triggering mechanisms actually worked. Your client could have distributed the canisters and kerosene around the house and then lit a match or left a lit cigarette."

"What about the blasting caps?"

"They wouldn't be easy to get, but he might have been able to find them if he knew someone in the construction business."

"Wonderful," I moaned. "Well, I appreciate you filling me in on the investigation. Let me know if anything else develops."

"I'll inform Mr. Shepard and I assume he'll pass the information on to you."

"I wouldn't make that assumption, but I know you have your protocols. Thank you, again."

When I got back to the office, I filled Bart in on my meeting with Stewart. He said what I'd found out didn't surprise him. It was looking more and more like our client was innocent, but it was going to be difficult to prove since the government and TI's competitors refused to talk to him. I suggested our best hope was that Mr. Brown's employer might be interested in discovering the truth. After all, they lost a key employee and, if a competitor was responsible, they'd be interested in nailing them for the crime.

Chapter 13

Indictment

When I got in work on Monday there was a message from Ben Stover. I prayed it wasn't bad news as I didn't feel like driving to Waco again. When I returned the call, Alice answered and seemed to be in good spirits.

"Hi, Alice. I was returning Ben's call."

"Oh, he went to the bank, but I can tell you why he called."

"Okay, what's up?"

"The grand jury indicted Ralph Herman."

"Oh, wow. They didn't waste any time."

"No. Larry has been working hard on the case ever since you called him."

"Well good. Did you have to testify to the grand jury?"

"No. I could never do that. I made Ben go. He testified yesterday for over an hour. They arrested Ralph within an hour of the indictment. He's in the county jail right now. I guess because of his prior arrest and the off shore account they set the bail pretty high. I understand he hasn't been able to make it."

"Great. So, what did the DA tell you he thought would happen? Does he think he'll plead out?"

"No. Ralph hired an attorney and says he's going to fight."

"Well, I guess you can't blame him. His attorney, I'm sure, advised him that it's difficult to prove embezzlement. He's probably thinking he can beat the charges."

"Larry thinks we have a good case. He's going to meet with Ron Jacobs, Herman's attorney and offer him a reasonable deal if he agrees to restitution."

"I hope he hasn't spent all the money."

"Larry says they've done an asset search and they think he owns a ranch. If we can show the money went into the ranch, the court might order him to sell it and use the proceeds to fund his restitution."

"That would be nice. I hope it all works out for you."

"Me too."

"So, how's the business holding up?"

"Up and down," Alice replied. "We've got a potential buyer. Ben signed a contract on Monday. If it doesn't fall through, we'll be able to unload a lot of our debt."

"Wow! That's wonderful. When are you supposed to close?"

"If all goes well, next Friday. All we have to do is get the lender to approve the loan assumption and we'll be home free."

"Well, let me know if I can help."

"There is one thing." Alice said. "Ralph called my daughter Peggy, you know, his ex-wife. She works at our Austin plant."

"He called from jail?"

"No, from the courthouse just before the grand jury began deliberations."

"Yeah. So, what did he want?"

"He told her he'd heard we were going to file bankruptcy and that she should start looking for a new job."

"Jeez. What a bunch of crap. She didn't believe him, did she?"

"Well, it upset her," Alice replied, "and she told the manager, Paul Brim about it."

"Uh huh."

"So, he just called a few minutes ago to tell me he's resigning."

"Shit! You've got to be kidding."

"I wish I were, but that's what he said. Apparently one of our competitors has been trying to recruit him and when Peggy mentioned the possibility of bankruptcy he got right on the telephone and accepted their offer."

"Damn. So, do have someone to replace him?"

"No, but that's not the worst of our problems. If our buyer hears that we're filing bankruptcy you know what's going to happen."

My heart sank. "Oh, shit. They're going to try to cut the sales price."

"Exactly and then what little equity we were going to pull out of the business will go up in smoke."

"Well. What are the odds the buyer will find out?"

"Pretty good, I'm afraid. He's scheduled to do an inventory at the Austin location tomorrow and if Paul's not there, he's gonna want to know why."

I didn't say anything. There wasn't anything meaningful I could say. It was like having to abandon your home just before a hurricane made landfall. You boarded up the windows, tied everything down, and made sure your insurance premiums were paid. There was nothing else you could do, but hope and pray there would be something left to come back to when the storm had passed. Unfortunately, Ben and Alice had no insurance and if their sale fell through, they'd likely be ruined.

"Do you want me to talk to Brim and try to talk him out of quitting?"

"No," Alice said. "We've known him for years and consider him a friend. We can't lie to him. Our financial situation is perilous and he's probably right to jump ship while he can."

"I know, but—"

"It's all right. We're going to talk to the staff and ask them to keep our situation confidential. Hopefully they will."

"Okay. Good luck. Let me know if there is anything I can do."

"I will," Alice said and hung up.

When the phone went dead, I just sat there trying to think of something I could do to help them. It was so frustrating to see the vultures circling over a client in trouble and not be able to do anything about it. I just prayed their employees would keep their mouths shut although I knew that was unlikely. The buyers were getting assets and the Stover's personal financial situation was irrelevant to the sale. Unfortunately, if they found out Ben and Alice were desperate to sell they would try to use that as leverage to get a better deal.

Human predators were far worse than their animal counterpart. They weren't acting instinctively to survive, but for their own profit or enjoyment. They were selfish, conscienceless creatures with no compassion for their victims whatsoever. Bottom line, they were manifestations of the evil of this world in its purest form. Unfortunately, they often operated within the letter of the law and therefore were untouchable. Enraged and frustrated, I silently cursed Ralph Herman for the affliction he had brought down on Ben and Alice. Damn him! Somehow I had to make him pay dearly for his transgressions.

Chapter 14

Technology Institute

Getting through TI security wasn't easy but after about forty-five minutes of jumping through hoops, Bart and I found ourselves seated outside the office of TI's HR manager, Robin Sylvester. We'd been promised by his secretary that he'd be with us shortly. Shortly turned out to be nearly an hour, but finally Mr. Sylvester came out and invited us into his plush office. We shook hands and introduced ourselves.

"So, you said you wanted to talk about Chester Brown," Sylvester said.

"Yes, we're representing Walter Stanley. He's currently the number one suspect in the Brown Family murders. Obviously, we're looking into other suspects and trying to gather evidence to move the investigation away from our client."

Sylvester grimaced, snapped his fingers, and pointed at me. "You represented that woman who vanished right in the middle of her trial, didn't you?"

I nodded. "Yes, Cheryl Windsor."

"Whatever happened to her?"

I shrugged. "I don't know. The police and the FBI are still looking for her."

"Huh. That was pretty bizarre. What was all that about a memory erasing device?"

I briefly related everything the public knew about the incident. He seemed fascinated with the story and had lots of questions. I didn't tell him I'd actually held the device in my hand and had a picture of it. Had I told him that, we'd never found out anything about Chester Brown.

"What we came to see you about, Mr. Sylvester, is information about Chester Brown's job and your competitor's interest in Mr. Brown. We believe the murder of the Brown family was a professional job. The fire's triggering device was just too sophisticated for our client to configure."

He frowned. "So, you think one of our competitors wanted to get rid of Chester?"

"Well, we don't know for sure, but that possibility exists and we have to explore it."

"I seriously doubt that was the case," Sylvester stated confidently. "Government contracting is very competitive and highly scrutinized by the FBI, CIA, Congress, the press—you name it. If anyone resorted to violence and got caught they'd be out of business in a heartbeat."

"Still. If the stakes are high enough, they may take the risk, don't you think?" Bart asked.

Sylvester shrugged. "I won't say it's never happened, and Chester Brown certainly was a valuable commodity, but why kill him?"

"We were told one of your competitors tried unsuccessfully to woo him away. Maybe they thought since he couldn't be bought it would be better if he were eliminated."

"Well, even if I agreed that was possible, how could we possibly help you? We certainly have no knowledge of any such plot to assassinate Mr. Brown."

"Right. But I'm sure you have your suspicions."

He thought for a moment and replied, "Well, the project Mr. Brown was working on is classified, so I can't tell you much about it. It's no secret that Almatech was our most aggressive competitor, though."

"Almatech?"

"Yes, Almatech Life Systems, Inc."

"When you say aggressive, what do you mean?" I asked.

"Well, they spent the most money wooing Congress and pitching the job to the Defense Department."

"So, why didn't they get the contract?" Bart asked.

Sylvester smiled. "They didn't have the technology that we had."

"Is it safe to assume that not having Chester Brown on their team had something to do with it?" I asked.

Sylvester nodded. "That goes without saying, but I'm afraid I've told you all I can on the matter."

He stood up. "I've really got to get back to work. I hope you find Mr. Brown's killer."

Bart stood up but I remained seated. "One last question, if you don't mind. If someone at Almatech did orchestrate the Brown murders, who would you put your money on?"

He gave me a wry smile. "What? You think I'm stupid? I'm not going to slander the CEO of a major U.S. corporation!"

I laughed. "Of course not. It was silly of me to ask."

I got up and Mr. Sylvester showed us out of his office. Two security men met us at the door and escorted us out of the building. On the record Robin Sylvester hadn't told us much, but reading between the lines I was sure the man we needed to be looking at for the Brown murders was the CEO of Almatech. When we got to the car, I asked Bart what his take on the conversation was.

"He didn't tell us a lot. I guess it being a classified project and all he's got to be careful. We probably could have gotten as much information reading the newspaper archives on the contract bidding."

"True, but we wouldn't have known what was important and what wasn't. This was much faster and more reliable. He officially told us nothing but indirectly pointed us right to our target. I'll have Paul Thayer do a complete report on the CEO of Almatech. I'd like to know more specifics about the project that they so desperately coveted and why Mr. Brown was so important."

"Right," Bart said. "Have Paul to do a report on Mr. Brown too–find out where he went to college, where he grew up, his work history, family, etc."

I nodded as I pondered the ramifications of this new information we'd gathered. If there was anything that was clear about this case it was that we were starting to wade into dangerous waters and further investigation would be at our own peril. I looked at Bart and smiled. He raised his eyebrows. He seemed to know what I was thinking.

Chapter 15

The Guide

When I got back to Dallas I pulled into the parking garage, found an empty space, and got out of my car. As I was walking to our office building, Alex Garcia suddenly appeared with a photographer.

"Stan. You're a hard man to catch."

"I have nothing to say to you, Alex," I replied without slowing down.

"I think you know what happened to Cheryl Windsor," Alex said. "Why don't you admit it?"

"You're full of shit, Alex, and you can quote me."

"There's a connection between Cheryl's disappearance and your son's death, isn't there?" Alex pressed.

I turned and glared and him. "Leave my son out of your wild speculations. He's dead for godsakes!"

"Don't you think it's odd that after nearly a year they haven't found his body?"

I felt like belting Garcia across the face, but that would just give his story more credibility. I looked straight ahead and kept walking like he wasn't there.

"I'm going to find out the truth eventually, Stan. You might as well save us all a lot of trouble and tell me what you know."

I didn't respond but kept on walking until I was inside the building. One of the building's security guards intercepted Alex to keep him from following me inside. When I got to the elevator and the door closed I breathed a sigh of relief. What an asshole. When I got to my office there was a telephone message from Mo. Seeing the message sent a surge of excitement through me. I didn't know why I was reacting the way I was, but I couldn't wait to meet this mysterious guide who was to be my confidant. I returned the call and waited anxiously for Mo to call me.

I suspected my reaction was due to Kulchz' description of a guide's role. She'd provide for my every need and he meant every need. I rationalized that it was only natural to feel good about having someone like that always there for you, even if you didn't intend to take advantage of all she had to offer.

Mo finally returned my call about a half hour later. He told me to come out to Lake Tawakoni to pick her up. Then it dawned on me. I'd have to find her a place to live, help her furnish it, and show her around. Shit, I'd have to take her shopping. After all, she was from another planet. Jesus! What had I gotten myself into?

The trip to Tawakoni went quickly. I'd been there so many times that I drove there pretty much on autopilot. When I saw the oil tank in the distance I started to get goose bumps. Aside from Kulchz, I'd never been up close to an alien. I had to keep telling myself she was human, just like me. It would be like being with a person from Mongolia. She'd just be a little different. After parking the car around the back of the tank, I opened the squeaky door, and walked toward the ladder that descended down into Kulchz' domain.

Mo opened the door when I gave a knock. Except for him the room appeared deserted. I took a deep breath and said, "Okay, don't keep me in suspense. Where's my guide?"

Mo smiled and pointed to staircase in the distance. "She's in the guest quarters. She'll be right down."

I took a seat where I could keep an eye on the door to the guest quarters. After a few minutes the door opened slightly. I swallowed hard. I don't know why I was so nervous, but I could hardly stand the suspense. Finally, the door opened fully and out walked a tall woman no more than twenty-five years of age. Her hair was light brown and from a distance it looked like her body was well proportioned. I knew as she came toward me, she'd be a very distracting companion.

She extended her hand, "Mr. Turner. Kulchz has told me all about you. I can't wait to get started."

"How was your trip?" I asked. "Did it take a long time to get here?"

Smiling, she said. "It didn't seem long at all. They just laid me down in a life support pod, injected me with DS, and when I awoke we'd landed. It just seemed like I had a good night sleep."

I shook my head. "Wow. That's amazing."

Mo handed me a briefcase. "In there you'll find her birth certificate, driver's license, passport, social security card, and some cash to set her up a bank account. We've already created her life history. You both need to read and memorize it. On her way here she was fully briefed on our situation and her role in helping you do your job."

"So, what's your name?"

"Tehra," she replied. "At least that was my name on Tarizon. Here I'm officially Maureen T. Connolly. I'd prefer you to call me Tehra, though, when we are alone. It will make me feel more at home."

A tingling sensation overcame me. She seemed so sincere and so anxious to please me. I really liked her and knew I was going to enjoy her company.

"Sure, Tera it is."

"Teh-ra," Mo said. "T-e-h-r-a."

"Gotcha. Tehra. Okay. Very good."

Mo helped escort us to my car and then we were alone. It was so strange knowing I had a woman from another planet sitting next to me. I didn't know what to say. I finally blurted out, "So, what do you think about this assignment? It must be very difficult being sent to Earth."

"No. Actually, I've been looking forward to it. I was born in Texas, you know."

"What!" I said turning my head to look at her.

"Yes, I was born in Grand Prairie. My father came here as part of the repopulation project many years ago. I lived here until I was seven years old. That's how I learned to speak English so well."

"Oh, that's right. I forgot about that," I said. "A lot of Tarizonians have been born on Earth."

"Yes, that's right. I'm anxious to see how Earth has changed in the last fifteen years."

"So, that means your birth mother is here."

She stiffened. "Yes, I suppose."

"Will you visit her?"

"No. No. I can't. She thinks I'm dead."

"Oh. That's too bad. I bet you miss her."

"No, my mother is back on Tarizon. I miss her."

"Right."

Tehra's birth mother seemed like a sore subject, so I made a note not to bring that topic up again. I couldn't imagine being in her shoes knowing that my birth mother was a few miles away, but not being able to go see her. As much as she protested, I knew that must hurt.

"There's a hotel near my office. I'm going to get you a room there for a week or two until we can find an apartment for you. There's no need to rush things. We'll have plenty of time to look around and find something permanent."

"Can't I stay with you?"

"Ah. . . . Well. My wife doesn't know about the Tarizon Repopulation Project, so as far as she's concerned you will be my new intern. It wouldn't be appropriate for me to bring my intern home with me."

"Oh, of course not. What am I thinking? A hotel will be fine."

"Since it's close to the office, I can pick you up in the morning and take you home at night. During the day we'll take some time off to shop and get you whatever you need to be comfortable."

"She smiled. That sounds great."

She seemed a little scared so I said, "Don't worry. I'm not going to just drop you off at the hotel. I'll go in and get you situated. We can have some dinner and watch a movie or something."

"A movie. I haven't seen one of those in years. That will be fun."

She had a little girl look in her eyes that made me smile. I felt good inside for the first time in months. I wondered if she was really excited about her new assignment or was it just a job for her. "So, how did you get this assignment?"

"Oh, I volunteered. Everyone wants to go to work on Earth. It's so beautiful here."

"So, you knew what you'd be doing before you volunteered."

"Of course, the Repopulation Project is important. Who wouldn't want to be a part of it."

I nodded. "So, what's Tarizon like? I guess you know my son is there."

"Yes. They told me that," she replied. "Don't worry, I'm sure he's fine. They treat visitors very well on Tarizon."

"So, is it like Earth?"

"It used to be a lot like Earth. At least that's what I've been told. Unfortunately, about eighty years ago there was a series of super volcanic eruptions that buried Tarizon in ash. The air is so polluted you can't see our sun except at the poles. The air is starting to clear there. I hear it's nice in Lortec and the Beet Islands."

"Wow. So, how does your population survive if the air and water supply is contaminated?"

"We've built gigantic domes over our cities. The air and water are filtered."

"What about the people outside the city?"

She sighed. "Life is difficult for them, but they've learned to adapt to the environment."

I could tell the conversation was making her uncomfortable so I let it go. There would be plenty of time to learn about Tarizon. My immediate problem was Rebekah. How was I going to explain to her that I'd be tied up all evening? When we got to the Harvey Hotel, I got Tehra a room and while she was washing up called Rebekah.

"Hi, honey. Sorry I didn't call sooner but my cell phone ran out of juice."

"Really? Where are you?"

"I'm out in East Texas trying to track down a witness. I won't be home until late."

"What witness?"

"A man who claims to have seen Mr. Wenzel and his children out on I30 the night they disappeared," I lied.

"Why didn't you send Paul out to track him down?"

Paul Thayer usually tracked down our witnesses. I hadn't called him in on this case because I was afraid he'd learn something I didn't want him to know. "Paul was busy and I got a lead on this guy and couldn't afford to let it go cold."

"So, how late will you be?" Rebekah asked.

"After midnight. Don't wait up."

There was silence. Finally she said, "Okay, drive carefully."

The phone went dead. I wasn't sure whether she believed me or not, but I couldn't think of a better excuse for not coming home. The next few weeks were going to be dicey trying to get Tehra settled without Rebekah suspecting something was up. Rebekah had a jealous streak and easily became suspicious if my routine changed. She was also very sensitive to my mood changes and was bound to notice the effect Tehra was already having on me.

After Tehra had freshened up we went to Bennihana's and had dinner. She watched the chef cook with great delight. When he was done she dug in, ate everything quickly, and asked for more. I was amazed at her appetite and asked her if she usually ate that much.

"No, I'm just so hungry. This is the first meal since I came to Earth."

"So, how long did it take you to get here? I know you said it seemed like a pretty quick trip, but it must have taken a while."

"They told me once it would take nine Earth months to get to here."

"So you haven't eaten in nine months!"

"Not solid food."

"Damn. No wonder you're hungry."

She smiled and took another bite of shrimp. An hour later we left Bennihana's and drove to a movie theater at LBJ Freeway and Webbs Chapel Road and saw Lethal Weapon 3. She loved it and made me promise to take her to another movie soon. When we got back to the hotel, I took her to her room to say goodnight.

"Will you stay with me tonight?" she asked.

"No. I'm sorry. I'd like to, but I have to get back to my family."

She seemed disappointed, but didn't put up a fuss. "Okay. So, I'll see you tomorrow."

"Oh, yes. I'll buy you breakfast and then take you to the office and introduce you to everybody. We've got lots of work to do, but I'll take time out to show you around Dallas. We'll even go to Grand Prairie so you can see if it's changed any."

She smiled. "That would be nice."

"Okay, then," I said. "Goodnight."

I felt like a school boy on his first date. Tehra was so sweet and innocent. It was going to be fun having her around, but I wondered how she'd adapt to her new role as my intern. Would she be able to convince people she was a native of north Texas? For the first time I started to worry about how Paula and Jodie would respond to her. There would be a lot of questions and I'd have to come up with a good excuse for hiring an intern without warning them. But there were always problems to deal with. At least dealing with this one would be well worth the effort.

Chapter 16

Surprise

When I came to the office the next day Stan was showing a young woman around the office. It was unusual for Stan to give office tours, so I was curious as to who she was and why he was giving her the VIP treatment. When Stan noticed me watching he turned and motioned to me excitedly.

"Oh, Paula. Come here," Stan said. "I want you to meet someone."

I strolled over nonchalantly and smiled.

"Paula,"this is Tehra."

I extended my hand and she shook it warmly. "It's a pleasure to meet you," she said.

"Tehra is going to be my intern," Stan advised, looking back at her and smiling broadly. She met his eyes and a wry smile quickly came and went. I did a double take.

For a moment I was speechless. Stan's announcement was a total shock. He hadn't had an intern in the past and hadn't told me he was considering getting one. I forced a smile. "Really? You didn't mention you were looking for an intern."

"Well, I wasn't, but that new client I mentioned to you, you know, the one who hired us to defend Charlotte Wenzel, he asked if I'd let Tehra intern with us for a year. She wants to be an attorney and would like to get some experience in a law office."

"Is that right?" I said evenly, trying to hide my shock.

"Yes, and since we've got two murder cases going, I figured I could use the help. It will be nice to have someone tagging along to help keep me organized."

That nearly cracked me up. This cute little girl was going to keep Stan organized? Ha! She couldn't have been a day over twenty-five and she'd be nothing but a distraction to him. From the way she was looking at him and hanging on every word, I wondered if she wasn't already infatuated with him. That would spell trouble if it were true.

I couldn't tell her nationality, but I suspected it was Asian or Middle Eastern. Her dress was, well, unusual—something a foreigner my wear not being familiar with the dressy-casual style of the American working woman. She wore no makeup, but was attractive nonetheless.

"So, where did you go to college?" I asked.

Tehra looked over at me. "UTD," she replied softly.

"Oh. Are you from around here?"

"I was born in Grand Prairie."

"Grand Prairie? . . .Wow. You could have fooled me. You don't look much like a Texan."

"No. I guess not. My mother is Greek and my father is Chinese—kind of an odd combination, I guess."

"No, not at all. . . .Well, it was nice to meet you. I guess I'll be seeing you around," I said biting my tongue. As I walked off, Stan and Tehra continued their tour. They were so giddy it was making me nauseated. I couldn't wait to go find Jodie. I wondered if she knew about Stan's new intern. She was in the library doing some research. She looked up when I walked in.

"Good morning," Jodie said.

"Did you hear about Stan's new intern?" I asked.

She shook her head. "No. Not until just a minute ago."

"What in the hell is going on?" I said.

"He didn't tell you he was hiring an intern?"

"No."

"Stan's been acting very strange lately," Jodie said thoughtfully. "First he takes on the Wenzel case when there is an obvious conflict of interest and now he shows up with an intern out of thin air."

"Apparently his new secret client is responsible for the intern as well as Charlotte Wenzel. He seems to be calling the shots for Stan these days."

"Who is this guy anyway?" Jodie asked.

"Stan won't tell me. He says the client wants to remain anonymous."

"But you and he are partners. You have a right to know."

"I agree, but I don't really feel like forcing the issue," I said. "If he doesn't want to tell me who the client is, I'll live with it, but who the hell is this intern?"

"Do you think Rebekah knows about her?" Jodie asked."I can't believe she's going to be happy about this."

"No. I doubt she does know. At least not yet. Should we call her?"

"No. I suppose not," Jodie replied. "We better let Stan break the news to her. She's going to be upset, though. It took her a long time to get used to me being alone with Stan all day. It was even worse when you came along."

Jodie was right. Rebekah was a jealous woman and she wouldn't like the idea of Stan running around with a twenty-five-year-old intern all day—particularly one as exotic as Tehra.

When I got back to my office, I couldn't concentrate. I was sick about this new girl in the office. Part of it may have been jealousy, I'll admit that, but just as much of it was the suddenness of it all and the odd circumstances of her hiring. There was something going on with Stan that he wasn't sharing with me, or even Rebekah, and that was unsettling.

After I'd gotten over the shock of Tehra joining the firm, I called Paul Thayer to get him started on a background check of the Almatech CEO. While I waited on the phone he did a preliminary computer check.

"Let me see. T. Robert Stout is the President and CEO of Almatech Life Systems, Inc. According to this short biography, he graduated from Harvard Law School in 1969, served in the air force for twenty years when he retired and joined Almatech in 1989. He became president and CEO in February 1992."

"That was about the time the secret project went out for bids. If he was so well connected with the military, I wonder why Almatech didn't get the contract?"

"I don't know," Paul said, "but I'll find out."

I told Paul all that we had learned about Chester Brown and

Almatech and what additional information we needed him to dig up. He said he'd have it for me in a few days. Before he hung up I asked him about Tehra.

"Paul, did you know Stan was hiring a new intern?"

"What intern?"

"Tehra, I think is her name."

"No. I don't know anything about it."

"Okay, just curious. Stan will tell you about it, I guess. Call me when you have anything."

After hanging up the phone I went looking for Bart for his take on the situation. Maybe Stan had told him about Tehra, but I doubted it.

Chapter 17

Price Cut

Over the weekend Tehra and I went apartment hunting. With the help of the classified section of the Dallas Morning News we were able to find a nice two bedroom apartment about ten minutes away from the office. It was right on the way to work, so it wouldn't be any trouble for me to pick up Tehra each morning. There was a Denny's close by too, in case we wanted to have breakfast before work.

I told Rebekah I had hired a new intern, but I was afraid to tell her much more in fear of alarming her. My concern turned out to be unfounded, however, as my announcement that I needed to work over the weekend on the Charlotte Wenzel case, elicited no more than a shrug from her. She said she had to take Marcia shopping for school clothes, so she wouldn't be home anyway.

While Tehra and I were out shopping for furnishings for her new apartment, I showed her around Dallas and reacquainted her with the geography of the area. She was amazed at how it had changed, but still remembered much of it. On Sunday I felt guilty about missing church and she sensed the tension. She asked if something was wrong.

"We usually go to church on Sunday," I said. "Do you worship a God on Tarizon?"

"Yes, there are many religions on Tarizon. I favor the Prophet Sandee."

"Sandy?"

She nodded. "Sand . . . ee, Sandee Branh, the Savior of our planet who united all the nations together and brought us, peace, liberty and justice. At least that's what they teach us."

"Why, you don't think it's true?"

"I believe in Sandee, but I'm not so sure the Central Authority always follows his teachings."

"Oh, so Tarizon is just like Earth–politicians have used the church for their own purposes?"

"Yes, the politicians and purists are constantly fighting for control of the church, unfortunately the politicians usually prevail."

"But, you can debate freely about it?"

"Yes, we are free society and are protected by the Supreme Mandate."

"The Supreme Mandate?"

"Yes. It's a little like your constitution but it was written entirely by Sandee Brahn. He took it to the nations of Tarizon and the people ratified it."

"He took it to the people singlehandedly?"

"He and his followers. Some claim God dictated it to him and he was just the scribe."

"Really? That's fascinating," I said shaking my head.

We talked for hours about our lives on Earth and Tehra's life on Tarizon. She was easy to talk to since I didn't have to worry what I told her. She seemed very open to me as well and I felt very connected to her even though we'd only known each other for a few days. She sighed when I told her it was time to bring her back to her hotel.

"I hate to go back to my room alone," she said. "You sure you don't want to join me?"

"I would love to, but I can't," I said with genuine regret. The disappointment in her eyes almost obliterated my resolve. I looked away quickly. "I'll help you move into your apartment next weekend. You'll feel better when you have a place of your own."

When I got home Sunday night Rebekah had little to say to me as usual. She didn't seem to care about what I was doing anymore. For the first time in my life I felt uncomfortable in my own home. If it wasn't for the kids I'd of packed a suitcase and left right then. If only I could tell her the truth that would change everything.

On Monday morning I left early to pick up Tehra for work. We stopped for a quick breakfast before we went to the office. When we arrived, Maria advised me that I'd gotten an urgent call from Ben Stover. I showed Tehra to her work station, asked Maria to help her set up her computer, and then went directly to my office to talk to Ben. He answered on the second ring.

"Stan. Thanks for returning my call."

"No problem. What's up?"

"Well, you're not going to believe this but we closed on the Austin property."

"Oh. That's great."

"Well, not really. We had to drop the price to salvage the deal after the rumors of filing chapter 11 started spreading."

"How much?"

"A hundred grand. I actually had to put in a few bucks to make the deal work."

"Well, at least you got rid of a lot of debt."

"Yeah, but I'd like to choke Ralph. I needed that hundred grand. I swear to God if I ever see that bastard again I'll kill him!"

"Well with any luck he'll be going away for a long time, so you won't have to worry about him. His cell mates will make his life miserable."

"I'm not so sure. Even if he is convicted he may thrive in prison. He's a real manipulator, you know."

"Is he?"

"Oh, yes. He knows how to get what he wants. I tried to get him to run for the city council here in Waco, but he said they didn't pay enough to make it worth his while."

"He's probably right on that score. If it's like Dallas they don't pay city councilmen squat."

"Anyway, I guess we're gonna need that chapter 11."

"Really? Business hasn't picked up?"

"It's our slow season. We've shipped all our Christmas orders already. Without the hundred grand from the Austin sale we'll have to shut down."

"Right. Well, we can't have that."

"Didn't you say we'd have at least four months to get a plan put together."

"That's right and you won't have to pay your vendors for at

least six months."

"Good. That will gives us time to collect some receivables."

I cringed at the thought of having to handle a chapter 11 case at the same time as we had two murder trials going on. A chapter 11 reorganization was a major undertaking and would drain hundreds of hours of precious time over the next six months. Unfortunately, I had no choice. Ben and Alice Stover wouldn't let anyone else handle it. They'd just throw in the towel if I refused to file it for them.

We agreed I'd meet them in Waco on Saturday to get all the information I needed for the filing. Then I'd come back to Dallas and put the petition and schedules together. On Tuesday or Wednesday I'd drive to Waco, they'd sign everything, and then I'd go straight over to the federal courthouse and file the case. After filing the paperwork I'd stay overnight so I could appear the next day for first day motions. A debtor-in-possession, as a business in chapter 11 was called, had to get permission to pay its employees and use cash collateral. In this case Ben had a good relationship with his banker so we weren't expecting any trouble.

After hanging up the phone I went to see how Tarah was doing getting her computer set up. Maria was hovering over her and she didn't look happy.

"How are you two doing?" I asked.

Maria looked up. "Not good," Maria said in a frustrated tone of voice. "How can you graduate from college and not know how to use a computer?"

Tehra looked at me and shrugged. "It won't do what I tell it," she explained.

I frowned not comprehending the problem. Then it suddenly occurred to me, she was probably used to much more advanced computers. These little HP desktops probably seemed pretty strange to her. "Ah . . . well, I think she's used to a Mac. It might take her a little while to learn DOS."

Maria shook her head. "Okay, I'll do the best I can, but I'm not a computer instructor."

I laughed. "That's all right. I'm sure you'll teach her whatever she needs to know quickly and efficiently."

Maria rolled her eyes. "Right."

After Maria was through with Tehra's computer lesson, I asked Tehra how our computers stacked up to what they had on Tarizon. She laughed. "I haven't ever seen anything like this since I was a child. My father took me to a museum once and I remember seeing something similar. Our computers on Tarizon are voice or thought controlled–no keyboard or mouse."

"You mean you just think about what you want the computer to do and it does it?"

"Something like that."

"Wow! That's amazing."

"They are a hundred times faster too," Tehra said. "Whatever you want done is completed almost instantaneously. I'm not sure I have enough patience to use one of your PCs."

"It's still a lot faster than doing it by hand," I noted.

"I know. I'm not complaining. I'll get used to it."

That afternoon I briefed Tehra on the Charlotte Wenzel case and gave her the file to look over. Besides being someone I could talk candidly with, I was learning a lot about Tarizon which would help me do a better job for the CIA. It also made me feel better about Peter being on Tarizon. I was starting to think of it as just another part of the world. If I could have only picked up the phone and talked to him, that would have almost made the situation tolerable.

Chapter 18

Indispensable

When I told Bart about Stan's new intern he seemed almost relieved. He said the firm was understaffed with only one paralegal for three attorneys and he was thinking about getting a pretty intern himself. I told him to forget about it. I assured him that between the two of us we could get all the work done. After thinking about it for awhile though, I understood Bart's relief. With Tehra hanging around Stan all the time he'd have little time for me.

It was a few days before I heard back from Paul Thayer about Almatech's CEO, T. Robert Stout and his interest in Chester Brown. "Apparently Chester Brown went to Harvard too, but never graduated," Paul noted. "While he was there, however, he met Stout and they became friends. I'm told that Stout not only held Brown in high regard but seemed to be fascinated my him. After Stout joined the Air Force they lost contact with each other. In fact, I can't find any trace of Chester Brown for about a seventeen year period starting shortly after he left Harvard to his employment by TI three years ago."

"How can there be such a huge gap in a person's history, particularly someone like Brown?" I asked. " He must have been somewhere."

"Speculation was that he went to work for a foreign government or maybe even a terrorist organization. He was somewhat of a renegade at Harvard and was disliked by his professors. Apparently he was brilliant and wouldn't hesitate to humiliate one of them if their theories were flawed. Some say he left Harvard without graduating because he'd learned all that he could there."

"Interesting, but if he'd gone to work for terrorists, TI would have never hired him."

"Yes, I wouldn't think so," Paul agreed.

"So, did you find out anything about the project they were working on?"

"Nothing official. But one of their recently laid-off staff members suggested it had to had to do with stealth technology. More than that he wouldn't say."

"Stealth technology? You mean like airplanes that can't be picked up by radar?"

"Exactly. Apparently TI is at the forefront of this research and Brown was in the thick of it."

"So, others may have wanted Brown dead too. Was he that critical to the project?"

"Apparently he was the project," Paul replied. "The project has languished since his death and TI is scrambling to find someone to replace him. If they fall too far behind schedule they could lose the contract and Almatech, being the runner-up in the bidding, would likely be asked to step up to the plate."

"What about Stout's Air Force background? What did he do the twenty years he spent there?"

"Lots of things. He started out as a pilot in the Vietnam War in 1969. When the war was over he went into military intelligence and worked in the field in covert operations for about ten years. His last four years were spent as a liaison officer between the FAA and the Pentagon."

"So, he had the necessary training and experience to set the fire trap in Brown's house."

"Without a doubt."

"Well, I guess I should go visit Detective Rhodes and fill him in on what we've found. Maybe this information will get him off our client as the primary suspect."

"It should, but I'm afraid Detective Rhodes may not relish the idea of taking on the CEO of a multi-million dollar corporation. Our client is an easy target with limited resources, but going after T. Robert Stout will be difficult and costly. I'm afraid unless we serve the necessary evidence for a conviction on a silver platter, the prosecution won't go in that direction."

"You may be right, but it's worth a try. I can't see that it will hurt our client in any way."

Paul agreed and said he'd keep digging into Brown and Stout's backgrounds. After he'd hung up I called Richard Francis, the assistant district attorney we'd met the night Walter Stanley was brought in for questioning. I told him I had some information I wanted to share with him. He agreed to meet me for lunch the following day at the Collin County Hospital cafeteria. It had become a favorite hangout for county officials after a world renowned chef, Ricardo Regori, had been sentenced to one year confinement in the Collin County Jail. Regori didn't want his skills as a chef to diminish while he was incarcerated, so he volunteered to be chief cook at the county hospital—an offer the county commissions could hardly refuse.

After setting up the meeting with Francis, I decided to call our client and fill him in on where we were at in the investigation. He was pleased when I explained what good progress we'd made.

"So, do you think I'm off the hook?" he asked.

"Well, I wouldn't say that. I'll know more after I talk to Richard Francis. It just depends on what he's uncovered since the last time we talked to him. There isn't anything I need to be worried about, is there?"

"What do you mean?" Stanley asked.

"You haven't forgotten to tell me anything, have you?"

"No. No. I've told you everything that is relevant."

I hated it whenever a client used the word relevant. It meant they were hiding something. "You let me decide if something is relevant. I need to know everything."

"I've told you everything," Stanley insisted.

I didn't press the issue, but I wasn't convinced he had told me everything. I just wondered what he had left out and if it would turn out to be important. I prayed it wouldn't.

Chapter 19

The Rub

The next day Tehra and I were the first to arrive at the office. I had told her on the way in that we'd have to postpone her move by a week since I had to file a chapter 11 for the Stovers. I could tell she was disappointed but she didn't complain. I had explained to her how Ben and Alice Stover had been good clients over the years and that I had to help them out in their time of need. She said she respected my loyalty and wanted to help.

Later, from behind my desk, I said, "You can come if you want, but it's not going to be very exciting. I'm going to be hold up in Ben's office gathering information about his company. I'm sure you could find something more interesting to do here in Dallas. Maybe you could do some shopping. I promise I'll help you move next weekend."

She was seated in a side chair across the desk from me. She leaned forward. "No. I'd rather be with you. I don't know anybody and it's lonely on the weekends. Besides, you'll be tired when you come back Saturday night and shouldn't be driving alone."

Her logic was impeccable and I certainly enjoyed her company, so I didn't resist further. I was learning a lot about Tarizon and I wanted to learn more. I guess it was a way to feel closer to Peter.

"Okay, then. I'll pick you up in the morning at seven. We've got to be there by nine."

She smiled, seemingly satisfied that she'd got her way, then her face turned serious. "I've been studying the Wenzel file," she said, "and I was wondering what you were going to do to prove her innocence."

I shrugged somewhat amused. "Good question." Tehra had figured out exactly where we were on the case—nowhere. I was clueless as to what I should do next. She smiled sympathetically.

"Any suggestions?" I asked hopefully.

"Well, you could find an alibi for Charlotte."

"I've tried that," I replied, "but until they found Jill's body we didn't even know the time frame needed for an alibi."

"But now you do. Charlotte wasn't there when Jill died, you know that, so all you have to do is find out the time of death and prove Charlotte was somewhere else."

"Okay, that makes sense. I guess we need to go talk to the medical examiner again and then get our client in here to see if she can help us figure out an alibi."

Tehra smiled. I was quickly learning that she was one smart alien. "So, is everyone on Tarizon as smart as you?" I asked.

She laughed. "Not necessarily any smarter, but the people on Tarizon get a far superior education."

"Do they?" I asked.

"Yes. With the help of powerful mind-stimulating drugs and advanced computer technology, learning is fast and efficient on Tarizon—usually just six to eight months to get the equivalent of a college education."

"Whoa! Don't tell my kids that. They'll all want to go to Tarizon."

She smiled. "No, they wouldn't. At least not now with the conditions that exist there. It's a world struggling for survival."

I shook my head trying to imagine what it must be like living in a constant haze and not being able to see the sun. I wondered how Peter was doing there. He was in a domed city, I knew that, so he could at least breathe. Was he happy? He seemed to be in the brief film clips I'd seen, but they were carefully selected, I was sure. Tehra must have sensed my worry. She sighed.

"Thinking of Peter?"

I turned and looked at her. "Are you physic too?"

She nodded. "Maybe, a little."

I laughed. "Jesus. A woman who can read my mind. That's scary."

"I can't read your mind, but I'm trained to sense your moods. What can I do to make you feel better?"

I considered her question for a moment and then replied, "I saw a clip of Peter in a restaurant with a judge and his daughter. I was wondering where they were and who was the girl."

"Oh. That must have been Counselor Garcia and his daughter Lorin. The restaurant probably was in the capital city of Shisk."

"Shisk?"

"Right. It's in Turvin, in the province of Soni."

"Hmm. Did you say Garcia? That's–"

She laughed. "Yes, another Earthchild. What can I say?"

"It's just an impossible situation to know Peter is out there but realizing I'll never see him again, at least in person."

"You don't know that. If you serve faithfully, they may bring Peter back or let you go visit him."

I frowned. "Do you really think that, or are you just trying to make me feel better?"

I wasn't stupid. I knew her loyalties were to Tarizon and she'd tell we whatever I wanted to hear. Besides, Kulchz or one of his men was probably listening, so even if she wanted to be honest, she'd have to be very careful.

She sighed. "Come here and sit next to me," she said softly. Our eyes met and I felt myself being drawn toward her She smiled wryly and patted the side chair next to hers. "Come here. You're all stressed out. I'll give you a rub."

"A rub?" I said amused at the term.

"A massage. You know what I mean. I'm very good at it. You'll feel much better when I'm done."

I shrugged and got up. My shoulders were quite tight and I could feel the beginnings of a headache coming on." I walked over slowly and sat down next to her as commanded.

"Close your eyes, take a few deep breaths, and try to relax," she said as she got up and maneuvered herself behind me. Her hands moved quickly over my neck and shoulders. The tension began to melt away as she worked seemingly effortlessly to beguile every angry muscle into submission. I almost moaned it felt so good. My head was beginning to clear and in just minutes I was feeling like a new man, then I heard footsteps. I opened my eyes and looked toward the door. Jodie's mouth was wide open. I stood up and smiled.

"Jodie. Good morning!" I said trying to hide my embarrassment. "Tehra's gives a hell of a massage if you ever feel stressed out." Jodie shook her head and walked away.

I looked at Tehra and rolled my eyes. "That felt really good, but I guess this isn't the place to be getting a rub."

She gave me a wink. "This weekend I'll give you a proper one when we are alone and there won't be any interruptions."

Her promise stirred a part of me that had been dormant for months. I went back to my chair and sat down trying to conceal my excitement. "Okay, that sounds promising," I said wriggling in my chair, "but I doubt we'll have much of an opportunity for that at Ben Stover's office."

She shrugged. "Don't worry. We'll find the right moment."

I raised my eyebrows and looked away. She stifled a laugh and tried to look serious. Finally she said, "I'll go see if I can set up an appointment for you to see the medical examiner."

I nodded. "Good idea."

Tehra left and went back to her work station. I wondered what Jodie was thinking. Would she think I was sleeping with Tehra? I sighed. Shit! Why had I let her give me a massage. How stupid could I have been! Jodie would go straight to Paula to gossip about what she'd seen. Now, if Paula didn't already suspect something, she'd definitely be convinced of it. That would really piss her off because she'd been trying to seduce me for years and I'd managed to resist her. I wondered if I'd be able to resist Tehra.

It wasn't long before Tehra was back proudly announcing that the Hunt County Medical Examiner had agreed to see us at 3:00 P.M. that afternoon. That was perfect since it would give us all morning to work on the chapter 11. We had lots to do since several motions had to be filed immediately after the bankruptcy case was opened. We could get drafts of those done before we had to leave for Greenville. It was about an hour to Greenville from Dallas so if we left at 1:00 p.m. that would give us time to get there and then get some lunch before our meeting.

About mid-morning, while we were in the midst of our work,

Paula looked in on us. She'd obviously talked to Jodie as she had an icy look on her face. I smiled and asked, "Hey. How's the case going?"

When Paula hesitated, Tehra got up and excused herself. Paula sat down in her place next to me. I was afraid I was about to get a lecture, but Paula restrained herself. Instead she began giving me a rather detailed account of her and Bart's progress on the Chester Brown case. I was impressed.

"That's great. So, with a little luck you'll have your man off the hook."

"Maybe, if he's not hiding something," she said and then recounted her fear that he was.

"He may not be. You never know. He may just be the paranoid type. A lot of people are like that. They can't imagine a day going by without some sort of trouble and they are always fearful of retribution for even the tiniest of transgressions."

"So, anything new on Charlotte's case?" she asked. I told we were going out to meet the medical examiner. She said she knew him and he'd be open and candid with me. Then she changed the subject.

"So, what's the real story with Tehra," she asked. "She's not just an intern. You don't think we're that stupid do you?"

I sighed. "No, you're right. She's a lot more than an intern, but I'd appreciate it if you cut me a little slack with her. With everything that's happened I need her right now."

She stiffened with anger. "Stan, you know I'm here for you. I've always been here. I'd do anything."

I nodded. "I know that, but it's complicated and I can't put you in danger. You'll have to trust me and, whatever you do, don't stir things up with Rebekah. You have no idea what's going on, so tread lightly, please."

Her eyes narrowed then she shook her head. "There was a time that we could talk about anything, a time when you trusted me–"

I took her hand and looked her in the eyes. "I do trust you, Paula, but this isn't about trust. It's about survival."

She frowned, pulled her hand away, and stood up. "Okay. Whatever is going on, I guess you'll fill me in when the time is right," she said sarcastically.

I nodded and she left. I hated not being able to confide in

Paula. She was right. In the past we'd always told each other everything. I wondered if she had any clue what was going on. I suspected she did, but hoped she wouldn't undertake any investigation on her own. If she did, there would be no way I could protect her.

Chapter 20

A Missing Steak

When Jodie told me she caught Tehra giving Stan a back rub, I was concerned. I felt my worst suspicions had been confirmed. Tehra had sunk her claws into Stan and in his delicate state he was too weak to resist her. What had happened to the incorruptible man I'd fallen in love with? He was a different man since Peter had died and Rebekah had turned away from him. He'd lost his zest for life and no longer seemed to care about his integrity and honor.

As I thought back over the years, I blamed some of what had happened to Stan on myself. He never cared about money until I came along and convinced him the practice of law was a business. I'd been wrong, I knew that now, but it was too late. Stan had changed. He was no longer the independent soul I'd grown to love and cherish. Someone had gotten to him and was jerking him around like a puppet on a string. I could see it, although whoever it was kept cleverly in the background. But who could be doing this to him? Who was so rich and powerful that they could corrupt Stan Turner and turn him into a docile pawn who'd be happy with a pocket full of money and a willing wench at his beck and call?

After I'd learned my suspicions were correct, I confronted Stan and he denied nothing. He told me the situation was complicated and dangerous. He asked me to stay out of his way and warned me that there would be dire consequences if I told Rebekah what I'd learned. He asked me to trust him.

Trust him? How could he expect me to trust him, when he didn't have enough trust in me to tell me what was going on. Why was he working for a man who was afraid to step out and let the world see him? It made no sense, unless the man was Mo. Was Stan working on some secret CIA project? That had to be it. That would explain a lot, but it wouldn't explain Tehra. Who the hell was she and why was she shadowing Stan so closely? Could she be watching him to make sure he did the CIA's bidding? But if they didn't trust Stan to do the job, why would they have assigned it to him? Nothing made sense.

Stan warned me not to look too closely into what he was doing. He said it would be dangerous for him and for me. I had no reason to believe he was lying on that point, so I decided to turn my head and look the other way, for now anyway. But I wasn't sure how long I could stomach that course of action. I cared too much for Stan and feared he might not be able to extricate himself from whatever nasty business he'd gotten himself into.

After a while I turned my thoughts to the day's tasks. I looked on my calendar and saw that Bart and I had an appointment with Detective Riley Rhodes and Assistant District Attorney Richard Francis. We were told to meet them in the 299th District Court's jury room on the fourth floor of the Collin County Courthouse. Apparently they were in trial and the jury was taking a late lunch. We shook hands and then sat across from each other at a long conference table.

"So, to what do we owe this pleasure?" Francis asked

I smiled politely and then told them about our investigation into Chester Brown and the CEO of Almatech, T. Robert Stout. They listened attentively, breaking in occasionally for a clarification, until I was finished. When I was done they shook their heads. Rhodes spoke first.

"That's all very imaginative," he said, "but according to your theory not only is Mr. Stout a suspect but so is every one of TI's competitors, not to mention a dozen national governments around the world."

"Yes, a very ingenious way to create reasonable doubt," Francis chimed in. I've got to hand it to you Paula, that's one hell of a strategy."

"It's not a strategy," I argued. "It's the truth. Don't you see it. Stout wanted that contract and now with Chester Brown out of the way, he's going to get it."

"Well, we've looked at Mr. Stout and some of TI's other

competitors, but we're having trouble getting over one thing."

"What's that?" I asked.

"Remember the dog . . . the German Shepard . . . what's his name?" Rhodes asked.

"Pretty Boy," Francis replied.

"Oh, right. Pretty Boy. Well, the thing is, Pretty Boy's been missing since the fire. Of course, you know about the feud that was going on over Pretty Boy."

I nodded. This wasn't sounding good. What did Pretty Boy have to do with anything? I braced myself for the worst. "Yes, our client told us about Pretty Boy."

"Well, Pretty Boy finally showed up," Rhodes continued. "It seems the arsonist lured him out the back gate with a big juicy steak. There was blood found on the stones in front of the gate. It's been analyzed and it is definitely blood from raw beef. It seems the killer didn't want Pretty Boy around to get in the way when he was wiring the place to go up in flames."

"So, that doesn't prove Stanley did it. Anyone could have bought a steak and lured the dog away with it," Bart argued.

"True enough, except as you will remember Stanley told us he ate alone the night of the fire. So we did some checking over at the Tom Thumb where he shops. The butcher remembers him coming in and buying two big 12 ounce steaks. There's even a record of it. So, the question is, who ate the second steak?"

"Maybe he froze it," I suggested.

"Yeah, well we thought of that so we checked his freezer."

"You've searched his house?"

"Yes, a few hours ago. But don't worry. We got a warrant."

"So, let me guess. No steak in the freezer."

"That's right," Rhodes said gleefully.

I shook my head in disgust. We'd walked right into an ambush. They sat there grinning at us like we were a couple of idiots. I stood up. "Well, it all sounds pretty lame to me," I said. "If you're so sure Walter Stanley is the perp, why haven't you arrested him?"

Rhodes smiled. "Well, it's funny you ask, because there's a squad car on the way to his townhouse right now."

Bart stood up and took my hand, "Come on, Paula. Let's go

find Roger. We're going to need to arrange bond."

We left quickly without looking back. I had never been so humiliated in my life. I vowed right then to prove Rhodes wrong. I knew Stanley couldn't have killed Chester Brown and his family over a fence or a barking dog. Whoever was responsible for all those deaths had no conscience and I knew Walter Stanley had one—a very strong one. I saw it in his eyes and the way he talked. He was no killer. Unfortunately my gut feeling didn't mean anything in court.

As a precaution we had previously arranged for Stanley to meet with Roger Rand just in case a bond became necessary. Unfortunately, Stanley had limited assets and if his bond were set over a quarter million dollars, he wouldn't be able to meet it. That would mean he'd have to sit in the county jail until his case came to trial. The county jail was better than Huntsville or one of the other state prisons, but it was no piece of cake either. The jail was old and dirty and the inmates were often hostile, especially to the white collar inmates being held there. It would be a dangerous place for Walter Stanley, particularly since he was accused of killing three innocent children.

Unfortunately, it was nearly six-thirty before they got Stanley to the county jail. The delay was no doubt intentional to make it harder for us to get him out on bail that evening. There weren't usually any judges on duty after five and unless you wanted to disturb one of them at home, your client would have to stay in jail until morning. Normally it was possible to run a writ at night and get a client out, but not when the charge was capital murder. It seemed Walter Stanley would be forced to spend the night in jail until there could be a bail hearing.

After we met with Rand, we headed for the county courthouse. Even if we couldn't get him out, we had a right to visit him. I was anxious to find out what he had to say about the two steaks he bought at Tom Thumb on the day of the murder. How could anyone be so stupid as to buy something like that where people knew him? It almost made me think it was a coincidence. While I waited to talk to Stanley, Bart got on the telephone to call a couple of judges he knew. If he could get in touch with one of them, they might agree to set a temporary bond.

About twenty minutes later the desk sergeant told me they were bringing Stanley into the interview booth and that I should go to room three. I rushed over to it, opened the door, and took a seat. It was a small room about the size of two telephone booths. I would be separated from Stanley by a thick glass window. We'd have to talk by telephone as the glass was nearly soundproof. A minute later a disheveled Walter Stanley took a seat. His hands were trembling as he picked up the telephone.

"I guess your meeting with the DA didn't go so well," he said.

"I frowned. "No. It didn't. You want to tell me about Pretty Boy?"

Stanley looked away. "I didn't go over there to set a fire. I was just going to let Pretty Boy loose to cause them some grief. I figured it was the least I could do after all the trouble he had caused everybody by putting up that damn fence."

"So, you lured Pretty Boy away with a steak and then what happened?"

"He was happy to be free. When he'd finished the steak he just ran off. That's when I noticed the fire."

"Did you see anyone else while you were there?"

"No. Just a couple telephone workers splicing some cables."

"A telephone crew?"

"Yes, they were working out of a yellow panel truck with a GTE logo."

"There were two men?"

"Yes."

"Can you describe them?"

"One was Latino. Medium height, short dark hair, and he walked with a limp."

"Hmm. What about the other one?"

"He was Anglo, tall, blond hair and a mustache. They both wore jeans and a beige GTE shirt."

"Well, I'll check with GTE and see who they were. If they were there when the fire was set, they should have seen something. I wonder if the police have questioned them."

“I don’t know. . . . Do you think I’m screwed?"

"It's not looking good, Walter. You should have leveled with us in the beginning. You made us look like fools today. Now we have no credibility with Francis. He's convinced you're his man."

Stanley nodded dejectedly. "I'm sorry. I know it was stupid, but I didn't figure anyone would ever know I let Pretty Boy out. I should have wrapped the steak in paper towels. When the blood started dripping, I knew I was in trouble."

There was a knock on the door and Bart stuck his head in. I turned around and raised my eyebrows. "Any luck?"

Bart shrugged. "Yes and no. I talked to Judge Milton and he said he'd set bond but it would have to be high since he hadn't seen our client or seen any evidence."

"How high?" I asked, and held my breath.

"A million."

"Shoot! So, we are out of luck?"

Bart shrugged. "I'm afraid so."

I turned and gave Stanley a sympathetic look. "Sorry, Walter, but I'm afraid you'll have to spend the night in jail."

He closed his eyes and buried his face in his hands. "I've never been in jail before. Do you think they'll rape me?"

"No. No. Not here. You're in for capital murder. They'll keep you segregated. You don't have to worry about being raped. You'll be fine until morning."

"I'm so scared. Do you think I'll be convicted?"

I shrugged. "I don't know. It's too early to speculate, but I do believe you're innocent, so you can rest assured I'll do whatever it takes to prove it."

Stanley seemed a little more relaxed when they led him away. I got up slowly and turned toward Bart. He took my hand and pulled me close to him. "Don't worry. We'll get him out tomorrow. You did all you could."

"Did I? I was so enthralled with our conspiracy theory that I totally ignored my gut feeling that Stanley was not telling us everything."

"I doesn't matter. Even if you had known about Pretty Boy the police still would have discovered it."

"Yes, but he wouldn't be spending the night in jail."

"Hey. A night in jail might be exactly what Stanley needs. He'll think twice before he withholds information again."

We left the courthouse and went home. Bart was right, Stanley had dug his own hole, but clients often did that and it was my job to dig him out. In bed later that night, I couldn't sleep. All I could think about was Francis and Rhodes laughing at us. That galled me. I had to have the last laugh. I just had to get Stanley off at all cost.

Chapter 21

Autopsy

Dr. Black stood up when his secretary showed us into his tidy office. It was furnished with cheap metal furniture and thinly upholstered chairs. He came around from behind his desk and shook my hand and nodded to Tehra. We sat across from him with some discomfort. They obviously didn't revere medical examiners in Hunt County or Dr. Black didn't like his guests staying too long.

"So, what can I do for you?" Dr. Black asked.

I explained that we represented Charlotte Wenzel and were there to find out what her daughter's autopsy had revealed. He frowned, swivelled around to his credenza and searched through a stack of file folders. Not finding the file he stood up and walked over to a file cabinet. After rummaging through it for a moment, he found what he was looking for and returned to his desk. He opened the file and studied it.

"Oh, yes. The body was found about a mile north of Hermits Cove near Point, Texas. It was in a heavily wooded area and the body probably wouldn't have ever been found had some hunters not accidentally stumbled across it."

"When was it found?"

"On Tuesday, I believe."

I wrote the information on a legal pad and looked up at the medical examiner.

"Did you determine a time of death?"

"The body had been there several weeks and had been ravaged pretty badly by wildlife, so I'm afraid I can't pinpoint it exactly. But, I'd say she was killed on the weekend after the family disappeared."

"So, that would be between August 2nd and 4th?" I asked.

"Yes."

"So, what did you determine to be the cause of death?"

"Well, that's what's strange about this case. The cause of death was head trauma. She seems to have fallen–fallen from some distance judging by the extent of her injuries."

I wondered what Dr. Black would say if I told him she'd fallen from a spaceship, but I repressed that idea quickly. "So, you think she fell off a cliff or out of a tree?"

"Possibly, but I'm thinking more likely it was an airplane."

"An airplane?"

"Yes, there are no cliffs near where she was found and few large trees. It's really rather puzzling."

"Hmm. Did you check airports in the area? Were there any small planes up over the weekend?"

"The sheriff is checking on that. My job is done."

I nodded and looked at Tehra. "Can you think of anything else we need to know?"

Tehra leaned forward toward the doctor. "Yes, one more thing. Who were the hunters who found the body? We should probably talk to them."

The doctor flipped through his file and replied, "John Sturgeons and Walter Creskey."

He turned the file around so we could copy their addresses. "Oh, one other thing," Tehra asked. "Were there any footprints or tire tracks near the body?"

He shook his head. "No, that's another reason I think she fell from an airplane. The only footprints were from the hunters and the wildlife that had been feeding on the body."

Tehra smiled and looked at me. I stood up, thanked the doctor and we left. Since we had been running late we hadn't eaten lunch before seeing the doctor, so I suggested we stop at a little café across from the courthouse. It was late so the place was deserted. A bored looking waitress showed up at our table and gave us menus.

"So, no surprises there," I commented. "I just wish Dr. Black could have pinned down the time of death a little better. Now we have to provide an alibi for the entire weekend."

"True, but unless Charlotte Wenzel can fly an airplane or had an accomplice who could, she's in the clear."

"You're right," I replied. "I'm sure that's got to be bothering Gary Shepard. How will he prove opportunity? He must have thought of that before he arrested her. . . . Shit!"

"What?"

"The informant, the one Shepard told Bart about hoping to get him fired, must have been real after all. Shepard must have somebody who's going to testify that Charlotte tried to hire him to kill her family. I can't believe this!"

"You think so? But, who would lie like that?"

"A jailhouse snitch. Somebody who's looking to get time knocked off their sentence. It happens all the time. I've just never seen it in the Collin County prosecutor's office. They are usually above that kind of thing, at least before Gary Shepard came on board."

"Can you find out who it is?"

"I don't know. They're supposed to inform us of any witnesses they plan to call, but they can wait until the last minute on the pretense that they haven't decided whether to call them or not."

"What will you do?" Tehra asked gingerly.

I shook my head. "I guess I'll talk to Bart about it. He knows the district attorney's policies and practices better than anyone. He should be able to help."

The waitress finally returned and took our orders. After we'd eaten we headed back to Dallas. It was late, so I took Tehra to her hotel before I went back to the office. I should have gone straight home but I had to check my messages and clean up my desk before calling it a day. When I got there I found a message from Mo, so I dialed his number. Surprisingly, he answered.

"So, how's Tehra working out for you?" he asked.

"Fine, she's a big help and it's nice to have someone to talk to, but you knew that, didn't you?"

There was an uneasy silence. "Yeah, well this project is very important and the Tarizonians don't take chances."

"So, who exactly is monitoring my every move? You don't personally have time for that, do you?"

"God no. Nor the patience, but I do get a daily report."

"I bet, " I grumbled. "So, what do you want? You didn't call because you were worried about Tehra."

"No. She's a big girl. She can take care of herself. No, actually, Kulchz was worried about the hunters that found Jill's body. He's afraid they might have seen something. He's considering . . . well . . . he's considering taking drastic action."

"Tell him not to worry. I'll handle it. They found the body weeks after it was dropped. They couldn't possibly have seen anything that would expose the project."

"That's what I told him, but he wanted me to discuss it with you."

"Tell him Tehra and I are going to talk to the hunters. We'll let him know if there's a problem, but I seriously doubt it."

"Good. Sorry to bother you. Now, go home. Why are you still at the office anyway? It's after seven. Go home . . . or better yet, go see Tehra. I'm sure she'd be happy to give you another rub," Mo laughed as he hung up.

Anger welled up inside me as I slammed the phone down. This living in a fish bowl was beginning to annoy me. It was so hard to believe that Tehra was part of Kulchz's game. She seemed so loving and concerned—almost like she was in love with me— but I knew it was a lie. She was one hell of an actress though, there was no doubt about that. Even knowing who she was, the moment she strolled into my life each day, I felt so safe and secure that I'd spill my guts to her without the slightest reservation. It was like she cast a spell over me that I was powerless to resist. The thought of going to her flashed in my mind. She'd give me whatever I desired—every fantasy I'd ever dreamed about could be lived and relished this very evening.

I took a deep breath and shook my head vigorously. What was happening to me? Why was I letting her get to me so? I couldn't go to Tehra for sex! Then they'd really have me. I could never go to her for that, no matter how much pleasure it might bring. I had to play the game, though—let them think they had me under their control—but somehow keep my wits. I didn't know how I'd do that exactly, but somehow I had to figure it out, or what little free will I had left in this world would be lost.

Chapter 22

Enlisting an Ally

A call to GTE proved a waste of time. They didn't give out information about their drivers or the routes they took, at least not over the telephone. They suggested I write a letter, but I had a better idea, I'd subpoena the maintenance survivor and make him drag all his records down to my office. I put Jodie on that task and had the subpoena delivered before noon. It didn't take long before I got an apologetic call from the manager in charge.

"I'm sorry. I didn't realize–"

"It's all right. Just tell me if you had a maintenance truck in the 4400 block of Collinwood Dr. in Allen on August 9th."

There was a moment of silence then a grunt. "No. There's no record of any activity in that area on the 9th, but there was an incident in Allen on that day that might interest you."

"What kind of incident?" I asked.

"One of our trucks was lost for awhile."

"Lost?"

"Yes, it seemed to have been stolen. Our men went into IHOP for breakfast and when they came out it was gone. That evening, however, the truck was returned to the same IHOP parking lot. It was very bizarre. We suspected it was the work of teenagers with too much free time on their hands. There wasn't anything missing out of the truck, so we withdrew our complaint with the police."

"Did the police check the vehicle for fingerprints?"

"Yes, but it had been wiped clean. I guess the kids had seen enough cop shows to know not to leave their fingerprints behind. Fortunately, our only loss was the cost of a few gallons of gasoline."

The theft of the GTE truck strengthened my belief that Stout was behind the fire. Finding evidence to prove that would be difficult, though, without help from the police or the DA's office. We'd already enlisted Paul Thayer's assistance with the case but his further involvement would be expensive. We'd already billed out most of Stanley's retainer and I could see his case costing a lot more than I'd originally advised him. Stanley would soon run out of money and we'd be working pro bono if I didn't think of something fast.

It occurred to me that it would be to TI's advantage to have a competitor under investigation. If we somehow proved they were involved in the Brown murders the company could go down in smoke and TI would be sitting pretty with its major competitor out of business. We hadn't got a particularly warm welcome from TI the last time we'd met with them, but things had changed. We had some evidence now of Almatech's involvement. I put in a call to TI's HR manager, Robin Sylvester, and he agreed to see me that afternoon. When I went looking for Bart to tell him about the meeting, Maria advised me he had gone to lunch with Bob Ralston.

I raised my eyebrows at the news that Bart was meeting with the DA. I wondered how that had come about. I asked Maria if Bob had called Bart or if Bart had contacted the DA. She said Bart had called and invited Ralston to lunch. She said she overheard Bart say something about wanting to make sure he got reelected. This new development intrigued me so much I nearly forgot about Sylvester. Luckily, Maria reminded me that I needed to leave. Thirty minutes later I was escorted into Sylvester's office. His secretary asked if I wanted a cold drink. I told her some water would be nice. He seemed very pleased to see me this time. I didn't know if it was because Bart wasn't with me or his perspective had changed since our last meeting.

"So, how's the investigation going?" he asked enthusiastically.

"Oh, it's having its ups and downs," I replied.

"So, tell me about it?" Sylvester pressed.

I sighed. "Well, although we've found considerable evidence to suggest the setting of the fire was a professional job, the DA is still convinced Walter Stanley is the one responsible for it and won't look at anybody else."

"What evidence do you have?"

"According to the arson investigator the triggering device was very sophisticated—something military or CIA. Our client remembers a GTE truck parked in the back alley behind the Brown house. It had been there a day or two and he'd seen a couple of workmen splicing cable. GTE confirms that one of their trucks was stolen the morning before the fire and returned the following evening."

"Really? That does sound interesting. So, what would you like me to do? I assume that's why you're here."

"Yes. We thought if Almatech is in fact assassinating your employees to get a competitive advantage, you'd be a little upset about it. We thought you might want to join in an investigation of their involvement in the Brown murders. Of course, we'd keep your involvement confidential."

"I know you'd try, but these things have a way of leaking out. If Almatech were to find out we were investigating them, they'd be extremely upset about it and they might retaliate."

"That's why our investigation is perfect for you. Nobody has to know that TI is involved. We just need some help with funding. Our client is just a private citizen with limited resources. Without your help he'll go down for the murders and Stout will get away with killing the most intelligent and talented employee TI has ever employed."

"Stout's got an alibi," Sylvester advised. "After you came by last week, we did some checking. He was in San Jose visiting one of his subcontractors."

I shrugged. "Well, I never thought he personally set the fire. I'm sure he has a team—some of his old running buddies, I bet—to do the dirty work."

"You're right He wouldn't be that stupid."

"So, you'll help us out?" I asked expectantly.

"I'm only the HR manager," Sylvester said. "I can't commit the company to something like this. I'll have to talk to our VP of Security, Tom Walston. I'll get back to you in a day or two."

I nodded. I hadn't expected an answer immediately and I doubted that even Tom Walston had the authority to commit funds for an investigation of a major competitor. This would be something the President or maybe even the executive committee of the board of directors would have to authorize. I felt good about the meeting, though, and began thinking of how to conduct an effective investigation once we had TI behind us. When I got back to the office I went straight to Bart's office. I was curious about his meeting with the DA.

Bart was on the telephone and motioned for me to take a seat. I did and waited impatiently for him to get off the phone. Finally, he said his goodbyes and hung up.

"Don't keep me in suspense. What happened with the DA?" I asked.

Bart's eyes narrowed. "How did you find out about that?"

"You think you can keep secrets from me?" I said wryly. "I've got spies everywhere."

"Hmm," he said. "Well, Stan asked me to check with the DA again about a possible snitch ready to testify against Charlotte Wenzel."

"What? But the DA already said that was a ruse."

"I know. But Stan was afraid maybe the DA really did have one or has found one since he took over the case."

"Okay," I said.

"So, I decided to do a little politicking to see if I could find out the truth. When I called Ralston I told him I was concerned about his re-election campaign and wanted to help him. He was skeptical but agreed to have lunch. We met at the On the Border in Addison, so it wasn't likely that our meeting would be noticed."

It was crowded and we had to wait about ten minutes before we were seated. The waitress brought us two beers and then took our orders. When she was out of earshot, Ralston took a deep breath and said, "All right, I'm here. Now what's this about my political career being in jeopardy?"

I took a swig of my beer and then looked him in the eye. "You know Gary Shepard is after your job, don't you?"

His eyes narrowed. "What? That's crazy. He hasn't been on the job here thirty days. How's he going to possibly run against me."

"He assumes he'll get a lot of media attention from the Wenzel case and be a household name by election day. But he knows that won't be enough so my guess is he'll orchestrate some kind of fiasco to embarrass you and force you to withdraw from the race. As you know, he'll get what he wants no matter what it takes."

"That's bullshit," Ralston chuckled.

"I know, it probably sounds like bullshit," I replied, "but I have it on good authority that it's true. He's been bragging about it to people."

"Why didn't he run in Houston? He already was a household name down there."

"My sources tell me the Harris County DA had something on him to keep him in line. That's why he so eagerly took your job offer. It was the first one he'd gotten from a decent size county—a county with a future. His political ambition goes beyond the DA's office, you know. He's got his eyes on Austin."

"Well, I don't believe you. I think you're just trying to get back at him for what he did to you and Paula."

"That was pretty underhanded and I won't deny that I'd like to get back at him for that, but that's not why I'm here. I don't want Gary Shepard being DA. I have a lot of respect for you and I want to help you keep your job."

"Well, your concern for me is very touching," Ralston said, "but if that's all you came here to tell me, you should have just sent my campaign treasurer a check and saved us both some time."

"That's not everything," I replied. "There is one other matter."

"What's that?" Ralston asked.

"These rumors Shepard has been spreading about having a snitch and then not having a snitch, have got to stop. We know you have someone in the wings who claims Charlotte Wenzel approached him about killing her husband."

"I don't know what you're talking about," Ralston protested.

"Okay, play dumb. It's your funeral. Just remember, though, if on the eve of trial you decide you need this snitch to testify and Stan hasn't had access to him, he'll be sure to let the judge know Shepard's been sitting on him for six months. And if the judge doesn't do anything about it, he'll go straight to the grievance committee of the state bar."

Ralston's complexion reddened. He got up angrily and put on

his coat. "Don't threaten me," he warned.

As he was leaving, I said, "Watch your back, Bob. I promise you Shepard's out to get you."

Ralston shook his head and stormed out of the restaurant. A moment later the waitress showed up with our orders. She asked me what had become of my friend. I told her he got some upsetting news and lost his appetite. She gave me a puzzled look and then said evenly, "Well, I hope you're hungry, because I can't take this back to the kitchen. Once it's on a plate it must be eaten or thrown away. If it gets thrown away, it will come out of my check."

"Don't worry. I'll cover it," I said with a smile. "I'm actually kind of hungry."

The waitress shrugged and tossed the bill on the table. As I ate, I wondered how long it would be before Stan got the snitch's name. Something like this was too important to ignore. If there was a snitch we had to learn as much about him as possible. The only way to deal with a snitch was to discredit him and that wasn't always easy to do.

Bart's confrontation with the DA bothered me. Even though Stan had asked for his help, he didn't have to go straight to the DA. He was playing hardball unnecessarily. I didn't want Shepard targeting Bart for more dirty tricks. There was no telling what he was capable of. We already had our hands full with T. Robert Stout. Soon he'd learn of our investigation and he was a professional killer with a security team that could kill anyone at will and make it look like an accident. The knot in my stomach began to twist and throb. Maybe working with your spouse on a high profile murder case wasn't such a good idea after all.

Chapter 23

Alien Sensation

On Friday while Tehra and I were preparing for our trip to Waco, Paula stopped in and brought us up to date on the Walter Stanley case. She told me about her meeting with Sylvester at TI and Bart's encounter with the DA. It amused me that Bart was getting a little revenge on Shepard, but I shared Paula's concern for their safety.

That afternoon Agent Lot of the FBI called. I didn't take the call as I still didn't know what to do about the lie I'd told him. If they discovered that we'd taken the memory gun off one of the kidnappers that would be obstruction of justice and we could all go to jail. Somehow I had to find someone who could pretend to be my client and talk to Agent Lot. Whoever it was would have to be damn convincing or Agent Lot would see through the ruse.

On Saturday I picked up Tehra and we headed down I-35 toward Waco. Neither of us had eaten breakfast, so we stopped at IHOP in Hillsboro to eat. I told Tehra about Agent Lot and the lie I had told him. I knew Kulchz would be listening and wondered what his reaction would be. Tehra agreed it was a troublesome problem. I asked her how the technology was transferred from Tarizon to the scientist in the U.S.

"I'm not a scientist nor am I involved in that process, but I do know that scientists from Tarizon do frequently visit Earth. That's part of a guide's job. In fact, that's what I was about to do when I got reassigned to you. I was supposed to meet some scientists and help them prepare for the trip back to Tarizon. If I hadn't been reassigned to you, I'd probably be traveling with them."

Anger welled in me as I thought of Tehra with other men.

What kind of government would use woman like that? I shook my head in disgust. "Do the scientists ever bring their wives and families?"

"Their mates, we don't have marriage on Tarizon. Each male is assigned a female mate for life. Few children are born on Tarizon, so I doubt they'd have any to bring. A scientist assigned to Earth might bring his mate, but it's not the usual policy. Most Tarizonian women are sterile due to the environmental contamination since the great eruptions. The men come here to find a fertile Earth woman. Often they stay and have several children before returning to Tarizon with the children."

"What about the poor women like Charlotte Wenzel who lose their families? That's pretty cruel, don't you think?"

"Yes, I agree it's a horrible sacrifice, but would you have our planet die?"

"No, but there must be another way?"

"We've tried everything to clean up the planet but it's such an incredibly monumental task it will take many generations to complete. In the meantime the repopulation project is helping to stem the rapid population loss that we've suffered in the last fifty years."

It was an interesting debate that we continued after we were back on the road. It was a hot August day and the weatherman had warned that temperatures would be in the triple digits. Dark clouds loomed ahead as we approached Waco. I prayed we'd get to Ben's place before the clouds unloaded on us. I'd driven through plenty of thunderstorms where visibility became next to impossible. We had a long tedious day ahead and I didn't want to get there already stressed out. Fortunately the skies held firm until we stepped inside Ben's place. A clap of thunder shook the building startling Tehra. Seeing the terrified look on her face made me wonder if they had thunderstorms on Tarizon.

"Well, I'm glad you made it okay," Alice said. "I've been listening to the weather reports on the radio and we're under a tornado watch until noon."

I nodded. "I don't doubt it. The sky looked pretty ominous all the way from Hillsboro."

Alice smiled at Tehra. "So, this must be Tehra. We've talked on the phone. It's good to finally meet you."

Tehra extended her hand. "Yes, it's so nice to meet you too. Stan has told me a lot about you."

"He has?" Ben replied. "Not all our dirty secrets, I hope."

I laughed. "No. Not those. I needed her help, so I kept my mouth shut. I didn't want her refusing to come down here with me."

Alice shook her head. "To hear us, you'd think we were gathering for a wedding rather than a bankruptcy."

"A reorganization," I stressed. "Let's be positive now."

"Right," Ben agreed. "We're going to straighten this mess out and get back on track."

"Exactly," I said patting Ben on the shoulder. So, where have you piled your mounds of records?"

Ben pointed to a double door that led into a conference room. I nodded and started toward it with everyone else close behind. Inside there was a long wooden table with dozens of stacks of papers and records. We all found a place to sit and I began asking questions about the business, its assets, and its liabilities. Occasionally, I would have to stop writing as Alice would rummage through paperwork to find the answer to a question. At noon we stopped and went down the street for a hamburger. Alice and Tehra were getting along well and seemed to have lots to talk about. While they were in the ladies' room I asked Ben how Alice was holding up.

"Not well, actually. She's worried sick about what Ralph will do next."

"What makes you think he'll do anything else?" I asked.

"Because he's obsessed with wrecking our lives. I don't think he'll be happy until we're both dead."

"Don't say that. In jail he'll have a lot of time to think. Maybe he'll realize he's brought everything on himself. It's certainly wasn't your fault. You were the victim."

"He won't see it that way," Ben said. "We were the ones who took away his freedom. Because he was once part of the family, I'm sure he never thought we'd turn him in. He feels betrayed, no doubt."

"Oh, so it's okay to steal from your family? Is that his logic?"

"I'm afraid so."

"Well, I really don't know what else he could do to hurt you," I said.

"Oh, I'm sure he's got a long list of possibilities. I just hope Alice is strong enough for whatever else he throws at us."

Ben's pessimistic attitude bothered me. What could I do to protect him and Alice from this lunatic? I couldn't think of a damn thing, yet there must be some way to stop him. I decided to contact Larry Wakefield who was responsible for Ralph until his embezzlement trial. Perhaps he'd have some ideas on how we could restrict Ralph 's access to his friends in the outside world. If Ralph had additional plans to hurt the Stovers, he'd need help.

After working all afternoon we finally completed all the bankruptcy forms necessary for the initial filing. It had been a long day and I wasn't relishing the idea of driving two hours to get home. Tehra offered to drive, but she didn't have a license, so I declined the offer. The weather was still bad and a line of thunderstorms was moving across central Texas from the west. I was hoping to beat the storms but ran right in the thick of them about twenty miles south of Hillsboro. The rain was coming down in sheets and it was nearly impossible to see the road.

Just past a little town called West, the sky turned an ominous green color and the wind whipped up in a frenzy. Debris began to blow across the highway and trees along the median were bending almost to the ground. Just as we saw the Hillsboro city limit's sign, a big branch came right at us. I tried to veer left and miss it, but the branch landed right in front of us. There was nowhere to go but over it. Our headlights were shattered as the branch hit, then we were jolted violently up and own as we ran over the branch. The car shifted left still entangled in the branch, but I was able to compensate by turning the wheel hard to the right. We finally skidded to a stop on the side of the road. I took a deep breath and looked over at Tehra.

"You okay!"

"I don't know," Tehra said breathlessly. "What's happening?"

"There must be a tornado close by. We should get out of the car and lie in the ditch beside the road."

"What?" She said looking at me incredulously.

"The tornado can toss this car around like it was a beach ball. We've got to get out now!"

As I opened my door and started to get out of the car there

was a clap of thunder and then the wind started to calm. By the time I got around to the other side of the car the rain had stopped. Tehra opened her door and got out.

"Maybe, we just got lucky," I said looking at the rapidly clearing sky.

"Good. I didn't really want to lie in the ditch."

I laughed and then started looking the car over for damage. The front end was smashed in a little bit and both headlights were broken, but other than that I couldn't see any damage. "Get back in. We'll see if she'll still drive."

Back in the car I started the engine and gave it a little gas. We drove along the shoulder of the road for a few hundred yards without difficulty. The only problem we had was our broken headlights.

"I guess we'll have to spend the night here in Hillsboro and drive home in the morning," I reasoned out loud. "We can't drive without headlights."

Tehra nodded. "No. That would be too dangerous."

There was a Best Western motel on the outskirts of town so we stopped and went inside to get a couple of rooms. A heavy set woman sat at the front desk reading a magazine.

"Can I help you?"

"We'll need two rooms for tonight," I said.

She frowned. "You got reservations?"

"No," I said as a sinking feeling came over me.

She grumbled something to herself and then started typing on the motel computer. "Sorry, I've just got one room left."

"Really? Hmm. How about the other motels in town? Do you think they might have some vacancies?"

"No, they usually fill up before I do. Your best bet would be Waxahachie about twenty miles down the road."

"Oh, we can't drive that far. We lost our headlights."

"Well, then you'll have to sleep together."

I looked at Tehra. She was smiling. I shrugged. "Okay, We'll take it."

The room wasn't anything fancy but it was tolerable. I turned on the TV and Tehra went into the bathroom. When she came out a few moments later she had changed into a pink pajama set with shorts and a tank top. My mouth fell open.

"You brought pajamas?"

She shrugged. "I like to be prepared for all eventualities."

Her legs were long and tanned. My pulse quickened. She moved quickly in behind me and started unbuttoning my shirt. I grabbed her hands.

"What are you doing?"

"Just hold still," she demanded as she jerked her hands free.

I felt her inspecting my back. Suddenly, there was a sharp pain in my shoulder. I jerked away and twisted around to look at her angrily. "Hey! That–"

She was holding up with a pair of tweezers what looked like a small electronic chip. She handed me a tissue to wipe the blood that was trickling down my shoulder. The wound hurt like hell. "What did you do? What is that?"

She put a finger across her mouth and climbed off the bed. I watched her in wonder as she took the device and set it on the air conditioning unit. When she returned, she pointed to her own shoulder and handed me a small knife and the pair of tweezers. My stomach turned at the thought of performing surgery on her. She pointed to a spot on her shoulder impatiently and then braced herself for the pain. I could see a dark spot which I assumed was the target of my surgery. I quivered slightly and then made a tiny incision above the chip. Then I plunged the tweezers into the hole and felt around carefully for the chip–trying not to cause Tehra too much pain. Once I had found it and gotten a grip on it, I pulled it out quickly.

Tehra took the tweezers from me without letting loose of the chip and placed it next to mine on the air conditioner.

When she got back to the bed she brought a tube of some sort of cream. She took a little and rubbed it on my shoulder where she'd made the incision. The pain immediately subsided. She motioned for me to put some on her incision, so I did.

She laughed. "That better?"

"Yes, what is that stuff?"

"Healing ointment. It's good for minor cuts and scratches. By morning you won't even be able to see where I took out the chip."

"Hmm."

"The hum from the air conditioner ought to give them a good headache, don't you think?"

"But won't they be suspicious?" I asked marveling at what she had done.

She shrugged. "We're entitled to a little privacy, don't you think."

"Sure, but–"

"They'll just think there's some interference. It happens all the time."

She put her finger over my mouth to end any further discussion of the matter and slipped behind me one more time. This time I felt nothing but pure pleasure.

"Now I can give you a proper rub," she said matter-of-factly. "And we can talk candidly for a change.

I sighed. "Sounds good to–oh, that feels so good. Ahhhh."

"Just relax," Tehra said as she worked. "Breathe deeply."

I started to respond but her caressing hands felt so good I could scarcely talk. They glided over every inch of my back and shoulders with expert precision. All the tension and anxiety that had been festering within me for months vanished. When she was done, she turned me over and started to unbuckle my pants. I grabbed her hands and stopped her.

"That was great, Tehra."I feel much better, but we should stop before we do something we'll regret."

"I wouldn't regret anything we did," she replied.

"Okay, then we better stop before we do something I'll regret."

She sighed and rolled off me sitting Indian style on her side of the king size bed. "I don't understand why you don't want to have sex with me. Don't you like me?"

"I do like you and having sex with you would be great, but I'm married.... Don't you feel bad about cheating on your mate?" I asked.

"No. I'm not cheating. He can't get me pregnant, so I have no choice but to find someone who can."

She said it as if it were an obvious fact. Our worlds were so different. It made sense, though. I could understand how fertility would be paramount on Tarizon, but this was Earth.

"You want me to get you pregnant?".

"Yes, of course. Every woman on Tarizon has a duty to get pregnant. I'm getting old and I have no offspring. I can't go home without at least one child."

I looked at Tehra with wonder and amazement. Giving her what she wanted would be so easy. She looked at me with such expectation. It seemed so surreal to be alone with a woman from another world. This had to be a dream. Her deep blue eyes beckoned me and all my resistence melted away. I leaned over and ran my fingers through her smooth black hair. She put her hand on my shoulder and gave me a wry smile.

Her skin was white as milk and without a single blemish. I wanted to touch it, to feel its texture. How could I be sitting next to a woman from another planet and not examine her? This was a once in a lifetime opportunity that I couldn't pass up. I reached out and ran my hand down her cheek. It was as smooth as silk. She turned her head and kissed my fingers.

My gaze went to her breasts and down to her stomach. I hadn't noticed it before but she had two slits on either side below her breasts. They were about eight inches long and opened and closed as she breathed. I lowered my hand and ran my finger across one of them. Tehra began to moan.

"What is that?" I said softly.

"A slova, but you would probably call it a gill," she replied. "I'm one-eighth Seafolken."

"Seafolken?" I asked.

"Yes, that is a race of humans on Tarizon who live in the sea. They are a superior race so it is a great honor to be part Seafolken." She extended her legs and spread her toes. There was a thin membrane between them. I stared at them in shock.

"So, you're a good swimmer then," I stuttered.

She laughed. "Oh, yes. I can swim half as fast as I can run and I can stay underwater for nearly ten minutes."

"Jesus!"

"So, do my fins turn you off, as they say here on Earth?"

"No, not at all. They're kind of cute. It's just that I've never seen anything like this before. It's going to take a little getting used to."

She retracted her toes and pulled her legs up to her chest. She seemed a little depressed. "Can I touch them," I asked.

She gave me an amused look and then extended her legs again and laid back on the bed so she was lying flat on her back. I crawled over and began examining her feet carefully. The skin was tough and a little course. I ran my fingers over every inch of them. When I looked up, her eyes were closed. She seemed to be enjoying my explorations so I ran my hands along her thighs looking for other parts of her anatomy that might be different, but everything else looked normal.

I felt bad that I'd given her such a clinical examination when the only thing on her mind was getting pregnant. I couldn't give her what she wanted obviously, but I decided it wouldn't hurt to at least show a little tenderness. I crawled up beside her, leaned over, and kissed her gently on the lips. That was my big mistake. Her eyes opened and she smiled up at me. Then before I could pull away she'd wrapped her hands behind my neck, pulled her lips to mine, and plunged her long reptilian tongue into my mouth. I felt a needle-like prick and then an incredibly wonderful feeling came over me. I tried to move but I my body wouldn't respond. Soon I drifted off into unconsciousness.

Chapter 24

Funding

When I got to the office on Friday, I looked in on Stan and Tehra to see what they were up to and discovered they were working frantically on Ben Stover's chapter 11. There were records strewn all over the big conference room and Stan was barking orders to Maria while Tehra was pouring through a tax return looking for something Stan needed. I decided not to interrupt them.

I grabbed a cup of coffee and walked back to my office to check my messages. The phone slip clip was bulging as usual. I pulled them off and began sorting through them. They all looked uninteresting except one that stuck out like a coyote in a chicken coop. It was from Ricardo Richmond and there were two big dollar signs next to his name. In the main body of the message it said he was calling about the Walter Stanley defense fund. I quickly dialed the number. It was the law office of Richmond, Jones, Fennell & Smith. I asked to speak to Mr. Richmond. The receptionist put me through the usual screening drill and then let me through.

"Ms. Waters. Thank you for returning my call."

"Well. All those dollar signs intrigued me."

He laughed. "Yes, that trick always works."

"So, what's this about the Walter Stanley Defense Fund?"

"Oh, yes. I got a call from someone who is very interested in insuring that your client gets a fair trial. I'm sure there are others who feel the same way, so this person thought it would be good to set up a trust to help fund his defense. They have asked me to be trustee and I have on my desk as we speak a check in the amount of $25,000."

"Wow! I'm speechless."

"Well, I doubt that, Ms. Waters. I happen to know you were

expecting a spontaneous outpouring of support for your client. Anyway, according to the terms of the trust I'm to pay any bills you send me for costs and expenses incurred in Mr. Stanley's defense."

"Twenty-five thousand, huh?"

"Yes, of course, that's just an initial contribution. I'm sure other contributions will be forthcoming if the need for them arises."

"Well, you know how a murder trial can go. I'm afraid it could get expensive."

"That's okay. Just keep your receipts. My client doesn't want you to spare any expense if it will lead to the acquittal of your client."

"Or exposing those responsible for this atrocity," I added.

"That goes without saying."

"Well, it's been a pleasure talking to you, Mr. Richmond. I'll call your secretary back to get an address to send the statements."

"You do that Ms. Waters, and have a nice day."

I hung up the phone and laughed. This guy was a real comedian. He seemed to be really enjoying our little covert operation with TI. I wondered if he was always so fun loving. When I told Bart about the phone call, he shook his head in disbelief.

"Well, I guess we better get Thayer over here," Bart said, "so we can brainstorm how we should handle the investigation. I'm not sure exactly how we should approach it."

"Good idea. I'll have Maria call him and set up an appointment. Why don't you go visit our client and tell him the good news. I know he's been worried about running out of money."

"I will, but I don't think we should overlook our other suspects. Perhaps you should meet with Paul and coordinate his efforts while I follow up on our other leads. That way we won't inadvertently miss something."

I nodded. "You're probably right. I've never seen a case with so many people with such good motives for murder. It's bizarre."

A little after noon, Stan stuck his head in and said he was ordering some Chinese fast food for lunch and wanted to know if I wanted anything. I put in an order for Mongolian steak and fried rice for me and cashew chicken for Bart as I knew that was his favorite. When the food arrived we all sat around the kitchen table and ate. I told Stan about Stanley's defense fund.

"That was pretty creative. I'm impressed," Stan said. "Don't tell Mo, though, he'll try to recruit you for the CIA. I bet they could use someone with your talents for raising money."

"No thanks. I don't want any part of that business. I value my life."

"Well at least with the CIA you have a little backup. You're all alone in the game you're playing."

I raised my eyebrows but didn't comment. Stan was right. TI would disavow having any knowledge of our investigation and if Stout felt threatened by it, he might try to derail it. In the process people might get hurt. Security would have to be a major consideration from now on. I made a mental note to discuss that with Paul when he came in.

Stan told us about his plans to go to Waco on Saturday to meet with Ben and Alice Stover, work all day Sunday putting the finishing touches on the chapter 11, filing it on Monday and then arguing motions on Tuesday. It sounded pretty intense to me, but I was more worried about Stan spending all that time alone with Tehra than anything else. There would be too many opportunities for them to get in trouble. I wanted to address that issue but couldn't think of a tactful way to bring it up. When Bart and I were alone I told him of my concerns.

"I can't believe Tehra. She hangs all over Stan–touching him, giving him back rubs. And she's with him every minute. I think she'd go to the bathroom with him if he'd let her."

"Well, she's his intern. They have to work together."

"Sure, but does she have to smother him? It's ridiculous and what's worse, I think Stan enjoys it."

Bart looked at me warily. "So, are you jealous?"

"No, it's not that. I'm just afraid Stan's going to get hurt. Tehra's going to destroy his marriage and then dump him. Hell, she's not much older than Reggie. He has no business getting into a relationship with her."

"Stan's gone through hell this past year. Leave him alone. If Tehra helps him forget all that's happened, then she may be just what he needs."

"What! I can't believe you're defending him."

"I'm not defending him. I'm just saying it's none of our business."

"Well it is my business. He's my partner and if she messes with him, she's messing with me and I have a right to protect my interest."

Bart shrugged. "Okay. Okay. But I think you're acting out of jealousy rather than good sense. Don't do anything rash. If you piss off Stan he may not want to be your partner anymore."

"I know. And I not jealous. It's just so frustrating. I know Tehra doesn't really care about Stan. She's got her own agenda. I'm a woman. I can feel it. I'm not sure what it is, but when she's through with him she'll dump him like an empty water bottle and never look back. With all that Stan's been through, I don't know if he could survive that."

When I was alone back in my office all I could think about was Stan and Tehra alone together in Waco. Would Stan give in to her? He'd shown remarkable loyalty to Rebekah in the past, but in his present state of mind I couldn't see how he could resist her. Had she been an ordinary woman, I don't think their relationship would have bothered me so much, but Tehra was very different from anyone I'd ever known. She looked almost normal, but I could feel that she was extraordinary. Who was this strange woman and why was she so interested in Stan? I just knew there was more to her than met the eye.

Later that afternoon Paul Thayer and a staff member named Lou Stallings showed up for our meeting. I couldn't tell them about TI's funding of the project so I said that Stanley had been able to borrow money from family and friends. Paul knew better than to question my explanation. I asked him how we should proceed.

"We need to identify Stout's staff and find out as much about each of them as we can," Paul said. I'm sure one of them was assigned the task of getting rid of Chester Brown. I'd bet whoever it was put together a team of ex-military to handle the job."

"Do you think they put together a team just to kill Chester Brown?" I asked.

"Maybe, or they assigned the task to an existing team that handled problems like that."

"Once we find out who was in charge of the hit," Stallings

added, "we can check out his whereabouts when the fire broke out."

"Can you track the parts used for the bomb and maybe find out who built it?" I asked.

Paul shrugged. "Maybe. I'll get with the arson investigator and see if that's a possibility."

We talked for several more hours and then Paul and Stallings left. I was starting to feel a little better about the case as it seemed we were finally making progress.

Just after five Bart called and said he wasn't coming back to the office but would meet me at home. He said he had some interesting news but refused to tell me what it was over the phone. I didn't know if he was teasing me or if there was a reason for his secrecy. Either way I was intrigued enough to quickly gather up my things and head for home. It had been a long week and I was ready to kick off my heels and relax for a change. When I got home I had expected to find Bart, but he wasn't there. When it got to be six-thirty, I began to worry in earnest. What had happened? He had called and said he was on his way home. I assumed he was somewhere in north Dallas or Collin County. If that were the case he'd have been home by now. Where could he be?

Chapter 25

Venom

In the blurry mist I saw Tehra leaning over me moaning."Oh, Stan. I'm sorry. I'm so sorry! I'll get you help." I tried to move but my body wouldn't respond to my wishes. Her voice faded . . .

Later, I don't know how long, I heard many voices, men barking orders, others talking excitedly. Someone was working on my arm, another adjusting my feet. "Get that IV in him stat! We're losing him," a man said sternly.

"Blood pressure 60 over 40," a second voice said.

"Shit! Is that thing working?"I could see glimpses of the men hovering over me and Tehra to the side, her arms wrapped around herself, tears flowing from her eyes. Then darkness returned.

My next memory was of the beeping sound of a heart monitor beside my bed. As the room came into focus, I saw I was in a medical ward somewhere. There were patients on either side and a nurse was hovering over one of them. I tried to sit up but realized I didn't have the strength.

The nurse looked over at me and smiled. "Well, Mr. Turner. You finally woke up. I was worried about you."

She strolled over and smiled down at me. "What happened?" I asked.

"That's what we were hoping you could tell us. Your illness is somewhat of a mystery."

I looked around for Tehra but didn't see her. "How long have I been out?"

She looked at her watch. "Almost twelve hours. Your wife is in the waiting room and I think the rest of your family is on their way.

"My wife!" I gasped. "When did she get here?"

"She called for the ambulance. She was with you when the spider bit you."

Relief fell over me as I realized the nurse must have thought Tehra was my wife. "A spider bit me?"

"A spider or flying insect. What else could get into your mouth and bite the back of your tongue?"

I swallowed hard and it felt like I had a needle in my throat. I grabbed it wincing in pain. "Shit, is there something still in there?"

"No. The doctors couldn't find anything but the bite marks."

"My tongue is swollen," I slurred.

"Not as bad as it was. When the paramedics got to your motel room it was twice the size it is now."

I shook my head rubbing my throat. A horrible thought suddenly struck me. What would I tell Rebekah when she showed up. I looked at the nurse. "I'd like to see . . . ah . . . my wife. You said she's in the visiting room. Can she come in now?"

The nurse looked at her watch again. "Well, it's not visiting hours yet, but I guess it wouldn't hurt. I'll call the front desk and tell them to send her back."

"Thank you," I said trying to manage a smile.

The nurse left and my thoughts went back to the previous night. I tried to remember what had happened but my mind was a blank. The last thing I could recall was marveling at the webs between her toes. What had happened after that? I just couldn't remember. The door opened and Tehra walked in quickly and came over to me.

"Are you okay, Stan?" she asked. "I've been so worried about you."

"I think so. What happened to me?"

She looked at me and asked, "You don't remember?"

"Not exactly." I told her.

She sighed. "Well, this was all my fault. I'm sorry. I didn't realize you'd react this way."

"What way? What are you talking about?"

She stuck out her tongue. It looked normal and then she extended it farther and a fold of skin shot out like two fangs. I recoiled. She closed her mouth and moaned, "Oh, I know it must seemed hideous to you, but it's really has a very useful purpose.."

"And what would that be," I asked with shock and amazement.

"It's called the tortiac and it's purpose is to stun fish so they won't thrash around and injure the Seafolken's throat or stomach before they die."

"You feed on raw fish?" I gasped.

"No. No. I don't live in the sea and rarely even go swimming. I've never actually used it for it's intended purpose. Tarizonian men actually like women with a tortiac. It usually just elicits a pleasant buzz like a few beers or a shot of alcohol. I've never heard of someone reacting the way you did. I'm so sorry."

I shrugged. "Okay, I forgive you, but now we've got a problem. The nurse said my family is on their way here."

"Yes, they said you might die, so I felt like I had no choice but to call them."

I nodded. "Of course, you did the right thing, but what did you tell them?"

"Only what the doctors said. You were bitten by spider most likely—a brown recluse I think that's what the doctor said. They are common around here apparently."

"Okay, good," I said. "What about the motel room."

She gave me a wry smile. "Oh, don't worry. I didn't mention your fascination with my anatomy."

A chill swept through me as I recalled her naked body. Her exotic feet and small gills below each breast were strange yet wonderful. I could imagine her gliding effortlessly through crystal clear water. She took my hand and I looked up at her.

"It will be all right. It was just an unlucky night. Your family won't be the least bit suspicious."

"What about the tracking device? Kulchz will be suspicious now that it has been removed from my shoulder."

"No he won't. I cut a slit in your belt and lodged it inside. As long as you are wearing it, he'll never know the difference. If you want some privacy take off the belt and put it somewhere noisy like I did in the motel."

I recalled her laying the chip on the air conditioning unit.

That was a clever trick but why would she want to deliberately deceive Kulchz? He would be extremely upset and if he found out and I'm sure she'd be severely punished for her actions. Had she developed some kind of attraction for me and wanted to protect me, or was there some other agenda that was driving her? I wanted to ask her, but this wasn't right time or place.

Despite Tehra's assurances that all would be well, I was still nervous, so I made her go over everything that had happened one more time to be sure our stories had no inconsistencies. Twenty minutes later Reggie, Mark and Rebekah rushed into my room. Tehra stepped back into the corner while they hovered over me. For the first time in months Rebekah showed some concern for my well being.

"Stan. Are you all right?" she moaned."How could a spider survive in a room? Don't they clean them everyday? You should sue their ass for this!"

"I doubt it was their fault. Maybe it crawled in when we opened the door. It could have been fleeing from the storm like we were."

"I don't care. You should sue them anyway. It's not right!"

Rebekah shook her head in disgust and then noticed Tehra for the first time. She stared a moment and then asked, "You must be Tehra?"

Tehra stepped forward and replied, "Yes, I am. It's nice to finally meet you."

Rebekah nodded but didn't offer her hand. "Yes, I wish it had been under different circumstances, though, . . . but it's a good thing Stan brought you along. If you hadn't have been there, he might have died."

She shrugged. "Yes, it was fortunate."

Rebekah measured Tehra for a moment longer and then returned her attention to me. "Marcia was at a music recital with a friend, so that's why she's not here. How long do you think they'll keep you here?"

"They have to let me out today. I've got to file a chapter 11 tomorrow in Waco. I have no choice."

"Well, it will have to wait if you're not well."

"I feel fine, except for the razor in my throat. I'm sure they will let me go home today."

"Oh. Is it painful?"

"Just when I swallow."

"Well, you can't drive. I'll have to drive you home. Tehra can drive your car."

"No, I can drive. I'll be fine. Besides, Tehra hasn't got her Texas driver's license yet."

Rebekah frowned and looked at Tehra. "Ah. I accidentally let it expire. I've got to retake the test."

"Well, Reggie can drive you home in Stan's car and I'll take Stan with me. There's no way I'm letting him drive today. They must have him on medication."

I nodded to Tehra hoping she'd drop the issue and go with Reggie. I was afraid any further protests might arouse more suspicions. Finally she acquiesced. As we were talking, the doctor came in. He was carrying a clipboard and looked stunned when he saw so many people in the room.

"Hi. I'm Dr. Thomas," he said. I introduced him to everyone and then waited to hear what he had to say.

"Well, you seem do be doing fine now. The swelling has gone down significantly, your temperature has dropped to normal levels, your blood pressure has come back, and all the blood work came out negative for toxins this go around."

"So, you're sure it was a spider bite?" Rebekah asked.

The doctor shrugged. "Not 100 percent. The symptoms are similar but not exactly what we'd expect. A sheriff's deputy searched the motel room and didn't find any spiders or even empty webs, so we may never know what it was. What we do know is that you are exceedingly allergic to whatever bit you and it's a good thing your friend got you over here quickly after you were bitten.

I looked over at Tehra. She turned away and hung her head. Rebekah saw my glance and looked at me suspiciously. I needed to change the subject.

"So, I can leave today?"

"I'd recommend you stay another day for observation. We don't want to take any changes and that would give us more time to do more tests."

“No,” I protested. “I've got to be in Waco on Monday and Tuesday. I've got a chapter 11 that must be filed."

"Well, I can't make you stay," Dr. Thomas replied evenly. "Chances are you'll be okay, but it's always better to be cautious."

We sparred with the doctor a little longer but finally he accepted the fact that I was leaving. Then Rebakah asked the inevitable question.

"Is Tehra going with you on Monday?"

I hesitated a moment. "Well, yes she was. I may need her."

Rebekah thought a moment. "Why don't I go with you since Tehra can't drive. You shouldn't be driving such a long distance. Besides I haven't seen much of you lately. It will give us time to catch up."

Actually, I liked Rebekah's suggestion. She seemed to have suddenly snapped out of her melancholy and I wanted so much for things to return to normal. It would be good to spend some time together. The past few months had been as close to hell as I ever wanted to get.

"Sure. That sounds wonderful," I said smiling broadly.

Tehra frowned but I ignored her. She'd get over it. After all she was here to help me and she'd unwittingly done that by waking Rebekah from her grief. Whether it was concern for me or jealously over Tehra's sudden appearance in my life, it didn't matter. It had worked and the woman I loved and thought I'd lost was back and that gladdened my heart.

Chapter 26

Threats

Bart finally made it home about 7:15 p.m. When I chastised him for being so late he apologized and explained that he was at a bar with Ruth Willis, the woman who allegedly was having an affair with Chester Brown.

"Well, was she pretty–worth losing a family over?" I said evenly. I felt a little jealous about Bart being at a bar with another woman even if it was business. I didn't say anything but I was sure he could sense the tension in my voice.

"She was good looking–sexy, but not the type you'd want to have children with."

"Hmm. Did she admit to the affair?"

"Yes, she did. She said it lasted about three months, and it wasn't the first time Brown had strayed from the nest. Ruth said he was dating an airline stewardess when she met him. He obviously didn't believe in fidelity and flirted openly with other woman, even when his wife was around."

"Nice guy," I replied. "Unfortunately, a lot of guys are like that. So what else did you learn?"

"Brown was frustrated with TI. He complained to Ruth that the people he worked with were stupid and incompetent. He also complained about not having the support and equipment he needed to do his job."

"Really? So what do you make of that?" I asked.

"I don't know. I guess Brown was a genius and he had little patience for those who couldn't keep up with him. Apparently the job he was doing was supposed to have been finished six months earlier but kept dragging on."

"So, what about the affair? His wife knew about it or, at least, suspected it, right?"

"Yes, she suspected it and made it crystal clear that she wouldn't tolerate it."

"Did she ever threaten divorce?" I asked.

"No," Bart replied. "Just the opposite. She told everyone she would defend her marriage and kill anyone who got between her and her husband."

"Well, if Ruth had been killed instead of Mrs. Brown we'd know who did it."

"Right."

"Do you think she could have been so outraged by her husband's continued infidelity that she set the fire? A quadruple murder-suicide, perhaps? She may not have intended to kill everyone, but something could have gone wrong. "

"No. From what I've been told she was a very loving mother and overprotective if anything. She'd never kill her children."

"So, what about Ruth? Does she have an alibi?"

"Yes, she was at work all day and went out with friends for dinner. Besides, she wouldn't have the technical knowhow to wire the fire's triggering device."

"True," I said. "Good point. So, we're back where we started."

"Not exactly. Ruth also told me that there had been other threats against Brown and his family and that he had reported it to management. She doesn't think TI passed the information onto the police, though."

"Probably not. They had enough trouble being behind on the project. So, how did he receive these threats?" I asked.

"In various forms," Bart replied. "Late night hangups, blank letters that reeked of smoke, and frequent vandalism—usually messages scratched on his car or burnt into his lawn. Nothing serious, but enough to keep a person on edge."

"Did they ever figure out who was behind the threats?"

"He suspected it was Stout," Bart said.

"Why?"

"Ruth said Stout had tried for months to get him to jump ship and come to work for Almatech, but he refused. He apparently offered Brown a lot of money, but when Brown refused he got belligerent and told him the world was a dangerous place and he should watch his back. It was a thinly veiled threat that Brown clearly understood, but couldn't do anything about."

"I wonder if TI knew about the threats. Sylvester didn't mention it."

"I don't know, but we need to talk to Chester Brown's co-workers. He may have told them about the threats or they might have seen some of the vandalism. If we're going to try to show reasonable doubt we'll need as many witnesses as we can find."

"I can call Sylvester and arrange it for you, if you want," I said. "I'm sure they'll give you access to anyone who worked with him."

"That would be great."

That night we went to a local Italian restaurant for dinner. I wasn't very good company because I was worried about Stan's trip to Waco. I didn't know why but I had an ominous feeling about it. I wanted to call Rebekah and warn her about Tehra, but I knew her condition was fragile and didn't want to make matters worse. Plus, I didn't know for sure that anything was going on between them.

"More wine, honey?" Bart asked.

"Huh?" I said looking up.

"Wine?" Bart said holding up the bottle.

"Oh, sure. Thanks," I replied forcing a smile.

"You look distracted. What's wrong?"

I took a deep breath. "Nothing, dear. I just had a long day."

Bart looked at me warily. I think he knew what was bothering me, but knew better than to press the issue. I smiled. I was lucky to have such a wonderful husband. I certainly didn't deserve him. Why was I so obsessed with Stan? I just couldn't stand the thought of him alone with Tehra.

Chapter 27

Stubborn Opposition

Rebekah and I got to Waco late Sunday night. We had a good talk on the way there and when we got to our room at the La Quinta Inn we were like a couple of teenagers ripping off each others clothes and frantically making love. We had sex again before we went to sleep and again when we awoke. It was the first time we'd been intimate since Peter had disappeared and all the pent-up emotions that had burdened us for so long came out like a raging bull.

On Monday morning Rebekah slept in and I went to the courthouse and filed the chapter 11 petition. Then I swung over to Ben's place to start notifying creditors. In my experience Chapter 11's were usually fairly routine and almost always amicable. The law was fairly clear on what could and could not be done, so the attorneys involved usually would negotiate any issues in good faith and enter into agreed orders routinely. Since Ben and Alice had always enjoyed a good relationship with their creditors and vendors, that's what I had expected in their case, but I was wrong.

Ben had alerted his banker, Tom Stenson, that we'd be calling at 1:00 p.m. but when Ben made the call Stenson refused to talk to us and directed us to his attorney Vernon Hunnicutt. I knew that was a bad sign. When I called Hunnicutt, he laid into me.

"We're going to oppose any cash collateral order. We know what your client is up to."

"What are you talking about? He's not up to anything."

I told him about the embezzlement and ensuing financial problems Ben and Alice had experienced. I assured him the chapter

11 was being filed in good faith.

"What about the offshore bank accounts? I have a witness who claims your client is liquidating our collateral and sending it to an offshore account. What does he plan to do, keep the company in chapter 11 long enough to collect all the receivables and then convert to chapter 7?"

"No, that's ridiculous. Who told you that?"

"One of Ben's ex-employees."

Suddenly I realized what was happening. Ralph Herman had talked to Stenson. I sighed in disgust. Was there no end to this asshole's meddling?

"Let me guess. Ralph Herman?"

Hunnicutt didn't respond. "He's been indicted for embezzlement for godsakes," I said. "You're surely not going to believe anything he says?"

"He claims to have proof and he's provided us with a lot of details on how it's being done. Unless you can prove that he's wrong we're not going to agree to let your client deplete the bank's collateral."

"You haven't seen any actual proof then?"

"No, but it's been promised to us. We'll have it at the hearing tomorrow."

I hung up frustrated. It was easy to toss out outlandish accusations, but difficult to disprove them. Sure, Ben and Alice could get up and deny everything, but that didn't necessarily prove anything. I needed to know what evidence Ralph was going to produce. I asked Ben if he had any ideas.

"No. I don't have any offshore accounts." He laughed. "Where would I get money to put in them?"

After we'd gotten all the bankruptcy notices in the mail and called everyone that needed immediate notification, I went back to the motel and took Rebekah to lunch. I told her what had happened and the trouble I was expecting at the hearing the following morning.

"How was he able to talk to the banker. Isn't he in jail pending his trial?" Rebekah asked.

"They let them make phone calls from the jail. I guess being the bookkeeper he knew the banker and just gave him a call. What I can't believe is that Stenson listened to him. It just blows my mind."

"So, what are you going to do?"

"Just plead our case as usual and hope this so-called evidence never materializes. I can't see how Herman could have any records to give the bank. He was supposed to have turned over everything in his possession to the DA after his indictment."

"He must have someone on the outside helping—a relative or friend."

"Possibly. We'll find out soon enough."

After lunch we went back to the motel. Rebekah was ready for more action, but I was in no mood for love making. What I needed was sleep. It had been an exhausting weekend and I needed rest. While Rebekah watched soap operas on TV, I slept. She woke me after the six o'clock news and said she was hungry. Ben and Alice had invited us out for dinner at seven so I just had time to take a shower and get ready before they came to pick us up. They were right on time. We went to the La Fiesta Restaurant and Cantina as they said it was the best Tex-Mex restaurant in Waco.

The place was packed for a Monday night and we waited quite a while to get seated. After we'd ordered and the bartender had delivered each of us a giant margarita, the topic of discussion inevitably went to Ralph Herman.

"I called my daughter," Alice said. "I told her what her ex-husband was doing to us. She said she thought about putting a bullet trough his head on more than one occasion, but never had the guts to actually do it."

Ben chuckled. "She should have said something. I'd of come and given her moral support."

We all laughed. "You didn't happen to ask her about his friends?" I asked. "I'd like to know who's helping him. He's got to have someone on the outside."

"I did," Alice said. "She said his best friend, Ike Eiseman, visits him at least once a week. They were high school buddies and roomed together at Cal State."

"What kind of business is Ike in?" I asked.

"He's an insurance agent—property and casualty mostly. He's got an office in Austin."

"So, how well do you know him?"

"Not too well. My daughter knows him much better. He used to hang around the house a lot when she was married to Ralph ."

"Has he ever been in trouble with the police?" I asked.

"Not to my knowledge, but he's no boy scout. He's been divorced twice and there were allegations of mental cruelty and physical abuse. His last wife had to take out a restraining order to get him to leave her alone."

"They're both right-wing fanatics," Ben added. "They hate Mexicans and Jews."

The more Ben and Alice told me about Ralph and his friend the sicker I became. It was clear we were dealing with intelligent but irrational adversaries. That meant it would be impossible to predict what they would do next. What we needed was an FBI profiler, but unfortunately we didn't have access to anyone with those skills.

As the evening wore on the conversation turned to Peter. Alice felt the need to offer her condolences. Personally I wished she hadn't brought that topic up. Rebekah was finally out of her despair and I didn't want there to be a relapse. She surprised me though, and talked about it freely.

"We were lucky to have Peter. He was a fine boy. I don't know why God chose to take him, but I've got to think he's in a better place."

Tears welled in my eyes as Rebekah talked about Peter. It wasn't fair that Rebekah didn't know the truth. I wondered now that the listening device had been removed from my shoulder and we could talk privately, if I couldn't tell her. How would she react? Would she be able to keep the secret? It would be a dangerous risk, but very rewarding if I could pull it off.

As the night wore on, I got more and more excited about the prospect of telling Rebekah the truth. When Ben and Alice dropped us back at the motel, Rebekah could sense something was up.

"What are you all keyed up about? You planning on getting into my pants again?"

"Why not? We're all alone."

She gave me a wry smile as she opened the door. She turned and leaned back for a kiss, but I brushed by her and went straight to the air conditioner. I turned the fan up high and pulled off my belt.

Rebekah gave me a bewildered look and started to say something, but I put my finger over my mouth and shook my head. She frowned but kept quiet. I motioned for her to go back outside.

Once out of the room, I took a deep breath and exhaled slowly. She raised her eyebrows in anticipation. I gazed into her brown eyes not knowing how to start. I finally said. "There's something you need to know, but you can never speak of it to anyone or we will both likely die."

"Huh. What secret?"

I put my hands on her shoulders and said earnestly, "I am dead serious. Unless you can promise me you will never speak of this to anyone but me, I won't tell you what it is."

"Why? I don't understand."

"You know I've done work for the CIA, right?"

"Yes."

"Well, this is a matter of national security. I could be arrested for treason for telling you this secret. But worse than that we'd both likely be killed if we were found out, before the government even arrested us."

She sighed. "Maybe you shouldn't tell me? I'm not worried about myself, but I'd die if something happened to you."

"I wouldn' t tell you except you have a right to know the truth. It will affect you most profoundly. I'm sure you will want to know this secret no matter how dangerous it will be for us."

She swallowed hard. "Then tell me. I promise to keep it to myself."

I smiled faintly and said, "Peter is alive!"

Chapter 28

Identifying the Enemy

On Sunday when I heard the startling news that Stan was in the hospital in Waco my first instinct was to rush down there to him. Bart cautioned me that I should resist that urge and let Rebekah handle the situation. He was right, of course. After all it was just a spider bite. How weird was that? But the fact that it happened when Tehra and Stan were alone in Waco disturbed me. I was too rattled to relax and enjoy the weekend, so I decided to go to the office while it was quiet and do some thinking. This Chester Brown case was starting to get complicated and I needed time to sort things out. Bart asked if I wanted him to come along, so we could brainstorm together, but I declined the offer. I needed some time alone.

When I got to the office, I noticed a late call had come in from Paul Thayer on Friday. I grabbed the message and anxiously called the number on the slip. It wasn't his usual number, so I assumed he was on the road. I was right. He was in California trying to identify the members of Stout's personal security team.

"Marty Ramirez is the squad leader," Paul said. "He's ex-special forces and served with Stout on a few intelligence missions. There are four others who regularly hang out with Ramirez–Pablo Crews, Tom Snider, Rich Walls, and Lisa Andretti."

"Lisa? A woman?" I said a little surprised.

"Yes, and she's the toughest one of the bunch. She once was on an LAPD SWAT team, but got busted for roughing up a couple gang members. The whole thing was captured on camera, so there was no whitewashing it."

I laughed. "Okay. We'll stay clear of her. So, where was this so-called security team when the Brown house went up in smoke?"

"Well, nobody around here seems to know much about their comings and goings. But I did discover that they travel in style–a private jet owned by Almatech."

"Really?"

"Yes. So, I checked all the DFW airports for the three days prior to the fire."

"Any luck?" I asked.

"Affirmative. Addison Airport has a record of their plane landing the day before the fire and leaving that same day."

"Really? That's pretty good. They come in, set the triggering mechanism to start the fire the following day, and leave town so they'll have an alibi when the fire erupts."

"Yes, and, according to the arson investigator, it would have been a perfect plan except the self-destruction mechanism on the triggering device malfunctioned."

"So, Ramirez and his team think they've committed the perfect crime?"

"Yes," Paul replied, "and Stout is up in his penthouse suite laughing as the government gets ready to turn the stealth technology contract over to him."

"But how does he plan to finish the project without Brown?"

"I don't know. He probably doesn't care. He'll milk $50 million from the government and then tell them what they want can't be done. After all two of the top technology firms in the country couldn't do it."

This was all making sense to me now, but how would it play with a jury? It seemed rather bizarre to say the least and then there would be the problem of the project being top secret. We couldn't bring in anybody from TI or Almatech to confirm its existence as they'd simply decline to answer any questions in the interest of national security. We might convince the judge that our inquiry did not concern any specifics of the project, but just the existence of it and the competition between TI and Almatech to get the contract that led to a series of dirty tricks and the Brown murders. Then again, the judge might tell us the entire top secret project was off limits and we couldn't mention any of it to the jury. In that case, we'd have nothing.

"You'll have to get more. Can you find out where they get outfitted? If we can show they purchased the materials for the triggering device, that would go a long way to proving they set the fire."

"That may be tough," Paul replied. "I'm sure they don't buy anything retail. They probably buy from the black market so there's no trail."

"Then find out who on the team is likely to have the requisite skill to build a sophisticated triggering device like they found in the Brown rubble. Then I'd like you to find out as much about that person as you can. He may the best shot we have at cracking this thing wide open."

"He won't talk even if you put him under oath on the stand," Paul cautioned.

"That's why you've got to get me more evidence. I've got to be able to force him to tell the truth."

"Okay. I'll see what I can do," Paul said,"but it won't be easy. We can't force people to cooperate like the police or the FBI."

"Just do what you can," I said and hung up. Paul's lack of confidence was annoying. We had plenty of money for a change, yet it didn't seem to matter. As I was thinking, I heard the door open and someone come in the office. Since it was Sunday I got up warily wondering who it could be. I was shocked when I saw Tehra sitting at her desk. She looked up when I walked in.

"Paula. Hi. What are you doing here on Sunday?" Tehra asked.

"I was going to ask you the same thing," I replied.

"Oh, Stan wanted me to finish up the bankruptcy schedules now that we've collected all the information we need. He and Rebekah will be here soon. They're going to take it to Waco tonight so they can file the case first thing in the morning."

"Rebekah is going to Waco?" I asked somewhat surprised at that development.

"Yeah. You know, just getting out of the hospital and everything, she's worried about him driving. It makes sense, I guess."

"Are you okay with that?" I asked.

Tehra's eyes narrowed. "Why wouldn't I be? I'm Stan's intern.

Whatever he wants me to do is fine."

"I know. But you must be a little disappointed."

She shrugged. "Sure I'd like to go to Waco. I've never been to bankruptcy court before, but there will be other opportunities. Stan says in a chapter 11 you have to go to court about something or other every week."

"Hmm. So I've heard."

"Besides, I'll have more time to shop for my new apartment."

"Oh, have you found an apartment?"

"Yes, Stan and I found one last week."

"Stan helped you pick it out?"

"Uh-huh. I've never rented one before, so he thought he'd better take care of it for me."

I just stared at Tehra for a moment. I couldn't believe Stan had helped her pick out an apartment. That was way beyond the call of duty. I made a mental note to check with Jodie to see if Stan helped her pick out her apartment. I wondered if his interest in her apartment was because he was paying for it and planned to spend a lot of time there. At least Rebekah was waking up to the danger that was lurking around the office. That could be the only explanation as to why she was going to Waco with him.

"So, what exactly happened to Stan last night? How did you two end up in a motel room together?"

Tehra told me they'd encountered a storm and the car headlights had been smashed when they ran over some debris on the road. It all sounded plausible until she got to the part about the spider. I didn't buy that. How could a spider survive in a motel room when it's vacuumed and cleaned each day? But someone or something had poisoned or drugged him and I couldn't see Tehra doing that. It was obvious she cared about Stan and wouldn't want to see him hurt. Something was going on though, and it was killing me that I couldn't figure it out.

Chapter 29

Nightmares

Rebekah's reaction to my revelation was first joy and excitement, but quickly turned to anger and bitterness. She couldn't accept the fact that Peter was alive but she would never be able to see him again. She had many questions and it took nearly two hours to explain what had happened to him and why he had been taken to Tarizon. She cursed the CIA for forcing me to work for them and the government for trading human lives for technology. She was quiet and introspective when we returned to the motel room. She picked up my belt and stared for a moment at the chip Tehra had embedded into the leather, then she shook her head and went to bed without a further word. For a long time she just laid there, her eyes glazed over.

Despite her obvious confusion over what I'd told her, I felt greatly relieved that she now knew the truth. I just hoped I'd done the right thing in telling her. I looked over at her and noticed she was weeping. I crawled over to her, dried her eyes with my fingers, and then put my arms around her. She put her head on my shoulder and I held her tightly until she went to sleep.

For a long time I just stared into the darkness wondering what lay ahead for us. Eventually, when I fell asleep, I found myself back in Hillsboro with Tehra. She was sitting with her legs crossed on the bed and I was sitting across from her mesmerized by her strange and exotic body. She wanted me and I wanted her but I didn't dare touch her. The consequences of such an encounter would be catastrophic. I looked away trying to retain control.

She smiled in amusement and then leaned forward and whispered in my ear. "Give me a child?"

I woke up with a start. Rebekah stirred but only turned over and went back to sleep. Fear shot through my veins like hot lead. I swallowed hard. Had I been dreaming or was the scene I'd played in my head a memory that I'd somehow suppressed? Could I have made love with Tehra? I cringed with horror at the thought.

In the morning I could feel nothing but dread and uncertainty. How would Rebekah be when she woke up and remembered the bizarre story I had told her? I feared she'd sink back into depression and all the progress we'd made these last few day would be lost. And what did Ralph Herman have in store for Ben and Alice today in court? Would it turn out to be nothing or did he have another grenade to throw in our faces?

Rebekah finally got out of bed and stretched. I opened my eyes and studied her. She smiled faintly and then walked into the bathroom. I yawned and then looked at the clock radio. It was 7:47 a.m. "If we hurry we'll have time to grab some breakfast at IHOP."

"Good. I'm starving," she replied.

At breakfast she was in such a good mood I wondered if she remembered what I had told her the previous night. Of course, I couldn't ask her about it. I just had to assume the knowledge that Peter was alive and well overshadowed the fact that we'd never see him again. On the way to the courthouse I caught Rebekah smiling at me several times. Finally, she said, "I'm sorry I've been so distant. I hope you'll forgive me."

I shook my head. "There's nothing to forgive. You've been through a lot."

When I looked over at her, she was focused on my belt where the listening chip was located. She looked up with a contorted look on her face and gestured at the belt with her middle finger. I burst out laughing.

We got to the courthouse about fifteen minutes before the hearing and found a seat in the gallery. We were number thirteen on the docket which I feared was a bad omen. A few minutes later Ben and Alice showed up and sat next to us. As we were waiting I noticed the bank's attorney, Vincent Hunnicutt. He motioned to me, so I got up and joined him outside the courtroom.

"So, have you heard from Herman this morning?"

Hunnicutt gave me a solemn look that made me nervous.

"Listen," he said, "your client has been a good customer at the bank for a long time and he and Mr. Stenson have become good friends. That's why I'm going to suggest you might want to withdraw your cash collateral request. I'm afraid if the judge sees the evidence that was handed to me today, he'll want to refer the case to the FBI."

"What!" I gasped. "What for?"

"Bankruptcy fraud," he said softly.

"Bankruptcy fraud? That's ridiculous."

He raised an eyebrow. "I'm not so sure. I've been given a signature card and bank statement from the Royal Bank, Grand Cayman Islands, for a bank account in the name of Stover Enterprises, Ltd. As of close of business on July 31st there was $107,332.00 in it. Today, of course, it's got but $52.08. Mr. Stenson said if you withdraw your cash collateral motion and move to dismiss the case, he'll give Ben forty-eight hours to bring the account current. Once the bankruptcy is dismissed, however, he'll want the note paid off."

For a moment I just stood there in stunned silence. Finally, I cleared my throat and asked to see the signature card and bank statement. He pulled copies out of his briefcase and handed them to me. They looked legitimate and were as damning as Hunnicutt had claimed. I wondered why Ben and Alice had hidden this from me, and where the money had been transferred. I couldn't imagine them doing something like this. It was a serious bankruptcy crime to conceal assets of an estate. They could both go to jail for many years and be fined hundreds of thousands of dollars.

I sighed. "Let me talk to my client," I said and excused myself. I went over to Ben and Alice and asked them to join me out in the hall for a chat. Alice turned white when I told them what Hunnicutt had said.

"It's not true," Ben protested. "I didn't set up this account."

I showed him the signature card but he continued to deny knowledge of the account. Alice shook her head and insisted it wasn't their account. "Before today you had no knowledge of this account or the money in it?" I asked urgently.

"No!" Ben replied. "But I bet I know who set it up."

I sighed. "Ralph Herman."

Ben nodded. "That's where he put the money he stole from us. Of course, he's moved it by now. This is all a game he's playing. The son of a bitch!"

"Damn it!" I moaned. "Now what are we going to do? If this comes up in the hearing the judge will have no choice but to get the FBI involved."

"No. We can't have the FBI snooping around," Alice warned. "No telling what other traps Ralph has set for us."

Hunnicutt motioned that our case was being called. "Okay, what do you want me to do? They're calling our case."

Ben shrugged. "We have no choice. Take the bank's offer. We'll dismiss the chapter 11."

I groaned at the thought of letting Herman win again, but Ben's decision was the right thing to do. Once the FBI and a federal prosecutor got on your butt, your life could go to hell in a hurry. I swallowed hard and made my way into the courtroom.

"Mr. Turner. Are you ready?" the judge asked.

"Yes, Stan Turner for the debtor-in-possession."

" Vincent Hunnicutt for Waco Commercial National Bank."

"Your Honor," I said. "The debtor has decided to withdraw its motion. The debtor is going to file a motion to dismiss their case."

"Very well," the judge said. "The motion is withdrawn."

"May we be excused?" I asked

"You may," the judge said. The judge nodded to the calendar clerk for her to call the next case.

"Star Bakery, Inc.," she read in a monotone, "Motion to Lift the Automatic Stay filed by Ford Motor Credit. . . ."

I turned and walked quickly out of the courtroom with Alice and Ben close behind. Rebekah was waiting for us and stood up when she saw us. "So, how did it go?" she asked.

"It was disaster," I said. "It seems Mr. Herman has struck again."

"Oh, no," Rebekah moaned. "I'm so sorry. That guy is really a bastard."

"Yeah, you're just lucky your banker likes you or it could have been a lot worse."

Just as I said that, two grim faced men approached us. One of them said, "Ben Stover?"

Ben nodded warily. "Yes."

The man pulled a badge out of his vest pocket and flashed it in front of us. "I'm deputy Charles Stanfield from the U.S. Marshall's office. I'm afraid I have a warrant for your arrest."

Ben's mouth dropped open and Alice let out a scream. "No! We didn't do anything." Alice started to attack the officer, so I grabbed her by the shoulder and restrained her.

"Don't interfere, Alice. There's nothing you can do now."

By this time a crowd of attorneys and spectators had gathered around. One of the marshals read Ben his rights while the other one cuffed him.

"Is that really necessary?" I asked. "I'm his attorney. Let me take him to your office and I'll surrender him there."

The Marshall brushed me aside and said, "Sorry, this is standard procedure."

I looked around and saw Rebekah with her hand over her mouth in shock. I motioned for her to come, grabbed Alice by the hand, and headed for the elevator. The marshals wouldn't let us ride down with them, so we had to take the next elevator. By the time we got down to the bottom floor the Marshals were gone. Then I realized they'd gone down to the basement which was restricted to law enforcement personnel.

Alice sobbed all the way back to her place. I told Rebekah to stay with her while I went to the Marshall's office to see about getting Ben out of jail. When I stepped into the lobby I was intercepted by Vincent Hunnicutt. I stopped to listen to what he had to say.

"Stan. I'm sorry about what happened. I had no idea what was coming down."

"I hope not. There's nothing like kicking a man when he's down. It's great sport. At least some people think so."

"It must have been Ralph Herman. He must have called the U.S. Attorney in addition to the bank."

"You're probably right. The son of a bitch!"

I started walking toward the elevator. "I'm going up to the Marshall's office right now to find out what the charges are and see about bond."

"I'll go with you. The bank is involved because the money was allegedly wire transferred from the company account at the bank to the Cayman Island account."

"Ben thinks it's the money Herman embezzled. That's why there's no money in the account now. Herman waited until he'd drained the account before he revealed its existence. How could he set up an account like that without Ben or Alice knowing about it?"

"He probably signed whatever Ralph put in front of them. They trusted him."

"Right," I said. "Because he was family. What a mistake. This guy is pure evil."

We went in the Marshall's office and asked about Ben. They said he'd been charged with concealing assets under 18 U.S.C. Section 152. They said I could visit him but he'd have to stay in jail until he was arraigned before the U.S. Magistrate the following morning. There wasn't much to talk about so I just assured him I'd do everything I could to get him out on bond and left. Hunnicutt promised to fax me a copy of everything he had when he got back to his office. I thanked him and went back to Ben's house to see how Rebekah and Alice were doing.

Rebekah opened the door when I got there and said Alice was lying down. She said her daughter was on her way over. While we were waiting, I got on the telephone to Roger Rand to see if he knew anybody in Waco who could handle the bond for us. Fortunately, he did know someone here and said he'd call them. He promised to call us back later that afternoon.

The fax from Hunnicutt came in about fifteen minutes later and I eagerly flipped through it. There was a signature card and account agreement both with Ben's signature on them. I gave them to Alice and asked her to look at them carefully. I wanted to know if there was any possibility that they were forged. She said they looked like Ben's signature but she couldn't be 100 percent sure. I told her we'd need to hire a handwriting expert because we had to prove these signatures were forgeries or Ben would surely be convicted.

Before we left Ben's place Roger Rand called back and said he'd arranged bond. All we needed to do was have Alice call Lucky Bonding in Waco in the morning and arrange to go by and fill out some paperwork. When Alice's daughter arrived, we left to have dinner and find somewhere to stay that night. It had been a horrible day and Rebekah and I were exhausted. As I lay awake in bed that night, I wondered what could go wrong at the arraignment. Would Ralph Herman have someone there to cause more trouble? I prayed to God that wouldn't be the case.

The next day I called Larry Wakefield, the McClennan County assistant DA who was prosecuting Herman. I asked him if he would agree to testify at the bond hearing. If Ralph Herman was the informant who provided information to the U.S. Attorney that led to the indictment, I'd want someone there to impeach him. I also arranged for some of Ben and Alice's friends and business associates to testify as to their character, ties to the community, and lack of flight risk.

When we arrived at the U.S. Magistrate's courtroom we were introduced to Thomas Stokely, the assistant U.S. Attorney assigned to prosecute the case. He was a tall stout man in his early forties. I told him we were quite surprised by the arrest and wondered what prompted it, but he had little to say about it. I asked him what kind of bond he would be asking for and he replied $500,000.

"That's a lot of money," I suggested.

He shrugged. "He's a major flight risk. The guy has at least one offshore bank account. How do we know he doesn't have other offshore accounts as well?"

"His business hasn't been that profitable to be sending money offshore. In fact, he barely survived this last year. Ralph Herman set up that account over a year ago and his embezzlement nearly put Ben and Alice Stover out of business. In fact, as of yesterday it's not nearly anymore. They are officially out of business."

"I'm not going to try the case today, Mr. Turner. Today I'm just going to do my best to keep your client in jail so he can stand trial for his crimes."

It was no use arguing. I'd done all I could, so I took a seat and waited for the magistrate to take the bench. A few minutes later he appeared and everyone came to their feet.

There were about a dozen matters on the docket and after eight of them had been finalized the clerk called Ben Stover's name.

"The United States of America vs. Benjamin T. Stover," the clerk announced.

Ben Stover was escorted to the defense table where I joined him. Stokely went to the lectern and addressed the court. "Your Honor, the defendant is charged with concealing assets in a chapter 11 case recently filed in this district. We have evidence that suggests he systematically extracted money from his business and deposited it to an offshore bank account for his own personal use and enjoyment. It appears his plan was to deceive his creditors by filing this bankruptcy. By failing to disclose material assets of the company's estate he committed bankruptcy fraud under 18 U.S.C. Section 152."

"What amount of bond are you requesting?" the magistrate asked.

"$500,000, Your Honor. We believe there is substantial flight risk as there may be other offshore bank accounts out there that haven't been discovered."

"Very well," the magistrate said. "Mr. Turner. What do you have to say about this?"

I stood up and replaced Stokely at the lectern. "Your Honor," my client has been a well respected businessman in Waco for over twenty-five years. He and his wife Alice have raised a family here, they own real estate, and, of course, they employ over twenty-five people in their two plants.

"What is particularly disturbing about this case is that the accusations that have prompted this arrest and indictment came from the very man who is responsible for Ben and Alice's Stover's financial problems—a man under indictment for embezzlement. In fact, the very offshore bank account allegedly set up by my client, we are pretty sure was set up by the accuser himself, Ralph Herman. We believe the money that was initially deposited into the offshore account was the money he embezzled from Ben and Alice Stover.

"Therefore, we would request that the defendant be released on his own recognizance."

"Thank you, Mr. Turner. "Mr. Stokely, you may call your first witness."

Stokely went to the lectern and said, "The prosecution calls Ike Eiseman."

A tall, slender man who looked to be in his early 30s stood up and approached the bench. He had a mustache and a smug look on his face. He took a seat and was administered the oath.

"Mr. Stokely, "Do you know the defendant, Ben Stover?"

He nodded. "Yes, I do."

"How do you know him?"

"I've been over at his office a few times on account of the fact that my best friend used to work for him."

"And who is your best friend?"

"Ralph Herman."

"Now; is Mr. Herman in jail right now?"

"Yes, because of that son of a–"

I stood up. "Objection!"

"Sustained. Watch your tongue, Mr. Eiseman. This is a court of law!" the Judge admonished.

"Thank you," I said and sat down.

Stokely continued, "Just answer the question, Mr. Eiseman. Your personal opinions are not needed here today. We just want to establish some factual issues."

Eiseman sat back and nodded.

"Now. Did I understand you to say your best friend, Ralph Herman, is in jail?"

"Yes. That's about the size of it. The Stovers had him arrested claiming he embezzled from them, but it's a lie."

"What happened to all of his personal property when he went to jail?"

"He left everything with me for safe keeping. I put it in my garage."

"Before Mr. Herman went to jail, would he confide in you?"

"Yes, he told me everything. You don't keep secrets from your best friend."

"Did something happen recently that prompted you to start digging through Mr. Herman's records?"

"Yes, I read about Ben Stover filing bankruptcy. I couldn't believe he was doing that since I knew he had a bank account in the Cayman Islands with lots of money in it."

"How did you know that?"

"Ralph made copies of everything in Ben Stover's office before he was arrested. I'd seen the bank statements. I just wanted to make sure my memory was correct before I called the FBI."

"So, were the bank statements there?"

"Yes, they were."

"Did Ralph Herman have anything to do with you bringing this information to the FBI?"

Eiseman shook his head vigorously. "Absolutely not, it was my idea. I was just trying to be a good citizen."

Stokely smiled and looked at me. "Pass the witness."

I knew Ben was screwed. Eiseman was lying through his teeth, but he was a good liar, and well rehearsed There was no way I was going to be able to trip him up on cross exam, so I made it brief.

"Mr. Eiseman. You testified you were Ralph Herman's best friend, right?"

"Yes."

"And you were close friends, so close you confided in each other, is that right?"

"Yes, absolutely."

"How did you feel when your friend was taken to jail?"

"I felt like shit. What do you think?"

"You were angry, right?"

He nodded. "Of course, I was angry. Nobody likes to see their best friend hauled off by the cops."

"Angry at Ben Stover, right?"

"Sure, I don't deny it, but I was angry because he stashed away hundreds of thousands of dollars and tried to pin it on Ralph . The son of a–"

"Objection, non-responsive?"

"Sustained," Mr. Eiseman. I warned you," the Judge said. "Anything else Mr. Turner."

I thought about asking one more question. Were he and Herman more than friends? But, I wasn't sure of the answer since Herman had been married to Alice's daughter. The cardinal rule in cross examination was never to ask a question you didn't already know the answer to, so I shut up.

"No, Your Honor," I replied.

It would do no good to continue the pissing match with Eiseman, so I sat down and watched him as he slithered by and took a seat in the gallery. Stokely said he had no further witnesses, so I called Alice's daughter who testified as to Ben's long history in Waco and his ties to the community. We also called the family's pastor who testified to his moral character and who said he was certain that Ben couldn't have done what the U.S. Attorney said he'd done. Finally, the judge made his ruling.

"Although it is clear that Mr. Stover has been a well respected businessman for many years in Waco, I can't overlook the obvious risk of flight we have here. Therefore, I'm setting bond at $500,000."

Alice let out a shriek in despair. There was no way she and Ben could come up with that kind of a bond. We all knew that. Ben would have to spend the next few months in jail until his trial. This was a federal case but I knew it was likely they'd keep him at the closest facility available which would be the McClennan County Jail. At least I hoped so.

Chapter 30

Dead End

Almost three weeks went by and little progress had been made tying Stout's security team to the Brown murders. They were professionals and had covered their tracks very well. The triggering device used to set the fire turned out to be made of many different parts that could have been used in a variety of products. Although Paul had been able to track sales of some of the components to the security team, it wasn't enough to prove anything.

As the trial date was set for early October our time to investigate was running out. It appeared our only hope was to prove reasonable doubt. We couldn't prove that Stout had ordered the murder of the Brown family, but we could point out a good motive, and with the security team in Dallas the day before the fire broke out, that was certainly an indication of ample opportunity. This was not concrete proof but it might be enough to create reasonable doubt.

But might is a shaky word, so we told Stanley he may want us to try to negotiate a plea bargain. We told him the DA probably would take the death penalty off the table and settle for life imprisonment, if he pled guilty to the homicides. At least then he wouldn't die.

"But I might as well be dead if I spend the rest of my life in prison," he replied. "I know I'm innocent and I have confidence you'll be able to convince the jury of that."

His confidence in us was flattering, but realistically there wasn't much hope of getting him off. Unreasonable expectations usually just made matters worse in this type of situation. It put undue pressure on the attorneys and gave the client a false sense of security. At a time when the client should be mentally preparing himself for the worst, he's getting ready to celebrate his expected exoneration. Then when he is convicted, the trauma is far worse than what it would have been had he been more realistic and prepared himself.

While I was contemplating all of this Maria stepped into my office and advised me Roger Rand was on the telephone. She said he had called for Stan, but when Stan wasn't available he wanted to talk to me. What could this be about?

I picked up the telephone. "Hello. Roger?"

"Paula, I'm sorry to bother you but Stan wasn't available–"

"I know. What's wrong?"

I just got a visit from Detective Kramer. He gave me a hard time about Charlotte Wenzel's bond."

"What? Why would he do that?"

“He doesn’t understand how she was able to post it. He wanted me to enlighten him.”

“What did you tell him?”

“I refused at first. I told him to call Stan, but he said he’d arrest me if I didn’t cooperate. He said there's no confidentiality between a defendant and a bondsman."

“So, what did you do?”

“I told him it was a cash bond, put up by one of Mrs. Wenzel’s admirers. Fortunately, that’s all I knew. Stan never told the identity of the person who put up the bond.”

“Don’t feel bad, he hasn’t told me either. . . . So, how did you leave it.”

“He said if he found out I was lying he’d put me out of business and arrest me for obstruction of justice.”

“Well, I’ll tell Stan what happened. Don’t worry about it. Stan will take care of it.”

After I hung up, I tried to think back to the last time a detective or assistant DA had tried to track down the source of a bond. Nothing came to mind. It was rare and I was shocked it was now happening. What difference did it make where Charlotte Wenzel got her bond? This wasn't an embezzlement, robbery, or a drug dealing case. Could Kramer and Shepard be looking for another motive? Or, were they looking for an accomplice? I made a mental note to discuss it with Stan after he got back from Waco.

Chapter 31

Snitch

On the Friday morning after my debacle in Waco, Paula caught me early with some alarming news. I tried to sidestep the conversation because I thought it was going to be about Tehra and I wasn't prepared to talk about her just yet. There was still a lot of sorting out to do after our strange night together in Hillsboro. However, it turned out that wasn't what was on her mind. The first bombshell was that Kramer and Shepard were poking into Charlotte Wenzel's bond. That was unexpected and a major cause for alarm as I had to protect the CIA involvement in the case at all costs. The second jolt was that the DA had finally designated the witness who claimed to have been approached by Charlotte Wenzel about killing her family.

A sudden sick feeling came over me. The fact that there was an adverse witness wasn't unexpected and something I could deal with later, but Kramer's attempt to track the source of Charlotte's bond money was alarming. If Roger Rand had disclosed where the money was being kept, I was in serious trouble. I called him.

"Yes. They threatened to put me out of business if I didn't tell them. What else could I do?"

"Shit! I wonder if they'll try to seize the money? They could claim it's tainted. That's just the kind of dirty trick Gary Shepard would jump on. Damn it!"

"I'm sorry, Stan. I should have–"

"It's okay. I put you in a bad position. I'm going to need to get the key to the box so I can move the money. We can't let them seize it. We may never get it back if that happens."

"All right. I'll meet you at the bank. I'll help you move it, but

I need to know where it is in case Ms. Wenzel skips out on me."

"Sure, I understand, but they'll probably be watching the bank. We'll have to be careful."

After I hung up, I called the bank and asked the office in charge of the safety deposit boxes if anyone had inquired about getting access to my safety deposit box. They said the police had been by, but didn't have a warrant so the box wasn't disturbed. I thanked them for that and then thanked God for giving me a little time to move the money. I figured Shepard would be out trying to get a search warrant or a seizure order at that very moment.

So, how could I clean out my safety deposit box without the police seeing me? It seemed impossible. They'd let me in but I'd never get out. I'd need a distraction about the time I wanted to leave. Whoever was watching the bank had to be lured away to allow me to escape, but what kind of a distraction could I set up in such a short time? Who could I enlist to create the distraction? Roger Rand was a possibility, but if he got caught he'd probably end up in jail and lose his business. Tehra? She might be able to do it, but I wasn't sure what her capabilities were yet and there wasn't time to find her and quiz her about it.

The more I thought about it the more I knew I needed help from Kulchz, and why not since this was his damn case. I felt in my pocket, grasped the telepathic modulator, and squeezed it. Supposedly, my thoughts would be immediately transmitted to my security team. They'd know what I needed done. But how could that be since I didn't even know what needed to be done. Then it suddenly occurred to me, I did know what I needed—a diversion like the aliens had used to abduct Cheryl Windsor.

When I got to the bank, Roger was pacing nervously out in front. Two men in suits were loitering across the street at a newsstand. A utility truck was parked a half block away. A steady stream of customers was entering and exiting the bank. There was no way I would know for sure if Kulchz' men were there to help me. I just had to assume they were. I parked across the street, grabbed my briefcase, and jogged over to Roger.

"You got the key?" I asked.

Roger nodded and handed it to me. "How do you plan to get

out of the bank without being stopped?" he asked.

"Don't worry about that. Just get in your car, drive two blocks south and wait for me to drive by. Then follow me."

"Why can't I wait for you in front of the bank?"

"Do you want to be charged with obstruction of justice? If Shepard or Kramer see you with me, they'll know you're helping me. I'm the attorney on the case so they can't directly attack me, but there is nothing to stop them from arresting you."

He looked at me skeptically. I wondered if I should tell him to close his eyes or his memory would be erased. But then how would I explain how I was able to leave the bank without being intercepted? No. I couldn't tell him. It would be too dangerous.

"Where are you going to take the money?" he asked.

"I don't know yet. It will depend on how things go. You'll just have to wait and then follow me to find out."

He nodded but didn't look thrilled with my plan. I slapped him on the shoulder, smiled, and said "Don't worry. I'll keep your collateral safe." Then I walked into the bank and didn't look back. The safety deposit vault was downstairs, so I went directly to the stairway, descended to the basement level and walked directly to the vault that housed the safety deposit boxes. The same lady who had set up the box for me was there to help me. I told her I needed to get into my box.

"Yes, sir. Do you have your key?"

"Yes," I said.

She leaned forward, opened a leather bound log book, and pointed to the first empty line. I signed my name and wrote in my box number in the column next to it. She got up and led me into the vault. Once I had my box safely in an inspection cubicle, I transferred the money to my briefcase and took the box back to its place in the vault. On the way out, I thanked the clerk then held my breath as I left the bank.

When the two men across the street spotted me, they started walking toward me. A cop disguised as a utility worker came at me from another direction. I quickened my pace and made it to my car just before the two men intercepted me. Once inside I lowered my head and covered my eyes tightly. There was a commotion outside and

I heard several screams. I could see faint blue flashes of light through the cracks between my fingers. When it was over, I sat up and looked at the scene around me. Some people were lying on the ground moaning. Others were wondering around aimlessly. I started the car and took off narrowly missing a lady staggering across the street. I looked in my rearview mirror and saw Kramer scratching his head and Shepard on one knee trying to stand up. Neither seemed to be aware that I was driving away.

Two blocks down the road Rand picked up my trail and we drove all the way to DFW Airport where I stashed the money in a locker. I was afraid to go straight to another bank as Kramer might have alerted them to be on the lookout for someone renting a box. I figured I'd leave it at the airport for a few days until the dust settled.

On the way back to the office I turned on the radio. They'd broken into regular programing to report what had just happened in downtown McKinney. "It a very confused scene downtown right now with police cars and ambulances just coming on the scene. We are in front of the First National Bank building and nobody is quite sure what's happened. There's obviously been a power outage, but that doesn't explain why dozens of people fell to the ground unconscious. Speculation is that there was some sort of gas spill or toxic release, but we haven't seen any evidence of that. Most of the victims on the ground appear to be waking up. They all look rather dazed and disoriented. Hopefully, nobody is seriously hurt."

It was a relief to hear that nobody had been hurt. I only wished I could have seen the look on Shepard's face when he discovered I'd slipped him. I wondered what he made of the chaos I'd left behind. It served him right, though, after what he had done to Bart, telling him there was a snitch knowing he'd obviously tell Paula. The bastard!

Now apparently there was a snitch, after all, ready to testify against Charlotte. I couldn't believe Shepard's gall dangling this witness in front of us but refusing to identify him. A couple of weeks later I was considering filing a motion to compel his identity when I got a manila envelope from the DA's office. After ripping it opened I quickly scanned the two-page pleading designating Son Lee as a witness. Lee's occupation was listed as a financial consultant. That was a pretty vague description and could mean anything from an insurance salesman to a loan shark. I suspected whatever this guy did, he was under indictment and was getting something from the DA for his cooperation. I told Jodie to have Paul Thayer check him out.

Chapter 32

Trial Strategy

August went quickly and before I knew it, thanks to the Speedy Trial Act, the Brown family murder trial was less than a month away. Paul Thayer had been working hard trying to find evidence to connect T. Robert Stout or his Almatech security team to the murders, but I hadn't heard from him for a long time, so I had Maria get him on the phone.

"Sorry I haven't gotten back to you sooner, but with your two murder trials and our regular workload, we've been up to our eyeballs," Paul explained.

"I bet you have been and ordinarily I wouldn't be so impatient, but time is running out. Have you been able to figure out who's our explosive's expert?"

"Yeah. We're pretty sure it's Rich Walls. That was his job on the special forces unit he served in before he retired. He's had the most extensive training in handling explosives and probably would have been the one called upon to rig the Brown triggering device."

"So, what do you know about Walls?"

"He's from Connecticut originally, graduated from Boston College with a degree in engineering, and joined the Army directly after graduation. Because he was a college graduate, they put him in officer training school and when he graduated they sent him to Vietnam where he served with the Army Corps of Engineers. When the war was over, he reenlisted and went to special forces training school. His file shows he's been deployed dozens of places around the world. His record during this time was exemplary. When his twenty-year hitch was up, he retired and went to work for a security firm that is now under contract to Almatech."

"Interesting," I said. "Do you have a photo of him? Maybe we can show his picture to people around the neighborhood in case someone might have seen him. In fact, get me pictures of the whole team. If we can find somebody who saw any of them, that could be huge to the jury. We don't have to prove they did it, just create reasonable doubt as to Walter Stanley's guilt."

"We've got photos. I'll get somebody on that task right away."

"Have them check the diner where the GTE truck was returned too. Maybe someone saw one of them drop it off."

After I hung up I went into Bart's office to discuss strategy. We had to decide pretty soon what our plan of attack would be. Would we just try to poke holes in the state's case and hope they couldn't prove it or promote our own theory about the murders? And, whichever way we went, should we let Stanley testify? Bart was on the phone with the medical examiner when I sat down in a side chair across from him. He motioned to me that he was finishing up. A couple of seconds later he hung up the phone and smiled.

"Bad news. The dental records came back and confirmed Chester Brown died in the fire."

"Was there any doubt of that?" I asked.

"Well, it was one hot fire and I was hoping maybe the bodies wouldn't be identifiable."

"But there were dental records?"

"Yes, I'm afraid so."

"Good," I replied.

"Good? How is that good?" Bart questioned.

"At least we know we have real victims."

Bart frowned.

I shrugged. "You know. In our last two murder trials none of the bodies could be identified, remember? It was . . . unsettling."

"Yeah, well that's why the mob loves to torch crime scenes. A lot of evidence is lost."

Bart didn't know about the alien involvement in our last murder trial. I didn't know much about it myself other than that they apparently had been living amongst us for some reason unknown to me. Stan was the one who risked his life to find out about them and what they were up to, but I had made it clear I didn't want to know. I was just glad they weren't involved in Stanley's case. I had enough other problems to worry about.

"So, Paul is sending us some photos of the Almatech security team. He's going to have some of his men show them to the neighbors to see if anyone might have spotted them."

"Good idea," Bart replied.

"So, if Paul comes up empty, what do you think we should do? We've got to make a decision soon."

"If we try to prove Stout is the killer and come up short it could make us look desperate. I think we'd do better just to show that Stanley isn't the killer type. We have to let him testify, of course, if we adopted that strategy."

"I don't know. He's kind of a wimp. Francis might tear him apart on cross examination."

"We'll just have to prep him thoroughly. Our only hope is that he comes off as someone incapable of murder. That's certainly my impression of him."

"Still, I have a bad feeling about dropping the whole case into Stanley's lap. It's our job to prove him innocent without risking self incrimination. I just hope Paul finds us a connection between Stout and the murders.. I'd hate to see an innocent man end up on death row because we couldn't do our job."

Bart sighed. "We're doing our job. What else could anyone do?"

I shrugged. "I don't know, but I can't stand the idea of losing. It's not an option. I'm going to talk to Stan. Maybe he'll have some ideas."

"Sure," Bart said. "Talk to him. I don't want to see Stanley die either, but you can't win them all. Did it ever occur to you that he might be guilty?"

I shook my head. "Sure. The idea crossed my mind a hundred times, but I rejected it each time. Like you said, I don't think he's capable of murder. It's just a gut feeling, but it's the way I feel."

Bart raised his eyebrows but didn't respond. I got up and went to Stan's office. He wasn't in yet, so I asked Maria to tell him to come see me when he made it in. She said she would. While I was waiting I started flipping through a dozen or so newspaper stories Jodie had dug up about the rivalry between Almatech and TI for the stealth technology contract. The reports were all pretty general and didn't provide much useful information, but I did notice that there was one reporter, Simon Barber, who seemed to know a lot about the competition between the two companies. I decided it wouldn't hurt to talk to him. I figured he might have information he didn't put in his stories for one reason or another. Maria got him on the telephone for me.

"Hi. Mr. Barber. Thank you for talking to me."

"Is this the Paula Waters, the attorney?"

"Yes, with Turner and Waters. I'm defending Walter Stanley in—"

"The Brown family murders. Wow! So, how can I help you?"

"Well, this is strictly off the record, okay?"

"Off the record? he replied tentatively. "How can I agree to that without knowing something about what you want to talk about?"

"Fair enough. As you can guess, we're trying to come up with alternative theories as to who might have killed the Brown family."

"Okay, that makes sense."

"I've seen some of your stories about the TI and Almatech competition for secret government contracts, and it seems you are the expert on that topic."

"Not everyone would agree with you, but let's assume that's true. Why are you interested in TI and Almatech?"

"Before I answer that, let's come to an understanding, okay?"

"All right."

"I've been investigating a possible link between Almatech and the Brown murders. I know it may seem far fetched that Almatech would be involved, but I have some evidence to suggest it. If you agree to help me with our investigation and keep it off the record, I'll give you the exclusive story should we be able to prove that Almatech was involved. I just don't want Almatech finding out that we're taking a close look at them."

"That sounds intriguing, but what you've told me already would make a nice story." Anger began to well up in me, but Barber didn't let it come to a boil; he hastened to add, "But, you'd deny it and then where would I be? . . . Okay, count me in."

"Good. Hopefully I'll be able to prove what I suspect and get my client off and you'll get a Pulitzer."

He chuckled. "I like you, Paula. You think big."

Barber agreed to meet me the following day for lunch. There was far too much to talk about by telephone. When I got off the phone there was a note from Maria that Stan had made it in. I got up and immediately went to his office. He was sipping a cup of coffee when I walked in.

"Stan. Good morning," I said.

He put his cup down and smiled. "Hi. How you doing?"

I sat down across the desk from him and replied, "Not too well, actually. I woke up this morning and realized the Brown murder trial was coming up on us fast."

Stan nodded sympathetically. "You could probably get a continuance."

"Yeah. I could, but I wonder if that wouldn't just help the prosecution shore up their case. I like going to trial quickly. It usually favors the defense."

"True. So, how is your defense coming?"

I brought Stan up-to-date on our theory that T. Robert Stout and Almatech wanted to torpedo TI's stealth technology contract with the government. He liked the theory and said it would play well with the jury and the press.

"So, you need some evidence that Stout ordered Brown's murder," he said.

“That would help,” I said. “We’ve got some circumstantial evidence, but it’s not enough.”

“Have you checked into terminated employees? A lot of times, after an employee has left a company, they’re not as protective of their employer’s secrets. Sometimes they're even eager to give up the dirt on them, particularly if they've been fired or mistreated."

"Yeah. I think Paul’s already talked to a few ex-employees. That’s how we found out the contract involved stealth technology.”

“Hmm. Did Brown have a secretary or personal assistant? They usually know what’s going on. You might want to talk to Mrs. Brown’s friends too. Women are usually more open than men. She’s probably got a friend who she’s spilled her guts to. Chester Brown probably knew who wanted him dead and told his wife. I doubt she’d keep that kind of information to herself. Try her parents too. They may have heard something."

"True. I'll look into that," I said feeling a little stupid since these were things I should have thought of on my own.

"Has anyone looked at Brown's computer or checked his email?" Stan asked.

"The police did that already and I'm supposed to have access to it in a week or two when their experts are through."

"Good. You might find something there. Did Brown have a calendar or diary?"

"Not to my knowledge."

"What about other competitors? They'll have someone watching TI and I'm sure would share any information they'd gather if it would help bring down one of their competitors."

"Maybe. I'm not sure how cooperative they'd be."

Stan sighed. "Well, it's just a thought. . . . What about General Accounting Office?"

"Huh?" I said.

"Don't they have to keep track of government contractors?"

"Ah. I don't know. Do they?"

"I think so. You may want to find out how they were keeping track of things. There may be reports that Almatech and TI had to provide them each month. No telling what you'd find in those reports."

"Thank you, Stan," I said standing up. "I knew you'd have some good ideas."

Stan smiled. "I'll give your case some more thought tonight," he said. "If I think of anything else, I'll let you know."

"Great," I said and left.

Stan's long list of ideas for getting more evidence left me feeling a little overwhelmed. How could I possibly do all those things? They were all good ideas but I'd never have time to follow through with them. I'd have to assign some to Paul and others to Jodie. Despite the enormity of the task ahead, I felt a little hope for the first time in weeks. Stan always managed to give me hope when I was feeling depressed and discouraged. Now, all I had to do was plow ahead and hope I'd stumble onto more evidence that would incriminate Stout and his security team.

Chapter 33

Civil War

My relationship with Tehra since Hillsboro had been strained, to say the least. Everything had been in such turmoil since that night, I hadn't had an opportunity to sit down with her and sort things out. I had put off helping her move into her new apartment too, but the time had come when it could be put off no longer. I met her at her hotel on Saturday morning for breakfast. Our plan was to eat and then go shopping for furniture and appliances. In the afternoon we'd move her things from the hotel into the apartment and put everything away. Some of the furniture we purchased would be delivered that same day, but most of it would come on Monday or Tuesday; but she could live in the apartment without it until it arrived.

She was sitting on a chair in the lobby when I got there. We had made it a practice to leave our tracking chips out of earshot when we were together. Mine was in the car. I assumed hers was still in her room. I walked up to her. "Good morning," I said cheerfully.

She stood up. "Oh. Hi. You made it."

"Yes. I promised you I'd help you move, so here I am."

"You didn't have a problem with Rebekah, did you?"

I shrugged. "Well, a little. She didn't like the idea of me helping you move in, but she's beginning to trust me again."

I couldn't tell Tehra that I'd told Rebekah about the aliens and that Peter was alive. I wasn't sure yet if I could trust her. I thought I could, but the consequences of being wrong were too great to take any chances.

"You told her you were helping me move?" Tehra asked seeming shocked.

I sighed. "Yeah, lying to her wasn't working. I figured I just better tell her the truth. It's not a crime to help your legal intern move into a new apartment."

"But, I thought she was the jealous type."

"I didn't say she was happy about it, but we've been through a lot together, so she cuts me a little slack now and then."

We went into the restaurant, leisurely filled our plates at the buffet, and took them to a corner booth to eat. A young waitress brought us coffee. Tehra dug in immediately and had cleaned her plate before I was half finished.

"You were hungry," I observed.

She laughed. "Yeah, I'm eating for two now."

My mouth dropped. "Two? You're pregnant?"

She smiled broadly. "Yes, isn't it wonderful?"

I just looked at her in shock. "But, I don't remember–"

"Yes, that's one of the side effects of the venom. It gives you a nice buzz but it also blocks any memory of the copulation."

I swallowed hard. "You knew I didn't want to have sex with you."

"What do you mean? You kissed me."

"But that didn't mean I wanted you to have my child."

She shook her head. "I'm sorry. I thought the kiss meant you would give me a child. I was so happy I didn't think to ask for clarification."

I took a deep breath. "You're right. Kissing you was a mistake. I don't know what I was thinking."

"You weren't thinking. You were reacting to your feelings."

My head was starting to throb. I rubbed my temples not knowing what else to do. What had I done? The worst part of it all was that I had no memory of it. The closest I had to a memory was the dream. How could this have happened? Did Mo and Kulchz know?

"Does anyone know you're pregnant?"

"No. You're the only one."

"How do you know for sure?"

"All women on Tarizon have a pregnancy sensor implanted in their uterus. The moment they become pregnant it is activated and sends out a signal to a monitoring device that tracts the babies vitals for the duration of the pregnancy. Mine came to life about the time they put you in the ambulance."

"Jesus! Do you realize what a problem this will be for me?"

"No. It won't be a problem. Nobody will ever know that the baby is yours. I'll go back to Tarizon and have the baby there."

"But I thought it was better to have the child on Earth and then take it back after it's a few years old."

"That is true, but I don't want to cause a problem by staying. I'll be all right."

"You can't worry about me. You've got to do what's best for the child."

She smiled. "I'm glad you feel that way. I would rather stay until the baby is older."

"What will Kulchz say when he finds out you are pregnant?"

"He'll be happy. Like I told you, all women of Tarizon are encouraged to have children. I'm doing my patriotic duty as a citizen of Tarizon."

After breakfast we went to Valley View Mall and shopped all afternoon. Tehra was in a great mood and enjoyed herself thoroughly. I wasn't so enthusiastic knowing that she was carrying my child. I still couldn't believe how it had happened. Then I started thinking about the baby. Would it have gills like Tehra? Would it have her webbed feet? Goose bumps broke out on my arms and legs just thinking about it. When we got to the apartment, I was exhausted and feeling rather depressed. While I was putting some appliances together Tehra came up from behind and began to give me one of her rubs. It felt good, but I just couldn't relax enough to enjoy it. I turned around.

"Don't you understand what this will do to me? Rebekah will sense that something is wrong. As soon as you start showing, she'll know what happened. My marriage will be over."

"I'll leave you before I begin to show. She'll never know."

I looked her in the eyes. She was a good woman. She meant me no harm. All she wanted from me was to have a child, nothing more. I wasn't mad at her. In fact, the thought of her leaving with my child was rather unsettling. How could I let her go? I already had one child I'd never see again. Could I live without another? She turned away.

"There is something else I should tell you. It will complicate matters even more, but you need to know."

"What?" I asked concerned with the gravity in her voice.

"Tarizon has been ruled by a coalition government. There are many political groups involved in the government, but the two most powerful are the Loyalists who support the Supreme Mandate and believe in Sandee, and the Purists who control the TGA and follow Tarizon's dictator, Videl Lai."

"The TGA?"

"Yes, the military–the Tarizon Global Forces. They will support Videl."

"Hmm."

"Anyway, civil war is about to break out on Tarizon and everyone will have to take sides soon."

"Take sides?"

"Yes. Maybe not openly at first. But eventually we'll have to choose between Vidal and the Loyalists."

"Damn! What are you going to do?"

"You'll have to choose too."

"Me? But–"

"Kulchz will support Vidal. He's a ruthless tyrant and will destroy democracy and liberty on Tarizon. I cannot follow him."

"But if you don't, what will become of you?"

"I'll have to seek sanctuary with the Loyalists. They will have friends and allies on Earth."

This was blowing my mind. How could the Tarizon Repopulation Project go on when Tarizon was in the midst of a civil war? Which faction would the United States support? I shook my head in disbelief.

"Will you stand with me?"

"Against Vidal Lei and Kulchz?"

"I don't know. This is all so sudden."

"Some say Vidal Lei intends to colonize Earth."

"What!"

"They say he doesn't believe Tarizon can be saved, so his plan is to conquer Earth and evacuate an elite portion of the human population of Tarizon here."

Just when I thought matters couldn't get any worse, I felt

myself slipping deeper into the quicksand. Now suddenly Tehra's pregnancy seemed insignificant to the plans of Vidal Lei to conquer Earth. There was no doubt I'd stand with the Loyalists, but I doubted my support would have much significance when the civil war broke out.

"I don't have any choice. I'd have to do what I could to protect Earth from an invader. How much time do we have before this civil war breaks out?"

"A few months, a year, I don't know exactly, but it will be happening soon. Your son Peter has already joined the Loyalists."

A chill shot through my veins. I just stared at Tehra for a moment trying to fathom her remark. "Peter's involved in this?"

"Yes. Kulchz spoke of it when I first arrived. He apparently was training with the TGA on Pogo Island and escaped with some fighter planes."

"You're talking about my Peter? He doesn't know how to fly a fighter."

"I don't know. I'm just telling you what I overheard Kulchz saying."

This was all too bizarre. Peter had no military training and couldn't possibly be involved in a civil war. It just wasn't possible. Tehra shrugged and took a deep breath. Why would she be lying to me about something like this? It didn't make any sense. If she was right, what did all this mean? Was Peter in danger? Obviously he was, if he was in midst of a civil war. He'd be in mortal danger at any moment.

"Okay. So, if what you say is true, what should we do?"

She shook her head. "I don't know. That's why I'm telling you. I need your help in figuring it all out."

I laughed. "You think I can help you figure this out. I'm sorry, but I didn't take intergalactic relations. A year ago I didn't even know alien life existed!"

"But you're smart and perceptive. Together we can develop a strategy for survival. We have no choice. We not only have ourselves to worry about, but our child as well."

Our child. Tehra had said all she wanted from me was a child, nothing more, but that apparently was a lie. She wanted not just a child, but a father, a mate, and most of all an ally to help get her through this impending civil war. But had she made a good choice in selecting me? This was all so overwhelming it made me dizzy to even think about it. I just looked at her and shook my head. She came over to me, put her head on my shoulder, and squeezed me tightly. I ran my hand through her smooth black hair and kissed her on the forehead.

"It will be all right," I said. "Don't worry. We'll figure something out. In the meantime, like Kulchz said, we've got to just act normal—just focus on the task that has been assigned to us. For now, that's the only way we can survive."

Chapter 34

Undercover

The following morning when I passed Maria in the reception area, she reminded me that I had a luncheon appointment with Simon Barber. She said she had made reservations for us at Vincent's. I thanked her and proceeded to my office. As I walked passed Tehra's cubicle, I couldn't help but look at her. What was she up to? I smiled.

"Good morning," I said. "How's it going?"

She shrugged. "Okay, I guess. There's just so much to do, I feel overwhelmed."

I nodded. "Welcome to the practice of law. You can work sixty hours a week and still never feel like you're on top of everything."

"How is Stan holding up after the Waco fiasco?" I asked.

Tehra sighed. "Not well. He feels so bad about what happened to Ben. He blames it all on himself, although I don't know what he could have done to prevent it."

"Yeah, that's why it's not a good idea to get too friendly with your clients. It's just too painful if you can't help them the way you'd like."

Tehra nodded. "Yes, I guess you're right."

"Anyway, I've got to get to work. Thanks for the update on Stan, he's not always very communicative."

Tehra smiled and I continued down the hall to my office. When I thought about it, I realized that was the first cordial conversation I'd had with Tehra since she'd come to work for us. Perhaps I had misjudged her. The rest of the morning went quickly as I worked on my witness and evidence lists for the trial. I added every person and every shred of evidence I could think of to the lists. I could cut out those I didn't need on the eve of trial once our strategy was set. The next step was to prepare questions for each witness and consider each piece of evidence for admissibility and relevance to our case. It was a long tedious process but one that had to be done early or it would probably never get done properly. At eleven-thirty I got my things together for my luncheon meeting with Simon Barber.

We met at Vincent's near North Park. I'd picked the location because they had corner booths that were tucked away and out of view of patrons coming and going. It was a good place to talk privately without fear that someone was watching or listening. We ordered and the waiter brought us some garlic rolls to work on while we were waiting for our entrees. Barber was medium height, in his mid-forties, and wore an expensive silk shirt. His long black hair was combed straight back, like what had been popular in the 60's. He was in mint physical condition for his age. I could imagine him working out in a gym every morning before the sun came up.

"Before we start," I said, "I want to thank you again for doing this."

He shook his head. "No thanks are necessary. This is for our mutual benefit, right?"

"Exactly. You get the Pulitzer, I keep my client from dying by lethal injection."

"Okay, then. How can I help you?" he said.

"First, I'd be interested in knowing how you got on to this story. It doesn't seem all that exciting on its face."

"You're right about that. It was by accident if you really want to know the truth. They were having a parade in downtown Ft. Worth and I got caught in the traffic. I was nearly an hour late for work and by the time I got to the assignment's desk, this was all that was left."

"So, how did it become your big obsession? I've read nearly a dozen of your stories about the rivalry with these two companies."

"Well, I believe in making the best of a situation, no matter how distasteful it may appear. Even though it didn't seem like much of a story in the beginning, when I started digging into to it I discovered a fascinating world of political intrigue. The more people I talked to the more curious I got about how it all worked and who were the important players."

The waiter brought our entrees and poured us some wine. Barber raised his glass and said, "Here's to a profitable relationship."

I nodded, raised my glass and smiled. "Yes, and to discovering the truth."

After he'd enjoyed a few bites of his meal, I continued my questioning. "Do you know anything about Chester Brown's history?"

"Sure, the basic stuff. I know he was a genius and that Stout was very upset when he went to work for TI. There's not a lot known about him. As I recall he disappeared for a long time and nobody seems to know where he went."

I told Barber what Paul had dug up on Brown and then asked, "Do you think Stout would have someone killed if he thought it would get him a lucrative federal contract?"

"Sure, if he was certain he could get away with it. Fear of getting caught would be a serious deterrent, though. I'm not sure he could afford to take that kind of a gamble. He has a lot more to lose than to gain."

"So, you're saying the stealth technology contract wasn't worth killing someone over?"

"Stealth technology? How did you know that? The contract specifications were supposed to be classified."

"Oh, right. Well, it's amazing what information you can get from a pissed off ex-employee."

"Which employee?"

"Ah. I think I'll keep that to myself right now. Later on I'll tell you if it looks like we're going to be able to substantiate our theory."

"All right. Well, if Brown was the key to the successful completion of the contract, then that would be a good motive for his death. Still, killing him would be very dangerous. If anyone ever found out it would be the end of Stout and Almatech."

"That's why I want to be sure Stout is responsible, before I start leveling accusations. Just suggesting that he might have done it would cause him grievous harm."

"What, an attorney with a conscience? I can't believe it," he teased.

I shrugged. "Well, I'll do what I have to get my client off, but reckless accusations have a way of coming back at you. It's important to at least look like you're searching for the truth."

"So, what can I do to help you find the truth?"

I told him about Stout's security team and told him we were

searching for away to prove they were at Brown's house. I told him about the sophisticated triggering mechanism which started the fire and made it spread so quickly the Brown's couldn't get out.

"I have a source inside Almatech that might help us."

"Who's that?" I asked.

"You don't need to know. I'll make contact and with them and see if I can get any information that might be helpful."

"Great. If we can show that anybody from the security team was at or near the Brown house the day they were in town, that would be enough to justify suggesting in trial that Stout and Almatech were involved in the murders."

"Yes," Barber said, "and justify a front page story. I'd want it to come out the same day that you disclosed it to be sure nobody beat us to the newsstand."

"No problem," I replied excitedly. "Just get me that link."

"Don't worry. If anybody from Stout's team was there, I'll get you the proof you need."

Simon Barber's assurances that he'd find the evidence I needed was nice to hear, but I wasn't going to get my hopes up. Actually, I was a little disappointed with what little information I'd gathered during our meeting. I wondered who this source was that Barber was going to contact. I hoped it wasn't a love-starved secretary that he was jumping. We'd need someone up higher in the Almatech hierarchy to get the kind of information we needed.

Chapter 35

Safe Haven

When I told Mo I needed to have a meeting with him and Kulchz, he didn't seem surprised. Of course, why would he? They were monitoring my conversations–at least most of them. They knew they'd been caught in yet more lies. Tehra and I drove out to east Texas and met them at Kulchz' headquarters beneath the oil storage tank. He'd made improvements since our last visit. The underground facility had at least doubled in size. We'd have gotten lost getting to Kulchz office had Mo not been there to guide us.

Just as we were about to go down, two guards confronted Tehra and told her to follow them. I tried to object but Mo restrained me.

"Don't worry. They're just taking her for a debriefing. She has to report on her assignment watching over you and they want to update her on current happenings on Tarizon as well as the project. And, of course, there's the pregnancy."

I looked at Mo in shock. How did they know she was pregnant? He gave me a wry smile. "Pregnant?" I replied feigning ignorance.

"They suspect that she is, but can't figure out when or how it happened."

I shook my head. "I didn't do it. At least, I have no recollection of doing it," I said truthfully.

Mo chuckled. "She hasn't been around anyone else, but we'll know soon enough. They'll test for parentage."

I felt myself getting hot with embarrassment. Mo seemed to

be enjoying my discomfort. "You wanted this to happen, didn't you?" I asked.

Mo nodded. "Kulchz did. He figured that would give him even more control over you."

I shook my head. "The bastard!"

"Careful!" Mo urged. "He's listening to you."

I bit my tongue and took a deep breath. Finally, Kulchz's door opened and we went inside. Instead of sitting on the plush sofas that we'd sat on in the past, we were escorted to a small room with a round crystal conference table surrounded by five matching chairs. A communications module was built into the center of the table. We took a seat and several seconds later Kulchz and two of his staff joined us.

"Well, Stan," Kulchz said gleefully. "I've got good news. You have honored Tehra by conceiving in her a son."

My heart skipped a beat. It was true. Somehow I'd gotten Tehra pregnant. "You're sure it's mine?"

"Yes, there is no doubt."

"And you know it's a boy?"

"Yes, and hopefully as strong and cunning as his father."

Cunning? What did he mean by that? Was that a compliment or a warning that he was on to Tehra and my attempts at privacy? I wondered if he knew Tehra wouldn't be on his side when the civil war broke out.

"Well, if he's anything like his mother," I replied. "He'll be a fine person."

"Yes, indeed. . . . So, Mo said you wanted to talk to me about an important matter."

"Yes, sir. Apparently there is a snitch prepared to say Charlotte Wenzel hired someone to kill her family. How am I supposed to deal with that?"

"Like you always deal with any other liar. Impeach his character. Prove he's a fraud."

"I know that, but do you know anything about this guy? He's not from Tarizon is he?"

"No."

"Did he know Charlotte? Was he her lover?"

"We don't think so, but she wasn't monitored. We knew where the children and Mr. Wenzel were at all times, but not Mrs. Wenzel."

"So, you can't help me?"

"No, other than to subject him to the memory gun."

I shook my head. "Only as a last resort. Using the memory gun could raise new questions. The FBI is still after me to explain how the bank's vault was opened and the contents of my safety deposit box removed. My little lie that a secret invention was the target of the thieves isn't holding water."

Kulchz looked at Mo. "Perhaps we could use this as a way to transfer some of the technology provided for in the treaty."

Mo nodded, "Why not? It's as good a cover as any."

"Fine," Mo said. "I'll have our scientist provide you a prototype of one of the inventions we are obligated to give your government under the treaty. I'll get an agent to pose as your client and you can turn the invention over to them."

"Really?" I said feeling much relieved. I hadn't expected Kulchz to solve this particular problem. I had mainly come to let off steam, but Kulchz had surprised me. I wondered if he was being so nice because of the civil war about to erupt on Tarizon. Was he hoping I'd remain loyal to him? That was probably it, I thought.

When Kulchz dismissed me, I was reunited with Tehra and we started back to the surface through the tunnel system that led underneath the lake to where the shuttle landed on an island in the lake called Hawk Island. In my mind's eye I remembered seeing the shuttle take off from Cactus Island at Possum Kingdom Lake. That was a night I'd never forget.

"You want to go see the launch pad?" Tehra asked.

"Could we?" I asked.

"I don't know why not. I've already seen it and you already know it's there, so it's not like it's a big secret."

"What if Kulchz doesn't think it's a good idea?"

"Then he'll have some of his troops stop us. If nobody bothers us, then we'll know he doesn't care if you see it."

"All right. I would like to see it."

Tehra nodded and said, "This way, then." She started walking down a tunnel. It was much cooler in the tunnel systems than on the surface. Water dripping from the ceiling formed into small pools that made navigating the tunnels treacherous.

"So, how was your debriefing?' I asked.

She shrugged. "Routine. They were mainly concerned about the baby. He's normal and healthy."

"He is? That's good."

"I'm going to name him Sophilo."

"Sophilo?"

"Yes, do you like it?"

"Sure, it has a nice ring to it. Is that a common name on Tarizon?"

"Yes. It means hero."

"Hero? . . . Hmm. That's nice."

As we continued to walk we passed several soldiers and Seafolken coming back from the launch area. Each of them gave us a hard look but nobody challenged us. Forty minutes later we reached our destination. It was located in a mammoth cavern under the island. Many crewmen and hundreds of Seafolken tended to the space shuttle that was docked just beneath the surface of the island.

"Oh, my God!" I said as I beheld the huge ship. I can't believe something that large can fly."

"I assure you it does. We're near the surface of the island here. There's a dome that conceals the ship. When it's ready to leave the dome retracts allowing it to take off. From above it looks like natural terrain."

"Jeez. That's amazing."

"These are small domes compared to the ones that cover our cities back home on Tarizon," Tehra noted.

"I bet. How tall must a dome of that size be?"

"Several hundred feet usually, but I know of one that is over 500 feet tall."

"That city must have one monster of an air conditioner."

"No. There are thousands of them, but they don't regulate the temperate–just the air quality."

Several soldiers stepped out of the tunnel and motioned to us. Tehra took my arm and led me toward them. They talked in their alien language, so I didn't know what they said but Tehra indicated we must leave as the ship was getting ready to test its thrusters. I nodded and took one last look at the mushroom shaped ship. I thought of Peter and wondered what he had thought when he was taken aboard a similar craft. Was he scared or too awestruck to think of his personal safety? Knowing Peter it was probably the latter. To think he was now a soldier in a civil war millions of miles away! It still blew my mind.

Tehra grabbed my hand again and I followed her back into the tunnels. The trip back to the surface seemed much quicker than the journey down to the launch site. Anticipation always had a way of slowing down time. On the way back to Dallas I asked Tehra if she'd heard anything about Peter or the civil war in her debriefing.

"Yes, there was a big battle on Lortec and the TGA was routed from the Island. Peter fought in the battle. He survived and is at Loyalists' headquarters somewhere in the Beet Islands."

"The Beet Islands?"

"Yes, it's a string of thousands of islands in the Southern Sea."

"So, the Loyalists won the battle? That's good, right?"

"Yes, but it is the just the beginning. The TGA has ten times the forces of the Loyalists. The Loyalists only won because they surprised the TGA. The war will be long and hard."

"So, has anyone here on Earth taken sides yet?"

"No, so far everyone remains loyal to the TGA, but it won't last. If the Loyalists aren't soundly defeated soon, many will desert the TGA. I must be ready when that happens."

"Ready? Ready for what?"

"To go undercover and hide from the TGA."

"But, where will you go?"

"I don't know. Will you help me find a place? A place for me and the others."

"Of course, but what if they find you?"

"Then they'll kill me."

"And the baby," I added.

Tehra nodded.

"Shit. We better start looking right away. I can't let them harm you and the baby."

"Dallas is a big city. There must be many places to hide."

"I suppose. I'll just have to give it some thought."

That night I slipped out of my belt and took Rebekah for a walk to bring her up to date on what was going on. I omitted the part about Tehra being pregnant. I still couldn't believe it was my child. She took the news about Peter badly.

"How can he be a soldier? Why would he do that?"

"He probably didn't have much of a choice. Anyway, he's not the youngest soldier that has ever served his country. He's almost 17."

"But he's my baby. It's not right. What if he's injured or killed?"

"You just have to have faith that God will protect him."

"God? The God who let the aliens take him?"

I frowned at Rebekah. "Come on. You think God only exists on Earth? I'm sure God is watching over Peter on Tarizon. He apparently has plans for him there."

"But why Peter? It's so unfair."

It took awhile, but I finally got Rebekah off the subject of Peter and told her about our need to find a hiding place for Tehra. She thought about it and then made a wonderful suggestion.

"What about the Double T Ranch?" Rebekah asked.

"The Double T Ranch. Hmm. . . . Yeah. That's a great idea."

The Double T Ranch was owned by an old client, Dusty Thomas. Thomas had been literally struck by lightning some time ago and killed, but his widow still lived on the ranch. She was a nice woman who would do anything for me since I'd successfully defended her husband when he was charged with the murder of an IRS agent.

The only trick would be getting Tehra there without Kulchz and the TGA knowing about it, but that would be a problem for another day. At least we had the beginning of a plan for the protection of the Loyalists forces on Earth.

Chapter 36

Obstruction of Justice

One afternoon in late September a cold front came through Dallas. At 3:01 p.m. the temperature was 101degrees and at 3:59 p.m. it was 59 degrees. When I stepped out of my car in my thin blouse and short skirt, I thought I'd stepped into a meat freezer. I wrapped my arms around me and hurried inside to my office. I'd gotten used to the Dallas heat and wasn't anxious for winter and cold temperatures to arrive.

When I sat down at my desk, I saw a message slip from Paul Thayer. I immediately picked up the telephone and gave him a call. Hopefully he had good news for me. The phone rang four times before he picked up.

"Paul? This is Paula Waters returning your call."

"Oh, hi, Paula. Thanks for calling me back. I just wanted to give you an update. We finally got a break."

"Thank God! What is it?"

"It seems one of the waitresses at the diner where they found the GTE service truck recognized one of the men on Stout's security team."

"Really? What's her name?"

"Blanche Reedy," he said and then briefed me on all that she had told him. "She says she remembers because he flirted with her briefly while they were eating. The man she recognized is Rich Walls. She also says Lisa Andretti may have been with him, but she's not as sure about her."

"That's fabulous. . . . Damn. We are so close to having enough evidence to go with this defense. Just a little more and I'd almost have a duty to bring all this up at trial. Any luck in the neighborhood?"

"No. Not so far."

"Well, keep at it. This was a huge breakthrough. Thank you,

Paul."

"You're welcome. I'll be in touch."

Paul's call lifted my spirits. If push came to shove we could go with our Almatech theory now and nobody would question our ethics. Although we couldn't prove Stout was behind the murders, the evidence certainly pointed in his direction. Enough so the jury might be sufficiently troubled to acquit Walter Stanley.

Being in such a good mood, I decided to spread my cheer into Stan's office. By the look on his face, I'd just got there in the nick of time. After I'd told him about our new star witness I asked, "So, what's up with you?"

He shrugged. "Oh, just the usual chap. I just got a trial setting in Ben Stover's case–January 7th–so, I was just trying to figure out how I was going to prove him innocent."

I took a deep breath and exhaled slowly. "Well, all you need to do is get Herman's buddy–what's his name?"

"Ike Eiseman."

"Right. If you could get Ikeie boy to tell the truth the entire case would crumble like a sand castle in a typhoon."

Stan nodded. "True, but the guy's a born liar. He's very smooth."

"Well, do you still have that truth serum?"

I was referring to a drug Mo had given Stan to use when we were desperate to get a witness to tell the truth. We'd actually used it on our own client to get her to remember something that had been erased from her conscious memory. It worked like a charm.

"Hmm. That's an interesting idea, but the last time we used it our client disappeared."

"True," I replied. "But we know that won't happen this time. I don't think Ralph Herman is married to an alien."

"No, he's not married at all. I'll give that idea some thought," Stan said giving me a wry smile. "Another idea would be to send you to the Cayman Islands to investigate that offshore account."

"Ah! Not this girl," I said emphatically. Stan was joking about the last trip I'd made to investigate an offshore bank account for a client. I'd gone to the British Virgin Islands and ended up in a hospital handcuffed to my bed next to a serial killer. I'd been arrested for suspicion of drug dealing, money laundering, possession, and aiding and abetting. It was all a setup and eventually the charges were dropped, but it soured my adventuresome spirit.

"Okay. I'll put Mo on it. He's the expert on money laundering. I'll call him this afternoon," Stan said.

"Good. Let me know what he finds out."

I nodded.

"I've got another problem," Stan said solemnly.

"What's that?"

"You know the little lie I told Agent Lot?"

"Yes. God, don't tell me he's contacted you again."

"I'm afraid so. He's called several times and I've been putting it off with one excuse or another."

"So, what are you going to do?"

"I've asked for help from Mo. I'm hoping they'll come up with something. In the meantime, if Agent Lot calls you, I'd plead ignorance."

"Don't worry. I don't know anything about your civil clients. I handle strictly criminal cases."

"Yeah, well you may be handling mine pretty soon if I don't figure something out."

I laughed tentatively. Stan was right. Lying to the FBI and removing evidence from a crime scene was a serious offense. If Stan went down for obstruction of justice, so would Jodie, and even I'd be incriminated since I was working on the case at the time too. That night I wanted to discuss all of this with Bart, but he didn't know about the aliens and I wasn't about to share that knowledge with him. It was better that he didn't know. If he found out, he'd be like Stan and have to know who they were and what they were doing here. But this wouldn't change anything. He couldn't force them to leave. The only result would be his life needlessly being put in jeopardy. No, I'd have to keep this to myself. There was no other way.

Chapter 37

Prototype

A week after our meeting with Mo and Kulchz, I was contacted by the man who was supposed to extricate me from my problems with Agent Lot of the FBI. His name was Alexander Tortoff. He was a large man with a full beard. He wore glasses and was rather sloppily dressed. He certainly looked the part of a man obsessed with his work rather than his appearance. When he came to my office for our meeting with Agent Lot he was carrying a large box.

An assistant helped him in with it and they set it down in front of my desk. The box contained a prototype of the air cleaning device that I had told Agent Lot about earlier. I had described it as a device that shot out a beam of light that cleaned and purified the air instantaneously. Tortoff had advised me that this actual prototype did that and much more and assured me he'd handle Agent Lot.

"This is my client Alexander Tortoff," I said to Lot.

"Good morning, sir," Lot said." Thank you for meeting with me."

"Agent Lot is with the FBI and they're investigating the theft of your prototype."

"Yes, that's wonderful," Tortoff replied. "Do you have any news?"

"No, but the bureau is working hard to find out who's responsible for the theft. Stan says it was some kind of an air cleaning device?"

"Yes. I call it the Eliminator. It removes 99.9% of all impurities in the air within seconds of its operation and scrubs all surfaces free of loose molecules. It will save millions of dollars to industries that use clean rooms or need a contaminant free environment for their operations."

"I see," Agent Lot said. "Do you know of anyone who might want to steal this technology from you?"

Tortoff pulled a sheet of paper from his coat pocket. "Yes, as a matter of fact I've made a list for you of our major competitors and those who have advised us of their interest in purchasing our technology. Any one of them would have profited by the theft of our prototype."

Agent Lot took the paper and glanced through the names. "There are quite a few names here," he noted. "You've had discussions with each of these companies?"

"No. Not everyone of them. We exhibited at a national trade show recently and these were the companies that expressed an interest in our technology. We've talked to many of them."

Lot's eyes narrowed as he went through the list of names. "You've been talking to the U.S. Army?"

"Yes. They are interested in it for use to combat chemical warfare. The Eliminator can remove toxic chemicals within its range within seconds and thus remove any danger to the personnel located there."

"Wow! I can see why someone wanted to steal this device."

"Would you like a demonstration?" Tortoff asked.

"Yes. Absolutely," Agent Lot replied.

Tortoff nodded and his assistant took the device and placed it on the corner of my desk. It was shaped like a Coleman Lantern cut vertically down the middle. The flat side was a clear substance and the curved portion a metallic grey. Tortoff pulled out a small fan, plugged it in to a socket on the wall, and placed it on my desk. The assistant pulled out a cotton bag and dumped the contents onto my desk as Tortoff turned on the fan.

In seconds the room was filled with a thick cloud of dust and flying debris. Agent Lot began coughing. My eyes began to water and I could feel the dust filling my lungs. The contamination got so thick I could barely see across the room. Just as I was about to suggest we evacuate my office, Tortoff pushed a button on the Eliminator. There was a flash of light and suddenly the room was clear. Agent Lot coughed once more and then looked around the room seemingly in shock.

"Whoa! That's incredible," Lot declared.

"Yes. Rather impressive, isn't it," Tortoff agreed.

"So, is there a danger someone could reverse engineer the Eliminator?"

"Probably not entirely, but it could greatly accelerate anyone's research in this area. We would very much like to get the prototype back."

"Is there any chance I could borrow this prototype so my people could photograph it and get its specifications? It might help in recovery the first prototype."

"Yes. We figured you'd want to do that, so you are welcome to take this one with you. There's complete documentation and schematics in the box."

Agent Lot's mouth fell open. "Oh. Okay. I really appreciate that. We'll get it back to you as soon as possible."

Tortoff shook his head. "Take your time. No hurry," he said.

Agent Lot thanked him, and with Tortoff's assistant's help, took the Eliminator out to his car. When he was gone I breathed a sigh of relief and thanked Tortoff.

"How do you know he'll pass the Eliminator on to the Army?" I asked.

"I've been negotiating a sale of the device to the Army with Colonel Martinez at the Pentagon. I was scheduled to go by there tomorrow and give them a demonstration. Before I came here today, I called him and told him I'd have to cancel our meeting since the FBI would be in possession of the Eliminator prototype for awhile."

"Oh. I see. When Martinez goes to the FBI to check out the device he'll find everything the Pentagon needs to reproduce it."

"Exactly, but the Pentagon won't let anyone know they have the technology and the FBI will give me back the prototype just like nothing happened."

For a moment I just stared at Tortoff thinking how clever he and Kulchz were. Then I wondered how many American children it had cost to acquire this new technology. I had no idea the number of children that had been taken each year for the Tarizon Repopulation Project, but I suspected it was in the hundreds of thousands. After all what good would the infusion of any fewer children do to a dying planet? There would have to be hundreds of thousands for there to be any significant impact on the population. Suddenly I felt sick. How could I continue to be part of this sinister project? Was the fact that I'd been recruited under duress keep me from going to hell? Somehow I doubted it.

My soul searching was interrupted when Maria stepped in my office and told me Martha Thomas was on the line. I was glad because I'd been trying to contact her about letting Tehra and her friends stay at her ranch for awhile. We talked for awhile about old times before I broached the subject.

"Listen, the reason I called is I need a favor."

"Anything," Martha replied. "You know I'd do anything for you."

"There are some visitors from out of the country who are trying to defect. There government will be very upset when they do it. They need to disappear for a week or two until the dust settles. Your ranch would be perfect."

"Are they communists?" she asked.

"I can't say where they're from for security reasons, but, needless to say, their government will try to find them to prevent the defection and to punish them for attempting it. It could be dangerous for you to keep them."

"That's okay. I'd be honored to help them. It's not everyday that you get an opportunity to help someone get their freedom."

"Thank you, Martha. You're a good person. I'll do everything in my power to keep you safe. If there is any damage to your ranch, I'll make it good. Don't worry."

"I'm not worried. I trust you, Stan. You know that."

I told Martha I'd contact her when the time came and then hung up. Maria immediately came on the intercom to advise me that Gary Shepard was on the line. I was curious as to why Shepard was calling. It was unusual for him to call me directly. I picked up the phone.

"Stan. That was pretty slick the way you emptied your safety deposit box the other day right under our noses. I'm not going to ask you how you did it, since I know you wouldn't tell us anyway."

"I don't know what you're talking about," I said. "What safety deposit box?"

"Okay, play dumb if you want. I just wanted to give you a heads up. We're going to find out how Charlotte Wenzel was able to post a quarter million dollar bond whether you voluntarily tell us or not. We've checked her financial situation and know good and well she didn't have that kind of money. She's obviously got a sugar daddy who's supporting her and we want to question him. He'd certainly have a motive for killing Mr. Wenzel, don't you think–so he could have Charlotte all to himself?"

"Assuming you're right, what's his motive for killing the children?"

"It might have been an accident or they were a distraction that he could do without."

“And you think Charlotte would sleep with the man who killed her children, accidently or intentionally?”

“Ah . . . well–”

"Come on. You're wasting your time," I said. "You’re not going to find out the source of Charlotte Wenzel's bond. Charlotte and I are the only two people who know where the bond money came from, and neither of us has any obligation to tell you. Roger Rand knows nothing as you already found out."

"There are other ways to find out," Shepard replied.

"Why do you even care? Hell, half the bonds posted these days come from drug sales or other criminal enterprises."

"The person who gave you the money for the bond obviously knows something about Mr. Wenzel's disappearance," Shepard said. "If you're withholding the identity of a material witness, I'll charge you with obstruction of justice."

Shepard's threats didn't bother me. After all, Kulchz would, no doubt, qualify for diplomatic immunity. He clearly was a guest of the United States government and protected by whatever treaty Tarizon and the United States were operating under. Fortunately, Shepard was too stubborn to realize he was at a dead end. I just hoped he'd continue down his little rabbit trail. It was a great distraction.

Chapter 38

Death Sentence

With less than a week before Walter Stanley was to go on trial for the murder of the Brown family, we still didn't have that last piece of crucial evidence to give us a fighting chance at proving our theory about the death of Chester and Gladys Brown and their three children. Paul Thayer's canvas of the neighborhood had failed to find anyone who had seen any of the Almatech security team near the Brown home on or before the tragic fire.

The sick feeling in the pit of my stomach was getting stronger each day and harder to ignore. My last hope for any new evidence rested with Simon Barber. He had assured me that if there was any evidence of Almatech's involvement in the Brown murder he'd find it. So, far he'd come up with nothing, but on several occasions he had said he was close to a breakthrough. I didn't know what that meant and he wouldn't elaborate. He just kept saying, "Trust me."

As I was about to take a break and go to lunch, he finally called. "Paula. Did I catch you at a bad time?"

"No," I said. "I was just going to grab a salad at the deli downstairs."

"Good," Barber said. "Let me swing by and I'll treat you to something better than a salad."

Since I hated eating alone, I jumped at the offer. He told me to meet him downstairs in front of the building in ten minutes. When I asked him if he had anything for me, he said he couldn't talk about it over the phone. After I hung up I went to the ladies' room to freshen up and then took the elevator to the lobby. He was already parked in front of the building when I walked out. As I strolled to his black BMW, I prayed he had some good news.

After a little chit-chat he got to the purpose of our meeting. "I'm sorry it took so long, but my source had a lot of trouble getting what you were looking for. It seems Stout's security team is off the company books. There was nothing in the company files about them."

"How can that be? They must be funded somehow."

"Yes. It took us awhile to figure it out. They actually work for a private security firm, Tripact Security. Almatech pays them $300,000 per year plus expenses. Unfortunately, there are no security team records in the possession of Almatech except a detailed invoice each month. We almost missed it, but on one of those invoices there was a taxi fare to Golden Cab Company on the day before the fire. We've checked with the company and we were able to get a record of three of the security team being transported to the Sheraton Hotel at Coit and LBJ in Dallas. That's just down the street from the diner where the GTE truck was taken."

"Three members?"

"Right."

"Hmm. That's quite a coincidence. Which three?"

"The receipt doesn't say, but the funny thing is, the flight log only shows Colonel Walls and Lisa Andretti coming to Dallas."

"Interesting. I wonder who else was on that flight?"

"I don't know, but I suspect you'll figure it out. When you do, don't forget our deal."

"I won't. You'll get your story. Don't worry."

By the time I got back to my office my spirits had risen immensely. I told Stan and Bart the good news and then went to my office to work on my opening statement and trial outline. I was excited now and, for the first time, anxious for the trial to begin. My only worry now was that Stout might somehow find out that he and Almatech were about to be attacked. I didn't want him to have an opportunity to defend himself and screw up Stanley's defense.

When it was time to go home that night, Bart came into my office with his coat on and briefcase in hand. I got the hint and started to wrap up what I was doing when Jodie rushed in. "You need to come watch the 5:00 o'clock news. They're doing a follow-up story on Cheryl Windsor and guess who they're going to interview?"

"Who?" I asked.

"Alex!"

I looked at Bart. He shook his head and then followed Jodie to the conference room. I reluctantly joined them. I had hoped never to see Alex Garcia again after our affair had been front page news but fate had decided to punish me one more time for my transgression. The media loved to dig up old love triangles so they were sure to be speculating as to whether Stan and I were lovers as well. The interview was being conducted by Ramona Mitchell and was just starting.

"Mr. Garcia, the Globe Inquirer published a story attributed to you about Cheryl Windsor mysteriously being abducted in the middle of her jury trial last year."

"Yes, Ramona," Alex replied. "I've been working on this story ever since Ms. Windsor's disappearance."

"In your story you allege that the aliens were involved in the abduction."

Alex smiled. "Yes, that's true."

"Isn't that a little far-fetched?" Ramona asked.

"No, not really. Not only was Cheryl Windsor abducted but a key witness in federal custody escaped as well. Remember the trial testimony about memory losses, time gaps, and crime scenes that were meticulously cleaned? These are not things that could be done by ordinary people. These were acts of alien beings that have infiltrated our society."

"I hear what you're saying, Alex. But what proof do you have that these aliens actually exist?"

"Well, do you remember the explosion that occurred out at Possum Kingdom Lake that same day that Cheryl Windsor disappeared?"

"Yes. The FBI has said it was unrelated to the Cheryl Windsor trial."

"Sure, that's the official line, but do you remember the photographs introduced into evidence showing that Martin Windsor was alive."

"Yes. That's what finally convinced the judge to declare a mistrial."

"Well, those photographs were taken at the exact location

where the explosions occurred later that night. So, there has to be a connection. Also, I can prove Stan Turner was at the scene of the explosion and was brought to the sheriff's office after it was over."

"So, you think Stan Turner was in on the abduction of Cheryl Windsor?"

Alex shook his head. "No, I think he had his investigators at the lake and they spotted the aliens with Cheryl Windsor, so Stan went out there to try to stop them from taking her. Unfortunately, he either got there too late, or wasn't able to stop them."

"In your story you claim the explosions were the result of the aliens blowing up the entrance to the caves that allegedly run under the lake to Cactus Island. Do you have any proof of that or is that just speculation?"

"Unfortunately, I have no proof of what happened at Cactus Island or in the tunnels under the lake, if they even exist. I think you should ask Stan Turner about that. He knows what happened to Cheryl Windsor and it's about time he told us."

"So, you haven't actually seen an alien?" Ramona asked.

"No," Alex said. "Not that I know of; however, the aliens could look just like us. You never know."

Ramona turned toward the camera, smiled broadly, and said, "This is Ramona Mitchell with Alex Garcia of the Globe Enquirer, who is asking some troubling questions about Cheryl Windsor's disappearance and attorney Stan Turner's knowledge of what actually happened that fateful day in court. Have aliens infiltrated our society? Does Stan Turner know the answer to that question? Hopefully by tomorrow night's newscast we'll have been able to talk to Stan to find out. Until then watch the skies and pray Alex Garcia is wrong. Goodnight."

Everyone turned to see Stan's reaction but he was gone. I called out for him but got no response. We searched the office but there was no trace of him or Tehra. I told Bart to check the parking garage to see if his car was there while I searched the office. A few minutes later he returned.

"His car is still there," Bart said. "I'm going to go check the john."

As Bart hurried away, I racked my brain trying to figure out where Stan would have gone. I thought maybe he'd left with Tehra to get some privacy while they tried to figure out the best way to respond to the news report, but why hadn't they taken his car? Then a horrible thought came to me. What if the aliens had taken Stan—afraid he might crack under the intense media pressure that would be coming down on him in the next twenty-four hours? My heart sank. What if they had killed him to protect their secrets. Was I next? They must realize I knew they existed. Oh, God! My heart began to pound in my chest. I couldn't breathe.

"Goddam you, Alex!" I cried.

Chapter 39

Media Crisis

Alex Garcia turned out to be smarter and more tenacious than I'd thought. Not only had he stayed on the Cheryl Windsor case long after it had gone cold, but he'd put the pieces together and come very close to figuring out the truth. I was afraid of what Kulchz' reaction to all this might be, so I thought it would be wise to contact him immediately before he had time to react. While everyone was glued to the TV, I got Tehra and we slipped out of the room. There was no time to take the car to East Texas, so I grasped the telepathic modulator and squeezed it. When I woke up, I was lying on a bed next to Tehra. We were in one of the crystal rooms I'd seen at Kulchz' headquarters. Tehra began to stir. She looked up at me.

"Are you all right?" I asked.

She sat up and put her feet over the side of the bed. "I think so," She said. "What happened?"

"I thought we should talk to Kulchz right away. I didn't want him to think for a moment that I might betray him."

"So, you used the TM?"

"Right."

Tehra nodded and stood up. " Where's Kulchz?"

"I don't know. I just woke up a moment before you."

Tehra looked around at the stark white walls. There didn't appear to be a door anywhere, but she walked over to the wall and said something in her alien language. A door materialized and she walked through it. I followed her immediately not wanting to be left in the room if the door closed after her. A lone guard stood in the hall outside our room. He motioned for us to follow him.

He led us through a complicated maze of hallways and tunnels until we reached Kulchz' office. He motioned to us to enter, so we went inside. Kulchz was seated at his desk. He looked up and smiled. "Mr. Turner. I trust your trip was satisfactory."

I shrugged. "I guess. I feel okay. How long have we been out?"

"Just a few minutes. We have to put you out for rapid transport. It's too traumatic for the conscious mind to handle."

I rolled my eyes and smiled. "I'm glad I was asleep then."

"So, why did you want to see me?"

"I think you probably know. One of the reporters from the Globe Enquirer is getting close to figuring out what happened to Cheryl Windsor. Fortunately, the Globe Enquirer is what we call a tabloid, so they don't have much credibility. What is disturbing is that the legitimate media is picking up on the story and there's going to be pressure on the FBI to look into it."

"So, how are you going to handle it?" Kulchz asked.

"Usually the best way to deal with the tabloids is to ignore them. If you respond to them, it just gives them credibility. That's why I wanted to talk to you. I didn't want you to think I had lost control of the situation."

"What about the FBI?"

"I figured that Mo could handle them. Where is Mo, anyway?" I asked.

"He's in Washington reporting to his superiors. He'll be back tomorrow."

I nodded. "Anyway. I just wanted to let you know that it might get nasty for a few days, but that nobody was going to find out about the Tarizon Project."

Kulchz studied me for a moment and then replied, "I'll trust your judgment for now, Mr. Turner. Mo assures me you are quite trustworthy, but the minute it appears your strategy isn't working, I'll have to take measures to protect the project."

I swallowed hard. "Yes, sir. I understand." I turned to Tehra. "We should get back. Paula's probably organizing a search party."

She nodded. "You're right about that."

Kulchz signaled to one of his guards, "Arrange transport for them back to Dallas."

The guard nodded and motioned for us to follow him. A few moments later we were standing in front of a small ship shaped like an arrowhead. There were two passenger compartments on both wings. Tehra was strapped in one and I in the other. Before we left they injected us with something and the world faded. When I woke up I was in Tehra's bed but she wasn't there. Then I heard banging on the door. I got up quickly and rushed into the living room. Tehra was opening the front door.

Paula barged in shaking her head. "What are you two doing? We've been looking everywhere for you."

"Ah. We just came here for a little privacy," I said. "I couldn't believe the BS your ex-lover was dishing out."

She sighed. "I know. What are you going to do?"

"Tehra and I have been talking about it, and we think the best strategy is to ignore the whole thing."

Paula frowned. "I don't know if you can do that. If you don't come out with a strong denial, people are going to think Alex is on to something."

"No, they're not. Nobody's going to believe there are really aliens running around."

Paula looked at Tehra. "Normally that would be the case, but the evidence is starting to pile up."

"It's all circumstantial. Garcia can't prove anything. No, I think the best thing to do is to ignore him and anybody who picks up on his story."

Paula signed. "Okay. I'll tell Ramona you have no comment."

"No, that sounds like we're hiding something. Tell her I think it's all a bunch of garbage and not worth talking about. Tell her I'm surprised she'd believe anything printed in the Globe Enquirer."

"Got it," Paula said. "I hope it works."

I smiled. "It will. Don't worry."

Paula looked at Tehra and then back at me. "Are you two coming back to the office," she asked, "or are you going to stay here together in the apartment all day?"

"We'll be back after lunch," I said evenly.

Paula looked over at Tehra again. Her eyes narrowed. "Tehra, are you gaining weight?"

My heart sank. Was she already showing?

"Ah, I suppose so. I've always had to watch my weight. I'm

going to have to join a health club, I guess."

After Paula had left I asked Tehra if she thought Paula might have figured out she was pregnant.

"No. I don't think so. I've only gained three pounds. She couldn't possibly know."

I raised my eyebrows. "I hope not. That would certainly complicate matters."

When we got back to the office there were lots of stares but nobody said anything to us. On my desk was a stack of phone messages from reporters and producers from local TV stations. I ripped them up and threw them in the waste basket. It was time to get back to work. The last thing we needed right now was a major distraction.

Chapter 40

The Brown Trial

It wasn't long after we'd sent out our subpoenas to Stout and his security team that we received an angry telephone call. Since the Texas criminal court only had subpoena power for a hundred-mile radius of the courthouse, we had to wait for our witnesses to come to Dallas in order to serve them. We'd got wind that they were coming to town for a meeting with EDC, one of Almatech's vendors. As they got off the plane just two days before the trial, each of them had been served by a Dallas Sheriff's deputy.

"Is this Paula Waters?" the voice asked curtly.

"Yes, it is. Who's this?"

"Carlton Stovers. I'm general counsel for Almatech Life Systems, Inc."

"Oh, yes. You must be calling about the subpoenas."

"Indeed I am. What could you possibly want with Mr. Stout and his security personnel?"

That was a fair question but I was afraid to answer it as it would telescope our trial strategy. If I didn't answer it, however, Stovers would go straight to the DA and get him all curious about what we were up to. I had to come up with something plausible, yet not alarm them.

"Well, I'm afraid I can't discuss that other than to say that each of these witnesses arrived in Dallas a day or two before the Brown murders. Since they travel in the same circles as Mr. Brown, we know their paths crossed. We believe they may have some relevant information about the murders."

"You're going to detain them for several days hoping they might know something that would help your client?"

"It's more than hope. We're pretty confident they do know something."

"Why don't I make them available to you this afternoon? You'll see that they know nothing and they can be on there way."

"That is very kind of you, but it's too close to trial to do that. I need every minute for to get ready."

"Do you realize how much it will cost Almatech to have it's chairman held up for a week?"

"No, but I suspect Mr. Stout can conduct his business from his hotel room for a week without much trouble. If you will agree to produce him within 30 minutes of my phone call, I won't insist that he sit outside the courtroom for the duration of the trial."

"I'm going to make some phone calls. This is ridiculous. Mr. Stout is not going to be held hostage here for a week."

We expected jury selection to take just a few days and the prosecution's case in chief almost a week. That would mean Stout and his men would have been detained more than ten days before we could even call them for the trial. I knew by reputation Stout wasn't a patient man and I didn't want to have to fight a major battle with him before the real trial even began, so I offered a compromise.

"Listen, I'll tell you what I'll agree to. If Mr. Stout and his men show up in court the first day, I'll have them sworn in and they can leave town as long as they agree to be back on 24 hours notice."

Stovers didn't immediately reply, but after a moment he said, "Well, that's certainly a more reasonable proposal. I'll talk to Mr. Stout and see if he can live with it."

"Good. If they get to court by 8:45 a.m. I'll have them out of there by nine."

I wasn't worried about Stout and his men not showing up. Being a man who lived off of government contracts, he couldn't afford to have an arrest warrant out for him for contempt of court. But if he did decide to blow it off, it wouldn't necessarily be a bad thing. I could introduce all the evidence against Stout and Almatech and then point out that they decided to run rather than answer the charges. A jury might just draw some interesting conclusions from that.

Before the November 11th trial was set to begin, we spent the weekend discussing prosecution witnesses, probing the weaknesses in the prosecution's case, preparing Stanley to testify, if need be, and going over every piece of evidence we knew would be tendered at trial. Paul and his men concentrated on making sure all of our witnesses had been served and would be in the courtroom by eight-thirty Monday morning. At eleven o'clock the night before the trial was to begin, I was still working on my trial outline. I couldn't decide in what order to call my witnesses. When Bart walked by on his way to the kitchen I asked him about it.

"Do you think I should call Stanley first or last?"

Bart thought a moment. "I don't know. I suppose you should get his testimony out of the way in the beginning. He can deny any involvement and then you can concentrate on our alternate theory."

"But if Francis rips him a part in cross examination the jury may not listen to our alternate theory."

"True. I suppose you could put on our other witnesses and see how it goes. If you feel confident that you've created reasonable doubt, then you won't need Stanley to testify."

"Right," I said.

"But if our theory doesn't go over that well, then you can call Stanley and hope he's convincing."

"How will I know how well it's going? We can't talk to the jurors," I asked.

"Maybe we should hire some mock jurors to sit in the gallery. We can question them at the end of each day to get their impressions on how your case is going."

"That's a good idea. Will you take care of that for me?"

"Sure, I'll get right on it."

"Thanks."

When I looked out my front window Monday morning, it was raining. The DJ on the radio indicated the temperature was 42 degrees. I hated cold weather as it was hard to dress for court. It would be cold on the drive in, but the courtroom would be warm once I got there. Bart brought me a cup of coffee and handed it to me as I was trying to decide what outfit to wear. A grey wool skirt and a fancy white blouse finally won out. Bart wore a grey suit and dark blue tie.

A mob of reporters met us as we entered the courthouse from the parking garage. Bart led the way through the throng responding with a curt "no comment" to any questions that were thrown out. Soon we were in the elevator and ascending to the sixth floor.

"Are you as nervous as I am?" I asked.

"No," Bart replied. "Second chair's a piece cake compared to your job."

I sighed. "Yeah, you've got that right."

Walter Stanley was already seated at the defense table when we entered the courtroom. He greeted us with an enthusiastic smile. Richard Francis and his assistant were conversing with Detective Rhodes in front of the bench. I nodded when our eyes met. I looked around automatically looking for Stan, but I knew he wouldn't be there. It didn't make sense to have three attorneys tied up on one case, particularly when Stan had his own cases to get ready for trial. If I needed him, though, he said he'd be there in a heartbeat. I didn't think I would, but it was nice to know he was waiting in the wings if needed.

At 8:30 a.m. the judge took the bench and we started the jury selection process. Richard Francis began by telling the jury panel about the case and then spent the entire day meticulously questioning each member about their lives, past experiences, prejudices, and knowledge of the case. It wasn't until afternoon on Tuesday that he finally turned the lectern over to me. As he had already done a thorough job, I didn't spend much time with any particular juror, but just chatted awhile about the case, the burden of proof, and what was expected of the jury. My objective was simply to establish a little rapport with each juror, so when the testimony began they would listen attentively to what I had to say. It was around three on Tuesday afternoon after the permanent jury had been seated that Richard Francis began his opening statement.

"Ladies and gentlemen of the jury. We are gathered here today because of a horrible tragedy that occurred on August 9th—a fire that took the lives of an entire family while they slept peacefully in their beds. Curtis Brown was a father, a husband, and an internationally renowned scientist for the Technology Institute. Gladys Brown, his devoted wife and his three young children also died in that same quickly spreading fire that we will show was deliberately set by the defendant, Walter Stanley.

"Why would Mr. Stanley, a neighbor and fellow member of the Collin Common's Homeowner's Association, want to kill Curtis Brown? Well, as with many tragedies the animosity sprung from a simple annoyance–Mr. Stanley's barking dog. Later, that escalated to complaints to animal control and the police and threats of physical violence. Stanley even blamed his divorce on Curtis Brown and his barking dog, Pretty Boy. Finally, perhaps the straw that broke the camel's back was a controversy that developed over a chainlink fence.

"The Covenants, Conditions, and Restrictions of the Collin Common's Homeowner's Association prohibited the construction of any fence without the approval and consent of the architectural control committee. The covenants further stated that only wood fences constructed of pine, cedar, or redwood were allowed. Mr. Brown, however, disregarded those covenants and had a chainlink fence built around his back yard.

"This infuriated Mr. Brown and prompted an altercation at the homeowner's association meeting on August 6, 1992, just three days before the fire. At the meeting the defendant yelled and screamed at Mr. Brown and the two almost came to blows. So, we will show that when Mr. Brown the next day called his fence contractor and gave them the go ahead to install the fence, that Mr. Stanley was outraged. So outraged, in fact, that he began to concoct a plan to make Chester Brown pay for what he'd done.

"Now I don't know what was going through Walter Stanley's head the day of the fire. Nobody but he does. Maybe when he went to Tom Thumb to purchase a steak to lure Pretty Boy away, his intention was only to burn the house down, not to murder five innocent people, but it doesn't matter. The judge will instruct you that if Mr. Brown went on the property to commit a felony and someone died, that is murder, even if he never intended to kill anyone.

"So, after you've listened to the testimony, scrutinized all the evidence, and considered the judge's instructions I'm confident you will come to the only reasonable conclusion, which is that Walter Stanley is guilty on all five counts of murder and that he should receive the maximum sentence for this heinous crime–death by lethal injection."

As Francis took his seat a low murmur erupted in the gallery. Walter Stanley swallowed hard and looked over at me. I tried to give him a reassuring smile, but I'm not sure it was very convincing. It was now time for me to give my opening statement. Whereas Stan liked to let the prosecution put on its entire case before he said a word, I believed many jurors made up their minds about a defendant's guilt or innocence the very first day of the trial. If that was the case, I wanted them to know that we had a defense and intended to prove it. Who was right? I don't know. So, when the judge asked if I wanted to make an opening statement, I said, "Yes, I do, Your Honor."

The judge nodded and I stood up and addressed the jury. "Ladies and gentlemen. Your Honor. Mr. Francis has told you a fascinating story about an alleged feud between Walter Stanley and Chester Brown that started with a barking dog and escalated to murder. If he is right then this feud will, no doubt, be right up there with the Hatfields and the McCoys. But remember the Judge's instructions. You must listen to all the testimony and weigh all the evidence before you make up your minds. And believe me, we will have a lot of testimony and tangible evidence pointing to other persons who had much stronger motives to kill Chester Brown than Walter Stanley.

"There hasn't been much said about Chester Brown yet. Well, let me tell you he wasn't just an ordinary citizen. Mr. Brown was a brilliant man who was the lead engineer on a top secret government project. Because it is top secret, I can't tell you much about it other than to say that if it was successful, it would have insured our military superiority over all other nations for decades into the future.

"In the next few days we're going to tell you about Mr. Brown's employer, Technology Institute, and its competitor, Almatech Life Systems, who fought a bitter battle to get a lucrative government contract. We will call witnesses who will put members of an elite Almatech security team in Chester Brown's neighborhood just days before the fire. More importantly we'll call upon the arson investigator who will tell you that this was not just your simple gasoline-and-a-match arson, but one that was created by a sophisticated triggering device that was way beyond the capability of the defendant Walter

Stanley to design and set up.

"As the Judge told you, the burden of proof rests with the prosecution. They must prove beyond all reasonable doubt that Walter Stanley is guilty. We're confident that when all is said and done Walter Stanley will be the least likely person to have killed the Brown family. Walter Stanley's only gripes were a barking dog and a chainlink fence; hardly motive for killing five innocent people. Almatech Life Systems lost millions of dollars because of Chester Brown's decision to work for TI. We will show that Almatech's CEO, T. Robert Stout, was bitter about losing that contract and vowed to somehow wrestle it away from TI. That would have been impossible with Chester Brown in the picture, but if he was dead that was a different story.

"So, please don't jump to any conclusions in this case until all the witnesses have testified and all the evidence has been presented. This is not a simple case as the prosecution would have you believe. It's very complex and there is a lot at stake, so please listen carefully and keep an open mind. Things may not be the way they seem. Thank you."

I sat down and looked over at the jurors. Most of them sat emotionless, impossible to read. One man, however, nodded slowly and smiled at me. Had what I said struck a chord with him? There was no way to know for sure, but I got a feeling I'd connected with this juror and he'd be listening to the upcoming testimony with an open mind. I just prayed the others would be doing the same.

Chapter 41

Sabotage

Paula insisted that she and Bart could handle the Brown trial. I protested, but she reminded me that I not only had Charlotte Wenzel's murder case coming up for trial soon but Ben Stover's bankruptcy fraud case as well. My problem was that I was at a dead end on both cases. I didn't know what I should be doing next to prepare for either one of them. One thought did occur to me, though. I had joked that Paula should go check out the bank in the Cayman Islands to see if there was any evidence that Ralph Herman had been there to set up an account in the name of Stover Enterprises, Ltd. If we could prove that, Ben Stover would be off the hook.

Due to the bank secrecy laws there was no way I would be able to get information on the account on my own, so the thought occurred to me that I should bring Alice along with me as a representative of the company. It would be a good diversion for her anyway and make her feel like she was doing something to help free her husband. When I called her she jumped on the idea.

"Yes, when do we leave?"

"Tomorrow if you're game," I said. "Could you drive up and meet us at DFW Airport?"

"No. Problem, just let me know the time and the gate and I'll be there. I'm so glad you called. Surely we can find some evidence to prove Ralph set up that account."

"You'd think so. Keep your fingers crossed."

I thought about enlisting Mo's help, but then thought better of it. I'd bring Tehra with me in case I needed her to babysit Alice while I checked out any leads. Since the FBI had probably already paid a visit to the Royal Bank, I decided it would be prudent to tell

Thomas Stokely, the assistant U.S. Attorney, my plans, so he could alert the local authorities that I was coming. I didn't want any trouble. I put a call in to him.

"I want to know immediately if you find anything," Stokely said. "I don't want any surprises on the day of trial."

"Don't worry. I'm hoping to find something good so you'll drop the case."

"Yeah, well I'm not holding my breath."

"We'll be leaving tomorrow and should be back by Monday. I'll call you either way as soon as we touch down."

"Good. I'll be expecting your call."

I was glad Stokely wasn't a jerk like many of the other prosecutors I'd been up against. He seemed genuinely sympathetic with my client's plight. Perhaps it was because he knew in his heart that Herman had set Ben up and was hoping we'd be able to prove it. But I'd known a few prosecutors who'd seemed nice on the surface, but were just looking for an opportunity to stick my client in the back. I had to assume Stokely was capable of that and be on my guard. There was too much a stake to do otherwise.

When I told Tehra we were taking a trip to the Carribean, she was excited. "Good. I was hoping to do some sightseeing before I return to Tarizon. All I've ever seen on Earth is Texas and the Gulf Coast."

"Well, we'll fly to Miami and maybe spend the day sightseeing and then catch a morning flight to the Grand Caymans. It's only about an eighty minute flight."

"Do I have time to go buy some sports clothes?" Tehra asked.

"Sure. You have the rest of the day. Buy a swim suit. I want a demonstration of your aquatic skills."

She smiled. "I usually don't wear a swimsuit in the water."

My pulse quickened. "Well, that wouldn't bother me, but if the other people on the beach saw your gills and built-in swim fins, it might be too much for them."

She shook her head. "What do you want me to do? Wear a wetsuit?"

I laughed. "I guess you're right. Anyway, we'll leave in the morning. If you don't find something you need today we can pick it up in Miami tomorrow."

"Great. This will fun!"

When I got home, I told Rebekah about the trip. She wasn't thrilled to hear I was going to the Carribean without her, but she and Alice were good friends, so when I told her the purpose of the trip she didn't put up as much of a fuss as I had expected. She did make me promise to be very careful, which I fully intended to do anyway after what had happened to Paula in the British Virgin Islands.

Bright and early the next morning I picked up Tehra and we drove to DFW Airport. We met Alice at curbside check-in and went together through security and to the gate. We had over an hour before our flight, so we stopped in at McDonalds and got coffee and some breakfast. While we were eating I asked Alice about Ben.

"He's hanging in there," she said. "I visited him on Sunday. I told him about the trip, so he's hopeful we'll find something."

"How's his health?"

"He's had a couple of episodes and had to take his nitro, but that's not unusual for him."

I shook my head. "I'm so sorry you're having to go through this. Ralph is a real bastard."

"I'm just glad we have you to get us out of this mess," Alice replied, "otherwise, there'd be no hope."

"Well, there's always hope. Sometimes you've just got to trust in God to get you through the day."

"Amen to that."

"Have you ever been to George Town?" Tehra asked.

"Yes, we stopped there on a cruise one time, but I swear I didn't open any bank accounts."

I laughed. "Yeah, I doubt I'd open one up either. I like having my money where I can get my hands on it in a hurry."

"I've never been even been to Miami," Tehra said. "I'm really looking forward to this trip."

“It’s been overrun by the Cubans,” Alice said. “It’s like visiting Havana.”

Tehra laughed. “Really? I can’t wait to see it.”

“One thing for sure, though, the Cubans know how to party. If you like to dance I’ll take you to one of the Cuban clubs in town.”

"That would be wonderful!"

"I doubt we'll have time for that," I interjected.

"Well, when we get you to the Grand Caymans, you've can swim with the stingrays. That's great fun. The water is so clear you can see every fish in the water."

"So I've heard."

"Again, I don't know how much time we'll have for sightseeing. Remember this is a working vacation."

"I insist you show Tehra all the sights of the islands. God only knows when she'll ever get back there again."

I looked into Tehra's eyes and saw a sadness I hadn't seen before. Was she regretting the fact that she'd have to return to Tarizon soon? I certainly didn't want her to go. She looked away.

"Oh, I suspect we'll find time to do a little sightseeing," I said, "and the Sundowner Hotel is right on the Seven Mile Beach. Maybe we can get in a little snorkeling."

When we got to our gate our flight was about ready to board. We sat down to wait and Alice excused herself to go the restroom. It suddenly occurred to me that Tehra had probably never flown in an airplane. Of course, she'd flown in a spaceship, but that was probably very different from a 727.

"So, what's it like to travel in space?" I asked. "Do you travel in seats like we do on an airplane?"

She shook her head. "No, as soon as you get aboard they put you in a transport cylinder, attach a breathing apparatus, monitors, a feeding tube, and then close it up. They immediately sedate you and you sleep for the duration of the trip."

"That sounds pretty boring," I said.

"Not really. It's like going to bed and waking up in the morning. It hardly seems like any time at all."

"How long does a trip to Earth take?"

"Almost a year. It's a long way to Tarizon. Luckily you don't age while you travel."

"Why is that?"

"I don't know exactly. There's a scientific explanation for it, but I wasn't very good in science."

"Me either. I'm not sure how I passed any math classes in

college."

Alice made it back just in time to board the plane. The captain advised us the flight to Miami was an hour and forty minutes. That would give me plenty of time to think about our game plan once we made it to George Town. I got out a legal pad and started thinking about possibilities. We'd visit the bank, of course, get copies of everything in the bank's files, but that might not prove anything. We needed witnesses—people who could verify that Ralph Herman or his buddy Eiseman had been in the Cayman Islands. That would go a long way toward meeting our objective.

I'd brought along pictures of Herman and Eiseman to show to bellhops and bartenders in hopes someone might recognize them. It was a longshot but if either had been in town somebody should have seen them. I asked Alice what Ralph would do for fun on the island.

"Scuba diving or deep sea fishing," she replied. "He was always a big sportsman."

"Okay, after we go to the bank tomorrow, we'll hit all the marinas and see if anyone remembers seeing our guys."

"There must be dozens of marinas," Alice remarked.

I nodded. "No doubt, but I don't know how else to do it."

"Why don't we split up so we can cover more territory. I'll hit the hotel bars while you two go to the marinas," Alice suggested.

I shrugged. "That's fine, but are you sure you want to be on your own?"

"Oh, yeah. I'm a big girl. Besides, I'm very comfortable in hotel bars."

I laughed. "Okay, whatever."

"That's a good idea," Tehra said. "We should split up too. I'll go to the scuba and gift shops and you can check out the deep sea fishing boats."

I folded my arms. "Well, I promise I'll take a bath tomorrow."

They laughed. "It's not that," Tehra said. "But Alice is right, we've got a lot of ground to cover. Someone must have seen Ike or Ralph, so we just have to keep looking until we find them."

When we got to Miami we caught a cab to our hotel and then went across the street to a the Lighthouse Restaurant for seafood. We stuffed ourselves and drank too much wine. At eleven we went back to our rooms. I was just climbing into bed when I heard a knock on the door. It had to be Tehra since nobody knew I was in Miami. I opened the door and she rushed past me.

"Why did you waste money on separate rooms. I'm not going to sleep alone when you're just down the hall."

"Yes you are. The last time we slept together I ended up in the hospital."

"I know. But that won't happen this time."

"Rebekah and Alice are friends. If she saw us together–"

Tehra shook her head. "It's so silly how you Earth people worry about who you sleep with."

"Well, that's just the way it is. I'm sorry."

"I'll go back to my room before she wakes up. I'm just so sick of being alone and you're the only person I can be with and not worry about them finding out my secret."

She was right. It had to be hard on her. I sighed and pointed to the empty double bed. "Help yourself." She looked at it, frowned, and then climbed into my bed. I shook my head, turned out the light, and climbed in beside her. I felt her arms encircle me and the warmth of her body as she cuddled up against my back. I didn't dare turn and face her. There was no kissing this girl. It was way too dangerous.

When I awoke the next morning she was gone. I wondered how she'd left without waking me up. I felt a little groggy. Had she had her way with me again? I struggled to remember but there was nothing there except the memory of her cuddling up behind me. The clock radio said it was 7:20 a.m. We had agreed to meet in the hotel café for breakfast at 8 a.m. Then we were going to hop a city tour bus and see the sights. The bus traveled a route all around the city and you could hop on and off at will. It was a good way to check out the sights and not be rushed.

After showering and getting dressed, I made it to the café just five minutes late. The ladies were already there talking excitedly. I slipped into a chair next to Tehra. She smiled when she saw me. A waiter came over and poured me a cup of coffee. It was a buffet so we all got up and filled our plates and then returned to the table.

"So, did you sleep well, Alice?" I asked.

"Yes, like a log. I was so tired last night," Alice replied.

"That lobster was something else, wasn't it?"

"Oh, God yes and the clams were so tender."

"Tehra, I noticed you really liked the sushi," Alice said. "Ben likes it too, but I've never cared for it."

"Cooking the fish takes out all the flavor," Tehra replied. "I've always preferred my fish raw."

"She's part dolphin," I remarked.

Alice laughed. Tehra gave me a look.

"Just kidding! She swims like a dolphin, though. At least that's what she tells me. I haven't actually seen her do it yet."

Tehra gave me another look. "You're in a good mood today," she said wryly.

"Yes," I replied. "I think it was the best night's sleep I've had in months. It's funny how you can just hit the pillow and wake up eight hours later with no memory of all that precious time."

Tehra stifled a smile. Alice said, "Yes, sleep is such a waste of time. Just think how much more we could accomplish if we had an extra eight hours every day."

"Unfortunately, most people would just spend it on the sofa, pigging out and watching bad TV," I noted.

"True," Alice said. "Fortunately, Ben and I never watched that much TV. We've always been in business for ourselves, so there was never time for it."

"Perhaps I'll show you my aquatic skills in the pool tonight, Stan," Tehra said casually.

I looked up. "Really? I can't wait for that."

Alice gave us a disapproving look. She must have taken it for flirting. I'd have to be more careful. I didn't want Alice calling Rebekah warning her about Tehra. That night after our excursion, Tehra asked me if I really wanted to go to the pool and see her swim. I said, absolutely, but later, when nobody was around and Alice was in bed. She agreed to meet me there a 11:00 p.m. When I arrived in my swim wear at the indoor pool I was relieved to see it was deserted. A few minutes later Tehra arrived wearing a white terrycloth bathrobe. When she took it off she looked like any other naked female athlete except for the two slits that ran down both sides beneath her breasts. Her feet appeared normal until she stepped into the water and her toes seemed to swell and protrude outward connected by a thick webbing. Her hands did the same thing.

"Whoa! How do you do that?"

"I don't know. It just happens when I get in the water."

I was a good swimmer and when I was young I had spent a lot of time in the high school pool near where I lived. In Boy Scouts I'd even earned my swimming merit badge by swimming a mile, but I was no match for Tehra who did three laps to every one of mine.

"You're slow and in terrible shape. You wouldn't last long living in the sea."

"Yeah. Maybe twenty minutes."

She laughed. "You should put a pool in your backyard and keep in shape."

"Have you been talking to my kids? They've been after me for years to get a pool."

"So, why don't you do it?"

"Rebekah isn't keen on the idea. She's a nurse and always fears the worst."

Tehra nodded. Her stomach was starting to bulk up a bit. She'd be showing soon. Then people would start to talk. I wondered how long it would take for them to figure out what happened. When I looked over at her she had a serious expression on her face.

"What's wrong?" I asked.

"I heard from the Loyalists. The civil war has come to Earth. It's time to choose sides."

"On, Jesus. What do they want you to do?"

"They said I should sabotage our base. They gave me orders on how to do it."

"How could you sabotage it by yourself? It's under heavy guard."

"There are Loyalists on the base who will help me. I have to find a way to get into the main control room. Once there I can initiate the self destruct mechanism built into the computers. I have the access and command codes."

"How much time will you have to get out after you do it?"

"Three minutes."

"Well, I've found a safe place for you to hide once it's over, but how will you get back to Tarizon?"

"The Loyalists have a ship on the way. It will be here in a few weeks. They'll take back anyone who wants to join the Loyalist's movement."

"Just a few weeks?"

"Yes, so you won't have to worry about our secret being revealed."

I sighed. "I don't care about that. I don't want you to go."

"Yes, you do. I can see it in your eyes. You love your family and would be devastated if anything happened to destroy that relationship." She shook her head. "It's funny, before I came to Earth I had no concept of love, but now I'm starting to feel its relentless power. So, it's a good thing I'm leaving. I'm not sure I could resist it."

"Relentless. Yes, love is that and more. You are starting to understand. . . . Okay, when the time comes, just tell me how I can help. I don't like Kulchz much and I want to do whatever I can to stop the abduction of innocent Earth children."

That night she went back to her room and I didn't see her until morning. We had an early flight to the Grand Cayman Island, so right after breakfast we went to the airport. We arrived in George Town before noon on Saturday. We had planned the trip for the weekend because we thought there would be more personnel working at hotels, bars, stores, and other resort facilities then than at any other time. This would thus increase our odds at finding someone who had seen Ike or Ralph. We had to find a witness or some other convincing proof that Ralph had set up the account at the Royal Bank or Ben Stover would probably go to federal prison. A man in good health might survive that ordeal and come out with many good years ahead, but with Ben's health he'd probably die in prison. It was an unbearable thought. I couldn't let it happen. I just couldn't let Alice down. The proof had to be here somewhere; in my heart I knew it.

Chapter 42

The Prosecution

The Stanley case was moving incredibly fast. On Wednesday Francis called his first witness, Detective Riley Rhodes. Rhodes was a man of small stature but he dressed well and talked with confidence and authority. The jury seemed very attentive. Francis asked him what he found when he got to the Brown house on the night of the fire.

"The Brown's two story townhouse was at the end of the street. When I got there, just a minute or so behind the fire department, there were three trucks working the blaze and several police cars parked in front and in the alley behind the house. The spectators who had been drawn to the fire were being kept across the street or down the sidewalk to the east. I parked on the side street and walked up the alley to the back of the house.

"The smoke was so thick and the fire so hot, I couldn't get very close. Flames were protruding out from the wood shingled roof. There were several explosions. A fireman had managed to open the garage door and I noticed that there were two cars in the garage, a black 1990 BMW and a grey 1992 Honda Accord. The Accord was on fire and already heavily damaged.

"Several firemen tried to enter the house to rescue the family but the fire was so intense they were forced back. It was pretty clear to me that there would be no survivors. I've seen a lot of fires, but none like this one."

"What was different about it?" Francis asked.

"Its speed and the intensity for one thing. It engulfed the house so quickly and completely that the firemen were helpless to do anything but watch. Normally, they can put a fire out very quickly and often save much of the structure, but there was no chance with this fire."

"So, while the firemen were trying to put out the blaze, what were you doing?"

"I secured the area as best I could and got a couple officers to begin looking for witnesses. While they were doing that I began a careful inspection of the perimeter."

"Did you find anything?"

"Yes, several things. First, there was evidence that a dog lived in the backyard. There was a dog run and a chain, but no dog. The back gate was opened and I found what appeared to be blood on the concrete stepping stones leading out of the gate."

"Did you find the dog?"

"I didn't, but Animal Control picked it up the following morning running loose several miles away."

"After the fire cooled did you inspect the premises?"

"Yes. There wasn't much left of the structure but we did sift through it and found charred skeletal remains. It's presumed the remains were of Mr. and Mrs. Brown and their three children."

"Were the bodies intact?"

"No, they were pretty well incinerated, but there were portions that could be identified as bones and body parts."

"Were you able to recover any records or personal property kept in the town home?"

"No. Everything was destroyed."

"Did you find any evidence as to what might have caused the fire?"

"The cause of the fire was arson. A lock was cut on the back gate, the back door into the garage was forced open with a crowbar it looked like, and there was an odor of kerosene everywhere. From the garage the perp was able to gain access to the kitchen and the rest of the house."

"Were you able to determine how the fire spread so quickly and consumed the home the way it did?"

"Well, we found remnants of several propane canisters not only in the garage, but in the kitchen and the living room as well. The arsonist may have placed the canisters in strategic points around the house and then opened them slightly so they would explode when the fire got hot. The electronic fire sensors were disabled as well."

There was a murmur from the gallery. Stanley swallowed hard and slouched in his seat.

"So, by engulfing the bottom floor in flames so quickly the perpetrator made sure the Brown family couldn't escape."

"Objection!" I said. "Calls for speculation."

"Sustained," the judge said.

Francis shrugged and continued. "Anything other than kerosene and the propane canisters?"

"No, nothing else that was obviously connected to the fire."

"Thank you, Detective," Francis said and sat down.

"The judge looked at me. "Ms. Waters, your witness."

There wasn't much to dispute about Detective Rhodes' testimony, but I did have a few things I wanted to clarify. "Detective, to summarize your testimony, it's your opinion that someone cut the lock to the Brown's back gate, forced their way into the garage, spread kerosene around the first floor of the dwelling, and then strategically placed propane canisters around the house so they would explode as the fire got hotter."

"Yes, that sums it up pretty good."

"Isn't it true the Browns liked to barbeque and kept several backup propane canisters so they'd never run out?"

"I wouldn't know about that."

"But the canisters you found could have belonged to the Browns? They did have a barbeque, isn't that right?"

"Yes, they had a fairly large one on their patio."

"Did you find any kerosene lamps in the rubble?"

"Well, yes we found some kerosene lamps used for camping."

"Yes, the Brown kids liked to camp, didn't they?"

"I wouldn't know—"

"Well, I assure you they did, so the smell of kerosene after the fire wouldn't be that unusual would it. Couldn't we presume that Mr. Brown would keep some around to use when they went camping or around the patio for ambiance?"

"Yes, but we smelled it all over the house."

"Was there any wind the day of the fire?"

"Well, yes. There was a moderate breeze."

"So, the smell of kerosene could have blown over the whole crime scene?"

Rhodes shrugged. "It's possible."

"What else did you find in the debris that you haven't told us about?"

"Huh? What do you mean?"

"Didn't you find some remnants of electronic equipment?"

"Well, yes. Mr. Brown was a scientist so there was a lot of electronic equipment in the house."

"Didn't you find any remains of the triggering devices?"

"That was not confirmed. I know the arson investigator thought he found some remnants of a triggering device, but what he found was inconclusive."

"But it's possible the fire was remotely set?"

Rhodes shook his head. "It's possible, but I don't–"

I didn't wait for him to finish. He'd said enough for me to go to my next question. How could Walter Stanley possibly have the expertise to disable the fire alarm and install a remote triggering device? It made no sense.

"Did you have an occasion to investigate the defendant's background?" I asked.

"Yes, we've done extensive background checks on Mr. Stanley."

"In the course of those investigations did you come up with any evidence that Walter Stanley had any knowledge or training in electronics, weaponry, explosives, or other related disciplines?"

"No, nothing along those lines came up."

"Then how do you suppose he could have managed to build and set a triggering device to remotely set the Brown fire?"

Detective Rhodes shrugged. "I don't think he did. It was simply a matter of kerosene and a match."

"But, assuming a triggering device were used, could he have done it?"

"Objection!" Francis exclaimed.

The judge looked at Francis. "I'll allow it."

Rhodes rolled his eyes. "I told you. I don't think he used one, but if he did, maybe he bought it from someone."

"Where would someone buy a triggering device like the one used to set the fire?"

"Objection, assumes facts not in evidence," Francis spat.

"Withdrawn. Sorry. Where would someone buy a triggering device like that?'

"Not at the hardware store, that's for sure," Rhodes snickered.

"Then where? " I pressed.

"I don't know. I've never bought one."

I nodded. "Nor have I. It's not something an ordinary citizen would know how to acquire, is it?

"No. I wouldn't think so."

"Thank you, Detective, no further questions."

The judge looked at Francis. "Any redirect?"

Francis shook his head.

"You may step down," the Judge advised. "Call your next witness."

Francis' next witness was the Collin County Medical Examiner, Dr. Winfield. He testified that there wasn't much left of the bodies after the fire had spent itself, but he had managed to confirm the identity of one of the children through dental records. He said he was unable to positively identify any of the other bodies, but that there were remnants of five distinct individuals in various parts of the house. Due to the time the fire broke out, he assumed they were all in bed asleep at the time of the fire. He indicated it was possible that they died in their sleep and never knew what had happened.

Charles Stewart, the arson investigator, took the stand next and confirmed much of Detective Rhode's testimony, however, when I asked him about the triggering device he disagreed with the detective.

"Yes, I found pieces of telephone receivers, parts of blasting caps, and other paraphernalia that would be used in making a remote triggering device."

"So, you don't buy Detective Rhodes theory that Walter Stanley just broke in, opened up the canisters, spread kerosene around, and then lit a match."

"Well, it could have happened that way but that is inconsistent with the physical evidence."

"Let's say for argument's sake that a triggering mechanism was used. Could Walter Stanley have configured the triggering device to remotely set the Brown fire?

He laughed. "There is no way a man off the street would have a clue how to use, let alone configure, that type of a triggering device. It is a highly complex piece of electronic equipment that would have to be handled by an expert."

"Thank you, Mr. Stewart. No further questions."

The judge looked at Francis. "Any redirect?"

Francis stood. "Yes, Your Honor. Mr. Stewart. Are you absolutely sure this triggering device started the fire?"

"Well, not completely but—"

"So, the mere presence of possible remnants of a device doesn't really prove anything conclusively. The fire could have been started by a match, right?"

"It's possible but why would there be remnants of triggering device in the rubble?"

"Perhaps these were remnants of other electronic devices that had nothing to do with triggering a fire."

"What about the blasting caps?"

"Maybe these pieces were left to throw you off. Have you thought about that possibility?" Francis asked. "It would have been easy for Stanley to take apart a telephone and then drop it near one of the canisters just to make you think the fire was remotely set."

Stewart shrugged. "Well, I guess anything's possible."

"Thank you, sir. No further questions."

After Stewart left the stand, the judge recessed the trial until the following day at 10:00 a.m. As I watched the crowd disburse, Stanley turned to me and asked, "So, what do you think? The prosecutor's case seems pretty believable, huh?"

I turned and smiled at Stanley. "Yes, it does and by the time Francis is done, a lot of people will think you're guilty, but then it's our turn. After we've put on our case a lot of people won't know what to think. At least that's what I'm counting on."

Stanley sighed. "I'm just so scared. What if they convict me? I don't want to die."

"Let's not even think like that," I said. "You've got to be positive. It's important not to look totally depressed to the jury. They may think you have a guilty conscience or have given up because you know you are guilty. I want to see you smiling once in awhile."

Stanley took a deep breath and shook his head slowly. "I don't know if I can do that. I'm not a good actor."

"Then start believing in yourself and in me so you don't have to act," I suggested.

He nodded. "Okay, I'll try to be positive."

"Good. I'll see you in the morning."

The bailiff took Stanley away and as he disappeared through a side door, a horrible feeling came over me. What if he was right to be pessimistic? What if the jury thought our theory was a bunch of crap and didn't buy a word of it? With five victims, Walter Stanley would get the death penalty. There was no doubt about that. Had we taken too great a risk insinuating that Almatech Life Systems and T. Robert Stout were behind the Brown murders? I prayed to God we hadn't.

Chapter 43

Rendezvous

Saturday afternoon we rented three cars and began to implement our revised and expanded game plan. Alice had a long list of hotels and restaurants to visit. Tehra headed to the scuba and dive shops and myriad of gifts stores wherever there were tourists. I went to the Marinas to see if Ike or Ralph had given in to their passion for deep sea fishing.

Starting at the Cayman Angling Club I acquired a list of recommended charter boats and guides. Each had a description of the trips they provided. The first one advertised a beautiful 44 foot custom performance open fishing vessel for up to six persons powered by three 250 horsepower Evenrudes that would get you to your destination in the blink of an eye. The perfect boat, they claimed, for deep sea or drift fishing over the Cayman Wall and catching your dream fish–a 100 pound tuna or a giant marlin. The luxurious fishing boat came with a fully equipped Penn International Reels, ice coolers, purified water, soft drinks, bathroom, and fresh water showers.

As I perused the rest of the brochure, a feeling of hopelessness crept over me. There were hundreds of charter boat companies. How could I possibly cover them all? Finally, I took a breath and began. At each location I talked to everyone I saw and showed them the two photos of Ike and Ralph. By mid-afternoon I'd covered about a third of the charter companies and had talked to hundreds of employees, fisherman, and anyone else I'd seen, but had come up empty handed. As I was leaving one of the marinas, a police officer approached me and flashed his badge.

"Hello, sir, I'm officer Stuart Brim with the RCIP."

"The what?"

"The Royal Cayman Island Police."

"Oh, hi, I'm Stan Turner."

"Do you have some identification?"

"Yes, of course," I said and fished into my pocket for my passport. I finally found it and handed it to officer Brim.

He looked it over and then asked, "What is your business today in the Cayman Islands?"

"Oh, actually I'm doing a little detective work. Your office should have been contacted by the Collin County District Attorney's office in Texas. I'm an attorney in Dallas and have a client who allegedly opened up a bank account here in the Caymans and stashed some money in it. He denies it and I'm trying to find evidence that perhaps someone else set it up."

He nodded. "Yes, we were told you would be here. You should have checked in at the Central Police Station before you started questioning people."

"Oh, I'm sorry. I didn't realize that."

"I guess we'll let it go this time. At least we knew you were coming. . . . Any luck in your search?"

"No, I'm afraid not."

"You've been showing some photos to people, I've been told."

"Yes," I said and pulled the photos out of my pocket. I handed them to the officer and he looked them over closely.

"Who are these two men?" he asked.

"Ike Eiseman and Ralph Herman. They are both from Waco, Texas."

He nodded and then handed back the photos. "I haven't seen either of these men, but if you'd like I'll run the names on our database and see if anything comes up. What exactly are you looking for?"

"Ah. Well, I need to prove that one or both of them were in the Cayman Islands during last June or July. We think one of them set up the account in our client's name and then transferred over a hundred thousand dollars into it without authority."

"Where can I reach you if I find anything?"

"I'm staying with two friends at the Sundowner Hotel."

He wrote the name down in a tablet. "All right. Thank you and good luck with your search."

Officer Brim left and I continued on to the next marina on my list. Several hours later I looked at my watch and saw it was 5:30 p.m. I had agreed to meet Tehra and Alice back in the lobby of our hotel at 6:00 p.m. so, I turned the car around and headed back to the hotel. Neither of them were there when I arrived. I waited until 6:30 p.m. but when they still hadn't showed up I went up to their rooms. Neither were in their rooms so I went to mine and called the front desk.

"Have you seen my friends Alice Stover and Ms. Connolly?"

"Yes, sir. They were in the lobby earlier, about quarter to six or so. They left with three men just before you arrived."

“They did?” I said confused by this revelation.

"What did the men look like?"

"One was tall, heavy set with a beard and the other two were medium height athletic types."

"Military, perhaps?"

"Yes, they did look a bit stiff."

The first thing that came to mind was Kulchz. I hadn't thought to tell him about the trip to the Caymans. Did he think we were trying to escape from him? Did he know Tehra was going to side with the Loyalists? If it was him, where would he be taking them? I went back into the lobby area where I was to meet them. They weren't there, but I did see a familiar face. I went over to him.

"Mo, what are you doing here?"

"I was going to ask you the same question." he replied. "Come with me. We need to talk."

There was no use refusing. I had to go with him even though I didn't know his intentions. Presumably he was bringing me to where they were holding Tehra and Alice, but I was wrong. We got into a waiting car and drove off.

"Where did you take Alice and Tehra?" I asked.

"Nowhere, Kulchz has them."

“Why?”

Mo didn’t respond but asked instead,“ Who removed your tracking chip?"

I swallowed hard. "How'd you know about that?"

"You've been seen places where you shouldn't be according to your body sensors. Obviously, someone removed it. It was Tehra wasn't it? She's the only who'd know where to find it."

I didn't answer. Why hadn't I put Tehra in hiding sooner? We shouldn't have waited for the civil war to officially reach Earth. How could that have been predicted? Anyway, it was pure stupidity to take such a risk. I hung my head in despair.

"Has she told you about the civil war on Tarizon?"

"Civil war?" I said not knowing whether I should come clean or not.

"Yes, there's been a military coup and the civil government, the Loyalists I believe they call themselves, is in exile. Kulchz thinks Tehra may be a Loyalists sympathizer."

"So Kulchz is part of the military coup?"

"Yes. He's a close friend to the new military leader who's taking over. Apparently he's been recalled to Tarizon—everyone has, in fact."

"Does that mean the Tarizon Project is over?"

He nodded. "Yes, I think that's a safe bet."

"So, where have they taken Alice and Tehra? They haven't taken them to Tarizon, have they?"

"No. Not yet. I've convinced them to leave Alice here with you, but Tehra must go back home."

I looked away. My heart was still pounding. How could this be happening? The civil war wasn't supposed to get to Earth for weeks. Damn it! I felt so helpless.

"So, how do we get Alice back?"

"I'm taking you to a rendevous point right now. They'll turn her over to us there. They'll have to erase her memory. I've convinced them you wouldn't try hypnosis on her. There'd be no point to that."

"No, Alice doesn't need to get involved in this. She's got enough of her own problems."

We drove in silence for another thirty minutes. Mo seemed sad and dejected. I wondered if he was upset that the Tarizon project was coming to an end. I supposed he was since it had to be one of the best assignments the CIA had to offer. “Would you like to go to

Tarizon now that you and Kulchz are such good buddies," I asked

He looked over at me and frowned. "He's no buddy of mine."

"He's not. You too seemed to get along pretty well."

"Just doing my job."

"Did he tell you his new commander wants to colonize Earth?"

"No, but if they wanted to do that they could have decades ago."

I told him what Tehra had explained to me about the civil war and what she thought would happen if the Loyalist lost. He looked at me and shrugged. "I'll be sure to put that in my final report. That should shake up Pentagon."

"Do you think your superiors will pass your report on to them."

He laughed. "No, probably not," he said and began slowing down. "Here's the spot. The exchange is to take place where the road goes over the seawall. See the lights up ahead? That's got to be them."

It was dark now and there was a lone set of headlights glaring at us. We stopped about a hundred yards from it and got out of the car. The street was wet and I felt the spray from the waves hitting the seawall. We walked slowly toward the lights. Suddenly two men emerged. They were carrying Alice who was limp in their arms. When we reached them, we took her and carried her back to our car. During the exchange I tried to look into their car, but the lights were too intense to see anything. I wondered if Tehra was also in there. If she was, this might be as close as I'd ever get to her. If only I had a weapon.

On the way back to the hotel Alice woke up and asked where she was. I made up the best story I could think of to explain what had happened.

"We're taking you to the emergency room. You must have eaten some bad fish or something."

"I don't remember eating anything," she mumbled.

"It made you very sick. You've been unconscious for several hours."

"Where's Tehra? Did she get sick too?"

"No, she's on her way back to Texas. There's been some kind

of family emergency. Don't you remember her telling us about it? She wanted to have dinner with us, but had to run to catch her flight."

"God. I don't remember anything. What kind of fish did I eat?"

"Oysters, I think."

"Oh, God. Bad oysters can kill you. Am I going to die?"

"No. You're going to be okay. We're going to the emergency room just as a precaution. I'm sure you'll be fine."

At the emergency room the doctors examined Alice but could find nothing wrong with her. They were perplexed by her lose of memory, but finally discharged her anyway attributing it to the number of rum and Cokes she'd consumed while she was checking out hotel bars. When we got back to the hotel she went straight to bed and didn't stir until 10:00 a.m. on Sunday. Although I could barely think with worry over Tehra and the baby, we continued our search for witnesses or evidence of Ike and Ralph's presence on the Island. Unfortunately, our luck didn't change and we returned to our hotel room depressed and dejected. Our only hope now was our meeting Monday morning at the Royal Bank. I just prayed someone there would recognize Ike or Ralph.

Chapter 44

Progress Report

The trial reconvened the next morning with Barbara Hines taking the stand. She testified she was the Brown's neighbor and was well versed on the feud between Chester Brown and Walter Stanley. She explained how the feud began with the Brown's dog barking incessantly.

"Did you ever complain about the dog barking?" Francis asked.

"No, I live to the east of Mr. Brown and there's a driveway and garage between his backyard and our house. I can hear the barking but it's not all that loud. The Stanley house is directly behind the Brown home and there is just a narrow alley between the two backyards. There is nothing to buffer the noise."

"Have you ever been in the Stanley house when the dog was barking?"

"Oh, yes. It was very annoying. I couldn't have lived with it."

"So, what did Mrs. Stanley do about the noise?"

"She and Mr. Stanley complained a lot to Mr. Brown and when that didn't work they called the police and complained to Animal Control."

"And did that do any good?"

"The police cited the Browns, but they didn't really do anything other than keep the dog inside for a couple of days."

"Are Mr. & Mrs. Stanley still married?"

"No, they're divorced," Mrs. Hines replied.

"Do you know what the cause of their divorce was?"

"It was due to the dog and Stanley's inability to effectively deal with the problem."

"How do you know that?"

"Mrs. Stanley told me her husband was spineless and let people walk all over him. She said she couldn't live in the house with that dog always barking so she had no choice but to move out."

"Why didn't they just both move?" Francis asked.

"Pride, I think. He wouldn't let someone drive him out of his own home. At least that's what I heard him tell Barbara during one of their arguments."

"So, you've testified there was great animosity between Walter Stanley and Chester Brown even before the chainlink fence went up, right."

"Yes."

"So, what happened when Chester Brown defied the architectural control committee and board of directors over the fence?"

"Stanley along with many others were livid."

Hines continued to testify about the board's refusal to grant Brown a variance and the confrontations between Brown and some of the board members. Then Francis asked her about the day of the fire.

"Did you see Walter Stanley on the day of the fire?"

"Yes."

"When and where did you see him?"

"It was in the evening before the fire. I saw him pacing back and forth in the alleyway."

"Pacing? What do you mean?"

"Well, he went out his back gate and stopped, then he walked up and down the alley like he was waiting for somebody or something."

"Was he carrying anything?"

"He had a brown bag and some kind of tool. I thought it was hedge clippers or something."

"Could you tell what he was doing?"

"No, not really, but he stood by the Brown's back gate for quite awhile."

"Thank you, Mrs. Hines, no further questions."

The judge nodded. "Ms. Waters, your witness."

I stood. "Mrs. Hines. You really don't know what Walter Stanley was doing in the alley, do you?"

"Not exactly, like I–"

"You don't know what was in the bag, do you?"

"Ah. Well I assume–"

"I don't want assumptions. Do you know for certain what was in the bag?"

"No, I do not."

"Did you see Mr. Stanley go into Mr. Brown's back yard?"

"No, from my bedroom window I can't see the Brown back fence, so I'm not sure if he entered the back yard or not."

"Did you see a GTE truck in the alley while you were watching Walter Stanley?"

Mrs. Hines frowned. "GTE. Ah . . . yes, now that you mention it. I did. It had been there a couple days. I figured they were putting in some new cable."

"Where was it parked?"

"Down the alley a ways. I don't remember seeing any workmen though."

"Mrs. Hines. Were you friends with Gladys Brown?'

"Yes, we were good friends."

"How would you characterize their marriage?"

"It was okay. They both loved each other."

"Did they have any serious problems that you were aware of?"

"Objection," Francis exclaimed. "Irrelevant?"

"Your Honor, in his opening statement Mr. Francis stated the Brown family was happy and they were innocent victims. I want to show that is not the case. Counsel has opened the door to this issue."

"Objection overruled," the Judge ruled. "Proceed."

"I'll cut to the chase, Mrs. Hines. Chester Brown was cheating on his wife, wasn't she?"

There was a murmur in the gallery. The judge sat up and put his hand on his gavel. The room quieted. Mrs. Hines swallowed hard.

"Well, I'm afraid that is true. There was a short fling with Ruth."

"Ruth?"

"Ruth Willis. She was a neighbor down the street."

"Did Gladys's Brown know about the affair?"

"Yes."

"Had there been confrontations between Gladys Brown and

Ruth Willis?"

"They had it out at one of the homeowner association meetings, if that's what you mean."

"Yes, exactly. So, there was more than just one feud in the neighborhood?"

Mrs Hines shrugged.

"Thank you, pass the witness."

Francis took Barbara Hines on redirect and I followed up with some more questions. The facts didn't change, however Barbara Hines really hadn't seen anything conclusive since her vantage point precluded her from actually seeing the Brown's back fence. After Mrs. Hines stepped down Francis called one of the crime scene investigators who testified about the crime scene and blood evidence collected there. Then he called the butcher who sold steaks to Walter Stanley the day of the fire. At five o'clock the judge recessed until Friday morning at ten.

That night we met with our five hired mach jurors to get their impressions of the prosecution's case so far. There were three women and two men. Three were white, one black, and the other Hispanic. Two were white collar, two workmen, and one housewife. It wasn't a perfect replication of the jury, but close enough to give us some valuable input. In today's session we wanted to find out what the jurors thought were the strengths and weaknesses of the prosecution case. First I asked them what they thought about Richard Francis.

"He seems like a nice guy,"#3 juror replied. "I like him."

"I like him too," #5 juror agreed. "He seems honest and sincere. I trust him."

I nodded. "Anything anybody doesn't like about him?'

There was no response. Great, they all loved him. "Okay, what about the defendant, Walter Stanley? How does he strike you?"

Juror #1 said, "He doesn't seem like a killer. I don't think he would have had the guts to set the fire."

"I disagree," #5 juror objected. "His wife divorced him. He'd lost everything because of Mr. Brown. I can see him wanting revenge. A fire is exactly how he'd do it and if he could set it remotely that's even better. He's a coward and this fire was a cowardly way to kill someone."

My mouth fell opened. Our whole theory of the remote triggering device had backfired at least with one potential juror. His argument made sense. The fact that Stanley probably didn't have the ability to rig a remote triggering device didn't seem to bother him. I made a note to really emphasis the complexity of the triggering device and the fact that Stanley couldn't have rigged it by himself.

"Okay, does anyone else feel that way?"

Juror #2 raised her hand gingerly. "He must have been pretty bitter about his wife leaving him. It must have been difficult for him to see Mr. Brown and his family coming and going everyday when he was all alone. The temptation for revenge must have been very strong."

"All right. What do you think of the defense's theory that a corporate competitor was responsible for the Brown murders?"

Juror #4 frowned. "We haven't seen any evidence of that."

"That's true. That will come when the defense presents it's case. I was just wondering what you thought at this point. Does it sound plausible or not? Are you anxious to see the proof?"

Juror #2 raised her hand slowly. I nodded. "I don't understand why Mr. Brown wanted to put up a chainlink fence. They are so tacky."

I chuckled. "I don't know, it does seem rather strange."

"He obviously didn't care much about property values," Juror #1 replied.

"The fence couldn't have been the reason the Brown's were murdered," #3 said. "It must have been something more significant. I like your rival company theory. It makes a lot more sense."

We talked another thirty minutes and then called it a night. The meeting had been fruitful in that I had confirmed my fear that the jury probably liked Richard Francis a lot and that they didn't much like Walter Stanley. The hope that came out of the meeting was that at least some of the jurors didn't believe a barking dog or a chainlink fence could be responsible for the murder of five people. If that were the case, when we put on our case against Almatech and T. Robert Stout many of he jurors would be listening and considering that possibility very carefully.

Chapter 45

Royal Bank

On Monday morning Alice and I went to the Royal Bank to visit with the bank officer assigned to the Stover Enterprises account. The bank was located in a modest four-story office building in downtown George Town. It wasn't at all what I expected. The people who ran this bank obviously were interested more in the bottom line than impressing anyone. We went to the reception desk and told them we had arrived for a meeting with our bank officer. She pointed to a sofa and asked us to take a seat.

Less than a minute later a dark-haired woman in a business suit walked over to us. She smiled and asked us to follow her. She led us down a hallway that ran between several large, plush offices with glass walls. I guess whoever ran the bank wanted to be able to keep a close eye on everybody. You couldn't pick your nose or scratch your ass without somebody seeing you. At the end of the hall was a conference room with a small table. The woman asked us to have a seat and wait. She asked if we wanted coffee. We accepted her offer.

A few moments later a tall, middle-aged man came in with a file and sat across from us. We introduced ourselves. He said his name was Ben Adams. The woman came back and set a cup of coffee in front of each of us. Adams opened the file and began studying it while we fixed our coffee. He flipped through some of the pages and finally cleared his throat and looked up.

"So, you are from Texas, I see?"

"Yes," Alice said. "Waco."

"Oh, Waco. My niece went to Baylor University. She really enjoyed Texas. She said it was hot, though."

"Yes, four or five months out of the year are quite hot," I said, "but our winters are mild and spring and fall are very pleasant."

"Is that right. Hmm. . . . So, what can I do for you?"

"This bank account is kind of a mystery to us," Alice said. "My husband and I own Stover Enterprises, Ltd. and neither of us can remember setting it up."

Adams frowned. "Well, somebody set it up obviously. Let me see," he said as he flipped through to the first page. "Oh, this is strange."

"What?" Alice asked.

"The RCIP has already been through this file. They've taken the original signature card."

"They have?" I asked somewhat surprised. Then I thought about it and figured the U.S. Attorney must have asked them to do it before they came down with the indictment.

"How could they do that? I thought our account was private."

"If there is an accusation of money laundering or other criminal activity sometimes the account can be examined by the authorities. It's rare though."

"So much for bank secrecy laws," I said.

"There is a copy of the signature card in the file. Benjamin Stover, General Partner is what it says on the card," Adams advised.

"Can I see that?" Alice asked.

"Sure," Adams said turning the file around so Alice could see the document.

She shook her head. "It's a forgery. It looks a little like my husband's signature, but it's much stiffer and jerky."

Adams raised his eyebrows. Well, we don't have any way of checking an initial signature. We compare it to the passport and driver's license but nobody here is an expert in handwriting analysis."

"Can I see the copies of the driver's license and passport?"

He turned a few more pages and then turned and showed us a photo copy of the driver's license. Alice grimaced. It was Dan's driver's license. There was no doubt about the picture being him.

"I don't understand. I know my husband never came to George Town and he keeps his driver's license in his wallet."

"Is there any way the person who opened the account could

have substituted the driver's license copy for the original one used?" I asked.

Adams thought for a moment. "Well, it would be difficult, but I suppose if the new accounts officer made the copy of the driver's license and then was called away or distracted he could have slipped in a substitute copy. But that's a bit of a stretch."

"But it is possible?"

"I suppose."

"Can we talk to the new accounts officer who opened this account? Maybe he or she will remember who opened it."

Adam looked through the file and said, "That would be Ms. Jenkins. I'll ask her to step in."

A few minutes later Ms. Jenkins stepped in but she didn't recognize any of the photos. "I'm sorry. I open so many accounts."

"It's all right," Adams said to her. She turned and left. "There is one other way we can figure this out."

"How's that?" I asked.

"The surveillance tapes. We're required to keep them for one year. I believe if we pull the right tape we can see who opened the account."

Alice sat up excitedly. "That would be wonderful!"

Adams smiled and stood up. "Give me a few minutes to find the right tape."

This was going better than I expected. Mr. Adams was being very cooperative. I was hopeful he'd find the surveillance tape, but something told me not to get my hopes up. I was right. A few moments later he came back with a glum look on his face.

"I'm terribly sorry, but I couldn't find the tape. It seems that it has been taken by the RCIP. It could be your FBI has asked for it."

"Probably," I said. "Maybe if I go over to the Central Police Station they'll have the tape and let us look at it. Do you have a record of who took it?"

"Yes, of course. I'll write the name of the officer, his station address, and telephone number. Hopefully he hasn't turned it over to the FBI."

We thanked Mr. Adams and left the bank. From a pay phone outside I called the detective but he was out. Then I remembered the officer who I'd met while I was canvassing all the marinas. I searched through my pocket and found his card. Luckily he was in. I told him who I was.

"Yes, Mr. Turner. How's your search going?"

"It was going pretty well until we discovered that someone from your office took the signature cards and the bank's surveillance tapes."

"Oh yes. We've been cooperating with the FBI on this case. We're getting ready to ship them to Texas for the trial."

"Is there any way we could look at the tapes today? We can come right over."

"Well, I suppose you have as much right to see them as the FBI. I better call them to be sure it's okay."

"That's fine. We'll have lunch and then be right over to see them. That should give you time to make the call."

Officer Brim agreed and I hung up. There was a restaurant down the street so we walked to it and went inside. I wasn't optimistic that we'd actually be able to see the tapes, but it was worth a try. We might get lucky. Alice was beaming with optimism.

"If the tapes show Ike or Ralph then it will be over, right? They'll have to dismiss the charges."

"I would think so, but I guess Ralph could still claim he set up the account at Ben's request.. It would be Ben's word against Ralph 's. He'd have a hard time explaining Ben's driver's license in the file, though."

"Yes he would. . . . Oh, I pray to God it shows one of them."

After lunch we went to the Central Police Station and asked for Officer Brim. He came out immediately and took us back to his office. There was a TV in the corner with a built in video player. He walked over to it and slipped in the tape.

"I called the FBI but the officer in charge wasn't available. I probably shouldn't be doing this, but I don't see how it could change anything by letting you take a look at it."

"Yes, your right. You've had custody of it since it left the bank so there's no danger of the evidence getting contaminated."

"No, so let's take a look," he said as he pushed the play button. "I've forwarded it to the date and time the person who set up the account supposedly arrived."

A picture came up of with a view of the new accounts desk. After a minute a man walked in.

"It's Ralph !" Alice exclaimed. "Ah ha! Look it's Ralph."

Tears began to run down Alice's cheeks as she pointed excitedly to the TV. Officer Brim seemed delighted as well.

"I've got more good news for you, Mrs. Stover. After I met Mr. Turner yesterday I started checking to see if there was any record of Mr. Herman being in the islands and I discovered he was involved in a barroom brawl the night after that bank account was set up. I've compared his prints from his arrest file with the prints on the signature card and they're a match.

"Oh, that's wonderful," Alice exclaimed. "This is such great news. Finally things are going right. We've got to call Ben and tell him."

"Thank you, Officer Brim. I really appreciate your help. This has been a very traumatic experience for Ben and Alice and hopefully now it will be over soon."

"Why does this guy Herman hate you so much?" Brim asked.

"He's an ex-son-in-law and I guess he never expected us to turn him in when we found him embezzling from us. He's been very bitter since he was arrested."

"Well, good luck to you."

We left the police station and went back to our hotel. Alice called her daughter to give her the good news and ask her to pass it on to Ben when she visited him at the jail. When Alice got off the telephone, I called the office to see how Paula's trial was going. Maria answered.

"The prosecution is putting on a good case. The jury loves Mr. Francis. Paula's worried by the time she's able to start putting on her defense that the jury will already have made up their minds."

"Well, that's always a danger, but Paula's pretty lovable herself. I'm sure when she gets going the jurors will listen."

"I told her that too, but you know how she can get sometimes. She's missing not having you at her side."

"She's got Bart. She doesn't need me."

"Yeah, well. I'm not so sure about that. Bart's a prosecutor at heart. He's not as helpful as he could be."

"Hmm. Well, I'll be home tomorrow, so tell her I'll be there if she needs me for anything."

I thought about what Maria had said. I wondered if Bart thought Walter Stanley was guilty. If he did, then he wouldn't be much help to Paula.

On the way back to our hotel I pondered what to do about Tehra. Was she still on the island or was she back in Texas? I wondered now that Kulchz and his men were leaving and the Tarizon Project was coming to and end, if it would be safe to tell Paula and Bart about the aliens. After giving it some thought, I realized it wouldn't be a good idea. The CIA would disavow any knowledge of the Tarizon project and I'd look like a lunatic if I brought it up. Even if I did have sufficient proof to make a credible case, what good would it do but cause fear and panic when the danger was already over? No, I'd have to keep my mouth shut, but at least the lies and deception would be over.

Chapter 46

Good Fortune?

On Friday morning, while I was gathering my files together to go to court, Maria told me that Stan had found exculpatory evidence at the bank in George Town that would get Ben Stover off the hook. I was excited and relieved to hear that and particularly glad that Stan was on his way home. On Monday I'd likely be putting on our defense and it would be nice to have Stan around in case I needed him. I don't know why but he had such a calming effect on me. Perhaps it was because, no matter how bad things got, he never lost his confidence and resolve to win.

At 10:00 a.m. the judge took the bench and the case resumed. Francis called several more members of the board of directors of the Collin Commons Homeowner's association who gave their rendition of the feud between Walter Stanley and Chester Brown. Their testimony added little to what had already come out and I detected that the jurors were finding the redundancy a little tedious. So, I didn't bother to cross-examine them. Finally Francis called Ruth Willis who testified that her short affair with Chester Brown had long been over and that she held no animosity toward Chester or Mrs. Brown. She also provided an alibi for the time of the murder. She claimed to have been out of town at a business seminar the night of the fire. Before she stepped down, however, Francis asked her one last question.

"Do you have any military experience, Ms. Willis?"

"Oh, God no," she replied.

"You're not an explosives expert are you?"

She laughed. "No, I don't think so."

"So, you wouldn't know how to set off a fire remotely with a telephone and a blasting cap?"

She rolled her eyes. "I think not?"

"Ms. Willis. Did you hire someone to set the Brown's house on fire?"

"No!" she exclaimed. "Like I said, the affair was over. Gladys had forgiven her husband, and we were cordial again. It was just a little sex, it didn't mean anything."

Francis smiled and nodded. "Your witness, Ms. Waters."

I stood up. Francis had made a joke of my mention of Ms. Willis' affair with Chester Brown. If I didn't cross-examine her the jury might think I was trying to mislead and confuse them with irrelevant evidence.

"Ms. Willis, I'm glad to hear that Mrs. Brown had forgiven you and Chester for the affair and that you all were, at the time of the murders, the best of friends. But isn't it true that you could just be saying that since Ruth and Chester are not around to dispute it? Why should the jury believe you?"

Willis stiffened. "Because it's true. The affair was just a mistake. You know how passions can get out of hand sometimes."

"Yes, and how many times did your passions get out of hand—once, twice, or was it over one hundred times?"

A lady in the jury box put her hand over her mouth. There were sighs of shock in the gallery. I had no idea how many times Gladys' and Chester had done it, but I figured it was more than once or twice.

"Oh, no. Not nearly that many times."

"How many, then?"

"Objection! Your Honor. The number of times is irrelevant."

"Overruled," the judge said. "You brought it up counsel."

"How many?" I asked again.

"I don't know, I didn't keep count."

"Did you do it more than once in a day?"

"Ah. . . . I suppose, sometimes."

"How many times a week on average would Chester slip away to see you and have sex? You did have sex every time he came over, didn't you?"

She shrugged. "I don't know."

"I can call your friend, Ally. She lives next door. I 'm sure you must have kept her up to date. Should I do that?"

"No," she snarled. "Leave her out of this. . . . Okay, three or four times a week, maybe. I didn't put a notch on the bedpost every time we did it."

"And your fling lasted, what, four or five months?"

She nodded. "Okay, let's do the math. Four times four is sixteen. Sixteen times five is eighty, times, let's just say 1.5 for multiple sex, so that equals 120. So, you had sex with Chester Brown over a hundred times, but Gladys didn't care. She'd forgiven you for it. Is that your testimony?"

Willis let out a barely audible gasp, looked up at the judge, and then shifted in her chair looking exasperated. "Yes, so what? It was just a mistake and Gladys fortunately was a forgiving person."

Although when I started the cross-examination I hadn't believed that Ruth Willis had anything to do with the Brown murders, I felt I'd hit a nerve and she was feeling guilty about something. When Francis asked her if she'd hired someone to set the fire, her answer was just a little too emphatic. I knew she hadn't killed the Brown family, but Barbara was hiding something and whatever it was it had her in a near panic. It was time to go in for the kill and see what developed.

"Barbara, what is it that you know about the Brown murders that you're not telling us? I don't think you killed them, but you know something about how or why they died, don't you?"

Willis swallowed hard, her face became pale, and she looked away. A tear trickled down her cheek and she swatted it away like it was a common house fly. She crossed her arms and closed her eyes.

"Tell us what you know, Ruth. There's no way you can hide it. It's going to come out anyway."

"Objection!" Francis exclaimed. "Counsel is on a fishing expedition and badgering the witness."

The judge's eyes narrowed. "Ms. Willis, do you know something about these murders? If you do, you must tell us."

"No, not really. It's just that . . . well . . . this might be all my fault."

There was murmur in the gallery. A man got up and rushed

out of the room. I motioned for Jodie to follow the man.

"Go on," the Judge ordered.

Francis stood up. "Your Honor. I've objected—"

"Objection overruled," the judge replied. "I think we need to hear what Ms. Willis has to say."

I said, "Go on, Ruth. How is all this your fault?"

"My ex-husband, Tim, is a very passionate man and loved me very much. When I left him two years ago it nearly killed him. After the separation I had to get a restraining order to keep him away from me. Many times he said he would kill the man who took me away."

"So, you moved down the street from Chester Brown not only to be close to him but to hide from your ex-husband," I suggested.

"Yes. I hadn't left Tim for another man but Chester was my first lover after the breakup."

"I see. So, what happened?"

"When Gladys Brown's PI discovered us together and reported it to her, she went ballistic and threatened to move out and take the kids. Chester loved those kids and couldn't let that happen. He said it was a bad time for a divorce and that it was over between us."

"Chester told you the affair was over?"

She lowered her head. "I'm afraid so, and I was so upset and hurt by it that . . . well . . . I told Tim all about Chester Brown and our relationship and let him think Chester had taken me away from him. He was livid, of course, and swore he'd kill him."

The gallery erupted in excited conversation. Reporters scrambled for the exits to phone in this startling development to their newsrooms. Francis jumped to his feet.

"Your Honor. Objection! This is pure speculation and highly inflammatory."

I looked over at Francis. "You bet it's highly inflammatory, but it's not speculation. Tim Willis made a death threat against Chester Brown and now he and his family are dead!"

The judge overruled Francis' objection and called a fifteen minute recess. Chaos broke out in the courtroom as everyone tried to fathom what had just happened. It suddenly came back to me that Bart and I had considered this scenario but never found any evidence to support it. The fear that immediately began to nag at me was that

Tim Willis might have an alibi. If he did and Francis proved he didn't have the capability of remotely triggering the device, then we'd lose credibility and the jury might be skeptical when we started pointing fingers at Almatech. Although what just happened might be a stroke of good fortune, it could easily turn out to be our undoing. I just prayed Tim Willis was alone watching TV when the fire was started.

Chapter 47

Breakthrough

After helping Alice to her car in the DFW Airport parking garage, I called the office to tell them I'd landed and see if there were any new developments. Maria told me that Paula had cracked a witness on cross examination and drawn serious blood. She told me to go straight to the courthouse as she and Bart needed help. I told her I was on my way.

When I got to the courthouse there was a ring of reporters around all the entrances. I tried to sneak in unnoticed but a reporter saw me and rushed over.

"Mr. Turner," the reporter asked. "What do you think of Ruth Willis' husband making death threats against Chester Brown?"

"I don't know what to think. I just heard about it myself a few minutes ago."

"Do you think the prosecution will drop the charges now considering this new evidence?" the reporter said.

I shrugged. "Probably not at this stage of the game. I imagine it will be up to the jury to acquit Walter Stanley. They certainly have good reason to now."

"Is Ms. Waters going to call Tim Willis?"

"I'm sorry. I've got to get inside," I said and pushed my way through the front door.

Jodie spotted me getting off the elevator a minute later and rushed over. "Stan, I am so glad you made it. You heard what happened, I guess."

"Yes, that's great. What's going on now?"

"Paula is still cross examining Ruth Willis. She wants you to talk to her ex-husband, Tim Willis. We need to find out if he has an alibi. If not, she wants you to serve him with a subpoena. Paul Thayer is checking into his background to see if he has any criminal history or military training."

"Any idea where I might find him?" I asked.

"Yes, he left here about thirty minutes ago. He either went home or to the General Motors assembly plant in Arlington. He works the second shift, I think. Here's his address."

Jodie handed me two pieces of paper, one with Tim's name, address, and the make and license number of his car written on it and the other a subpoena commanding him to appear as a witness in the trial. I looked them over. "Okay, I'll go straight over there. I just hope he'll talk to me. I can't serve this subpoena, though. We'll need a process server."

"I know. I called Jeb Lewis. He'll be downstairs in front of the clerk's office waiting for you."

I nodded and left. If Tim Willis had heard his ex-wife's testimony he'd be scared and probably skip work. He'd avoid going back to his apartment too. If he did go back, it'd just be to pack a few things for the road. My only hope would be that he'd linger too long and I'd catch him before he left. I found Jeb and we left in my car to look for Tim. When we arrived at his apartment complex, his car was still parked outside. I told Jeb to wait in the car. I wanted to talk to Tim first, if possible. I approached the front door cautiously and knocked. The door immediately opened and a young woman appeared.

"Hi," I said. "I'm looking for Tim. Is he around?"

"Ah. . . . No, I haven't seen him," the woman replied.

"But isn't that his car?" I pointed to the blue Buick in the parking spot directly in front of the apartment.

She looked at it blankly.

"I'm not a cop," I pressed. "My name is Stan Turner. I'm an attorney. I just want to talk to Mr. Willis for a minute."

"He's not here," she insisted.

"Come on. I know he's in there. Tell him I just need a minute or two."

She closed the door and I waited. After a few moments Willis stormed out and headed for his car. He was carrying an overnight bag. I rushed over to him.

"Mr. Willis. If I could have a word with you."

He shook his head. "I don't have time right now. I've got to get to work."

"Do you usually take a suitcase to work?"

"I told you, I don't have anything to say."

As he opened the door and slid in behind the steering wheel I motioned to Jeb.

"Wait one minute," I said. "I've got something for you."

Tim frowned and when he saw Jeb he tried to close the door, but I had a hand on it. Jeb thrust the subpoena into the car and dropped in on his lap. He glanced at it and grimaced.

"What's this?"

"You've been served," Jeb said. "You must appear tomorrow as a witness in the Walter Stanley murder case currently in session in the 199th District Court of Collin County, Texas."

"Like hell I will," he said and started the engine. He tried again to close the door but I held it firmly.

"I would take this subpoena seriously," I warned. "Failure to respond to it could result in a bench warrant being issued for your arrest."

"Well, we'll see about that," he said and pulled one more time on the door. I let go and it slammed hard. He stomped down on the accelerator and took off with all his tires squealing.

When we got back to the courthouse, Jeb filed his return of service with the clerk and I went upstairs to report to Paula. The trial was in recess and Paula and Bart were talking in the private hallway in front of the court clerk's office. I went up to them.

"Well, Tim wouldn't talk to me, but we did get him served. I wouldn't count on him showing up, though. It looked like he was leaving town."

"That's what we were hoping he'd do," Bart said. "Running makes it look like he's guilty."

"Well, good. So, has Francis finished putting on his case?" I asked.

"Yes, he just closed and I'm about to call my first witness."

"Who's that going to be?" I asked.

"The dispatcher at the Southwestern Bell service office," Paula replied. "Then we'll put on the waitress from the diner."

"You're still putting on your Almatech defense?"

"Yeah. Bart and I talked about it and there isn't any downside since we don't have to prove either theory. All we need to do is confuse the jury."

"What about tomorrow?"

"Tomorrow I'll call Tim but he won't show, of course. After that I guess it will be Stout and his men."

"That should be interesting."

"Yeah, I figured I'd let you cross-examine Stout," Paula said evenly.

I looked her and laughed. "Yeah, right."

She sighed. "Just a thought."

"Hey. I heard you did a number on Ruth Willis?"

"Well, not really. I just saw a crack in her story and hammered away at it."

The door to the judge's chambers opened and the bailiff yelled, "All rise." The judge took the bench and asked everyone to be seated. "Call your first witness, Ms. Waters."

"Yes, Your Honor, the defense calls Norman Rusk."

The bailiff went out into the hallway and brought Norman Rusk to the stand. He testified that he was the maintenance supervisor for GTE. Paula asked him if there were any missing trucks on the day of the fire.

"Not on the day of the fire, but the day before we had a missing service truck."

"Could you describe it?"

"It was a 1990 Chevrolet van."

"What color?"

"White and blue."

"How did you find out it was missing?"

"Two of our service men went into IHOP for coffee and when they returned for the vehicle it was gone."

"Was it subsequently recovered?"

"Yes, the following night someone returned it to the same parking lot."

"Was there anything missing from the truck?"

"No, and there was no damage. Apparently someone just wanted to borrow it for a day."

After Norman Rusk stepped down, Paula called Martin Ramirez, the good-looking, blond leader of Stout's security team. He walked briskly to the witness stand exuding great confidence. Stout lawyers were sure to have thoroughly prepared him for his testimony, so I didn't expect Paula to get much out of him, but I was wrong. He turned out to be quite open and friendly. He even asked Paula to call him Marty. He must have known he couldn't hide his relationship to Stout so he'd better be straight and try to win over the jury with his charm.

After asking about his background and training, Paula asked him how he was employed.

"I own a security company, Tripact Security. We do contract work for the defense industry. Currently we have a contract with Almatech Life Systems, Inc."

"I see. What services do you provide under this contract?"

"General security for the CEO and board of directors."

"What does that entail?"

"Objection, Your Honor," Francis said. "I don't see the relevance of this witness."

"Your Honor," Paula replied. "We need this witness to lay a foundation for our defense. The relevance of the witness will be apparent when we call our next witness."

"Very well," the judge said. "Objection overruled. You may answer the question."

"We have someone assigned to each board member 24/7 and two men on the CEO," Ramirez said. "We do advance work on their schedules, background checks on anyone they meet, screen mail, monitor and check security systems–that sort of thing."

"Who is the CEO?"

"T. Robert Stout."

"In the course of your contract with Almatech were any

members of your team in Dallas on August 8th or 9th of last year?"

"Yes, one of the board members flew to Dallas on business and I sent two men with them."

"Which two men?"

"Actually it was a man and a woman–Rich Walls and Lisa Andretti."

"Could you tell us about these two team members–their background and training?"

"Sure, we got Colonel Walls when he retired from the Marine Corps. He spent the first nine years of his military service as an artillery officer and the last eleven in intelligence. Lisa Andretti was an ex-LAPD officer who spent seven years in their SWAT Division."

"So both of these employees were knowledgeable and competent in armaments and explosives?"

"Yes, they both had extensive training in all aspects of security and law enforcement. Armaments and explosives would have been part of their training."

"Do you have any knowledge of what Walls and Andretti did in Dallas the two days they were here?"

"Just what I read in their reports."

"Do you have those reports with you?"

"Yes."

"Do the reports indicate that either Ms. Andretti or Colonel Walls visited the home of Chester Brown?"

"No. According to the reports they were nowhere near Chester Brown's house on either of those two days."

When it became time for Francis to cross-exam the witness he declined but reserved the right to cross-examine him at a later time. Paula next called the waitress at the IHOP, Blanche Reedy. The jurors watched the pretty brunette intently as she took the stand. Paula questioned her about the GTE truck that went missing and then handed her a photograph of Rich Walls.

"Do you recognize this man?"

She nodded. "Yes, he was in the restaurant that same night the GTE truck disappeared."

"Are you sure about that?"

"Oh, yes. He and I hit it off and I gave him my phone

number. We were supposed to get together later that night."

"Did you?"

"No. He never called. You know men."

"Right," Paula said. She took the photo back and showed her another one. "How about this lady—did you see her?"

"Yes. She was with Colonel Walls but not as a couple. He said she was part of his team."

"Did he tell you why they were in Dallas?"

"Yes. He said he was babysitting some bigwig."

"I see."

"How far is the IHOP you work at from the Collin Commons Condominiums?"

"Just a mile or so. We get a lot of business from there especially on the weekends."

After Paula was through with Blanche, Francis took her on cross and got her to admit that she didn't know how Colonel Walls or Lisa Andretti had gotten to the IHOP nor did she see them take the GTE Truck. He tried to get her to say that the GTE Truck was stolen while Walls and Andretti were in the restaurant but luckily she remembered otherwise.

"No, they both had left when the GTE crew came in. It was probably forty-five minutes later that the truck was discovered missing."

"So, Colonel Walls and Lisa Andretti could have stolen the vehicle?"

"Yes, I didn't see them take it, but they could have."

"Thank you. No further questions."

After Blanche stepped down the judge recessed the case for the day. I was glad because I was worried about Tehra and needed time to think. There had to be some way I could rescue her. There was no telling what Kulchz would do to her now that the civil war had reached Earth and she was the enemy. The only problem was how to get to her. I was but one man and she was in the custody of hundreds of Tarizonian soldiers and Seafolken slaves. The odds of my rescuing her were exceedingly remote. If I even tried, I'd likely get killed or captured. Nevertheless, I had to do something. I couldn't just sit around and hope for the best.

Chapter 48

Missing Witness

As expected Tim Willis was a no show on Friday morning. In order to take advantage of his absence I had to make sure the jury knew about it, so when the judge asked me to call my next witness I said. "The defense calls Tim Willis."

The judge looked at the bailiff. "Please bring in Mr. Willis," the judge said.

The bailiff raised his bulky frame and waddled to the door. After a minute he came back. "Mr. Willis is not here, Your Honor."

"Not here?" I exclaimed, "but I subpoenaed him. He was served last night. Did you search the hall for him?"

The judge shook his head. "Check one more time. If he's not here, I'll issue a warrant for his arrest."

"Thank you, Your Honor," I said gleefully.

"In the meantime, Ms. Waters. Call your next witness."

At this point in our case I had to connect the dots, so to speak. I'd shown that part of the Almatech security team was in Dallas the two days before the fire. I'd established that they were near Chester Brown's house. It was clear they were capable of building and installing a complex triggering device to set the Brown fire, and they'd kept their visit to the Collin Commons neighborhood a secret. Now what I needed to do was inform the jury of the intense rivalry between TI and Almatech and explain Chester Brown's critical role in developing stealth technology. Robin Sylvester took the stand and testified on all these points and more.

"So, how did the death of Chester Brown impact Almatech?"

"Well, because TI doesn't have Chester Brown anymore

Almatech's competitive advantage has improved dramatically. Brown was the backbone of the stealth technology team and it will take them years to find the talent necessary to make them competitive again in this area."

"So what does that mean in dollars and cents?" I asked.

"Millions. As you probably know these defense contracts are very lucrative and whenever the bids go out the competition is intense and often bitter. Brown's death was the best thing that could have happened to Almatech all year. In fact, thirty days following Brown's death TI stock had dropped 22% and Almatech Life Systems, Inc. had gone up 17%"

Francis came back on cross exam and got Sylvester to admit he had no knowledge of any plot by Almatech or anyone else to kill Chester Brown. He hammered the point that corporate competition, especially for government contracts, is often intense and bitter but that rarely does such competition result in physical violence. He reminded the jury that this was America where free and spirted competition was a way of life.

I didn't object to Francis' speech because it didn't matter. The jury had gotten my message. I could see it in their faces. They weren't stupid. They knew that when millions of dollars were at stake businessmen, hell anybody, might resort to violence and murder to get their hands on it. After Sylvester stepped down the judge called a short recess. Although there was a chance the jury might vote for acquittal now, it was only a fifty-fifty proposition and I didn't like those odds. I needed one last witness to shift the momentum in my direction. The problem was I didn't have any more witnesses that could really contribute anything. I could call Walter Stanley, but that was risky, particularly since he was such a wimp.

During the break I decided it was time to unleash Simon Barber. He met me in the parking garage where we could talk freely.

"You got your story ready?" I asked.

"You bet. It's ready to go to press.'

"Good. I'm going to recall Marty Ramirez and hit him with the Golden Cab receipt. Do you have anything else for me?"

"Yes, as a matter of fact my source came across something quite interesting."

"What's that?"

"It seems that Marty Ramirez and Ruth Willis know each other."

"What? You've got to be kidding."

"No. My source found her name and telephone number on the back of an envelope in his trash can."

"That's pretty careless. Your source must be pretty close to Colonel Walls to have access to his trash."

"Not that close, really, but she does have a key to his office. I guess since you're about to stick your neck out I should tell you. My source works in the secretarial pool at Almatech. She's been there for years, and accordingly, is invisible to them."

"Why would she stick her neck out for you like this?"

"I met her when I was doing a story about the merger of Almatech and Varden Enterprises many years ago. She'd been with Varden for almost ten years when the merger took place. Unfortunately she was a few months short of vesting and lost her pension as a result. She was very bitter. They didn't pay secretaries very well at Varden but she'd stayed on because the pension and fringe benefits were good. Unfortunately, Almatech didn't have much of a pension and paid secretaries even less than Varden. She was so bitter, I decided to befriend her and help her out financially."

"I see. So, what do you think it means?" I asked. "Do you think they are involved?"

"It's possible, but it would be difficult due to the distance between them."

"Okay, call your editor and tell him to go ahead with your story. Then let's go back upstairs and shake things up a bit."

It suddenly all made sense to me. I couldn't wait to get Ramirez back on the stand. He was a lying scumbag and I wanted to let the world know it. After Barber had made his call, we returned to the courtroom. Bart was talking to the court reporter when I walked in. I assumed he was getting my evidence marked for submission to the court. I looked for Stan but he wasn't anywhere to be found. It irritated me that he'd miss such an important moment. I wanted him to see this. Damn him!

The door suddenly opened from behind the bench and the bailiff yelled, "All rise!"

The judge took the bench and Bart rushed over and took a chair next to me. When the gallery had quieted, the judge said, "Call your next witness, Ms. Waters."

"Yes, Your Honor. We'd like to recall Martin Ramirez."

"Very well, Bailiff, call Mr. Ramirez back to the stand."

Walls stepped inside the courtroom and made his way to the witness stand. He didn't look too thrilled about being recalled, but he took his seat and forced a smile. I smiled back and asked, "Mr. Ramirez. I believe you testified earlier that Lisa Andretti and Colonel Walls came to Dallas on August 8, 1992 to work security for one of the Almatech board members who had meetings in Dallas?"

"Yes, that's correct."

"I'm going to show you what's been marked Defendant's Exhibit 22 and ask you to identify it."

I handed Ramirez the paper. He looked it over and said, "Yes this is a copy of the invoice for our services for that trip."

I nodded. "Does the invoice confirm that Colonel Walls and Lisa Andretti were the only two security officers to accompany the board member to Dallas?"

Ramirez' eyes narrowed. "Yes, that's correct," he said slowly.

"Where were you on August 8th and 9th, Mr. Ramirez?"

His body stiffened. He looked at the judge and then to the jury. "I was at my home in Alexandria, Virginia," he finally said.

"Yes, and I'm sure you have witnesses who could testify to that."

He frowned and twisted his neck nervously. "I'm sure I could find someone, if need be."

"Yes, a man in your business could arrange just about anything," I said coldly. "Mr. Ramirez, I'm going to show you what's been marked Defendant's Exhibit 41 and ask you to identify it."

Ramirez took the paper and squinted. "I don't know. It looks like a receipt for a cab ride, but I've never seen it before."

"It's from the Golden Cab Company of Dallas, Texas and is dated August 8th, right?"

"That's what it says."

"Can you tell from the receipt where the passengers were taken?"

"Objection!" Francis exclaimed. "He said he's never seen it before. Calls for speculation."

"Sustained."

"Okay," I said. "You've never seen it before. I'll buy that. What's interesting about it is the number of passengers that were transported from Addison Airport to the Sheraton Hotel. It's says three passengers were transported."

"Yes, Colonel Walls, Lisa, and the board member."

"That would make sense, except the board member was transported to the hotel by limousine provided by the host company where he was having his meetings."

Ramirez shrugged. "Then it must be a mistake."

"Is it a mistake? Isn't it true that you were the third occupant of that cab?"

"No. That's ridiculous. I didn't go to Dallas."

"Do you know a woman named Ruth Willis?"

Ramirez froze. His eyes narrowed. He rubbed his neck nervously. Finally he shrugged. "Sure, I've seen her name in the papers. Didn't she testify yesterday?"

"Don't play games with us, Mr. Ramirez. You know Ruth Willis quite well don't you? Didn't she hire you to kill Chester Brown?"

The gallery erupted in conversation. The witnesses' face reddened in indignation. Reporters began writing furiously. Francis jumped to his feet and glared at me.

"Objection! Your Honor. "This is outrageous! Counsel is testifying and trying to mislead the jury. Move for an instruction to disregard."

The judge frowned. "Ms. Waters. You know better than that. Ask a question and wait for a response."

"Your Honor!" Francis moaned. "Will you instruct the jury to disregard counsel's attempt to testify?"

"The objection as to the form of the question is sustained. The jury will disregard counsels remarks. Ms. Waters. Do you have any further questions?"

"Yes, Your Honor. Mr. Ramirez. Do you know Ruth Willis other than from what you've read in the papers?"

Ramirez took a deep breath and nodded. "Yes, we've met before."

Ramirez stuck to his story about being at home in Virginia when the murders took place, but he did admit to a one night stand with Ruth Willis many years earlier. It was enough to give the jury pause. There were now two more likely persons responsible for the Brown murders. Whether it was Tim Willis killing them to get revenge or whether Ruth Willis had hired Marty Ramirez to kill Chester Brown out of anger, it didn't matter. Either was better than a barking dog. At least I hoped so. It was hard to predict what a jury would make from all of this, but I felt I'd done all I could to create reasonable doubt. Now the decision rested with the jury. After Ramirez stepped down, I rested.

Chapter 49

Rescue

After helping to get Tim Willis served I drove out to Lake Tawakoni to see if the Tarizonian base was still there. I wanted so desperately to rescue Tehra. I couldn't imagine what fate lie ahead for her if she was forced to go back to Tarizon as a prisoner of war.

From the surface I couldn't tell much. I'd have to go down into the tunnels to find out if anyone was still there. If they were that would be a good sign. Kulchz would surely destroy the base moments after they left. I pulled open the door into the storage tank that camouflaged the entrance to the base. The ladder down into the tunnels was still in place. As I stepped inside a man grabbed me by the collar and yanked me to the ground. Before I could even think about resisting he had a rag in my mouth and had me pinned down.

When I looked up, I saw two pulsing green eyes and a half-human face. Fear shot through me like a hot blade. Then a woman spoke.

"Stan, do not resist. We mean you no harm. Are you here to rescue Tehra?"

I tried to talk but the rag prevented it. The monster pulled the rag from my mouth but didn't let me up. "Yes, is she still here?" I gasped.

The woman looked human but was dressed in a military uniform. As she spoke a half dozen other soldiers crowded around her. Some were human and others were like the beast who had me pinned. Then I realized the monsters were the Seafolken that Tehra had told me about, humans who lived in the sea. I struggled to free myself.

"Let him go," the woman said to the man. He stood up

immediately and extended his hand. I took it and pulled myself up. "I'm Lorrah. Tehra told us you had a place where we could hide."

"You're all Loyalists?"

"Yes," Lorrah replied. "We must leave immediately. We will soon be missed and then they will come looking for us."

"What about Tehra? We can't leave her."

"She's under heavy guard. There is no way to rescue her now."

"Are you sure? There must be something we can do." "We can't leave her here."

"We'd need heavy weapons and all we have are our personal protectors. We couldn't assault the detention center without heavy guns."

"Tehra said her orders were to sabotage the ship and keep it from leaving. Aren't you going to try to do that?"

"This is the first time we've been together. We've had no time to make plans."

"Well, you better make them now. Isn't there any way to keep the ship from taking off? That would give us more time to figure out a rescue plan. We might even figure out how to permanently disable the ship."

A Seafolken stepped up. "I'm one of the onboard mechanics. I think I could cut a few power intakes and prevent take off. Once done, it will take hours for them to find the interruptions and repair them."

"Great. That's exactly what we need. You should do it."

"Yes. Go at once, Pulgan," Lorrah ordered.

Pulgan walked briskly to the staircase and disappeared into the tunnels. I took a deep breath and exhaled slowly. How could we possibly rescue Tehra without weapons? Then an idea hit me.

"What about picking weapons up as we went along? I asked.

"What do you mean?" Lorrah asked.

"Well, each guard has a heavy weapon, right?"

"Yes," Lorrah acknowledged.

"Well, can't your men take out a few guards quietly by surprise and take their weapons. There's only a half dozen of you. It shouldn't take long to get you fully armed."

Lorrah nodded. "Yes, there are single sentries all along the tunnels about a hundred yards apart. Since we haven't been identified as Loyalists as yet, we can go back into the tunnels and each engage a sentry. It will have to be a coordinated attack. If the guards suspect any trouble, we won't catch them off guard and the plan will fail."

"Then once you have the weapons you need, you can go rescue Tehra."

"Yes, that will be our plan. You'll have to wait for us here. You'd be immediately recognized in the tunnels if you came with us."

"Yes. Of course," I said a little relieved. It wasn't that I didn't want to help them, but I was no solider and would likely endanger the mission if I accompanied them. Lorrah looked at her watch and then barked orders to her troops in her alien language. They immediately began moving toward the tunnels.

"Wait here. When we return, I'm sure we'll have to leave in a hurry."

"Okay," I said, wondering how I was going to transport eight people.

Lorrah rushed to the ladder and slid down. She hit the ground hard and I heard her running. Outside I got on my cell phone and called Martha Thomas.

"Martha!"

"Yes."

"This is Stan Turner. It's time. I need you to come help me transport our guests. You better bring the Suburban."

"All right. Where are you?"

After giving Martha directions I hung up the telephone and called the office. I wanted to see how the trial was going. Maria answered and told me the trial was going well and Paula was feeling optimistic. She asked me where I was.

"Something came up with another client. I may be tied up for awhile. It's a pretty serious situation. Would you call Rebekah and tell her I'll be home late tonight?"

"Sure, but why don't you call her yourself?"

"Ah. . . . Oh, I've got to go. Thanks. See ya."

If I called Rebekah there'd be too many questions, questions I couldn't answer. It was better she not know what was going on. She'd just worry and that would do no good. The thought occurred to me that helping the Loyalists may not be such a hot idea. Hanging around here waiting to assist their escape could end up costing me my life. If things went wrong I'd likely die in the crossfire.

Despite this growing fear, I couldn't force myself to leave. I'd promised to help them and I couldn't betray their trust. Besides, if Peter was now somehow involved in the Loyalists' movement, I had to support it in hopes that someday we might be reunited. It was a slim hope, but hope was hope. As I was grappling with my fears, I saw the alien ship begin to lift off of the island where it was hidden.

"Oh, no!" It was taking off. All was lost. Then suddenly the ship lurched and began to fall. There was a terrible explosion and the island exploded into a fiery inferno sending debris all across the lake. I just stared at the spectacle in disbelief. What had happened? Was Tehra still on the ship when it took off? My heart sank as I feared the worst.

I rushed back into the tank and peered down into the tunnels. Smoke shot up from the shafts and quickly overtook me. I began to cough, struggled to breathe, and was soon forced back outside. The island still glowed from the explosion and smoke billowed high up into the sky. I wondered how the authorities would spin an explosion on a deserted island in the middle of Lake Tawakoni. An airplane crash? That's how they'd explained the explosions at Possum Kingdom Lake. It had worked then and would probably work again. I decided that's what I'd tell Martha too since she didn't know her guests were from outer space.

As I was analyzing the situation, I saw headlights approaching. Was it Martha? Who else could it be? I prayed it wasn't the local authorities responding to the explosion. As the vehicle got closer I saw it was a Suburban and breathed a sigh of relief. The car stopped and Martha got out. She pointed to the island.

"Stan, what happened? Was there a crash?"

I shrugged. "Ah. . . . I don't know. It looks that way. I just got here a few minutes ago."

"Why did they land on the Island? There's an airport in Greenville."

"Right, but there can't be a record of their arrival. At least not yet until political asylum has been granted."

"Oh," Martha said tentatively.

"It's been almost half an hour since the explosion and I haven't seen a single survivor."

Suddenly there were footsteps and voices approaching. Out of the smoke a figure appeared. When the smoke around her cleared I saw it was Lorrah. I rushed over.

"You made it out. I thought you'd all been killed."

"We almost were."

"Listen, my friend Martha is here to take you to her ranch where you can hide out. She doesn't know that you are from Tarizon. She thinks you are from another nation on Earth. Don't tell her anything, okay?"

"Right. We won't."

"Did you rescue Tehra?" I asked anxiously.

"Yes, not only Tehra but all the passengers from the ship."

"Oh, thank God! Where are they?"

"Your CIA has captured them and are taking them away. We managed to elude them."

There was coughing in the distance and then several soldiers stumbled out of the tank. A moment later Tehra emerged, black from the soot and smoke, but alive and well. We embraced.

"Oh, I'm so glad to see you. I didn't think I'd ever see you again."

"Yes, that was my fear as well. I was very surprised and delighted to be rescued."

We held each other happily for a moment and then Tehra pulled back, her eyes widened. "Oh, I found someone else you're going to be happy to see."

I frowned, wondering who that could possibly be. She looked over at a man and two children seemingly in shock just outside the door of the tank. She motioned for them to come over. The man walked slowly toward me. He looked strangely familiar but wasn't someone I'd ever seen before. The children however were a spitting image of their mother.

"Mr. Wenzel?"

"Yes."

"But I thought you'd gone back to Tarizon months ago?"

"I was scheduled to, but when my daughter was accidentally killed, we were delayed and missed our ship. We've been waiting in the base for the next shuttle."

"Well, I don't think there will be any more flights back to Tarizon for a while. I guess you'll have to stay on Earth until the war is over."

"Yes. I'm not so sorry about that either. I love my Earth wife and didn't really want to leave her. If it hadn't been my duty to return to Tarizon, I would have never left."

"Well, your wife is in a lot of trouble right now. She could well have been convicted of your murder."

"Yes, but I was assured that wouldn't happen."

"Well, I was trying to prevent it, but there were no guarantees. With your return, though, the charges will be dropped. The only problem is how to explain where you've been."

"Yes, what will I tell the authorities?" Mr. Wenzel asked.

I shrugged. "I don't know, but we'll think of something. I'm just so happy you made it off the ship. Let's get you home. I think your wife will be glad to see you."

"You don't think she'll be angry when she finds out the truth?"

"Yes, she'll be livid . . . but, I suspect, she'll get over it. The important thing is that you are all together and will never be separated again."

Lorrah, Tehra, and the others climbed into the Suburban with Martha Thomas. The Wenzels came with me. Tehra wanted to come with me too, but I reminded her that Kulchz was probably searching for her. Her apartment would not be safe and she certainly couldn't come home with me. She reluctantly acquiesced.

I told Martha I'd come by in the morning to check on everyone and discuss future plans. She agreed and drove off. On the way back to Dallas I called Charlotte Wenzel and told her I was on my way to see her. She wanted to know why, but I was afraid to tell her for fear someone might be intercepting the call. She said she'd leave the light on for me.

As we drove toward Dallas, I wondered how best to handle Gabriel Wenzel's return to the living. In order for Charlotte to be exonerated people would have to see that he was alive. Since he was sitting right next to me that shouldn't have been a problem, but I had a nagging fear that Kulchz and his men might show up at anytime and snatch Gabriel and the kids away. He wouldn't be happy when he found out they'd escaped from the ship. I'd ditched my tracking device, so I wasn't worried about Kulchz tracking me, but he and his men could be lying in wait anywhere to ambush us. I needed to get Gabe in front of some witnesses soon, but how?

Chapter 50

Closing Statements

On Monday morning both parties had finished and the judge asked for closing statements. This was our opportunity to sum up the case for the jury and convince them to vote our way. By this time most of the jury members had made up their minds, so the closing argument was addressed to those few jurors still undecided. Unfortunately, we had no way of knowing which jurors were on the fence, so we couldn't focus our attention on any one juror. Each side was given thirty minutes to close. Francis elected to break his closing into segments–twenty minutes to start and ten minutes to get in the last word. This was the prosecution's right since they had the burden of proof.

Francis stood up and walked toward the jury box. "Ladies and gentlemen of the jury," he said. "I want to thank you again for acting as jurors. Jury service is a wonderful public service and you should be proud of what you are doing here today.

"I know some of you have been intrigued by the ingenious stories the defense has been telling these last few days. I've been quite entertained myself, but these stories are just that–stories, pure fiction. Ms. Waters is a great storyteller, but her motive is to confuse you with conjecture and possibilities. She hasn't come close to proving anything. She wants you to think there is reasonable doubt as to who murdered Chester Brown and his family, but there isn't. We know it was Walter Stanley.

"It is undisputed that Walter Stanley and Chester Brown were engaged in a bitter feud over a barking dog. Stanley's wife couldn't stand the constant barking so she called animal control, the police, and her attorney trying to get relief. She asked her husband to do something but his attempts to reason with the Browns failed. Eventually the feud led to a divorce which Walter Stanley blamed on the Browns.

"So, when Chester Brown advised Walter Stanley and the Collin Commons Homeowner's Association that he was installing a chainlink fence in disregard of the association rules and the clear dictates of the Covenants, Conditions, and Restrictions of Collin Commons, Stanley was outraged, so outraged that he decided to end the feud once and for all by killing the Brown family.

"Although Ms. Waters would have you believe an elaborate triggering device was used to set the fire, it isn't true. Several of our witnesses have testified that the fire was started by a match and a can of gas. Ms. Waters would like to complicate things but don't listen to her. This a very simple case. Walter Stanley blamed Chester Brown for his divorce pure and simple. When Brown defied the homeowner's association over the chainlink fence it was obviously an intentional act calculated to incense Walter Stanley and the other members of the Collin Commons Homeowner's Association who had sided with Walter Stanley over the barking dog.

"I know that some of you may feel sorry for Walter Stanley. Perhaps Chester Brown went too far in defying Stanley and the Board of Directors. Perhaps he should have taken stronger measures to quiet his dog. Perhaps he shouldn't have built a chainlink fence. But did his errors in judgement justify murder? Did Walter Stanley have the right to lure the Brown's dog away, break into their house, douse it with kerosene, and set it on fire? . . . You know the answer to that. We have mediators, arbitrators, and courts of law in America to settle disputes. There is no justification for this cold blooded, calculated murder of five human beings. Three innocent children who knew nothing of this ridiculous feud were killed. Their lives were stolen by the callous, selfish acts of Walter Stanley, a pathetic man who couldn't face up to his own shortcomings and had to blame them on others.

"You all have a duty as jurors to render a just verdict. We have proven beyond any reasonable doubt that Walter Stanley set the Brown house on fire. We produced the butcher who testified Walter bought two steaks. We showed you the blood evidence proving that Stanley opened the gate and lured the dog away so he could enter the house. We produced a neighbor who saw Stanley in the alley just before the fire. We established a motive–the bitter feud between these families. "Whether Walter Stanley intended to kill Chester Brown and his family or just destroy their house doesn't matter. Breaking and entering and setting the fire is a felony and if someone dies during the commission of a felony, that is as much murder as if Stanley had stuck a knife into Chester Brown's heart.

"Thank you all again for your jury service. I am confident that you will now fulfill your oath to render a fair and just verdict by finding Walter Stanley guilty of murder."

Francis bowed slightly and then took his seat. The judge looked at me and said, "Ms. Waters."

I got up and smiled at the jurors. "Your honor, ladies and gentlemen of the jury, I too am confident that you will render a fair and just verdict here today. I have watched you throughout the trial and have observed your keen attention to the testimony and evidence presented. For that reason I know that you must realize the prosecution has failed miserably in meeting its burden of proof.

"I'm sure you remember the judge's instructions in this regard. The defendant is presumed innocent and in order to convict him of murder the prosecution must prove beyond any reasonable doubt that he caused the death of Chester Brown and his family. If you think back the only thing the prosecution has proven is that Walter Stanley let the Brown's dog out. There is no evidence that Walter Stanley broke into the Brown house or set the fire. The prosecution would like you to draw that inference but you don't have to. If the prosecution can't meet their burden of proof then you should find the defendant

innocent.

"The prosecution complains we are trying to confuse you by advancing two very plausible explanations for the Brown murders. They claim Walter Stanley killed five human beings over a barking dog and a chainlink fence. We produced a suspect who'd made death threats against Chester Brown because he thought he'd stolen the woman he loved. Isn't that a more plausible explanation for the fire and subsequent death of the Brown family? The jilted lover wanting revenge is the oldest motive for murder in the book, yet the prosecution calls it fiction.

"We produced compelling evidence that Ruth Willis hired Marty Ramirez to kill Chester Brown. We know that Ruth Willis was upset when Chester dumped her. We also know that Almatech Life Systems stood to gain millions of dollars by Chester Brown's death. These are all much more compelling motives for murder than a barking dog and a chainlink fence.

"As jurors you have the obligation to consider the testimony and physical evidence and give it the credence you think appropriate. That means you can use common sense in determining a verdict. Common sense tells us that the death of the Brown family wasn't the result of a barking dog and a chainlink fence. Sure, we haven't proven who killed Chester Brown and his family or why they were killed, but we don't have to. All we have to do is create reasonable doubt.

"If you're not sure who killed Chester Brown then you must find Walter Stanley innocent. If you think there is any chance that Tim Willis followed through on his death threat or Ruth Willis hired Marty Ramirez to remotely set the Brown house ablaze, then you must find Walter Stanley not guilty.

"Thank you for being such a serious and attentive jury. I have no doubt you will render the correct verdict in this case by setting Walter Stanley free."

A wave of relief swept over me as I sat down. It was over for me. Now all I had to do was listen and wait. Francis got up and finished his closing argument, but the jury wasn't paying much attention. I could see they were already deliberating. The weight of their task would weigh heavy on their souls until a decision was made. I didn't envy their job. When Francis was done, the judge gave his final instructions, admonished them to keep their deliberations confidential, and sent them to the jury room.

"Nice job," Bart said smiling. "You knocked 'em dead."

"I don't know. It was hard to read them," I said with genuine concern.

"You did great, Paula," Stanley concurred. "Thank you so much for everything. No matter what happens, I couldn't have had a better attorney."

"Thank you," Walter. "I'm glad you feel that way."

The momentary relief I'd felt at the conclusion of my closing statement began to wane. Worry began to creep into my mind as I feared the jury would think our alternative theories were pure speculation and fiction as the prosecution claimed. A knot began to well in my stomach. Bart must have seen my crumbling confidence as he put his arm around me and squeezed me tightly.

"Don't worry, honey, your theories make much more sense than the prosecution's. The jurors aren't stupid. You don't kill someone over a barking dog. They'll acquit Stanley."

Whether Bart really believed that or was just trying to make me feel better, I didn't know, but it was nice to hear. I took a deep breath and said a silent prayer for Walter Stanley. His life was in the hands of twelve strangers. That had to be scary. I looked over at him and noticed he was trembling. I couldn't imagine being in his position, all alone with his life in the balance.

Chapter 51

Celebration

After pondering the question of how to document Gabriel Wenzel's return, I picked up my cell phone and dialed Paula's friend at the Dallas Morning News, Jane Witherspoon. If she met us at Charlotte's home, she could bear witness to the fact that Gabriel and the children were alive. I dialed the number. After a long wait while they searched for her, Jane finally came on the line. She was obviously surprised to hear from me.

"Stan. It's been awhile. How are you?"

"Wonderful. What are you doing right now?"

"Right now? Ah, just finishing up a story."

"How would you like a nice scoop on the Charlotte Wenzel case?"

There was a pause. "Yeah, sure. What's up?"

"I can't talk about it on the phone. Meet me at Charlotte Wenzel's house in thirty minutes and bring a cameraman."

Jane had lots of questions but finally agreed to hold them until we met. I wondered if I should call Gary Shepard or let him find out on the ten o'clock news that his case had disintegrated. I finally decided to go over his head and invite Bob Ralston to the party.

Looking over at Gabriel Wenzel, I said, "You're going to need some kind of a story as to where you've been these last two months."

He nodded. "Right. What do you suggest?"

"We obviously can't tell the truth. That would be a disaster for both of us. There is one plausible explanation that might work."

"What's that?"

I explained my idea to Gabe. He didn't like it much because

it cast him in a bad light, but since he couldn't think of a better explanation for his absence, he agreed to it.

When we got to the Wenzels home, Charlotte was so shocked and excited to see Gabe and the children she nearly fainted. After she'd recovered and had a chance to hug and kiss all of her family, she thanked me profusely for bringing them home. As we were celebrating, the doorbell rang. I was sure it was Jane Witherspoon and her cameraman, so I motioned for Gabe to follow me to the door, which he did.

"Jane, come in," I said. "I want you to meet someone."

Jane smiled and stepped inside. "Okay."

"You'll probably want to be rolling that camera," I said to the cameraman. The cameraman shouldered the camera and a green light came on. I stepped aside so that Jane could see Gabe and the children. "Jane, I'd like to introduce Gabriel Wenzel."

Jane's mouth dropped, then a wide beaming smile appeared. She picked up the microphone, looked into the camera, and said, "I'm in the home of Charlotte Wenzel where a celebration is in progress. What's the occasion? Well, nothing less than the resurrection of Charlotte's husband, Gabriel Wenzel and two of her children."

Jane moved up next to Gabe so they could both be seen on camera. "Mr. Wenzel. This is such a shock. Where have you been these past few months?"

Gabe sighed. "Well, it's a long story and I'm embarrassed to tell it, but I guess I owe it to everyone to explain what happened."

"Yes, we are all very interested. Your wife's been on trial for murder. Please tell us where you and kids have been."

"Well, Charlotte had been complaining for a long time that I hadn't been spending enough time with the children, so I decided to take them hiking at the lake."

"Lake Tawakoni?"

"Yes. Charlotte had wanted to do some shopping so I called her from the office and told her I'd take pick up the kids on Friday so she could go shopping with her friends. She thought that was a great idea so I got kids from school and we went to the lake. Unfortunately–" Tears began to well up in Gabe's eyes and his voice cracked. "Unfortunately, Jill ran off when I was busy with other kids.

She apparently saw a coyote and thought it was a dog. Oh, God. It was so terrible. The animal didn't like being chased and turned on her. By the time I got there she'd been mauled. I tried to save her but she died in my arms."

"So, you couldn't get her to a hospital?"

"No, she was dead. The coyote severed an artery and she bled to death in minutes. I was devastated, I didn't know what to do. All I could think about was how Charlotte was going to react to what had happened. I just couldn't face her, so I decided to run."

"Where did you go?" Jane asked.

"I hid out awhile in a rundown motel in Longview but the case was getting so much publicity we moved on to Louisiana where we'd be less likely to be recognized."

"So, what made you come back now?"

"As time went on, I realized that I couldn't let Charlotte go on trial for my murder. I loved her and had to make things right. It was time for me to take responsibility for what happened and face the consequences."

Jane shook her head, "Well, this is quite a shocking development. I'm speaking with Gabriel Wenzel who everyone presumed was dead since he and his children went missing last August. In fact, his wife Charlotte had been charged with his murder and was scheduled to go on trial in just a few weeks.

Jane walked over to me and asked, "Mr. Turner. Have you advised the District Attorney of this development?"

"Not yet. I did invite him to this interview but I haven't seen him yet."

Just then the doorbell rang. Hoping it was Rob Ralston I strolled briskly to the door. It was Gary Shepard and Will Kramer, even better. I smiled and invited them in.

"Gary, I don't know if you've met Gabriel Wenzel."

Shepard's face contorted like he'd been hit with a Taser gun. I felt better at that moment than I had in years. Not only had I wrapped up a murder case, but I'd brought a family back together. To make it even more memorable, I'd seen Gary Shepard's look of shock and utter dismay when he realized Gabriel Wenzel was alive and his plans to oust Rob Walston as DA had just gone up in smoke.

When I got back into my car I just sat there a moment and thanked God for bringing order to the chaos that had plagued me since Mo and the CIA had come into my life. For the first time since this horrible nightmare began, I felt confident it would all soon be over. Why it happened, I'd never know, but I was sure God had his reasons and would provide guidance for the challenges that still lay ahead.

Chapter 52

Verdict

The jury deliberated the rest of the day and it wasn't until six o'clock that evening that the judge let them go home for the day. I figured a quick verdict would favor the prosecution. If they believed Francis had proven his case beyond all reasonable doubt, then they wouldn't have much to talk about and would come back with a quick guilty verdict. On the other hand, if they believed the prosecution's case was weak or that one of our alternative scenarios was plausible, they'd have lots to talk about and a decision might not come for days.

The next morning Jodie and I brought Stanley and the Sheriff's deputy guarding him a dozen Duncan Donuts and coffee for breakfast. We ate in the attorney's conference room adjacent to the courtroom. Stanley looked pale and there were dark circles under his eyes. It was apparent he was beginning to crumble little by little under the gravity of the situation. Watching him pace back and forth like a caged animal made me uneasy and I prayed the jury would render their decision, one way or another, quickly before he had a nervous breakdown.

For lunch we ordered pizza. It was hard just sitting around twiddling our thumbs while we waited for the jury to make a decision. Time crawled like a crippled snail. Stanley's pacing was giving me a headache and Jodie looked like she was ready to hit him over the head to make him be still. Finally at three that afternoon we got word the jury had reached a verdict. Within minutes the courtroom was full of spectators and the judge ordered the jury be brought back in. Once they had been seated, the judge asked them if they had a verdict.

The foreman stood up."We do, Your Honor," the foreman

replied.

'What is your verdict, then?" the Judge asked.

"On the charge of the murder of Chester Lewis Brown, we, the jury find the defendant not guilty. On the charge of the murder of Gladys Brown, we, the jury find the defendant not guilty. . . ."

The gallery erupted in bedlam as the judge dismissed the jury, set Walter Stanley free, and left the bench. Stanley shook my hand and then gave me a big hug. Francis, the gentlemen that he was, came over and congratulated me. He said I was very imaginative and told a good story. I didn't know if that was a compliment or not, but it didn't matter. We'd won. Bart was ecstatic as he'd gotten sweet revenge for his untimely firing. The only disappointment that afternoon was the absence of Stan. I wanted him to see my victory, but he was nowhere to be found. I feared he was in some sort of trouble.

When I got back to the office Maria said my friend, Jane Witherspoon, had called. She wanted to know what was up with Stan. He'd called her to set up a meeting and she wanted to know what it was about. I tried to return the call but she was out. Why would Stan want to meet with Jane Witherspoon? I looked at my watch and saw it was nearly 6:00 p.m. The news would be on soon and perhaps I'd find out. When I saw Gabriel Wenzel on the screen I nearly jumped for joy. What a stunning day for Turner and Waters. Jodie and Maria joined me in front of the TV. We all laughed and cried joyful tears.

"This calls for a celebration," Jodie said.

I nodded. "You're damn right! Why don't you call the Adolphus and see if we can get a banquet room."

While Jodie and Maria made plans for the party I tried to get Stan on his cell phone, but as usual he had it turned off. How in the hell did he get Gabriel Wenzel to come out of hiding? His story was plausible, but something about it didn't feel right. I wondered if it was the truth or just a story. Either way Gabe would be facing his own legal problems now due to his failure to report his daughter's death and allowing his wife to go on trial for murder. Under other circumstances I could see the DA overlooking his improprieties, but since the DA's office had wasted over a hundred thousand dollars of the taxpayer's money, I couldn't see them letting him off the hook.

At 6:45 p.m. I finally reached Stan and congratulated him. I told him about the party and suggested he go get Rebekah and the kids and go straight to the Adolphus. He said he wouldn't miss it for the world. I hung up the phone and left to go home to shower and change. Bart had gone straight home after the trial, so I called him and told him about the party. He said he'd already started partying and that I might have to drive. I laughed and told him not to worry about it. I'd be the designated driver for the evening.

At 7:30 p.m. we arrived at the hotel and were directed to a private banquet room. There were already twenty-five or thirty people drinking cocktails and eating hors d'oeuvres. Bart brought me a glass of white wine and pointed to an incredible spread of hors d'oeuvres—crabmeat and crayfish with tiny green beans, trout, potato salad, seared rolaide of beef—to name just a few of the delicious looking treats. I grabbed a plate and loaded it up.

As I was feeding my face I spotted Charlotte and Gabriel Wenzel talking to Jodie. Their kids were running around having a great time with some other children who'd come with their parents to celebrate. I saw Paul Thayer and his wife getting drinks. There were clients, reporters, and friends of friends all having the time of their life. I noticed Walter Stanley talking to a group of reporters and Maria and her husband at the hors d'oeuvres stand loading their plates. Finally, I spotted Stan and his family entering the banquet room. I rushed over.

"Stan. Rebekah. You made it!"

"Yes," Rebekah said. "Look at this. How did you put this all together so quickly?"

I shrugged. "I can't take the credit. Jodie and Maria arranged it."

"Congratulations!" Stan said. "You finally got to be first chair in a murder trial."

"Yes, but I was a little disappointed you weren't there to watch."

"Yeah. I'm sorry about that, but it couldn't be helped."

"Yes, now I understand. How the hell did you find Gabriel Wenzel?"

"Well, that was a bit of good fortune, I'm afraid. I can't take much credit for it."

I had lots of questions, but this wasn't the time or place to get answers, so I dropped the subject. The party went on for hours and when it came time to go home I was too intoxicated to fulfill my duty as designated driver, so we got a room and stayed the night. Stan and Rebekah did the same thing, but not because they were too drunk to drive. They just wanted some time alone. It had been a great day, and I felt proud and content until the thought occurred to me. Tomorrow I'd have nothing to do!

Chapter 53

A Sad Farewell

The next morning I had a hangover that would have made a bloody Irishman proud. My head throbbed and the light sent piercing darts of pain through my brain. After I'd had a cup of coffee and some aspirin, my head began to clear and I remembered there was a camp of refugees at the Double T Ranch in Wylie. I wondered how Martha Thomas was handling them.

After eating a nice breakfast compliments of room service, we got our things together and headed home. By noon I was on my way to the Double T Ranch. It was a forty minute drive, so it gave me time to think about the logistics of hiding a dozen aliens for an extended period of time. Since the Tarizonian shuttle had been destroyed it was no telling how long we'd have to house them.

When I rolled up the driveway I saw Tehra and Martha sitting on the front porch. I wondered what Martha would do if she knew she was talking to an alien. I had told her they were aliens, but not from another planet. She just thought their visas had expired. I got out of my car and strolled up to them.

"Well, it's about time you got here," Tehra remarked.

"Yeah, well we did a little partying last night. I had a bit of a hangover this morning."

"It serves you right partying and not inviting us," Tehra teased.

"Well, it would have been a tad dangerous for you to come, I think."

Looking at Martha I said, "So have your guests given you any trouble?"

"No, not at all. I've enjoyed having them. It's usually so quiet around here. It's nice to have the ranch jumping again."

"Well, when they wear out their welcome be sure and tell me. I don't know how long they'll need to stay."

"Actually, it won't be but a few days," Tehra said.

I frowned. "A few days? How's that?"

"I got a message this morning. Our friends from home are coming to get us."

"You're kidding! How did they find you?"

"I left them my number." Tehra said smiling.

I didn't know what that meant. Apparently she had some sort of communication device that the Loyalists had used to communicate with her. I was ambivalent about her leaving. It was risky having her around, yet she was carrying my child. I had feelings for her, but I couldn't give in to them without endangering my marriage. It was good she was leaving. There was no doubt about that.

Martha asked if I wanted a glass of lemonade. I told her I did and she got up to go get it for me. That gave me the opportunity to talk more freely with Tehra.

"So, a ship is coming for you?"

"Yes, it will be here the day after tomorrow."

"That soon?"

She nodded. "It was a shuttle that was working out of Arizona. There were enough Loyalists aboard that they hijacked it. Now they are flying around the Earth picking up recruits."

"That's great. Will it go back to Tarizon?"

"Yes, just as soon as it's full."

I just looked at Tehra. I didn't know what to say to her. I looked away.

"It's for the best," she said.

I nodded and then squinted at a shiny object in the distance. It looked like a small Lear Jet and it was flying low. As it got closer it dove straight at us.

"We've got company! I yelled. Take cover."

I grabbed Tehra's arm and we ran across the driveway away from the house with Martha fifty yards behind us. There was a flash of light and a shrill noise before Martha's house exploded knocking us off our feet. Two more fighters followed the first and blew up the barn and a storage shed. I looked on in shock not knowing whether to run or stay put. Tehra pointed to a drainage ditch about twenty yards away. We made a mad dash for it as the three fighters swung around and took another run at us.

This time around Martha's truck was blown up and three of the Loyalist's recruits were incinerated by one of the blasts and lay smoldering on the concrete. Martha came running toward us screaming in horror. She was laden with soot from the billows of smoke pouring from the house. Her arm was bleeding badly. I intercepted her, dragged her into the ravine and forced her to the ground.

"Stay down!" I screamed.

"My arm, it's killing me," she moaned.

I looked around for something to wrap it with.

"I'm so sorry, Martha. I never dreamed they'd find us."

"Who? Who are they? Why are they trying to kill us?"

"They must have followed you here," Tehra said. "That's the only way they could have found us."

"Or maybe when you contacted your friends they were listening."

She shrugged. "It doesn't matter. We've got to get out of here."

I tore off one of my sleeves and wrapped Martha's arm to stop the bleeding. She was breathing heavily and I feared she'd pass out on us at any moment.

"We'll be sitting ducks if we try to move," I replied.

"There's some four wheelers behind the barn," Martha screamed. "If we stay along the perimeter of the farm the trees will protect us."

Tehra looked at me. I nodded. "Let's go."

As the fighters flew by a third time we got up and made a run for what was left of the barn. Fortunately, three of the four wheelers were not damaged. As I got on one of the vehicles, I smelled the foul odor of burning flesh and turned to see two more fallen aliens, their bodies badly burned and mutilated by the lasers. I felt sick and turned away trying to avoid vomiting.

Soon we were racing as fast as the four wheelers would let us along the perimeter of the farm. The tall oaks and thick Bradford Pear trees made it difficult for the fighters to get a beat on us. Finally, they disappeared and we stopped to catch our breath.

"Do you think they've gone?" Martha asked.

"It looks that way," I said. "But they may be back."

When we got back to the main house there were five aliens still alive. Six had been killed and the Double T Ranch was in shambles. The scene reminded me of the string of bad luck that had befallen Dusty Thomas and his ranch. In his youth Dusty had nearly been killed by a falling branch after a lightning strike. His first wife spent his life's savings, ran up a pocket full of credit cards, and then divorced him. A few years later he'd had a heart attack while plowing, fell of his tractor, and broke his leg. Then there was the tornado that leveled the house and barns. In recent years much of the ranch had been seized by the IRS and sold at auction. Finally, an IRS agent was murdered in front of the big house while serving a warrant and Dusty was hunted down by the FBI and charged with the crime. He was later tried for that murder but acquitted.

We thought it best to evacuate the ranch before the police and fire department showed up. There was no way we could have explained what had happened. I looked up as I heard sirens in the distance. Martha ran to her neighbor and borrowed another truck. We threw the dead bodies in the back, covered them with a tarp, and got the hell out of there. As we drove away, I had no idea where we were going. All I knew as we had to get as much distance from us and the ranch as we could.

That night we camped out at one the Oklahoma state parks on Lake Texoma. Tehra managed to contact the Loyalists and gave them our new position. The following day just before dawn the huge ship glided over the lake shooting out blue lightning ahead and behind the ship. Once it was overhead it hovered effortlessly above us.

"I wish I could stay," Tehra said. "I'd like to live here with you."

"I'd like that too if circumstances were different."

She sighed. "I'll find Peter when I get back to Tarizon and tell him how I met his father."

Tears began to well in my eyes. "If you do see him, tell him we love him and we miss him terribly."

"I will," Tehra said squeezing my hand. "Take care of yourself."

"Me! You're the one who'll be walking into a civil war."

She shrugged and then joined the others on the shore of the lake including the dead soldiers whose bodies were laid out in a row. Suddenly there was a hissing sound and both the living and the dead floated up into the ship within an invisible tube. It was an incredible sight that left me breathless.

When I got home an hour later, Rebekah wanted to know all that had happened. I told her everything and assured her the alien project was finished. She breathed a sigh of relief.

"Thank God. These past two years have been the worst years of our lives. I curse the day you met Mo and got involved with the CIA."

"Don't worry. Those days are over," I said and took her in my arms. "Paula will be happy too. She hated all of this."

"I don't blame her. It's been horrible."

As I held Rebekah, I thought of Tehra somewhere out in space. How could that be? I wondered if she'd really look for Peter when she got to Tarizon and, if she found him, tell him about her adventures on Earth. It was all so incredible, I could scarcely comprehend it. Then a strange calm came over me. Someday I'd see Peter again. Somehow he'd make it back to Earth and we'd be reunited! I just knew it!

Chapter 54

Outburst

In early spring the following year I got a call from Ben Stover reminding me that Ralph Herman's trial was starting the next week. He and Alice really wanted me to attend the trial. I told him I really couldn't afford the time away from the office as I was involved with a trio of doctors who'd enlisted me to set up a defensive estate plan for them. They had been plagued by ex-wives, frivolous lawsuits, and the IRS and wanted to be able to practice medicine without constantly being distracted by someone after their money. It was one of those projects that involved creativity rather than legal prowess and had been a nice change of pace.

"Alice and I'd really feel better if you came," Ben pleaded. "We'll pay you for your time."

"Do I have to remind you that you're bankrupt?"

"I don't care. We'll find the money."

"It's not the money," I said. "It's just I'm deluged with work right now."

There was silence on the other line. I could feel Ben's anxiety through the phone line. I couldn't stand it.

"Okay, I'll come down for the last day of the trial and sit with you and Alice during jury deliberations."

"Well, I guess that's better than not coming at all," he said gloomily.

"Come on. You're in good hands with Gary Wakefield. He's a good prosecutor."

"I know, but he could probably use some help. You know Herman's a smooth talker. He'll probably have the jury eating out of his hand."

"I doubt that," I protested. "There's a lot of evidence against him."

"True, but every time we take Ralph Herman for granted he burns us."

Ben was right. It was uncanny how Herman could hit you with a grenade when you least expected it. Could he possibly escape conviction? We just couldn't let that happen.

"Listen, Ben. Don't worry about. I've got an idea how to insure Ralph gets what he deserves. Jodie and I will be there to give Wakefield a hand if he needs it."

"Good. I feel so much better now. Alice will be thrilled."

After I hung up, I asked Jodie to come and see me. We had a plan to concoct to be sure the truth about Ralph Herman finally came out. On a previous case we had been desperate to get a witness to tell the truth so I had asked Mo if he could get us some truth serum. We were shocked when he provided us with the CIA's latest brew. The directions were simple. A few drops directly on the tongue or a half teaspoon in a liquid. Luckily I had a little bit left.

On Wednesday of the following week I got a call from Ben. He told me the case was winding down and would likely go to the jury on Friday.

"I'm really worried. Ralph testified today and he's very convincing. He went on and on about my poor health and how forgetful I've become. He says it got so bad, he was practically running the company for me. He still claims I authorized him to set up the accounts and that he just did what I told him to do."

"What about the missing money?"

"He says I've got it stashed away somewhere. Wakefield says he's going to have to recall me and Alice as rebuttal witnesses to try to undo some of the damage he's caused."

"I can't believe this. Didn't Wakefield try to discredit him?"

"Yes, it's not his fault. Ralph's a snake. When Wakefield brought up his surreptitious trips to the Cayman Islands, he claimed that I gave him detailed instructions on how to set up the accounts and then blurted out the fact that I had been arrested for bankruptcy fraud."

"What! I thought the judge ruled that was not relevant and couldn't be mentioned at trial."

"He did, and Ralph was admonished for bringing it up but big deal. The jury still heard it."

I took a deep, frustrated breath. I told Ben we'd be there in the morning and not to worry.

The next morning Jodie and I worked out our plan to dispense the drug to the witness on the way to Waco. The truth serum seemed to have worked on the last witness we tried it on, but her testimony was interrupted so we didn't really know for sure. Another uncertainty was that she was a willing participant in the use of the drug. Today our witness would not know that he had been drugged and it might not work as well on someone who fought its effects.

Another worry would be if the judge found out what we'd done. It would be considered obstruction of justice and we'd be immediately arrested and I'd lose my law license. But we couldn't let Ralph Herman get away with his crimes and it looked like that was exactly what was going to happen if we didn't take matters into our own hands. It didn't feel like we were doing anything wrong, since the truth serum was supposed to make the witness tell the truth. What could be wrong with that? But, I knew the judge and the bar association wouldn't see it that way. I discussed the situation with Jodie and told her that she probably shouldn't help me, but she wouldn't hear of it.

We conferred with Wakefield when we arrived at the courthouse and he advised us that he was taking Ike Eiseman on cross when the trial resumed. That was perfect as Ike seemed to be the best candidate for the truth serum as he would have less resolve to fight off the effects of the drug than Herman. I pointed out Eiseman to Jodie and she went off to implement our plan.

It was a simple plan. Jodie would sit next to him and strike up a conversation and then invite him to have a cup of coffee. While he wasn't looking, she'd slip in the truth serum. As I entered the courtroom, I saw them walking off to the courthouse cafeteria. I shook my head. Female charm was the deadliest weapon in the universe.

Inside, I saw Ben and Alice and went over to them. Alice and I embraced and Ben shook my hand fiercely.

"Thank you for coming, Stan. You don't know how much this means to us."

"Well, I want to see that bastard put away as much as you guys."

"Yeah, well," Alice muttered, "that's not looking so good right now."

I smiled. "Don't be pessimistic. The jury is pretty smart. They'll be able to sift out the truth, particularly after Wakefield gets through with Eiseman."

"Did you give him a few pointers, I hope?" Ben said. "So far he's coming off as a pretty decent lad. He's as good a liar as Herman."

"We met this morning and discussed how to handle the cross. I think he'll do just fine."

Ben looked at me warily. I gave him a wry smile in return. "Well good, then. Maybe the momentum will shift. I sure hope so."

As we continued to talk the bailiff stood and said, "All rise!"

The judge scurried into the courtroom and took the bench.

"Be seated," he said. "Let's see. I believe Mr. Wakefield, you were about to cross Ike Eiseman."

Wakefield rose. "Yes, Your Honor."

"Bailiff, bring in Mr. Eiseman."

The bailiff nodded and went out into the hallway. A moment later he returned and said, "Mr. Eiseman is not here, Your Honor."

The judge frowned. "Where is he?"

The bailiff shrugged. "I saw him sitting in the hall thirty minutes ago. He must have gone to the restroom or something."

The judge shook his head angrily."Well find him and get him back here. I want to get testimony wrapped up today, if possible."

"Yes, sir," the bailiff replied and went back out into the hall.

A jolt of fear shot through me. Had Jodie had a problem? They should have been back from having coffee by now. I got up and went into the hallway outside the courtroom. It was empty with the exception of a lawyer talking to his client outside another courtroom. Then I heard the elevator bell ring and arguing.

"You shouldn't have strayed off like that. Everyone is waiting for you. The judge is really mad."

"Hey man, chill. I was just getting' a cup a coffee. Jeez."

The bailiff had Eiseman by the arm and was pulling him toward the courtroom. I backed out of the way. Jodie was nowhere to be found. We had agreed she would make herself scarce after spiking the coffee so that nobody would connect us as being together. I followed them into the courtroom and took a seat.

"Well, Mr. Eiseman. I'm glad you could join us," the judge said sarcastically. "Please retake the stand."

"Yeah. Whatever," Eiseman said jovially and staggered to the stand.

Ralph's attorney looked at Eiseman nervously. He must have sensed something was awry. Ralph frowned as Eiseman smiled broadly at Wakefield.

"Your witness," the Judge said.

Wakefield nodded. "Mr. Eiseman, you testified yesterday that Ralph Herman was your friend, is that right?"

Eiseman looked at Ralph and smiled, "Yes, my best friend."

"And you've been friends since childhood, isn't that correct?"

He nodded. "Yes, since grammar school."

"So, for a relationship to last that long you must look out for each other–watch each other's back?"

"You got it man. That's what friends are all about."

"So, has Ralph ever . . . you know . . . covered for you, as they say?"

A broad smile came over Eiseman's face. "Yeah, sure. Like when I wanted to get out of the house, I could always count on Ralph to cover for me. I'd do the same for him."

"So, you'd lie for him and he'd lie for you?"

Eiseman nodded. "Sure, why not?"

"And you covered for each other in other ways too, I suppose. Like at school maybe?"

Eiseman squinted a moment then a big grin came on his face. "Oh, you mean like if he wanted to cheat on his girl?"

"No. I was thinking more like with tests and exams. Did you or he ever cheat on an exam–maybe get the questions in advance or get the answers from one of the smart kids in the class?"

He laughed. "Oh, yeah. You don't think we actually studied all that crap, do you?"

"No, of course, not. So, did Ralph ask you to help him skim money from Ben Stover?"

Eiseman rolled his eyes and twisted his head in a weird manner. "Yeah, what a deal, huh? Stover was so loaded he never missed it."

"Objection! Your Honor," Jacobs shouted, "there is something wrong with this witness."

"Yeah, he finally decided to tell the truth," Wakefield spat.

The judge took a deep breath and turned to the witness. "Mr. Eiseman, are you feeling okay?"

A big smile came over Eiseman's face. "Never better, Your Honor."

"Have you been drinking?"

"Just coffee, Your Honor."

The judge studied Eiseman for a moment and then shrugged. "Objection overruled. You may continue, Mr. Wakefield."

"So, did the money go into the offshore account?"

"Right, pretty slick, huh?"

Ralph stood up and pointed his finger at Eiseman. "Shut up! You lying son of a bitch."

Jacobs grabbed Ralph 's shoulder and tried to sit him down. Ralph turned and shoved him hard, sending him crashing to the floor. There were screams from the gallery and the jury just stared at the melee in shock. Two bailiffs came running over and tried to seize Ralph but he fought them like a raging bull and they were unable to restrain him. Finally a sheriff's deputy intervened with a billy club and Ralph collapsed to the floor unconscious.

Within five minutes the paramedics arrived and took Ralph away. Chaos continued for several more minutes until the judge finally banged his gavel and the courtroom quieted down. Then he sent the jury to the jury room to wait until as he put it, "things were sorted out."

"I move for a mistrial, Your Honor," Jacobs snarled. "This incident has irrevocably prejudiced the jury. There is no way my client can get a fair trial now."

"Your Honor," Wakefield replied, "this incident was caused wholly by the defendant. You can't grant a mistrial when it was the defendant's misconduct that caused the problem. If you did that, all any defendant would have to do to thwart the court is have a temper tantrum like Mr. Herman just had."

The judge nodded. "I would agree with you counselor, if this was completely the defendant's fault, but you have to admit Mr. Eiseman was a different man here today from the one who testified yesterday. I'm ordering he be subjected to a physical examination to be sure he wasn't under the influence of alcohol or some other personality changing drug."

The judge looked up and met my eyes. "Mr. Turner. What business do you have with this court?"

A chill swept over me. I stood up tentatively. "Ah. Just a spectator, Your Honor. Ben and Alice Stover have been long time clients."

"Well, Mr. Turner, you have a reputation for your courtroom antics. Is it just a coincidence that you are here when all hell breaks loose or did you say something to Mr. Herman or Mr. Eiseman that could have set them off?"

I shook my head. "I haven't talked to either one of them, Your Honor."

"Uh huh. Well, I sincerely hope you had nothing to do with what happened here today."

I didn't respond because I didn't want to have to lie to the Court. I just shrugged and walked out of the courtroom. My heart was pounding. What if they found traces of the truth serum in Eiseman's blood? We'd be screwed. I had no idea what was in the truth serum as Mo had delivered it in an unlabeled bottle and never revealed to us its formula. I had to find Jodie and decide what to do. Should we hang around for the results of the test or go into hiding? My head began to throb as I saw my legal career going down the toilet.

Jodie was sitting on the hood of my car when I got to the parking lot. I told her what had happened. She said there was a Denny's down the street where we could talk. I told her I needed something stronger than coffee. She raised her eyebrows and then said she thought there was also a Bennigans that would have a bar. I opted for that idea and we found it just a few blocks farther down the street. After we'd had a couple of drinks, we talked strategy.

"Let's not panic," Jodie said. "Maybe they won't find anything in Eiseman's blood."

"I hope not. I don't know what will happen if they do."

"Even if they did, how would they prove how he got it?" Jodie added.

"True. If the drug acts like alcohol Eiseman won't remember a thing tomorrow."

"That's right. So, relax. All is not lost."

I felt a little better after talking it out with Jodie and getting a few drinks under my belt. We had one more drink and then ordered dinner. An hour later we left to find a motel to stay the night. When I got to my room I called Ben and Alice and we discussed what had happened. They both said they felt good about the day's events and were anxious to find out what the judge would do in the morning. I wasn't as anxious as I feared there was trouble ahead.

As I lay in bed trying to sleep, I prayed God would just get me through one more day. I thought back to the past year and wondered how I'd made it this far. Now that Rebekah was better and the CIA was finally out of my life, I needed some tranquility. I couldn't take another catastrophe in my life right now. It would be the end of me. Why hadn't I stayed home and ignored Ben and Alice's plea? Why was I seemingly compelled to drop everything and come running when clients were in trouble? It was a curse.

The alarm clock startled me. I rolled over and squinted at the display. It was seven-twenty-nine a.m. I sighed. Just a little over an hour and my destiny would be sealed, one way or another. After showering and getting dressed, I called Jodie's room and asked if she was ready to get some breakfast. She said to give her ten minutes.

At eight-forty-five I left the motel and drove to the courthouse. Jodie stayed at the motel still concerned that Eiseman might see her and remember their brief encounter. Fortunately, Ralph's trial hadn't garnered a lot of media attention, so the gallery was only half full even after yesterday's excitement. Ralph was at the counsel table but his hands were in cuffs. He had a bandage over his left temple where he'd been hit with the billy club. The jury box was empty. At nine a.m. the judge took the bench and immediately addressed the parties.

"Yesterday's events have caused this court much concern," the judge said. "The defendant's outburst and the witness's strange behavior might well influence the jury's decision, yet the medical exam conducted on the witness did not show that he was drunk or otherwise under the influence of a controlled substance. Therefore, I am denying defense counsel's motion for a mistrial. Mr. Wakefield, you may continue with your cross examination."

Wakefield stood up. "Your Honor, after the incident last night defense counsel and I talked and reached an agreement for a plea in this case."

The judge sat up in his chair. My mouth fell open. Alice twisted in her chair and looked over at me, eyes wide. Relief flooded through every vein, muscle, and joint of my body. I couldn't help but smile gleefully. God had come through one more time.

"Well, that's good news," the judge said. "Please state your agreement for the record."

"The defendant has agreed to plead guilty to theft over $25,000 but less than $100,000 which is a felony in the third degree under Chapter 31 of the penal code. Under our agreement the prosecution would recommend a minimum sentence of two years conditioned on restitution of $100,000. The prosecution is prepared to accept that plea subject, of course, to the court's approval."

The judge nodded. "That seems quite reasonable. Will the defendant be able to come up with $100,000?" the judge asked.

"I'm told, Your Honor, that Mr. Herman is in possession of certain real estate that he paid more than $100,000 to acquire. He has agreed to turn that property over to the state for liquidation."

"Very well, then. Mr. Jacobs, is this your agreement?"

Jacobs stood up. "Yes, Your Honor."

"Then the agreement is approved. Bailiff, call in the jury so I can advise them of the plea."

The bailiff got up, went into the jury room, and, a moment later, led them back into the courtroom. The judge explained to them what had happened, thanked them for their service, and then dismissed them. We caught one of the jurors as he was leaving and asked him what he thought the verdict would have been had the defendant not pled out. Without hesitation he replied, guilty.

Apparently the defendant's outburst pretty much did him in.

His attorney must have realized it and strong-armed his client into the plea. If Ralph had lost, he'd have been looking at a felony of the second degree which carried a maximum sentence of twenty years. I doubted Ralph much liked the idea of a plea bargain, but he wasn't stupid. He couldn't take a chance on conviction and end up serving twenty years.

I'd managed to outrun an avalanche of trouble and thanked God for seeing me through it. It felt good knowing Ben and Alice's would be getting a second chance with their $100,000 stake compliments of Ralph Herman. Except for Peter's absence, everything seemed almost back to normal. Of course, normal for me could still be pretty intense.

Other Books About Tarizon

The Tarizon Saga

Unification (2014)
Shroud of Doom (2013)
Desert Swarm (2013)
Cactus Island (2006)
Act Normal (2007)

The Tarizon Trilogy

The Liberator (2008)
Civil War (2009)
Conquest Earth (2010)

Other Books by William Manchee

The Stan Turner Mysteries (10 volumes)
The Rich Coleman Novels (3 volumes)
Go Broke, Die Rich (Non-fiction)